Praise for
Snitch

"A wonderful, fully developed ensemble cast makes *Snitch* an entertaining, engaging read. Rene's flair for a comedic, well-turned phrase shines here. *Snitch* is worth snatching."
—SUSAN MEISSNER, author of *Widows and Orphans*

"*Snitch* is an engaging crime novel, balanced between sheer whimsy and genuine human drama."
—CHRIS WELL, author of *Tribulation House*

Praise for *Scoop*,
book one of
The Occupational Hazards Series

"…deserves being read out loud to a significant other who can laugh and cry along with you. Highly recommended."
—ChristianFictionReview.com

"This is a rollicking evangelical ride through the television news world, reminding readers why Gutteridge is such a delightful read."
—*Publishers Weekly*

"The writing is excellent, the action is fast-paced (not a single slow paragraph!), and I was honestly challenged by Hayden's upfront, candid faith. A fantastic book—I can't wait to read more of Rene's work!"
—ALISON STROBEL, author of *Violette Between*
and *Worlds Collide*

snitch

NOVELS BY RENE GUTTERIDGE

The Occupational Hazards Series
Scoop
Snitch

The Boo Series
Boo
Boo Who
Boo Hiss

My Life as a Doormat

The Storm Series
The Splitting Storm
Storm Gathering
Storm Surge

snitch

a novel

Rene Gutteridge

WaterBrook
PRESS

SNITCH
PUBLISHED BY WATERBROOK PRESS
12265 Oracle Boulevard, Suite 200
Colorado Springs, Colorado 80921
A division of Random House Inc.

Scripture quotations and paraphrases are taken from the Holy Bible, New International
Version®. NIV®. Copyright © 1973, 1978, 1984 by International Bible Society. Used by
permission of Zondervan Publishing House. All rights reserved.

The characters and events in this book are fictional, and any resemblance to actual persons
or events is coincidental.

ISBN 978-1-4000-7158-6

Published in association with the literary agency of Janet Kobobel Grant, Books & Such,
4788 Carissa Avenue, Santa Rosa, CA 95405.

Library of Congress Cataloging-in-Publication Data
Gutteridge, Rene.
    Snitch : a novel / Rene Gutteridge. — 1st ed.
      p. cm.
    ISBN 978-1-4000-7158-6
    1. Las Vegas (Nev.)—Fiction. I. Title.
    PS3557.U887S65 2007
    813'.6—dc22

                                2007003309

Printed in the United States of America
2007—First Edition

10 9 8 7 6 5 4 3 2 1

*For Brian Worel,
a gifted actor who has brought many
of my characters to life right before my eyes.*

HAZARD

PERCY MITCHELL HAZARD was born January 7, 1940, in Dallas, Texas, and passed away June 8 at the age of 65. He was born to Gordon and Ethel Hazard and raised in Austin, Texas. He was baptized at the age of fourteen at Christ the Lord Church. He married Lucy Boyd in 1962, and shortly thereafter moved to Plano. He worked as the manager of a feed store for two years before becoming a computer manager at the unemployment office. A dedicated and hard worker, he spent twenty-eight years of his life there until he was replaced by a computer and became unemployed. Determined to provide for his family, he and Lucy started their own successful clown business, The Hazard Clowns, entertaining children and adults alike. Many people knew him only as Hobo, but his family and friends knew him as a loving and kind man, full of wisdom and laughter. He is survived by his children: Mitchell, 26, married to Claire; Cassie, 24; Hank, 23; Mackenzie, 22; Hayden, 20; Avery, 18; Holt, 16. He will be greatly missed, but is now safely in the hands of his loving Father in heaven. Funeral services will be at Chapel Christian Church on Tuesday at 10:00 a.m.

HAZARD

LUCILLE "LUCY" MARGARET BOYD HAZARD was born February 15, 1945, in St. Louis, Missouri, to Gilbert Boyd, a pastor, and Wanda, a homemaker. She was raised in Louisville, Kentucky, where she spent most of her life until her family moved to Austin, Texas, where she met and married her husband, Percy. She had a long and distinguished career as Inspector 49 at Hanes until 1992, when the company was forced to downsize to 42 inspectors. As her husband lost his job three weeks earlier, they decided to start a clown business. Along with running The Hazard Clowns, this special woman homeschooled all seven of her beloved children. She went to be with her Lord on June 8. She is survived by her children: Mitchell, 26, married to Claire; Cassie, 24; Hank, 23; Mackenzie, 22; Hayden, 20; Avery, 18; Holt, 16. She died happily alongside her husband and will be laid to rest next to him at Resurrection Cemetery. She will be greatly missed by her family who adored and loved her. Funeral services are Tuesday at 10:00 a.m. at Chapel Christian Church.

Chapter 1

M ack Hazard stood near her parents' coffins. Though side by side, they seemed too far apart. Her hand glided across the marbled texture that swirled over each top, but she kept her attention on the approaching crowd. Without fail, each person reached out to touch the caskets. Mack grew rigid every time it happened, but took a cue from her oldest brother, Mitch, and tried to seem courteous.

Mitch shook hands and patted backs, reassuring everyone at the graveside that things would be okay. Except he hadn't reassured Mack. He had called a family meeting for later. Maybe the reassurance would come then.

Mack tried to ignore her sister Cassie, who continued to wail louder than a windstorm. Thankfully, that meant Cassie attracted most of the hugs.

Hank stood by a tree he'd retreated to after the service, tracing the grass with his toe. She could see his solemn features, and she swallowed to hold back tears. Cassie was crying enough for everyone.

Mack looked through the crowd to find Hayden, her younger sister by two years. Of her six siblings, she was closest to Hayden, and being separated from her now caused a strange tickle of panic.

Suddenly, two arms reached from behind and pulled her into a hug. Mack's first instinct was to body slam the owner of the arms—she didn't like hugs, and she detested anyone grabbing her from behind. But after all, this was her parents' funeral. It had always bothered her mom that she was so physical. After one brutal game of Thanksgiving flag football, Mack answered her mother's worries with, "Then you shouldn't have had any boys." Her mother replied, "Go get an ice pack for your brother's forehead."

Mack pulled forward, causing the arms to release. She turned around, forcing a smile. When she saw Cassie, she dropped the smile. "You know I hate that," Mack said.

"You should try it," Cassie said. "It brings out your eyes."

"I'm talking about the hug."

"Oh. I thought you were talking about my mascara."

"That's kind of tacky, isn't it?"

"Blue is tacky. Black is classic."

"I mean wearing it at all. Mom wouldn't approve."

Cassie glanced at the coffin beside them, and tears rolled down her face. "If you must know," she said between sobs, "Mom once told me it looked nice, but that it would put Dad in the grave if he ever saw me wearing it."

Mack gestured to the other coffin. "Well, he's right here."

"Our parents are dead and all you can complain about is my mascara?" She blotted her eyes.

Mack sighed. "I'm going to check on Hank."

"You should try crying," Cassie said. "It'll make you feel better."

"No, it won't."

"How would you know? You never cry."

"That's because it never makes me feel better." Mack left Cassie and approached Hank, who now fiddled with a piece of bark.

"Did Mitch tell you about the meeting?" Mack asked.

Hank didn't look up. "Yes."

"What do you think it's about?"

"It's what families do when their parents die. They have meetings."

"We already had two meetings. One at the coroner's and one at the funeral home."

"Maybe he's going to reveal a deep, dark family secret."

Mack offered a wry grin at Hank's statement. She was the only sibling who appreciated his dry sense of humor.

"Oh no," Mack said suddenly.

"What?"

But Mack was already elbowing through the crowd toward Hayden. She could only see half of Hayden's face—the other half was blocked by weird old Mr. Stewart, who had the breath of a man expired twice over.

"Excuse me," Mack said, squeezing through a circle of well-wishers. "I'm sorry," she said as she pushed through another cluster. She touched Hayden's shoulder. "Mr. Stewart," Mack said, "I'm sorry, but we have to go. We're having a family meeting."

"A family meeting? About what?" Hayden asked.

"I'll tell you on the way," Mack whispered and headed toward the car.

Mr. Stewart wasn't easily thwarted and he followed behind, hammering them with one question after another. He was a nosy man, too, a character trait his DNA seemed to anticipate by placing a large mole at the tip of his nose. Mack opened the door for Hayden, nearly pushing her in, and closed it. She turned around and was nearly bowled over by his breath.

"Mackenzie," he began. Mack bristled. She hated being called Mackenzie. No one in her family dared to use her full name. Her parents had taught her to be kind and courteous to those who didn't know her well, but Mack's idea of kind and courteous was letting Mr. Stewart keep the blood inside his nose. "I am one of your company's best clients."

It was true. Mr. Stewart hired more clowns in a year than a circus used in a lifetime, which was exactly why Mack kept a very close watch on him. There was something odd about a person who liked clowns that much. She should know. Her parents' clown company had been successful, and Mack, like all the Hazard kids, had been a clown since she was young.

Mr. Stewart peered at her. "I demand to know what's going on. First of all, were your parents murdered?"

Mack clenched her fists behind her back. "Why would you think they were murdered?"

"The rumor is that they went to Las Vegas for their vacation, and we all know what kind of city that is."

"Mr. Stewart, they were not murdered. It was just an unfortunate incident."

"Incident? Accident? What?"

Mack glanced at her sister, who offered a feeble smile. If Hayden hadn't been nearby, this would be the moment for Mack to take things to an entirely new level. But Hayden didn't like violence and would probably faint if Mack got aggressive.

"Well?" Mr. Stewart asked.

"Look, we don't really understand it ourselves," Mack said through clenched teeth. "But it boils down to an overly ambitious serenading guitar player, a hundred-foot extension cord, and a rack of mood lighting." She felt no need to mention the hot tub.

Mr. Stewart's jaw dropped. Mack shook his hand and said, "We'll talk soon." That's what her father used to say, and he meant it literally. For Mack, it meant Mr. Stewart would not end the afternoon prostrate on the grass.

She walked around to the driver's side door while Mr. Stewart continued blabbing his concerns and Hayden tried to answer him with kindness. Mack didn't wait for the conversation to end before she pulled away from the curb.

As she rolled down her window for some much-needed fresh air, she got the feeling that the family meeting hadn't been scheduled just so they could trade more condolences.

Her instincts proved right. Mitch stood in front of the family in their parents' living room and announced the sale of their clown company to Clowns Inc. As a result, every Hazard would receive enough money to go to college if they wanted to, and to start a new life.

Hayden bolted from the room in tears, and the rest of the family didn't seem to be taking it much better. Mack spent half an hour in the backyard calming Hayden, reassuring her that everything would be okay, and then she went back inside to see how the rest of her siblings were coping.

Cassie was crying on Claire's shoulder. Mitch had mentioned Claire's pregnancy along with the announcement of the sale, but the news that they were all going to be aunts and uncles wasn't the main topic of conversation. Mack lingered by the mantel looking at family photos until Cassie went into the kitchen, then approached Claire.

"Congratulations," Mack said.

Claire looked surprised. She touched her belly and smiled. "Thanks, Mack."

"I always thought it would be great to be an aunt. Mom's sister, Aunt Nell, was fun. Every summer we would spend a week at her house. Some of my best memories…" Nell died a few years ago, and Mack still felt the hole in her heart.

"I told Mitch not to announce the pregnancy today, but he wanted everyone to know. He kept calling it a sign of hope, a sign that life was going on." She shrugged. "I just didn't think it was a good time."

Mack glanced at all the somber faces. "We'll look a whole lot more excited once the shock wears off. The shock about the company, I mean. This is a lot for everyone to take."

"You don't look upset," Claire said.

"I'm learning to control my anger."

"Oh. Well, uh, good. What will you do now that you're no longer a clown?"

Mack smiled. She knew exactly what she would do.

Chapter 2

Five Years Later

L aura Gates hunched over the bowl of cocktail peanuts, her fingers toying with them, rubbing their skins off just for something to do. The noise of the bar couldn't drown out her elation. This was a big day.

"Captain Gates?"

Laura looked over to see Mack Hazard sliding onto the stool next to her. She wiped the salt off her fingers and offered a hand. "Hello, Mack."

"It's been a while," Mack said, her nearly constant smile still in place. "How are you doing?"

"I'm captain of property crimes these days. I'm dodging egos instead of bullets."

Mack laughed. "Both can be bloody. Congratulations."

"Not my dream job, but I can't complain." She caught the bartender's attention for another drink, then turned to Mack. "I've been keeping up with you since that day at the convenience store."

"Oh…thanks. I don't think about that much anymore."

"Who would? Nearly got yourself killed. Not something you want to daydream about, right?" Laura grinned and plunged her fingers back in the peanuts. "I've got some news for you."

"What?"

"I got word you were interested in the undercover program."

"Yes, I've been accepted. Now it's a matter of paperwork and figuring out where to put me."

Laura leaned onto the counter, clasping her salty hands together and meeting Mack's curious eyes. "I got myself a task force."

Laura threw a few peanuts in her mouth, chomped on them, and studied Mack's expression. She had met Mack two years ago during a hostage situation inside a convenience store. The gunmen had no idea an off-duty officer was there. Mack risked her life to save the clerk. Laura was first on the scene and never forgot this young woman's face. Mack had walked out with a calmness that seemed to defy human nature.

During the debriefing, Laura asked Mack how she had managed to stay calm.

"I prayed, ma'am. I started praying and never stopped."

Laura had liked Mack from then on. Driven, focused, serious, but not self-absorbed—Mack reminded her of herself when she entered the force. Something told Laura this girl was somebody worth investing in. Nobody had helped Laura, shown her the ropes. She swore once she got to a place where she had the influence, she'd seek out other women with great potential and make them into something.

"Task forces are tough to establish," Laura continued. "You have to go through miles of red tape and get approval from people who have no business approving anything. After that, you have to stand in front of a group of men who don't think you belong there in the first place and sell the idea that you've got a worthy cause."

"I see," Mack said, but she looked confused.

"I've spent months compiling information on the rise in auto theft. This morning I took my information to the sheriff, the division deputy chief, the assistant sheriff for law enforcement operations, and the office of legal affairs. I threw in a bunch of numbers, mentioned how these thefts are affecting places like Lake Las Vegas too, and how the paper was going to run an investigative piece on what the city is doing to protect citizens from auto theft…and presto! Task Force Viper was born." She glanced at Mack, who was taking in every word. "I make it sound easy," she added, "but they don't just hand out task forces." She smiled. "The Financial and

Property Crimes Bureau is the most underfunded bureau we have. Borrowing officers from Boulder City and Henderson will help with the cost. And it doesn't hurt that auto theft affects the upper-class residents."

"So what does all of this have to do with me?"

Dennis Norton, an officer who worked in narcotics, appeared out of nowhere, grinning like he'd just discovered gold. It was the same over-the-top grin he used every time he tried to get Laura to go out with him.

"I'm busy," Laura said to him.

Not only did Dennis never get the hint, but he also never got the direct approach. At the moment, he seemed particularly fixated on a basket of fried food he was holding. His eyebrows bobbed up and down, apparently trying to express a message.

Laura always found it odd how meticulously groomed Dennis's pencil-thin brows were.

He pointed to the basket of food. "Jalapeños."

Laura groaned. "Dennis, I'm a little busy here." She hated running into him, but at Hippo's, a bar so popular with cops that the drink specials had ordinance names, it was unavoidable. Dennis and his buddies served as reminders of everything that led to her being passed over for narcotics.

"Come on, Laura." He pointed to a table of officers who were sitting nearby and gawking. "I've told them all about how you can do this."

"It's not a big thing."

"It's not a big thing? Lieutenant Martin tried it and almost had to go to the hospital!" He glanced back at his posse and gave them the thumbs-up. "These babies are so hot that the juice burns your skin. We've all got bets going. Come on, please..."

"*Then* will you go away?"

He nodded eagerly and held out the basket. Laura snatched four and stuffed them in her mouth, chewed until she could swallow, and then smiled.

"Did you see that?" Dennis roared, returning to his table. "Come on! Pay up!"

Laura went back to her peanuts, glancing at Mack. "I was in a car wreck when I was eighteen and lost the ability to taste spicy foods. Let's just keep this between you and me, okay? That jalapeño trick comes in handy sometimes." Laura leaned toward Mack. "You've got to hold your own against the boys, Mack. You can't let them think they're better than you." The bartender brought her a bourbon, and she sipped it. "You're a good officer. Brave. Intelligent. A little idealistic, but that's nothing we can't work on. You've certainly proven yourself over and over again, Mack. I got my task force. And I'm willing to put your name on the short list."

Mack stammered, "But I haven't even started the undercover program. I just got accepted—"

"Do you want this or not? I can make it happen. But you need to want it."

A smile replaced Mack's concerned expression. "No jalapeño-eating skills required?"

"Not unless you want to scrape the taste buds off your tongue."

Chapter 3

R on Yeager opened his eyes at the sound of his wife's voice.
"Your coffee's ready," Nan said. She was smiling, but Ron knew it wasn't a happy smile. In the thirty years they had been married, Nan was never happy before ten in the morning.

He felt the weight of a coffee mug balanced on his chest. He rubbed his eyes with one hand, the other hand holding on to the mug, then pushed himself to a sitting position. Nan had come up with this morning ritual of putting the mug on his chest ten years into their marriage when she'd finally tired of spending thirty minutes each morning trying to wake him up. If he rolled over to try to go back to sleep, hot coffee would spill all over him. She hadn't done this in years, mostly because these days he kept a regular bedtime schedule.

After setting the mug on the bedside table, he watched Nan open the drapes. Squinting, he groaned and lay back down. "I thought we agreed to stop doing this."

"Doing what?"

"You know what."

"Serving your coffee to you in bed?"

Ron chuckled. *Right, such innocence.* After all these years, she was still feisty. "Yes, that."

"We did. But that was before you agreed to go back on the streets."

Ron stretched. "I'm not going back on the streets. Your stubbornness is clogging your ears."

"You're two years from retirement. Why in the world would you want to go back on the streets?"

Ron sighed, rolled out of bed, and shuffled to his bathroom sink.

"First of all, this isn't a big deal. There's a task force, and they want to talk to me this morning about it. That's all."

"Who is *they*?"

"Captain Laura Gates is heading it up."

Nan turned. "Gates? As in James Gates?"

"His daughter. She was just a baby the last time I saw James."

"Does she know you served with him in Chicago?"

Ron shrugged as he ran the toothbrush over his teeth. "I don't know. I just got the voice mail, so I don't have much information."

Nan joined him in the bathroom, splashing water on her face from the sink on her side.

"Captain Gates is in charge of property crimes. No idea why she wants to talk to me."

"Hey, don't act like you're too good for property crimes. Narcotics beat you to a bloody pulp. You could use something less exciting."

"Property is where old detectives go to die."

"No, it's where smart cops go until they can pull their pension, which they know they can't spend if they're dead."

Ron turned to face her. "I haven't seen you this riled up since I brought that pound of dope home and hid it under the bed."

"I am *not* riled up," Nan said, applying her makeup. "And I wasn't riled up then. I just thought you could have used more common sense. Especially since it came with a briefcase filled with forty thousand dollars."

"It wasn't my fault the lab closed at five. Some of us don't work eight to five."

Nan shot him a look and shoved the Aleve bottle into his hands before heading for the kitchen. "Nobody who has to take eight Aleve in a day should be back on the streets."

Ron poured two in his hand and trailed behind her. "Would you rather I end up like Eddie Givens, going around taping orange stickers to abandoned cars on the highway?"

"Eddie hasn't been shot at, now, has he?"

"Eddie chain-smokes and lives for his bowling league."

Nan opened the fridge and pulled out jam. "Don't expect a big breakfast. I'm retired. The best I can do for you is a couple pieces of toast."

Ron poured himself some orange juice, kissed her on the cheek, and slowly walked back to the bedroom. She was cute when she stewed.

He pulled slacks and a long-sleeved cotton shirt out of the closet. He managed to get dressed in under ten minutes, a new record. He didn't want to be late. He'd spent the last eight years sitting at a desk in front of a computer, first doing profiling, then, after a transfer to a new building, working with intelligence. He'd been counting down the days until retirement. His career had flown by up until last year when it suddenly slowed to a crawl, and he figured the next two years would crawl as well. Maybe this task force would speed things up.

Nan brought his toast into the bedroom on a plastic plate. She smiled a little as she set it down, and Ron let out a laugh. In recent years, they'd always shared breakfast together at the table. Before that, Nan brought it to the bathroom. He would insist he didn't need to eat, and she would insist he did. Then he would grab three or four bites while getting ready. That always seemed to satisfy them both.

"You don't have to say yes," Nan said, observing the uneaten toast.

Ron pulled her into a hug. "Don't worry, my dear. They're not going to send an old man into any dangerous work. Maybe they want me to head up the retired police officer's fund-raising campaign."

"I just don't have a good feeling."

"I have a better chance of dying of boredom at my current job than I ever did on the streets."

Those steely eyes that had followed him out the door every day of his career, the ones that told him she would be okay if he didn't come back, reflected back a rare vulnerability. "You're worried?" he asked.

She ordered him to eat his toast and then went back to the kitchen. He sipped his cooled-down coffee. Back in the day, it would've been caffeinated, but thanks to high blood pressure and heart palpitations, he just drank it for the fat in the cream he wasn't supposed to be adding.

He straightened his shirt and checked his watch. *Time to go.*

"I'm out the door," he hollered as he grabbed his keys, badge, and wallet.

She came from the kitchen and looked him up and down. "Slacks. Haven't seen you in those on a weekday in a long time." Ever since he was transferred to intelligence, he'd worn jeans to work. Nobody noticed or cared.

"How do I look?"

A tender smile passed over her lips. She pulled his cane out of the umbrella holder next to the door and handed it to him. "You're kidding yourself if you think you can make it through the day without this."

"I was going to grab it."

"Uh huh." She kissed him on the cheek. "Don't forget to take your medication at noon."

Ron parked at Area Command downtown and took the elevator to the third floor, where he found Laura Gates's office. Her door was open, and he could see that her window framed a nice view of the dazzle and glare of Las Vegas. She was concentrating at her desk and didn't see him, so he gently knocked.

"Captain Gates," Ron said. He stuck out his hand as he stepped toward her desk. "Sergeant Yeager."

She glanced at his cane, then offered a professional smile and the handshake of a three-hundred-pound man. She had the same red hair and green eyes as James.

"Thank you for coming to see me," she said, gesturing toward a chair. He set his cane against her desk and tried to sit down like he didn't have a metal rod in his leg.

"The last time I saw you, you were a baby."

Captain Gates looked surprised.

"I patrolled with your father up in Chicago."

"I knew you were in Chicago, but I didn't realize you served with him."

"Just a couple of years. He was a good man."

"I began my career there."

"Really? I thought James moved to Oklahoma."

"We did. Dad served out his career in homicide there."

"How is your father?"

"He's fine."

"Tell him hello for me."

Captain Gates rose to close the door behind him as she said, "So let me tell you why I've asked you here." She returned to her desk and sat down. "In the last couple of years, we've seen a surge in auto theft, particularly in the nicer parts of town. People are starting to get upset, and the politicians are making some noise. Of course, nobody wants to take into account the budget cuts we've endured over the last couple of years, but that's a whole other story." She folded her hands over some papers on her tidy desk and smiled. "Thus, the task force."

"You're spreading the cost among several agencies."

"That's right. I've been authorized to bring in officers from Boulder City, Henderson, and North Las Vegas." She paused, looking over a sheet of paper in front of her. "I'd like you to command the task force."

"Me?"

Laura smiled. "You're surprised?"

Apparently his expression was speaking for him. "I just...I haven't been involved with a task force in...well, in years. And by years, I mean decades."

Laura laughed. "Nobody is counting your gray hairs."

Ron rubbed his head. "That's because I'm bald."

Laura gave a nod toward the cane. "Did you get shot?"

"Car wreck."

"Oh."

"It hasn't stopped me from doing my job."

"I like your attitude," she said. "And I'm not worried."

"Captain Gates, as flattered as I am that you have asked me, I am curious. I haven't exactly been on the radar screen in a while."

"Your record keeps you on the radar." She opened the file in front of her. "I'm familiar with your cases here in Las Vegas and back in Chicago too."

Ron looked down. He hadn't left Chicago on the best terms.

"Sergeant Yeager, I can read between the lines. I know what the court documents say, and I know what the police reports say."

"What exactly would be my assignment?"

Her understanding voice took on a more professional tone. "I want you to put together a UC team."

Ron tried to hold back a laugh. "Undercover?"

"This theft ring is big, and I want to bring it down from the top."

Ron shifted. His leg ached when he sat in one position too long.

"Sergeant Yeager, you're not telling me you're too old for this, are you?" she said with a hint of teasing.

Ron smiled. "No, but my leg might be trying to tell me something." Ron leaned forward and locked eyes with her. "There are a lot of UC officers around here. Why not bring in one of the guys from narcotics?"

Captain Gates seemed to have expected the question. "Narcotics already has their hands full and their resources exhausted. Besides, I want the best." She stood, walked to a nearby table, picked up a stack of folders, and handed them to Ron. "This is the long list of available officers. I'll give you until the end of the week to make the short list, only five officers. There's an office down the hall where you can work until we secure the area we'll be using."

Ron stared at the folders on his lap.

"Something wrong?" Captain Gates asked.

"Uh, no. No. I'm just… It's a lot to process."

"You get your pick, Sergeant Yeager. There are a lot of excellent officers who would jump at an opportunity like this. I only have one request." She pulled a single folder from her drawer and handed it across her desk to him. "I want this officer on the task force."

Ron opened the folder, pulled his bifocals out of his shirt pocket, and slid them on his face. "Mackenzie Hazard?" Ron flipped through her history, noticed she didn't have any undercover experience, then looked up at Captain Gates. "Why her?"

"She's someone I've taken under my wing. Someone with great potential. Don't hesitate to let me know if you need anything. I'm counting on you to be resourceful but pragmatic. You've got full access. Dig as deep as you need to. There's a summary of the auto-theft problem we're dealing with at the bottom of those files. Our task force is only authorized for six months, so we're going to have to be swift."

Ron stood, trying to tuck the stack of folders under his arm so he could grab his cane. "Six months?"

"Not my timeline. I asked for a year. Didn't get it."

"I'm going to need time. I won't send the team out into a UC operation until I know they're ready."

"There're at least two dozen experienced officers in that pile. I think you'll be able to find the perfect team." Captain Gates stood and offered her hand. "Welcome to Task Force Viper."

"Viper. That stand for something?"

"No. I just thought it sounded sexy."

"Nothing catches criminals like sexy."

Laura grinned and waved him to the door. Ron made his way down the hallway, careful not to let the folders slide out from underneath his arm. He found the office: a small, windowless box with a wobbly looking desk and an empty file cabinet. He dropped the folders to the desk, then tried out his chair. It leaned to the left. This was really going to help his back problems.

He stared at the white walls.

As the saying went, undercover work is a young man's game. Ron smiled.

Maybe. Maybe not.

Chapter 4

The Henderson sky glimmered with stars that could never be seen on the strip. Not many were visible in Henderson either, but at least a few popped through the megawatt city glow. From where Jesse Lunden stood on this cool evening, he could see the Vegas valley spread wide, its lights twinkling inside a sprawling desert bowl.

Elliot Stillman, nicknamed Dozer for his excessive napping tendency, stood a few feet away. Without a technical support team, there was nothing to do but wait. Dozer's eyes, fixed and focused, also held fear. Jesse stepped to his side. "You ready?"

Dozer nodded. They'd been working undercover together for three years, and before that they had worked the same patrol shift. Dozer stood more than six feet tall and had the build of a linebacker. Jesse was barely five-eight. When they worked an undercover case together, they made a great duo. With every introduction, the attention always shifted to Dozer because of his size. But they knew the importance of respect, so Dozer would lean down, Jesse would whisper something in his ear, Dozer would pretend to disagree, and then Jesse would hit him.

The reaction was always the same. The bad guys' faces told the story. The big one could beat them up, but the little one called the shots.

This time, though, Dozer was going in alone. Jesse's cover might have been blown, and they didn't want to take any chances. The meeting with the dealer was delayed for three weeks while they scrambled to get Dozer in. But now they had their big break.

One of their informants had provided them with a potentially big break by introducing them to Carlos Vinetti, who had eluded law enforcement for three years. He wasn't a big-time dealer, but they believed he had bigger connections. The meeting was to take place in eight minutes: a pound of marijuana for seven hundred and fifty dollars.

Jesse would be the "eyeball," positioning himself in the Laundromat across the street from the apartment building. Their other partner, Gundy, would stay in the Suburban a few blocks away and take notes. Jesse checked his watch. Dozer did the same.

"Dozer, you're going to be fine. They're going to be more scared of you than you are of them."

"That's what my mom used to say about bees until she got stung thirty times."

"We've got your back. I'll keep track of anyone going in or out of the building, and I'll be in constant communication with backup, okay? Just go in there, make the deal, and we're done." Not optimal conditions. Usually they tried to set up a buy in the relative safety of a parking lot. But Vinetti had insisted on this apartment.

Dozer nodded. "I've got to go." He climbed into a Mustang that looked too small to hold him. He pitched a thumbs-up and offered a steady smile before he drove off.

Gundy hopped into the driver's seat of the Suburban. Jesse got in his truck, then drove to the back of the Laundromat and went inside to the office. It had a perfect view of the front of the apartment building.

Jesse checked his watch. Ten o'clock. Outside, the Mustang roared into a parking spot.

"Dozer's here," Jesse radioed to Gundy.

"How's he look?" Gundy asked.

Jesse watched Dozer get out of the Mustang with the duffel bag. "Like the kind of guy who could kick a puppy." Dozer always wore the same expression when he went undercover.

Jesse watched him open the front door and disappear inside. After five minutes, Jesse gave an update to Gundy. "There's been no activity since Dozer went inside."

Jesse's agitation built as he slumped in his seat with nothing to do but watch and wait. He would be in there himself had he not run into a patrol officer at 7-Eleven three weeks ago. Jesse went in with one of Vinetti's contacts to buy cigarettes and beer on the way to what was supposed to be a buy. A guy he'd served patrol with five years earlier recognized him and came over to say hello. Jesse tried to make a scene, telling the officer he didn't know him and to back off. But the officer had called him by his real name. There was little Jesse could do. The officer quickly caught on to what was happening and tried to cover, but it was too late. The officer called the UC office the next day to apologize, said he hadn't heard Jesse had gone undercover. Luckily, their informant still had credibility, and Dozer was connected within two weeks.

Vinetti's Navigator pulled to the front of the building. He and another man got out and walked into the building.

"Vinetti's here. He's got Matt with him. They just went inside."

"Okay," Gundy said.

Jesse was about to check his watch when he saw movement on the west side of the building. A man dressed in a dark hooded sweatshirt and jeans was climbing up the fire escape. Jesse leaned forward, pressing the binoculars against the glass window. The man reached beneath his sweatshirt and pulled out a tire iron. He wedged it underneath the windowpane and popped it up.

"Uh…Gundy?"

"Yeah?"

"There's a guy on the west side of the building. He's breaking into one of the apartments."

"Stop screwing around, Jesse. Just keep an eye out for Dozer."

"I'm not kidding. There's a guy breaking into an apartment."

"Really?"

"Yeah."

"Well, just sit tight. Don't worry unless he comes out with a TV."

Jesse glanced again at the front doors, then back to the west side of the building, where he could see the man climbing into the apartment. He checked his watch again. It had been fifteen minutes. The deal should've gone down already.

"Any sign of activity?" Gundy asked.

"Nothing."

A few more minutes ticked by. Jesse couldn't sit any longer. He rolled the chair back, stood, and looked out the window. A sneaker, then a leg, then a body emerged out of the second-floor apartment. The man was holding a—

"Gundy?"

"Yeah?

"He's coming out with a TV."

"Please tell me you're joking."

"Looks like a flat-panel. He's making his way down the fire escape. I'm going after him."

"You can't leave Dozer."

"I'll be right next to the building. He'll be fine."

"Jesse, wait!"

Jesse raced toward the front door of the Laundromat. The burglar was just a few feet from the bottom of the fire escape. An old El Camino sat parked in the alley. Running as fast as he could, Jesse crossed the street and pulled his weapon.

"Police! Freeze!"

The hooded thief looked up, his face wide with surprise. Jesse was still fifteen yards away when the man threw the TV and jumped from the fire escape. The TV crashed to the ground, and as the man's feet hit the pavement, he stumbled, then ran toward his car.

But before he could get his door open, Jesse slammed him against the hood. Whipping the burglar around, Jesse pushed his head down and cuffed his wrists.

"Jesse, what's happening?" Gundy's voice crackled through the radio.

"Hold on," Jesse said as he noticed something bulging underneath the thief's shirt. Pulling it up revealed a baggie tucked into the waist of his pants. "You're not going to believe this," Jesse said into his radio.

"He's on the FBI's Ten Most Wanted list?"

"Not quite. But he's got at least an ounce of Mexican black tar heroin. I need an officer here to secure him."

"Where are you?"

"In the alley to the west of the building."

"I'm sending Carson to the south side. Take him there. I'm going in to cover Dozer."

Jesse grabbed the man by the arm and began to lead him toward the back of the building. But as he did, he heard tires squealing from the front of the building. "Gundy? Is Carson there yet?"

"No, he's about five blocks away," Gundy said.

"Where are you?"

"About two blocks away."

"Come with me!" Jesse pulled his cuffed prisoner to the front of the building. They rounded the corner in time to see Vinetti's Navigator speeding off. "I don't see Dozer!" Jesse said into his radio. "I'm going in."

"You can't. We don't know what's going on in there."

"Something's not right."

"You're telling me," the thief said. "I don't want to have anything to do with this. And aren't you supposed to read me my rights? Just leave me here. I won't go anywhere—"

"Shut up," Jesse said, his back against the front wall of the building. He pulled the thief beside him. He drew his weapon and listened for any sound.

"Are you going to get me shot?" the thief asked.

"Shut up."

"I'd like to see a badge. You don't look like a police officer."

Jesse cut his eyes sideways. "Can you just stop talking for one second? You're a thief. Surely you know how to be quiet and sneaky."

"What about that guy on the radio? He said not to go in, that we're going to get killed."

"He said he doesn't know what's happening in there. Now shut up."

"That's a good way to get yourself killed. I always know what's happening inside an apartment before I go in. I'm no idiot. You surprise someone, and the chances of getting shot go way up." The thief was staring at Jesse's gun.

"I know what I'm doing."

Jesse peeked around the corner. The front doors were glass, but all he could see was a dark hallway and stairs that led to the next floor.

"Gundy, what's the apartment number?"

"One-zero-eight. What's going on?"

"We're going in."

"We? Who is we?"

"Me and the…the thief."

"Burglar," the man said.

"You were supposed to hand him to the backup team!" Gundy said.

"Yeah," the thief agreed.

Jesse switched off his radio, rounded the corner with the thief in tow, and pushed open the front door. He could see the apartment, its door wide open, no movement inside. He signaled the thief, whose eyes grew rounder by the second, to be quiet.

They walked forward. As they neared 108, the thief whispered, "Maybe you should take the handcuffs off of me. You'll probably need them for whoever it is you think is in that apartment."

"Whoever has the cuffs on is less likely to get shot," Jesse whispered back.

Jesse stood against the wall next to the open door and listened for conversation, but heard nothing.

With the thief in one hand and his gun in the other, Jesse moved into the doorway. A card table occupied the center of the room, along with three chairs, a phone, and old pizza boxes.

Dozer's duffel bag sat on one of the chairs.

The thief whispered, "Would've been a waste to break into this apartment…"

Jesse tightened his grip on the man's arm, making him wince in pain.

To the right was a small hallway. As Jesse stepped forward, he could see an empty bedroom. On the other side of the hall, the bathroom. The light was on.

A few more steps and he would be able to see who was in there. They both noticed simultaneously how squeaky the thief's tennis shoes were on the cheap laminated floor. The thief shrugged. "What? I got 'em off a tourist at the MGM Grand."

Suddenly Dozer came out of the bathroom.

"What are you doing?" Jesse shouted. "We're all wondering what happened to you! Why were you in the bathroom?"

"I was looking at myself in the mirror."

"Why?"

"They saw right through me. I stood there with the meanest look I'm capable of, and I don't know, they just got nervous. I think it's in my eyes, you know? I look mean, but my eyes are screaming, 'I'm about to arrest you!'"

"You're being too hard on yourself."

"No, I'm not. I'm no good at this, Jesse. The only time anything goes my way is when you're with me."

Jesse radioed Gundy to tell him to stand down. "So what happened?"

Dozer threw his arms up and walked past them in the hallway. He turned and pitched a thumb at the thief. "Who is he?"

"A thorn in my side."

"You still haven't read me my rights," the thief said.

"You have the right to remain silent or I'll duct-tape your mouth shut."

"Now you're going to torture me?"

Jesse dragged him over to the chair and thrust him into it. Jesse uncuffed him and recuffed him with his hands in front, then grabbed the duffel bag from the chair next to the thief.

"Hold this."

"Why?" the thief asked.

"Because now I'm going to torture you." He grabbed the thief's hands and shoved the handles of the duffel bag into them. Jesse unzipped the bag. The thief gasped as he stared at the stacks of cash inside. Jesse turned back to Dozer. "Talk to me, Dozer."

"I came in, we started talking, nothing big. And then when it came time to make the deal, Vinetti started acting really strange. He kept asking me for more information about myself."

"What'd you say?"

"I asked him why he was asking so many questions." Dozer shook his head. "And then it started getting weird. Vinetti whispered to the guy next to him and then…" Dozer was staring at Jesse's belly.

"What are you looking at?" Jesse asked.

Dozer pointed. "What's that?"

"What?"

"Sticking out of your waistband? That baggie."

"That was going to get my electricity turned back on," the thief said, sighing, his eyes still focused on the money.

"Is that black tar heroin?" Dozer asked.

"This guy had it on him when I arrested him for trying to steal a TV."

"I went in to steal the TV," the thief explained, "and found this in a drawer. Figured it was a nice bonus for all my hard work."

"You pried open one lousy window." Jesse rolled his eyes at Dozer.

Dozer let out a loud and frustrated sigh. "See what I mean? I'm the one that goes in to make the buy, and you're the one that comes out with the drugs." Dozer marched out the apartment building's front door.

"He's kind of whiny for a cop, isn't he?" the thief said.

Jesse grabbed the duffel bag, zipped it back up, and twirled the burglar toward the door. "Let's go. And for the last time, shut up."

Ron pulled into his neighborhood and turned left on Glouster Street. It had been a long time since he'd worked this late, and he still had more work to do. He hadn't realized it was dark outside until he went to the break room for coffee. Nan didn't sound happy when he called to apologize. The chicken Tetrazzini she'd ordered from Schwan's would be cold, but he could nuke it for three minutes if he found time to "fit dinner into his busy schedule."

He saw a blue car parked in front of his house, which he recognized as their pastor's Civic. After pulling into the driveway, he turned off the engine and hobbled quickly into the house. A visit from the pastor after ten o'clock usually signaled bad news.

Nan sat in the living room with Pastor Kyle across from her on the sofa. Both had cups of coffee in their hands. As Ron walked into the room, Kyle stood.

"Hi, Ron," Kyle said, shaking his hand. Ron couldn't remember seeing him look that nervous since the day he arrived at their church fresh out of seminary, barely twenty-four years old. Ron had always liked the kid. He had a wide-eyed youthfulness about him. A little timid for Ron's taste, but Kyle was a hard and eager worker, always making himself available to anyone who needed him. And over the past two years, he'd managed to trim his average sermon length from one hour to forty minutes.

"What's wrong?" Ron asked, looking at Nan, who didn't bother standing or making eye contact.

Kyle smiled meekly. "Uh…Nan asked me to come over."

"Why?"

They both looked at Nan, who just stirred her coffee and sipped as if it were the only interesting thing in the room.

Kyle cleared his throat. "Uh…well, I'm here to pray for you."

"Pray for me?" Ron laughed, which finally caused Nan to look up at him. "Why do I need Pastor Kyle to pray for me?"

Nan set down her coffee. "Well, Ron, you tell me. It's ten o'clock. When's the last time you weren't in bed by nine forty-five?"

Ron glanced at Kyle, who looked like he wanted to sink into the carpet. Kyle said, "Listen, this is probably none of my business. In fact, I usually try to get to bed by ten thirty myself, so—"

"Oh, no you don't." Nan stood and gestured toward Ron. "I realize the man can appear intimidating when he wants to, but he doesn't intimidate me, and you shouldn't be intimidated either."

"I'm just standing here," Ron said. He turned to Kyle. "I'm just standing here."

"Look at him! He uses a cane!"

"Listen, I'll let you two sort this out. You're welcome to set up some counseling time with me if you—"

"Pastor Kyle," Nan said firmly, hands on her hips, "you told me you could do this."

"When you called, you sounded very upset, and it sounded urgent, so I came right over."

"It is urgent."

Kyle's gaze bounced between them. "I thought she said you were in the street. That's why I told her to call 911."

"You called 911?" Ron asked Nan.

"I said he's going *back* on the street."

"I'm not going back on the street," Ron said.

"I'm still not sure what the street has to do with this, but—"

"Go ahead," Nan interrupted. "Lay your hands on him and pray the devil out of him."

Ron couldn't help but smile as he watched Kyle's gaze slowly work its way from Nan to him. "Um…"

"It's okay, Kyle. I'm sure I could use some prayer. But," Ron said, "why, exactly, are you praying for me?"

"Nan was trying to explain… Well, she's worried that you've, um…"

"He's having a midlife crisis," Nan said emphatically.

Kyle looked relieved that he didn't actually have to say it.

"Why would she think that?" Ron asked Kyle.

Kyle stuck a finger under the collar of his polo. "She said that you're, um, you're having delusions…"

"Delusions?" Ron cracked another smile.

"She said you're…" Kyle looked at Nan for help, but Nan was too busy glaring at the smile on Ron's face. "Uh, her words, not mine, but she says you think you're an undercover agent."

Ron's smile grew into a belly laugh.

"Stop laughing!" Nan said.

"Mr. and Mrs. Yeager, I can certainly recommend some good Christian therapists and—"

"First of all, Pastor Kyle," Nan said, "I told you that he's thinking about going back on the street to do undercover work."

"How would you know that? All I said was that I was going in for a meeting," Ron said.

"That was early this morning. Now it's late at night."

"So?"

"The only thing that would keep you away from chicken Tetrazzini is undercover work. I wasn't born yesterday. And neither were you, which is the whole point here."

Ron and Nan stared at each other for a moment, then looked at Kyle, whose mouth appeared to have frozen in midsentence.

Nan said, "Are you going to pray for him or not?"

"You're an undercover agent?" Kyle asked. "For real?"

"An undercover officer. Used to be."

"But...but I thought you were a...a..."

"Yes?"

"I'm sorry, I just assumed you were, uh, semi-retired."

At least he managed a graceful ending, Ron thought.

"I can't believe this," Nan said, her eyes narrowing. "See what I've had to live with for thirty years? He just walks into a situation and takes complete control of it. We've been sitting here for twenty minutes, you and I, and you assured me you would pray for him, and here he is, and you're not going to pray for him, are you?"

Kyle looked at Ron, and Ron crossed his arms, just for effect.

"Ron, stop it," Nan said with exhaustion. "Fine, I give up." She threw up her arms and headed down the hallway mumbling. The bedroom door slammed. Kyle still looked dumbstruck.

"You really do undercover work?" he asked.

"That was a long time ago. I've been working a desk job, so, as you put it, I'm semi-retired."

"So you're not going to be doing undercover work anymore?"

"I've been called back for a short assignment, but just as a supervisor."

"Wow," Kyle said. "That sounds exciting."

"Listen, I'm sorry you had to come over at such a late hour. I don't want to keep you."

"No, no, it's fine." Kyle shook his head. "It's so weird. You just don't know things about people. I would've never expected that about you."

Ron smiled and moved to the front door, opening it as he said, "That's what makes a great undercover officer. Good night, Pastor Kyle."

"Oh, yeah. Right. Good night." Kyle stepped out the door. "I'll be praying for Nan."

"Thanks."

Chapter 5

As the sun rose over Las Vegas, Ron sat on his back porch studying files and stroking the fur on his lab, Magnum. He hadn't slept well because of the excitement and the pressure to move quickly. He still didn't understand why Captain Gates had chosen him, but he wasn't going to second-guess her now.

The back door slid open, and Nan walked out with two plates. She set one in front of him. "Eggs over easy?" he asked, looking up at her. "I thought you were retired."

"If you're going to keep these long hours, you're going to need something more than toast to make it through."

Ron looked at the plate. Not just eggs, but sausage and biscuits, too. Turkey sausage and whole-wheat, high-fiber biscuits, but at least she was trying.

Nan sat next to him at the patio table and stared into their swimming pool. "What time did you get up?"

"Four."

She glanced at him. "My father is eighty-seven, and he gets up at four every morning. That should tell you something."

Ron shoved his plate aside and turned to face her. "I'm going to train some kids, and we're going to bust up an auto-theft ring."

"Did you happen to mention your experience is in narcotics?" She took a bite of eggs and studied the pile of folders. "What are those?"

"Officer profiles. I'm going to have a team of five."

Nan raised an eyebrow. "Five? The county must be feeling generous."

Ron nodded. Most of his years in undercover work, teams had been limited to two or three people working together at a time.

"Any promising apprentices?"

"I've already been told an Officer Hazard is on the team. Someone Laura wanted. It's up to me to pick the other four."

"Hazard. Hope he doesn't live up to his name."

"She."

"A she?" Nan's eyebrows rose. "Times have changed."

"Yeah, but as you always like to point out, women don't come with big egos."

Ron pointed to the open folder beside his plate. "This guy from Henderson, Detective Lunden, looks promising. Has a lot of experience, but not a lot of successful deals. Looks like he's a bit of a problem child."

"Like *you*, you mean?"

"That's a bad thing?" Ron asked with feigned innocence.

Nan laughed and shook her head. She knew problem children were harder to manage and control, but that they also made the best undercover cops.

Nan used her fork to chase a bite of sausage around her plate. "Do you remember Roberto Hector?" she asked.

"I still have his photo hanging on my wall at work. What about him?"

"All you ever told me about that case is that you nailed this big mob guy."

"We did."

"Special Agent Doughtery from the DEA called the next day to apologize to you, but you weren't home yet. He assumed you told me the whole story."

"What whole story?"

"That there was nobody available for backup, not a single DEA agent. That you went out there alone and waited for three hours. That while this big mob guy was walking back to his car from the restaurant, you grabbed him, cuffed him, shoved him into your car, and the rest is history." She waited for Ron to look at her. "Doughtery called to apologize because he said that you had to put yourself in an enormously dangerous situation and that they should've worked harder to get a DEA agent there."

"That was years ago."

"It was also really stupid. You knew I'd tell you how stupid that was, right? That's why you didn't tell me. I figured you weren't going to tell me what you'd gotten yourself into this time, either. So I phoned Laura Gates."

"What? Why would you do that?"

"To find out what's really going on."

"What did she tell you?"

"That you're supervising an auto-theft task force."

"That's what I told you." Ron tried to simmer down.

"Captain Gates doesn't know you like I do. You were barely thirty, with three small kids at home, and yet you were willing to die that night." Nan's eyes softened. "Your kids are grown and gone. Your wife's getting old and cranky. Your heart's working overtime as it is. What's to keep you from risking it all again?"

Ron reached for her hand and took it gently into his. "I've been at a desk for nearly eight years. Everybody thinks I'm an old man with nothing to offer. This is my chance to make a difference again. I see the weaknesses. I watch these young guys come in with their preconceived notions, and I see the weak links. But they don't want to listen. They look at me like they wish I'd just go away."

"Honey, your whole life has been about your being in control. Maybe that's what you're struggling with. Everything is moving around you, and you're standing still. But at some point, we have to just accept our time has come and gone."

"My entire career you've resolved not to worry about me. Let me do this. It makes me feel alive again."

He saw the hurt in Nan's eyes before she looked away. He regretted the words already. He'd been married long enough to know what Nan was thinking: *Why don't I make you feel alive?* "Don't take this personally. Just think of it as my new hobby." He smiled, but he could tell he wasn't making Nan feel any better.

She stood and picked up her plate. "I know you. You can't go into something halfheartedly. You're going to pour yourself into this just like you did all those years ago, when I would go days without seeing you. I've loved these past few years because, finally, this all became just a job to you. You clocked in and clocked out and that was it. But now the fire in your eyes is back. You're going to dive deep, just like the old days."

"You've seen me in the pool. I'm a horrible swimmer." Ron chuckled.

"What difference does it make? Nothing I say will change your mind. You're as stubborn as you've always been." She turned to walk back inside. "Just be sure to leave me a list of songs you'd like played at your funeral."

Inside O'Connor's, Brandi Brown stood behind the bar, wiping shot glasses and arranging them inside the cabinets. She could hear Mason in the back, laughing at something she was sure only he thought was funny. Except for that laughter, the bar was quiet, the chairs still stacked on top of the tables. She loved this time of day. The morning sun caused a still haze to hang in the air. This was her best thinking time before the busyness began around eleven, when the doors opened and Elliot came in to sit on the third stool from the end. For about three weeks now, he'd been showing up every day, ordering the same thing, and staying for exactly forty-five minutes. She wondered where he came from, what his story was, but she never asked. She just served Enormous Elliot—as she had secretly nicknamed him—his Guinness and minded her own business. Brandi checked her watch. Usually by this time, Mason was getting the register ready and putting the chairs down. But he was talking to someone, and the rules were that she stayed out of it. She'd heard Mason open the back door thirty minutes ago. An unfamiliar male voice asked if anyone else was here.

She never heard Mason's answer. They'd gone into the office and shut the door. She decided to pull down the chairs herself. That was Mason's job, but Mason probably wasn't in the mood for responsibility. Her arms ached by the time she'd set the last chair on the floor. By eleven Mason still hadn't surfaced.

She went to unlock the doors and flip the Open sign. She grew anxious as the minutes ticked by. Mason had been spending more and more time in Vegas. She wondered if he was making plans to go again. He was rarely gone for more than a night, but she still hated not knowing the purpose of his trips. She didn't dare ask, as she knew that she was always one question away from being back on the street.

She wiped down tables and cleaned the counters, anticipating Elliot's arrival. He usually plopped himself on the barstool at 11:03. She stopped cleaning and stepped into the hallway that led to the office, hoping to hear something. All she heard was a muffled conversation, and since she didn't want to get caught eavesdropping, she went back to the bar. The bell chimed and in walked Elliot, fifteen minutes late. Brandi smiled. She was starting to enjoy his company.

"Hi," she said.

"Oh, hi." A hint of a smile was all he could muster this morning.

"Guinness?" she asked.

"Sure."

"You okay?"

Elliot's eyes widened as he looked at her.

"Sorry," she said, trying to laugh away the awkwardness. "I should leave you alone."

"What makes you think something is wrong?" he asked.

She handed him his glass and shrugged. "I just get feelings about people. My mom used to call 'em hunches. Besides, you're usually here earlier."

Elliot stared into his drink. It didn't look like he wanted to talk. Not that he was ever chatty, but he did usually ask how she was doing. And sometimes he talked with Mason.

She left him alone, but she couldn't shake the nagging feeling that Elliot needed someone to talk to. She made her way back to him. He didn't look up as she wiped the counter in front of him.

"I hate the sound of slot machines," he said.

"Excuse me?"

"That sound they make. That horrible metal against metal, ding-ding-ding, grating-on-your-every-last-nerve sound that makes me want to bury myself alive—"

Brandi smiled. "You may be living in the wrong state."

He glanced up at her. "This bar is pretty quiet. I like that. And believe me, Henderson is still much better than Vegas."

"I know we don't know each other well," she said softly, "but I have this feeling that something is bothering you." She tried to let him see the caring side of her that her mother used to brag about when she was a child. "Sometimes it's easier to talk to a stranger. You should hear the things people tell me." She laughed again, trying to break the ice, but Elliot didn't even smile.

"It's the slot machines, okay?"

Brandi raised an eyebrow. "Okay…"

He looked around the bar. "Where's Mason?"

Brandi felt disappointed. She was trying to be nice to Elliot, and all he wanted to know was Mason's whereabouts? Then it dawned on her that maybe he wanted to make sure Mason wasn't going to come around. Maybe he liked the idea of talking to her alone.

"He's busy. Been busy all morning."

"Doing what?"

Brandi glanced up at him. "Anything but worrying about me and this bar."

Just then the back doors swung open and Mason walked through, followed by a man with a hard stare. Brandi looked away and grabbed her cleaning rag.

"You got the keys?" Mason asked her. She hated when he talked to her like they had nothing more in common than the fact they were both human beings.

"What keys?" she asked.

"To the register." His voice was low. Brandi glanced at the man behind Mason. He looked annoyed…and familiar. Had he been in the bar before?

"What for?" she asked, reaching into her pocket to pull them out. She looked at Elliot, who was back to studying his drink.

"What's with the questions?" He grabbed the keys out of her hand and started to open the register.

"What are you doing?"

A mixture of anger and embarrassment swept over Mason's face. "What's your problem?" he whispered.

"We've got to put this in the books. We can't just take cash out of the register. We finally got everything straightened out—"

"Look, it's nothing. It won't be missed. Now shut up."

Mason pulled open the register and grabbed a handful of large bills. Then he looked under the tray and turned to Brandi. "Where's the rest of the money?"

"What money?"

"This isn't all of the money."

"I put it all in there. From the bag."

Mason let out an angry sigh, counted the twenties in his hand, and turned to the man behind him. "Looks like the lady here got greedy."

"I didn't take any money!" Brandi said.

Mason shoved her backward. "I told you to shut up. We'll discuss this later."

"What's the problem?" the man said.

Mason counted the twenties a second time. "Look, I'm a hundred dollars short. I can get it to you by the end of the week."

Brandi held her breath as she watched the man's eyes. She glanced over at Elliot. He looked like he was trying to mind his own business.

"We agreed on nine hundred and fifty dollars."

"I know," Mason said. "Like I said, the chick here must've gotten greedy. You know how it is, trying to control a woman."

Brandi wanted to defend herself. She hadn't taken the money and didn't know where Mason had gotten that idea. But the man standing behind Mason looked like he wasn't in the mood for any more trouble, so she clutched her dishrag and tried to remain calm.

"I swear, I'll get you the rest by the end of the week," Mason said. "Maybe by the end of the day…"

The strange man's eyes darted around the room, noticed Elliot, then looked back at Mason. "All right, fine. But you know what happens to people who don't pay up."

"I'm good for it. This is just a minor glitch. It won't happen again." The man nodded, and Mason said, "Let's go back to the office."

"Just hand it over. You have what you want; now give me what I want."

Brandi stood perfectly still. Mason handed over the money. The man stuffed it into a satchel. Brandi's eyes met his, and she suddenly felt terrified, as if she had stared into those eyes before. She watched him reach into his bag, and the next thing she knew, he had pulled a gun.

"Police! Freeze!"

She stumbled backward, dropping her rag and crashing into a cabinet full of shot glasses. She turned, scanning for Elliot. But when she saw him, she gasped.

He pointed a gun at her and held out a badge.

Chapter 6

"F reeze!" Dozer shouted. "Don't move!"

The woman behind the bar trembled so badly she seemed unable to stand still. She looked over at Mason Capps, who was stringing together a long sentence of cuss words.

"Shut up," Jesse said to Capps. "Turn around. Dozer, secure the woman." Jesse cuffed Capps and then patted him down.

He was just about to tell Dozer to lock the front door of the pub when he heard, "Jesse?"

Jesse looked at the bartender.

"You *are* Jesse!" she said. She looked familiar, but Jesse was having a hard time placing her.

"You know this girl?" Dozer asked as he cuffed her.

"Ma'am, just be quiet, okay?" Jesse said.

"Don't call me ma'am! Don't you recognize me?"

"Uh…" Jesse glanced at Dozer.

"Name's Brandi," Dozer said. "That's all I know."

Jesse squeezed his eyes shut. And then it came to him. He'd just been punched by a visit from his past.

"Brandi Brown," she said, and if she'd been able to put her hands on her hips, he could tell she would have. "Hello? Henderson High? Senior year?"

Jesse's face warmed with embarrassment. Capps stood next to him and looked as confused as Jesse felt.

"You know this guy?" Capps asked her.

They all looked like they wanted an answer.

"She was my, uh, prom date," Jesse finally said.

Capps let out an angry laugh.

"She doesn't seem to be involved here, Jess," said Dozer. His emerging grin wasn't helping matters.

"You're going to cut her a deal because she went to the prom with you?" Capps asked. "My lawyer will have a heyday with that one."

"Shut up, Capps. You don't have a lawyer."

"I'm not involved," Brandi said, shooting a wounded gaze toward Mason. "I don't know anything about what's going on."

"Thanks for being a stand-by-your-man kind of woman," Capps said. "Get me away from her. I don't even want to look at her."

Jesse sighed and was leading Capps out the back door when Capps added, "But you might want to take a look in her purse."

"What are you talking about?" Brandi asked.

"Why?" Jesse asked.

"It's in the back office."

Jesse looked at Dozer and turned to the back office.

Brandi pulled away from Dozer. "You're a creep, you know that?"

The three men looked at one another, unsure to whom she was referring. Then they watched her eyes focus on Dozer. "You said your name was Elliot!"

"It is," Dozer said.

"So you were just pretending to be nice to me?"

Dozer sighed and looked at Jesse for help, but Jesse wasn't about to offer any. For the moment, Dozer was alone with the woman's wrath, but soon enough, she aimed her fiery stare straight at Jesse.

"What?" he asked.

"You were a lousy prom date."

Dozer started laughing.

"Why was I a lousy prom date?"

"Oh, please. Don't act so stupid," she said.

"Yeah. Don't act so stupid." Dozer smirked.

"Dozer is a stupid name. You should stick with Elliot," she said.

"It's a nickname," Dozer said defensively.

Now Jesse was laughing.

"Look," Capps interrupted, "as much as I would love to walk down memory lane with the three of you, I want to get one thing straight. She's as much a part of this as I am."

The laughter stopped. Capps said, "I'm telling you. Check her purse."

Jesse walked over to the desk. He picked it up and looked at Brandi.

"He's lying," Brandi said.

Jesse unzipped it and pulled out a baggie of cocaine and a hundred dollars.

"No!" Brandi shouted. "No!" She looked at Capps. "You put that in there!"

"Come on," Jesse said. "Let's get them out of here." They walked toward the back door where officers were waiting.

Suddenly Brandi yanked herself away from Dozer. As Jesse turned around, he saw her trip Dozer, who landed hard on the floor. Scrambling back up quickly, he pushed her against the wall, and she kicked him in the shin.

Dozer was trying not to wince in pain. "Lady, you need to chill," Dozer said, grabbing his shin with his free hand.

"Suddenly I'm a lady again?" she shouted.

"Maybe you two should call for backup," said Capps.

Jesse pushed Capps out the back door. The bright midday sun made everyone squint. Jesse handed Capps over to another officer and glanced back at Dozer, who was trying to get Brandi out the door without having to heave her over his shoulder like a potato sack. Once outside, he promptly stuffed her into the back of a patrol car.

"Read them their rights," Jesse said to the officers standing by their cars. "You might want to emphasize that 'remain silent' part to the chick."

Ron pulled a turkey sandwich, an apple, and a baggie full of chips out of a paper sack. It had been a long morning. He had spent the first half narrowing the list of people he wanted to interview for the task force and the second half reviewing the case files. One pattern caught his attention: several of the stolen cars were minivans, some of them later models.

Someone knocked on his door. He looked up to see a young woman wearing a uniform and a serious expression. "Sergeant Yeager?"

"Yes?"

She walked toward him and stuck out her hand. "Mack Hazard."

Ron stood and shook her hand. "Hello. Good to meet you." He offered her a seat next to his desk. Gates had told him this woman would be on the team, and he was curious about what prompted her insistence. He figured he might as well put her through the interview process. He pulled her file from the stack and opened it.

"Says here that you worked three years in patrol in Boulder City."

"Yes sir."

"And then you transferred here, still working in patrol."

"That's right."

Ron scanned the file again. Although she was certainly a reliable officer and had even been involved in a hostage situation, he didn't see anything that screamed UC. Ron studied her. She was average build, had shoulder-length blond hair pulled back in a ponytail, and didn't seem to be wearing a stitch of makeup. "So, Mackenzie—"

"Mack, sir, if you don't mind."

"You don't go by Mackenzie?"

"Not since I could talk and voice my opinion about it."

Ron smiled. Okay, so she was opinionated. And, judging by her body language, also trying to make a good impression. "Tell me about yourself."

"I love police work, and I love God. I'm a Christian, and I don't make any apologies for it."

"Huh." Ron looked down at the folder.

"If that makes you uncomfortable, sir, I'm sorry. But you told me to tell you about myself, and that's me."

Ron closed the folder and threaded his fingers together, thinking about the episode with Pastor Kyle. "Very funny. You almost got me."

Her expression didn't budge.

Ron cracked a smile. "Let me guess. You want to pray for me."

The young woman looked puzzled. "Well, sir, if that's what it takes for me to get on this team, I'd be happy to. I've been praying about it every day, but I will admit it's been difficult. I want to do this so badly, I'm having a hard time asking God for his will."

"Come on," Ron said. "I'm onto you." Ron glanced to his doorway and back to Mack. The police department had a long history of practical jokes. The jokes were often what made the days and nights bearable. Ron himself had been responsible for so many practical jokes they'd nicknamed him Jester. "Gates was in on this, wasn't she? Nan must have told her about our pastor coming over to pray for me. It's funny. Really. I get it now, so you can stop pretending. But I have to ask, are you really Officer Hazard, or did they hire you to act like her? Are you an actress?"

"I did work for many years as a clown."

Ron couldn't stop himself from laughing. "A clown, good one." He looked at her file picture. It did look an awful lot like the woman sitting across from him. "Nan has got to be in on this."

"Who is Nan?"

"So what were your instructions?"

"Um…I was told that you wanted to speak to me and that I should come by your office as soon as possible."

"Come on, drop the act."

"What act?"

"Let's just get this over with. Go ahead. Pray for me."

"Sir, the last time I did that, I nearly got fired. So you're going to have to give me explicit permission."

Ron felt like he was going to start laughing all over again. He looked at her, but she remained seated. "Right. Permission. Okay, permission granted. Get over here and lay hands on me. And make it a good one."

"Sir," she said, "you do understand—God does all the work, not me."

Ron couldn't hold it together anymore and started laughing uncontrollably. He couldn't remember the last time he had laughed this hard. He waved the girl over. If this really was Officer Hazard, she was one heck of a prankster, which meant she was most likely going to make a really good UC officer. As she walked to the other side of his desk, Ron stopped her and grabbed her hands, flipping them over to look at the palms. He'd once fallen prey to Jimmy Whatts's red-dye prank. Jimmy would walk by and give you a friendly pat on the cheek or neck, leaving a bright red handprint that you would only notice if you happened to look in the mirror. He got away with this four or five times before he became Hands-Off Jimmy, and no one allowed him to touch them.

"Hands off, sir."

Ron dropped her hands and cleared his throat. "Oh, uh…sorry."

"I've done a lot of praying, but not once has anyone ever examined my hands." A suspicious eyebrow popped up.

Ron sighed. The joke had definitely run its course. "Make sure you pray about my midlife crisis."

"No offense, sir, but I think you're a ways past the 'mid.' But I will ask God to heal your leg."

"Okay…" This was getting less funny by the second.

Ron sat still as she prayed for him. He kept expecting her to start cracking up, but she didn't. Her prayer was short, to the point, and twice mentioned his "later-life crisis." Then she returned to her seat.

"May we continue with the interview?" she asked.

Ron stared at her, bewildered. He'd known lots of good pranks, but this seemed more like an epic. He was about to tell her this when he noticed Captain Gates standing in the doorway.

"Sergeant Yeager, I need to see you outside for a moment."

Ron stood, grabbed his cane, and walked out into the hallway.

"Were you in on this?" Ron asked her.

"What?"

"The joke."

"What joke?"

Ron glanced toward his office door. "Is that Mackenzie Hazard in there?"

"That's what I wanted to speak to you about. She's… I don't know how to say this delicately, so I'll just say it. She's very religious."

"Please tell me you're joking."

"I thought I should forewarn you. She's an excellent police officer, but the whole religious thing could be a lot to manage."

Ron's smile faded.

"What's wrong? You're religious, aren't you?"

"I am, but—"

"Did you see the report on the convenience store robbery? She saved a hostage."

"Her file looked good, but she doesn't have any undercover experience."

"She has a lot of potential. She'll be a good addition to the team." Gates studied him. "Don't tell me you've never worked with a female undercover officer before."

"I have. Just not a former clown."

"If the worst thing she has in her record is a clown background, more power to her, you know? Let me know when you've got your team assembled. We've almost got a location ready where you can set up your operation."

Ron watched Gates disappear around the corner. He took a deep breath and walked back into his office. Mack Hazard sat right where he had left her. But she was hunched over, and her hands were clasped together. Was she praying again?

When he cleared his throat, she sat upright. "Yes sir?"

"Sorry about the interruption," Ron said as he made his way back to the desk. "Now, let's get back to your file, here."

"All right." She stared intently at him.

"Look," Ron said. "About that crisis thing…I was just joking. I'm not really having a life crisis."

For the first time, he saw her smile. "And I guess that cane is just a prop too?"

Chapter 7

Jesse walked into the Henderson police station. It was after five and the office was nearly empty, just the way he liked it.

He went upstairs to Greer's office. He knew the chaplain liked to stay later than most, and this was the best time to find him.

Greer sat at his desk, reading his Bible. His office was a peaceful place—a slice of paradise in the middle of nonstop chaos.

As usual, Chaplain Greer didn't notice Jesse standing in his doorway until Jesse said, "*Hello,* Chaplain!" Jesse laughed as the chaplain picked his Bible up off the floor. "Surprised you, didn't I?"

"Yes," Chaplain Greer said. "Just like you do every time." He offered a small smile.

"It's just too hard to resist." Jesse plopped down in the leather chair. "I had a weird day."

The chaplain set his Bible on the desk and took a deep breath. "Jesse, I am always here for you if you need me. But we've talked about this before. I'm not a priest. You don't have to confess things to me."

"You're not my priest. You're my good-luck charm."

Chaplain Greer shook his head. "Jesse, we've been over this. I thought you were working on your superstitions."

"I am. Most don't seem to be doing much good, like the dry ice in my bathtub. And the rabbit's foot. I've outgrown that one, but you are the exception. Ever since the day you prayed for me at the hospital, not one bad guy has pulled a gun on me. And there's that one other little detail—that I didn't die."

"But like I've told you before—"

"Chaplain Greer, I appreciate your humility. I really do. The police department could use more people like you. God knows there are enough egos around here to warrant a second building. But you and I both know there's something unique between us. I have to tell you what happened to me today."

Chaplain Greer glanced at his watch. "I've got to deliver a care package to the Samson house. His wife had triplets."

"This won't take long."

"All right." Chaplain Greer took out his stopwatch. "You've got ten minutes. Just remember, no matter how much you tell me about your sin, it's God who forgives, not me."

"I know, I know. So I'm doing a deal this morning, and it goes down as planned, except for the girlfriend."

"What about her?"

"Turns out she was my prom date."

"Prom date?"

"Back in high school."

"What a coincidence. Listen, I need to get going—"

"Wait, there's more. We arrest her because she's got cocaine in her purse, right? So then she starts yelling at me and tells me I was a lousy prom date."

Chaplain Greer leaned back in his chair and crossed his arms. "Jesse, this is nothing compared to last week when you lost your temper and punched a hole through the wall. And the week before that when you cussed out your superior. I'm not sure being a lousy prom date actually qualifies as a sin."

"Well, having to arrest her just makes things worse."

"That can certainly dampen a date."

"I mean today. I had to arrest her today."

"Okay…so what's the problem, exactly?"

"You've been talking a lot about forgiveness. Maybe I should say I'm sorry."

"Maybe she was just angry that you were arresting her."

"I thought of that, but…I really was a lousy prom date."

Chaplain Greer slid his Bible into his briefcase. "Jesse, as much as I'd like to continue with this, I really do need to go visit the Samsons. They already have three kids. This makes six. These are the sort of people who need a chaplain."

"Do you think I should apologize?"

"Did you ask God?"

"I'm asking you."

"Proms aren't my area of expertise." He stood and reached out to shake Jesse's hand. "I'm sure you'll know what to do."

"Why won't you tell me what to do? You always tell me what to do."

"Jesse, I really do have a great deal of patience. And I am happy that you are concerned with the moral choices you make. But you have to believe me when I say I had nothing to do with the fact that you made it through that shooting. A lot of people were praying for you. Not just me. The person you need to be thanking is God."

Jesse followed the chaplain out of his office. "What good is having a chaplain if he doesn't help you through things?"

"I am helping you, Jesse. I promise. I'm helping you by not helping you."

He watched Chaplain Greer walk down the stairs and out of sight as his cell phone rang.

"Hello?"

"Detective Lunden?"

"Yes."

"This is Jackie Taylor from property crimes in Las Vegas calling on behalf of Sergeant Ron Yeager. He would like you to come by his office this afternoon."

"What's this about?"

"I don't know, sir. I'm just supposed to ask if you could come by, anytime after three o'clock."

"Sure. Fine."

"Thank you. I'll tell Sergeant Yeager you'll be there."

Jesse slid his phone into his pocket. He'd be there. But first he had an appointment with a former prom date.

Laura waved Ron in. "How's it going?"

"Fine. I've got a couple of guys coming in this afternoon and one tomorrow."

"Good."

"I wanted to ask you about these reports. I've been reviewing them all morning. Something struck me as strange."

Laura set down the papers she'd been holding. "What?"

"There's definitely been a spike in auto theft over the past eight months. But there's an interesting pattern emerging about the kinds of cars that are being stolen."

"What about them?"

"Some don't fit the profile. Look at this. On the third week of September, three minivans were stolen."

"You know you've got a problem when minivans are being stolen," Laura said, grinning.

"Yeah, I guess," Ron said. Laura could practically see the wheels turning in his head. "It just seems odd."

"The task force was approved in large part because this is starting to affect the middle and upper class. That's how I had to sell it. But if it doesn't play well in the press, then it doesn't play."

"I've never worked in property crimes. Maybe minivans are a hot item."

"They do have those flip-down televisions."

"Right." Ron smiled. "Your dad hated television, didn't he? He always had his nose in a book. Does he still enjoy reading?"

Although she prided herself on a good poker face, Laura knew she was horrible at hiding her emotions when it came to her dad. "Dad and I haven't really… We don't speak."

Ron apparently needed to brush up on his poker face as well. "Really?"

"We had a falling out a while back."

She could tell Ron wanted to know more. "He didn't want me going into police work. He was adamant. But that's all I ever wanted to do. I guess we just don't understand each other. He's a stubborn man, and that's what made him so good at what he did." She paused. "If there's nothing else, I need to get back to my work."

"One more thing."

"Yes?"

"I want permission to train my team the way I want, with nobody else in the middle of this. We've got limited time and a lot of work to do."

Laura nodded, but she was suppressing a smile. Ron Yeager was going to serve his purpose well, and he didn't even know everything there was to know about that purpose.

Jesse waited in front of a Plexiglas window for Brandi Brown with the same nervous jitters he had before prom. The last time he'd seen her, she was a petite brunette with a kind smile and a passion for partying. Now she was a blonde, and there wasn't much kindness in her smile. Then again, she had been arrested by the guy who dumped her for a redhead with a fake ID.

The door opened and the guard brought Brandi to her seat. Bewilderment and anger flipped back and forth across her face. She picked up the phone when Jesse did.

"Brandi, you're probably wondering why I'm here."

"Well, I'm not wondering about whether or not my hair looks good in an updo." She leaned forward. "Mason is a liar. He planted that stuff on me."

Jesse studied her drawn face and sunken eyes, trying to find anything resembling the girl he knew from high school. Life had done a good job of beating her down.

"Look," she said. "Yeah, I use. Not all the time. I'm trying to get off of it, you know? And I've been doing good. I work at the bar. I hold down a job. I have weak moments. But not very often. Mason is the user. You gotta believe me."

Jesse had rehearsed what he was going to say all the way to the jail, but now that she was sitting there hoping to get a favor from him, it seemed incredibly awkward, not to mention irrelevant.

"Brandi, the fact that you were there was a… We didn't realize you were connected with Mason other than working at the bar. But that's not why I'm here. I just wanted to tell you that I'm sorry for ditching you at prom."

Brandi looked at Jesse as if he'd suddenly morphed into a monkey.

He continued. "Look, back in high school I was a real jerk. I was just out to party and be an idiot. I'm sorry if I hurt you that night. I really am."

"That was, like, a decade ago."

"I know."

"You came all the way here to tell me you're sorry for…for… Wait a minute. I thought you got the stomach flu."

Jesse looked down. So *that* was the lie he couldn't remember. He knew he'd come up with something. Not very original.

"You ditched me for someone else?"

"I'm a loser. *Was* a loser, I mean." Jesse scratched his forehead, trying to draw sympathy yet not look too pathetic. "Brandi, I just want to apologize to you."

She started laughing.

"What's so funny?"

"The whole night I was wishing I would've gone with Sean Andrews. When you got the stomach flu and left, I thought I was the luckiest girl alive."

"You didn't want to go with me?"

"I said yes because I was afraid no one else would ask me. But you were in your own little world. I drove, you never opened the door for me, and I was the only girl without a rose or carnation. Plus, you danced like an idiot."

"If I remember correctly," Jesse blurted, "you were drunk before we even got there."

"That was my only hope of having any fun."

Jesse hung up the phone and left. Chaplain Greer was going to hear about this. Apologizing in person was not all it was cracked up to be.

Ron wasn't sure what he'd been expecting, but the young man sitting across from him definitely was a bit of a surprise. Lamar Takahashi's dark African American skin, hazel Asian eyes, and blond, curly hair practically assaulted the senses. Ron had certainly encountered many different cultures and races, but never so many wrapped up into one person.

Lamar droned on for five minutes about his career in patrol, until finally, looking as if he needed to add something more exciting, he said, "My mother is black, my father is Asian, and I was raised in Australia by an American nanny. I came to the United States when I was eighteen, became a citizen, and I've been here ever since."

"It says in your file you're interested in doing UC work."

"Yes."

"Why? What interests you about it?"

"I don't know."

"I've got a lot of people who do know, so you might want to give me a bit more than, 'I don't know.'"

"Maybe it's because my nanny wouldn't ever let me out of the house."

Ron glanced at his notes. "You've been a patrol officer for eight years. You've flunked the promotional exam twice."

"It's a stupid test."

"What makes it stupid, exactly?"

"It has nothing to do with the street. The test is a bunch of rules and regulations that you should know, sure, but at the end of the day, it's all about instinct."

"What makes you think you would be good at undercover work? We have to follow the rules and regulations just like everybody else. This is no place for a maverick."

"True, but it's no place for those who worship the policy and procedure tests either, is it?"

"We still have to draw lines in undercover work, or we're no better than the people we're bringing down. You have to understand that and never compromise."

"I understand."

Ron studied Lamar. "Lamar, what languages do you speak?"

"Just English."

"Oh. Um, what about accents? Do you do any accents?"

"I do a nice John Wayne impression."

"Anything else?"

"No."

"I was just hoping, with your background, you could bring some cultural diversity to the table."

"I can make stir-fry taste like barbecue."

"That's quite a talent."

Lamar leaned forward. "I know this is what I'm meant to do."

Ron saw it in Lamar's eyes. Ambition. A love for it. He stood. "I'll let you know, Officer Takahashi. Thanks for taking the time to come in."

Jackie buzzed him. "Sergeant Yeager, Detective Lunden is here."

"Thanks, Jackie."

"Oh, and Sergeant Yeager?"

"Yes?"

"Your wife called, wanted to remind you to take your heart medication."

"Thanks," Ron said, sighing. He glanced at Lamar, who was studying the cane leaning against his desk. He shook Lamar's hand. "I'll be in touch."

He watched Lamar leave and then took out Jesse Lunden's file. Time to meet his problem child.

Chapter 8

Rhyne Grello watched Bobby drive the minivan through the large garage door and into the warehouse. He pulled the warehouse door closed as Bobby rolled down the window. "Where do you want it?"

Rhyne pointed to the far corner.

"Over there?" Bobby asked above the noise of four men working to disassemble a Lincoln. "Why?"

"Just do it."

"We're ready to take a load out to Griffin's shop."

The side door opened, and Mason Capps strolled across the concrete toward Rhyne. "Give me a minute, will you?" Rhyne asked Bobby. The minivan rolled past, and Mason approached, his hands stuffed in his pockets and guilt written all over his face.

"Heard you had a long night."

"I posted bail; let's just drop it."

Rhyne turned toward his friend. They'd known each other since they were seven years old. Their parents used to play poker together every Friday night, and their dads worked at the same casino. Mason had always been the irresponsible one, the one who got them caught when they were doing something wrong.

"We can't afford this," Rhyne said bluntly. "There's too much at stake."

"Look, it went down in Henderson. It was my first time."

"You assured me you weren't dealing on the side."

"It was stupid, okay? I admit it. Can we just get past this?" Mason nodded toward Bobby. "So are we going to Griffin's tonight?"

Rhyne shook his head and said, "I'm getting word Griffin's may go down. I don't want to risk it."

"So whadda we do?"

"Hang tight."

"We could turn three thousand dollars tonight."

"Or turn up in jail."

"C'mon, Rhyne. You're going to let some rumors stop you? Griffin's good for it. We already know that."

"We don't want to be in the middle of a shakedown."

"We've heard rumors about Griffin's for months. Nothing has happened."

"We're going to sit on this, Mason."

"What am I supposed to tell the guys?" Mason asked.

"Maybe you could give them a lesson about how greed can take you down." He gave Mason a hard look. "I've been telling you that for years. You're always in a rush."

"We strike while the iron's hot. If we wait, somebody else will bring the goods to Griffin's and then we got nothin'."

"Nothing?" Rhyne nodded toward the minivan. "That's something."

"Yeah, that was quick," Mason said, the excitement obvious in his voice.

"Don't say anything. I told the other guys my sister needed it fixed."

"What can I say? You haven't told *me* much."

Bobby approached and Rhyne nodded toward the Lincoln. "Finish that up, then head into Henderson; try to drop a few parts at Davey's."

"Henderson," Bobby groaned. "The yuppie place that always asks questions."

"It's a formality. They ask so they can say they asked. They don't care what the answers are. As long as we keep it small, they're not going to get nervous. Now get back to work and stop giving me a hard time."

Bobby walked back over to the Lincoln. Rhyne turned to Mason and lowered his voice.

"We leave in three hours."

Jesse rounded the corner and entered the first office on the right, as the secretary had instructed. An older man sat at a desk with his attention on a folder. The office was nearly bare.

"Sorry," he said as the old guy looked up. "I think I have the wrong office."

"Who are you looking for?"

"Sergeant Yeager."

"That's me."

"Oh…" *kay. Is that a cane leaning against his desk?*

"Come on in."

Jesse stuffed his hands in his pockets. He would normally try to get a feel for the person based on the office décor, but since the walls were bare, he just dropped into the chair and looked at the man.

"Thanks for seeing me on such short notice." Yeager removed his bifocals, and Jesse wasn't entirely sure he could see without them.

"Sure," said Jesse. "You are aware I have no idea what this is about, right?"

"I'm trying to keep this under the radar a bit. We're setting up an undercover task force—Task Force Viper."

"Who is *we*? Isn't this the Property Crimes Bureau?"

"Yes. We're losing about two cars an hour. I need some good UC officers who can help me bring down an auto-theft ring."

"You're heading it?"

"Captain Laura Gates is. She appointed me to lead and train the UC team."

"Train?" Jesse laughed. "I've been working undercover in narcotics for three years. I don't need training."

The sergeant looked at the folder on his desk. "I've read your file. You do have a lot of experience." He paused and looked up. "But in three years, you've closed less than forty percent of your cases. There's always room for improvement."

Jesse crossed his arms. "Look, with all due respect, I don't think I'm interested, okay? I've got a good thing going in Henderson."

"Sure."

"It's nothing personal."

"I understand. You think narcotics is where the game is."

"Sergeant, maybe you'd have better luck with some of the vice guys. They all stay a couple of years in Henderson, but some of them are itching to get out."

"Interesting."

"For some of the less experienced UC guys, auto theft would be a step up."

"But it's a step down for you."

"No insult intended. I just like working narcotics."

"A six-month stint in this task force could widen your radius of experience."

"I could give you a few names of guys who might be more of what you're looking for."

The sergeant smiled. "You're not what I'm looking for?"

"I'm flattered. But I don't have any interest in doing auto theft."

Sergeant Yeager closed his folder. "Thanks for the offer of names. But I just have one more spot to fill. And actually, one of the guys I just brought on gave me your name. Said you were one of the best."

"Who's that?"

He looked down at a paper on his desk. "Elliot Stillman."

"Dozer?" Jesse blinked. "Elliot signed on?"

"About three hours ago."

Chapter 9

W hat do you think you're doing?" Jesse said as Dozer swung open his front door. He didn't seem surprised to see Jesse. Despite Dozer's apparent grogginess, he still looked guilty. They walked to the living room where Sarah was rocking Emmy.

"Hi, Jess," she said.

Jesse tried to mind his manners. He'd learned long ago never to get on a wife's bad side. Even when she's not your wife. "How's Emmy doing?"

"Fighting sleep, like usual. She's only three months. Sleep is what they're supposed to be doing."

"So she doesn't take after her father, then," Jesse said with a smile.

Sarah laughed. "Not yet."

"Let's go to the back patio," Dozer said. "You want something to drink?"

Jesse shook his head and followed Elliot out the back door. A small table sat between two lounge chairs. The air was cool and felt good in his lungs.

"I was going to tell you," Dozer said. "I just haven't had a chance. Grace has been sick, Taylor needed help with her homework, and Emmy's got the colic thing going." Dozer sighed. "I knew you'd be upset."

"Why would you take this? We've got good things going in Henderson."

"*You've* got good things going. I'm still feeling my way through. You got me on in narcotics, and I really appreciated that. But ever since then, I've been following your lead, trying to get better, but not doing so great. Sergeant Yeager promised some training, and I could use that. I think it would be interesting to explore auto theft. I can't do UC work forever, and I don't really like narcotics that much." He leaned back into his chair. "I've

wanted to get in with Vegas for a while. It's better pay. Sarah could quit
her part-time job. It's only a six-month task force, but it could get my foot
in the door." Dozer reclined in the chair. "Yeager mentioned you were
coming in later, and I told him you were really good, that you'd be a huge
asset to the team. I was hoping you might sign up."

Jesse stared into the small backyard, the moonlight washing out the
green grass. "I've wanted to get into Vegas narcotics forever. But this is auto
theft. Not my sweet spot. Plus, I get to do things how I want to do them
now. If I move into Vegas, it's a new ballgame. Bigger city, more hoops to
jump through. Plus, how old do you think Yeager is? Dozer, swear to me
that when we get that old, we'll get desk jobs and take our bathroom breaks
every fifteen minutes. I mean, did you see the guy's cane?"

Dozer didn't answer. His head had fallen backward and he was snoring lightly. Jesse nudged him, but he was out. He rose and found Sarah
still in the living room. Emmy's wide-awake eyes were focused on the ceiling fan. "Narco Polo is out cold." Jesse swore the guy had narcolepsy, but
getting him to go to the doctor was like getting Jesse to go to the doctor.
Impossible.

She smiled. "Sorry about that."

"I wouldn't have it any other way. Besides, I don't want to have to
come up with a new nickname for him… Do I need to carry him to his
room or something?"

"Nah. He'll eventually wake up and stumble into bed."

"All right. Well, good luck with Emmy."

"Thanks, Jess. See you soon."

As Jesse walked toward his truck, he couldn't help but wonder what
life would be like working UC without Dozer. He began to wonder if he'd
made his stupidest career move yet. Or *non*move. Either way, it was a good
thing he'd never considered Dozer a good-luck charm.

Ron walked up the sidewalk to his home ready to bite someone's head off. Pastor Kyle's car was parked out front again. When Ron stepped through the front door, Pastor Kyle stood abruptly. Nan had crossed the line, but Ron suspected she already knew that.

She sure didn't look nervous when he glared at her.

"Hi, honey," she said with a smile.

Kyle, on the other hand, was practically shaking. Ron decided he might as well have some fun. He gave Kyle a look that instantly made Kyle grow pale. The look worked on bad guys, but it worked even better on good guys. "What's going on here?"

"Ron, knock it off," Nan said. "You're scaring the poor kid to death."

"Why is Kyle here again?"

"You're being rude," Nan said, still sitting comfortably on the couch.

"I'm sorry to just drop by," Kyle said quickly, fumbling his fingers around each other, "but Nan said I could stay until you got home. And she's cooking."

"Stay for dinner? Nan's cooking without Schwan? Kyle, you may be about to witness your first miracle."

"Who is Schwan?" Kyle asked.

"Our private chef."

"Funny, very funny," Nan said from the couch. "Keep it up, and I'll be cooking for one."

Ron turned to Kyle. "So why are you here?"

"I wanted to talk to you about your career."

"My career?"

"I'm just curious about it, that's all," Kyle said. "I think it sounds really interesting."

"Oh, it is. Fascinating," Nan piped in from the couch. "If you're lucky, he might even show you his guns."

Ron dialed back the expression. Kyle looked as genuinely curious as he did frightened. Ron gestured toward the couch so they could sit.

"Nan was telling me all about your career in undercover work," Kyle said, sitting as far away as he could from Nan.

Ron set his cane in the corner. "That was a long time ago. I haven't done undercover work in a while."

"Nan says you're back."

"I'm not back; I'm just training some kids and leading a task force."

"You even talk like them!"

"Like who?"

"The cops on those TV shows. I watch all the *CSIs*, all the *Law & Orders*. I had no idea a man in my congregation did this for a living!" Kyle's eyes were wide with excitement.

"Kyle, I'm flattered that you find my work interesting. But those television shows, well, they don't always paint an accurate picture of—"

"I've been intrigued with undercover work ever since I saw *Donnie Brasco*."

Nan chuckled.

"And *24*. Do you watch *24*?"

"Kyle," Ron said, "I know it sounds fascinating. And it is certainly interesting and can be exciting, but it's not quite like the movies."

"But it's dangerous work, right? I mean, it's really dangerous."

"Actually, patrol officers on the graveyard shift have a much more dangerous job. For that matter, any patrol officer."

"Really?"

"Undercover work is very controlled and planned. Every time patrol officers pull someone over or get a call, they have no idea what they're walking into."

"But it's got to be crazy pretending you're a bad guy. Have you ever been shot?" Kyle's eyes were so wide now that Ron wondered if something more exciting might be going on behind him.

"No."

"Have you had to shoot someone?"

Ron didn't want to go there. "Kyle, look, as much as I'd like to keep talking about this, I'm sure you need to head home and get some sleep. I know how tiring the ministry can be."

Kyle's shoulders slumped. "I don't really have anything going on tomorrow." He looked at Ron. "I was hoping I could hang out with you."

"Hang out with me?"

"I've got a sabbatical coming to me."

"Aren't you a little young for a sabbatical?"

"It's a postmodern thing," Nan said, shrugging.

"Postmodern? We're barely out of the dark ages," Ron said and grimaced, thinking of their relic of an organist.

"The denomination makes me take one every year," Kyle said. "I promise I'll stay out of your way. I just want to watch what you do."

"Kyle, all you would be doing right now is watching me fill out paperwork. Lots of it."

"Oh." Kyle looked like he'd just heard the news of a relative's death.

"Besides," Ron said, trying to keep the conversation light, "isn't the point of a sabbatical to rest? To spend time connecting with God?"

Kyle sighed. "I do that every morning. And every evening. The most excitement I've had all week was when Nan called me and told me you were in the street. Turned out you weren't, but then I found out you're an undercover police officer." He shrugged. "Maybe we can go to lunch sometime. I mean, I know a lot of this stuff is classified, but maybe you can tell me some of it."

Ron laughed. "Kyle, it's not classified."

"I heard that undercover officers work out of a separate office and that the other officers don't even know where they're located."

"That's to protect our identity. If we're ever followed, the trail doesn't lead back to the police department."

"See! See? That's what I'm talking about!"

"Look, Kyle, I appreciate your enthusiasm for my work, but you've got an important job too. You have an eternal impact. Mine is more of a twenty-to-life kind of deal."

Kyle's gaze found the carpet. "Yeah, I guess."

"Look, why don't you stay for dinner. I'll tell you some stories from my undercover days."

"Really?"

"Sure."

Kyle stood and pumped Ron's hand enthusiastically. "Thank you." He looked at Nan. "And thanks for the dinner invitation."

"Sure," she smiled.

Ron led Kyle out to the back patio. "We love eating out here. Make yourself comfortable. What do you want to drink?"

"Do you have iced tea?"

"I'm sure we do. I'll be back in a few minutes."

Ron walked into the kitchen where Nan was chopping vegetables for a salad. She threw up her hands in protest. "I didn't invite him over. I swear. He was lingering, and I felt trapped. So I asked him what he liked to eat. All I could get out of him was ham sandwiches."

"He just showed up?"

"About thirty minutes ago." She opened the fridge, and her voice became quiet. "I got a call today from the eye doctor wanting to know if you would like to pick up your contacts or have them shipped to the house." She turned to face him and folded her arms. "You're getting contacts? You haven't ever worn contacts."

"The bifocals aren't helping my image any. You should see the way these guys look at me. I might as well be dead and in a coffin."

"You think getting rid of your bifocals is going to help? What about that cane? And in case you haven't noticed, what hair you have left is white."

Ron sighed and leaned against the counter. "It's a different world, Nan. Maybe I don't belong anywhere but behind a computer. I've interviewed at least a dozen officers, and still only have three who are willing to work on the task force. Back in my day, any one of us would've jumped at a chance to work a case like this. Maybe it's me. Maybe they take one look at me and wonder if I'm going to make it to the six-month deadline before I croak."

"Stop it. You're stealing all my best lines. Please tell me you took your heart medication."

"I did. But the last thing I need is for them to see me popping heart pills."

"What about your problem child?"

"Wasn't interested. Likes working yuppie narcotics cases in Henderson." Ron took a glass from the cupboard and filled it with ice. "Remember Rodney Beavers?"

"Sure."

"When I was just starting UC work, Rodney was like a mentor to me. He was in his late thirties, and of course I thought he was over the hill, but he had a ton of experience. I learned some of my best tricks from him. I remember one time we were doing this big buy, and I was posing as the money man. We flew a rented airplane in to meet him, just to make it look like we were rolling in cash. I knew in order to sell the part of a big buyer, I was going to have to verify the product as cocaine. Rodney showed me how to dip one finger into the bag and then lick the finger next to it. It worked perfectly."

"So does your cholesterol medication, when you take it." She dropped two pills into his hand and poured him a glass of water.

"These guys don't want a mentor. They think they already know it all." Ron swallowed the pills. If he didn't take the bull by the horns, he would get chased around the ring like a rodeo clown. He sighed again and looked at Nan. "What do we have on our calendar tomorrow?"

She looked at the calendar hanging by the fridge. "You've got an appointment with your heart doctor at four thirty."

"Cancel it."

Nan turned. "Cancel it? It takes three months to get an appointment."

"My heart's fine. We're going shopping."

Nan's fists planted against her hips did plenty to express her anger. "Shopping?"

"At Wal-Mart."

"Wal-Mart? You wouldn't be caught dead at Wal-Mart."

"Trust me," Ron said. "This is going to be fun." He took Kyle's glass and started to walk to the back porch.

"What exactly are we getting at Wal-Mart?"

"A glimpse of what the next six months are going to look like."

"Where are you going?"

"To take Kyle his iced tea and invite him to go shopping with us tomorrow."

"What?"

Ron smiled a smile he knew would cause Nan to grind her teeth. She hated not being in the loop, but he also knew she would go through the roof if he told her what he was planning.

Ron joined Kyle at the patio table. "It's a great evening," Kyle said. "Thanks for inviting me to stay for dinner."

"Our pleasure, Kyle. You're our pastor. Like…um…one of the family."

"You're kind."

"Which is why I wouldn't ask just anyone for this favor."

"You need a favor? From me?"

"It's a pretty big one."

"Please don't hesitate. What is it?"

"I'd like you to help me train these UC officers."

Kyle's mouth trembled with a nervous grin. "You want me to help you train undercover agents?"

"Officers. Yes."

Kyle was shaking his head with astonishment. "I can't believe it." He looked up at Ron. "What do you want me to do?"

Ron lowered his voice, just for effect. "I can't give you all the details right now. And we're going to need to keep this to ourselves. Can you be here tomorrow at two?"

"Yeah, sure."

"I want you to pose as an undercover officer I'm recruiting for the task force."

Kyle thought for a moment. "What should I wear? I've got slacks in every color and three pairs of jeans. I could rip a couple of holes in my jeans."

"Just show up looking like you usually do. No need to destroy any clothing."

Kyle looked down at his pressed cotton shirt and his tan khakis. "Like this?"

"Yep."

"You're sure? Won't I stick out like a sore thumb?"

Ron smiled. That was the idea.

Chapter 10

L aura liked the stillness of the early morning. She was in her office every day before the sun came up, and she got more work done in those two hours than during the rest of the day. An unexpected knock on the door broke both the silence and her concentration. She looked up to see a young man with earrings, tattoos on his arms, and a severe case of bedhead. "May I help you?"

"Detective Lunden, ma'am," he said. "You're Captain Gates?"

"Yes. What can I do for you, Detective, besides get you some hair gel?"

He blinked, like it was too early to process how he should respond. "May I come in?"

"Sure."

He closed her door and sat down. "I was invited by Sergeant Yeager yesterday to join a task force called Viper. I work UC in Henderson."

"That explains the hair."

"I met Sergeant Yeager. Nice guy. But…"

Laura smiled. "You were expecting someone younger?"

"It's no knock on him. It's just that you don't see someone that old, normally, in that kind of position. I mean, as part of a task force doing undercover work. Did he come out of retirement or something?"

"Sergeant Yeager is about twenty months away from retirement."

The young man clasped his hands together and looked for the right words. "The truth of the matter is that I would love to work with the Vegas unit. But not in property crimes. No offense, but my life is in narcotics."

Laura looked down at her desk. She once thought that would be her life too. "I understand, Detective. So why are you here?"

"I thought maybe if I worked this task force, you could put in a good word for me with the Vegas narcotics team."

"So you want to use this task force as a stepping stone?"

"I would give you everything I've got. I wouldn't just ride the wave."

"Look, I can't guarantee you anything." Laura hardly had any pull with narcotics. They didn't want her years ago, and they didn't want her or her opinions now. She caught his eager gaze. "You would do well to work for Sergeant Yeager. I had my pick of a lot of people, and I hand-picked Ron. Doesn't that make you wonder? It should."

"I've been working undercover for three years."

"But you haven't been working for Ron. He's one of the best. And he did it for nearly twenty years."

"I'm sure he has a lot of experience, but—"

"Have you ever heard of the Ki Club?"

The detective shook his head.

"You won't find a trail of paperwork on it, but if you worked in Chicago, you would know about it."

"What is it?"

"An informal organization that existed almost five decades ago. You didn't get into the Ki Club unless you did a buy for a kilo or more of cocaine."

The young man shrugged. "That's terrific. I've done a lot of deals for a kilo of cocaine."

Laura leaned on her desk. "Let me guess. All of those deals were controlled buys done by an informant, or repeated buys by you. You developed sufficient probable cause, obtained a search warrant, executed it, and when you searched the location, you found the drugs you were looking for."

"Sure. That's how it's done."

"The only way to get into the Ki Club was to do a hand-to-hand deal for a kilo of cocaine. Have you ever done a hand-to-hand deal for that much, Detective?"

He shook his head.

"Once you were in the Ki Club, you were assigned the bigger cases and you were working with some of the best around. Sergeant Yeager was in the Ki Club." Laura folded her hands together and looked directly into Detective Lunden's eyes. "You strike me as a guy who didn't go into police work for the pay or the pension. You love what you do."

He nodded.

"You have ambition. I can understand that. I had ambition too. But if you join this task force, Detective, I want you on board a hundred percent. You give me six months of your undivided attention. Period. After that, you can follow the job leads wherever they take you."

He stared down at the carpet.

"We could use a talented officer like you," she added.

That sealed the deal.

Jesse sat in his truck outside the Wal-Mart Super Center, clutching a white envelope that read, DO NOT OPEN UNTIL YOU'RE IN THE PARKING LOT. As if he didn't have reservations before, now he was on some kooky assignment.

He turned off his engine, tore open the envelope, and pulled the piece of paper out.

YOU HAVE TWO HOURS TO IDENTIFY THE FOUR OTHER
MEMBERS OF YOUR TEAM WITHOUT BEING DISCOVERED. AT THE
END OF THE TWO HOURS, WRITE DOWN THE DESCRIPTIONS OF
THE PEOPLE YOU THINK ARE YOUR FELLOW OFFICERS. THEN
RETURN TO 1159 FOSTER DRIVE BY 5:30 P.M.

Great. So this was what he was in for—stupid games and Undercover 101.

Jesse sighed and decided there wasn't much use complaining since he would be the only one to hear the complaint. He got out of his truck and went around to the back, where he opened a new container of socks. Since this was just training, he chose white. There was no point in wasting the clearly superior luck of colored socks on training. He peeled off his old socks, pulled the tag off the new ones, and put them on. He slipped into his tennis shoes, laced them tightly, then went back to the cab of his truck. Reaching inside the console that sat between the two front seats, he grabbed the bullet he kept there and rolled it between his hands three times. Then he positioned his framed picture of Elvis so it faced him. "Here it goes," Jesse said, knocking knuckles on the glass.

Jesse tossed the instructions on the seat, shut the truck door, and trudged forward. He checked his watch as the doors swooshed open. He was greeted by a voice announcing sales on bananas and Hanes underwear. An old woman, clutching smiley-face stickers and wearing a blue vest, rolled a shopping cart toward him.

"Anybody walk through these doors within the last few minutes and not ask for a cart?" Jesse asked.

The woman pushed her glasses up the bridge of her nose. "Sir, hundreds of people walk in and out of these doors in an hour."

"But you didn't notice anyone specifically not take a cart?"

Her greeter cheer diminished. "Is there something you need, like an aisle number or the location of the restrooms?"

This woman wasn't going to be helpful. But a shopping cart might—especially a two-seater for children. "I just need that cart," Jesse said. "The one that holds kids."

Granny Greeter looked him up and down. "Where are your kids?"

"Uh…parking the car?"

"This cart is for mothers with children, especially wily ones. They have the straps to belt them in so they can't run around the store."

"My wife's meeting me here. With our two kids, who will probably be on a sugar high from the party they just finished."

She looked suspicious. "What are your children doing out of school?"

"They're homeschooled. Now, may I have the cart?"

"Your wife is welcome to come get the cart when she arrives, as long as she has the kids." She glanced at his hand. "No wedding ring?"

"Had to sell it to pay the kids' dental bills."

"Right."

Jesse sighed and grabbed a regular cart, rolling it away from Keeper of the Carts. He grabbed a few packages of diapers and other random items so he would look like he was actually shopping. He figured he would start on a main aisle and then formulate his plan.

As he passed the small appliances section, he thought about yelling, "Gun!" Everyone but a cop would run screaming for the door. A cop would run toward the chaos.

He opted against this approach, imagining the stampede of innocent customers and injuries and lawsuits. He decided to wander each aisle and look for people who didn't seem the least bit interested in shopping. A man walking with his hands stuffed in his pockets and no cart. Someone standing at a clothing rack but looking elsewhere.

Forty minutes passed quickly. Jesse pulled his cart out of the hair accessories aisle. He had been distracted by the extensive selection of gels when he noticed a man passing the aisle. The man had medium-dark skin, blond hair, and plenty of tattoos. When Jesse caught up to him, he was admiring a pink infant dress and glancing around suspiciously like he might just shoplift it. Jesse smiled. *Bingo.* He would bet his lucky socks this guy was one of them. He made a note of his clothes and watched him for a few seconds longer. He was definitely not shopping for little girls' clothes. He started to turn around, and Jesse quickly slipped behind the underwear rack and out of sight.

He went through the automotive area but didn't see anything unusual. He wondered why he hadn't run into Dozer when he suddenly spotted him in the video game section…playing a video game.

"What are you doing?" Jesse asked, stepping up beside him.

Dozer glanced at his cart, then returned his attention to the game. "Diapers. Nice touch."

"Aren't you supposed to be looking for the other UC cops?"

"Yeah. Did that for a while. Got bored. This kid finally stopped playing, so I jumped on it. This is that new Xbox 360 game I was telling you about." His thumbs were flying fast over the buttons as a dragon breathed fire over an entire village. "Yes!"

"Dozer, seriously. You're not going to stand here and play video games, are you?"

"Look, I wandered around for almost an hour and all I noticed was a store full of weird people wandering around. I mean, this assignment might be easy at Macy's, but at Wal-Mart, you've got every kind of person in the world."

"I think that's the idea, Dozer," Jesse said, removing the joystick from his hands. "Come on, we've gotta finish this. We've got less than an hour. There is no way I'm going to let some other guy beat me."

Dozer looked longingly at the video game. "Thanks a lot. The wizard just got incinerated."

Suddenly, a distraught young woman near the photo lab desk caught Jesse's attention. She was gesturing toward the back of the store.

"I can't find her anywhere!" she said to the clerk.

Dozer glanced at Jesse, and they both walked closer.

"The last time I saw her, she was near the bathroom."

The photo lab tech picked up the phone and started dialing.

"Ma'am?" Dozer asked. "Are you okay?"

"Have you lost a child?" Jesse asked. If so, they would need to monitor the front doors immediately.

"No," she said, her voice trembling, "it's my grandmother. Gammy. She went off to use the restroom. I went to look at a magazine, and then she didn't come out for a long time, so I went to check on her and she wasn't there." She looked around, panicked. "I don't know what to do. She's got a bad memory. Not Alzheimer's, at least they don't think so. But she's forgetful and sometimes gets lost, which is why"—tears welled in her eyes—"Mom asked me to go with her to Wal-Mart. Last time Gammy went alone, she couldn't find her car."

"Does she have any identification with her?" Jesse asked.

"No. I have her wallet in my purse. What am I going to do? What if she went outside? What if she's wandering down the street?"

Jesse turned to the lab tech. "Get your security guy to canvas the parking lot looking for an older woman, okay? And have your greeters keep an eye out for…" Jesse turned to her. "What's her name?"

"Marie Holmes."

"What is she wearing?"

"A purple cardigan and a long off-white skirt."

"You got that?"

The lab tech nodded and finished dialing the number.

Dozer said, "I'll take the back half of the store. You go to the front."

Jesse nodded as Dozer rushed off. "Where do you think she might go?" Jesse asked.

"I've looked in all her favorite places…crafts, the bakery, by the sugar-coated cereals." She drew a tissue from her purse and blotted her eyes. "Should I call the police? I think I should call the police."

"Not yet, ma'am," Jesse said calmly.

"But maybe I should fill out a report. A missing persons report."

"This is a big place. Your grandmother is probably testing the hand lotions." This brought a smile from the woman.

"I would just feel better calling the police." She started to pull out her cell phone.

"Ma'am," Jesse said, "I am a police officer."

She raised an eyebrow. "Are you just trying to make me feel better?"

"No. I'm really a cop." She was staring at his tattoo. "Plainclothed."

"Oh. Well—" She stopped for a second and looked at her cell phone. "Hold on a second." She flipped it open. "Hello?... Gammy! Where are you? What...? Why did you...? Okay, fine. Just stay put. Don't move!" She snapped her phone shut, and relief washed over her. "She's at the car. She thought I'd headed out. Thank you." She reached out to shake his hand.

"You're welcome. I'm glad she's okay. Let the Wal-Mart staff know you found her on the way out."

"And thank your... Is he a friend?"

"Partner."

"Ah. Well, thank him too." She rushed away and Jesse turned, glancing at his watch. Thanks to Gammy, he only had thirty-five minutes left.

Chapter 11

R on looked up from the papers piled on his lap and watched Nan clear the breakfast dishes. He wanted to finish reading the profiles his agents had written before heading off to work. Nan continued back and forth between the table and the kitchen without a word.

Last night had been a brilliant success. After the officers made their best attempts to identify the other UCs at Wal-Mart, they joined him at the house for a silent cocktail party. Ron had gotten the idea from an academy instructor. He'd thrown a similar party for his class where everyone had to read body language to figure each other out. Then they had to write profiles about what they learned from body language alone.

Only Kyle seemed particularly fond of the exercise, but Ron learned a lot from each of them. No one had spotted all of the fellow officers at Wal-Mart. Mack had come the closest, pegging everyone but Kyle. Jesse had identified Lamar and Dozer, of course, but that was it. Apparently he didn't like losing to a girl, especially one pretending to have lost her grandmother.

Nan was an entirely different matter. Ron had asked her to prepare for a cocktail party, but didn't tell her about the silent aspect until the party began.

"You're quiet," Ron said as she took his plate.

"Oh," she said. "Is it over? I thought maybe we were still playing the quiet game."

"Are you still mad about that? I told you it was a training exercise."

"Yes, five minutes before the guests arrived. If I'd known the entire cocktail party was going to be silent, I would've prepared something a little crunchier."

Ron laughed.

"Maybe it was a training exercise for you," she said.

"What does that mean?"

"One of these years I might just stop speaking to you."

Ron tried to suppress his chuckle and failed. Nan's eyes softened, and he could tell she was getting a kick out of bugging him about it. She dropped two pills in front of him, "So I have to ask, what was the point of this activity? Why not just ask them to write up profiles on themselves?"

"I'm learning everything I need to know about each officer by what and how they wrote their profiles of the *other* officers." Ron took his pills. "Plus, that was a perfect setting to study body language. They all have a lot to learn."

She folded her arms. "And what, exactly, was your plan for Kyle? He wandered around the room doing this weird thing with his eyes, like he was trying to spy on everyone."

"I just wanted to see what they would do with him." Ron smiled. "He seemed to be enjoying himself."

"A little too much. I don't think this is what they had in mind when they granted him a sabbatical."

"Nothing wrong with some excitement. I don't think he's too damaged."

"Just don't do anything crazy, okay? He's our pastor. If it came down to it, God would be on Kyle's side, not yours, so don't do anything stupid."

Ron laughed. "I'm not worried about Kyle. He had fun. I'm worried about Mackenzie Hazard."

Nan turned. "She looked pretty tough."

"She's not."

"How do you know?"

"I just know. She's smart and naive, all at the same time." Ron shook his head. "I would never have picked her for undercover work."

"I could spot your problem child from a mile away. Something about how he kept heaving his chest and rubbing his arm muscles."

"He was outsmarted by Mack. By definition, all undercover officers are problem children. That's what makes them good at what they do. That's also why I'm worried about Mack."

"You just said she outsmarted the guys."

"She doesn't have a lot of real-world experience. She'll be a good pupil, though. Jesse, on the other hand, already thinks he knows everything. Dozer, as they call him, doesn't have enough confidence in himself for undercover work."

"The guy that fell asleep in the chair?"

"Yeah. And Lamar, well, he's as typical as they come."

"You got all that by reading what they wrote?"

"Yeah."

"That talent would've come in handy when our lovely daughter went through nine years of puberty. I should've just stolen her diary and let you dissect it. By the way, she's coming to dinner Saturday and bringing her fiancé."

"His name is Jeff."

"I know his name. But this is her fourth fiancé. Why waste the time remembering his name when he'll be gone in a month or two?"

"Anyway," Ron sighed, "I wish I would've had more time to come up with a team, but I had to do this fast."

The doorbell rang. Nan looked at Ron, then at the clock. "Who would be here this early?"

Ron grabbed his cane and made his way to the door while Nan rushed down the hallway to get her robe. He peered through the peephole and opened the door. "Kyle? What are you doing here?"

Kyle smiled through bloodshot eyes cupped by dark bags. "I've been creating an identity."

"A what?"

"An identity." Kyle walked past Ron into the house and rolled up his sleeve. "Check this out."

As far as Ron knew, Kyle had never before said the words "check this out." But that minor issue was overshadowed by the image Kyle was proudly showing off on his forearm. "You got a tattoo?"

"It hurt like the dickens, but isn't it awesome?"

Ron leaned in. It was barely the size of a dime.

"It's Chinese," Kyle said, and then he snickered. "It's so clever. You want to know what it says?"

Ron glanced down the hallway, praying he wouldn't see Nan.

"Check it out. Faster Pastor."

"Faster Pastor?"

"It was my nickname in seminary. I took a speed-reading course in college, and all the other MDivs were always jealous because I could read so much faster than them."

"Oh. Yeah. Um, clever." Ron felt beads of sweat popping onto his forehead.

"I was going to get my ear pieced—"

Ron was going to have to up his heart medication.

"—but then I decided against it. However, I did go get some hair wax." He pointed to his hair. "I've used hair gel for years, but apparently the new rage is hair wax. The lady said it will give my hair more texture." Kyle smiled. "Makes me look like a whole new person, doesn't it?"

Nan came breezing down the hallway.

Ron turned to Kyle and whispered. "Quick! Roll down your sleeve!"

Kyle nervously obeyed.

"Good morning, Kyle," Nan said. "What brings you by this morning?" The words were courteous but the tone didn't match.

Ron spoke. "Kyle just came by to thank us for the cocktail party."

"Uh…" Kyle glanced at Ron, then at Nan. "It was a very nice party. Thank you."

"I'll walk you out," Ron said, taking Kyle by the arm and leading him outside to the street where his car was parked.

"What's wrong?" Kyle asked.

"Kyle, what are you doing? Why would you get a tattoo?"

"You said you needed me to help you train the officers. That I was going undercover."

"That was just for last night. At the cocktail party."

"But my sabbatical is three weeks long. What am I supposed to do for three weeks?"

"Kyle, I appreciate your enthusiasm, but I can't really use you beyond what you did last night."

"Have I been compromised?"

Besides the fact that Kyle had watched too many episodes of *Alias,* he was also a bad liar. Nan, who had a talent for spotting lies, was peering out the window at them.

They noticed her gaze and instantly took on more casual demeanors. At least the kid could adapt. "Maybe I could be an informant," he said. "A good citizen informant. I've read about people doing that."

Ron had used a good citizen informant once—an elderly widower named Howard who passed the time watching cars come and go from the house across the street.

Ron paid Howard a visit one evening when he was bored. Howard told him the neighbors across the street seemed suspiciously unfriendly, but thought a story about how he was dying from cancer might work to get some drugs. At around midnight, two men entered the house and Howard made his way across the street with his walker. He knocked on the front door, gestured to his kidneys, handed over some money, and within a few minutes, Howard was rolling his walker back across the street holding a baggie full of drugs. Unfortunately, after the bust, Howard grew paranoid and called Ron every day for months claiming the mob was after him, until he died of natural causes at the age of eighty-nine.

"Well?" Kyle asked. "What do you think?"

"Kyle, informants are people who have connections to criminals. Do you know any criminals?"

Kyle seemed to be giving it serious thought. "No, I don't think so. Except maybe Mildred at church. Some of the elders think she's stealing money and aspirin out of purses."

"Listen, I thank you for your help, but—"

"I could keep helping you train your officers. I had so much fun last night at Wal-Mart, and then at that freaky silent party thing."

Ron imagined the "freaky silent party thing" only worked because Kyle didn't get to say anything.

"Please, Ron," Kyle said. "I'm not married, so I don't have any family to spend time with. I'm done with school, so I don't have any studying—"

"A sabbatical is a time for rest and reflection."

Kyle sighed. "I guess."

Ron worried that Kyle was bored this early in his career, but he could feel Kyle's pain. He'd been feeling a similar boredom for years. He'd spent so many years in the adrenaline rush of undercover work that when he moved to a desk job, he had to do something to feed the need for that rush. So he'd started racing cars. Three years later, an accident ended any hope of more excitement. He'd shattered his leg and gained a cane.

What was the harm in letting Kyle pose as a task force recruit for a few more days? It would be interesting to see how the other officers handled him. The profiles they'd written on him were hilarious. All of them suspected Kyle wasn't really undercover material. Mack Hazard noted that Kyle seemed like "the kind of person who liked to serve others and had a kindness and gentleness about him."

Throwing Kyle into the mix could train them to cope with the unexpected.

Ron glanced at the window and saw that Nan was gone. He looked back at Kyle. "All right."

"Really?"

"Yes, but"—Ron held up a stern finger—"this is temporary. A week at the most."

"I understand." Kyle grinned and shook Ron's hand. "Thank you."

"Just remember your calling is as a pastor. Don't lose yourself in this. And let's just keep it between us."

"Got it."

"I'll be in touch," Ron said.

Kyle sprinted back to his car. He drove off waving. Ron waved back. He would use Kyle to play head games with his team and learn how well they could handle out-of-the-ordinary circumstances.

Turning to head back into his house, Ron yelped as he nearly ran into Nan, who had snuck up behind him. She seemed pleased to startle him.

"Just remember, if something happens to Kyle in this stunt of yours, you're the one who's going in front of the ministry board to explain the whole thing."

Chapter 12

R on sat at the end of a small conference table waiting for his new
protégés. He had scheduled the meeting for 7:30 a.m. just to see the
condition they all arrived in. Mackenzie Hazard was ten minutes early,
bright-eyed and eager. It didn't bode well that she was clearly a morning
person. She had some long nights ahead of her.

Dozer walked in, sat down, and slumped in his chair. True to his nickname, he looked like he could fall asleep at any moment.

Lamar looked tired, but not exhausted. He worked the graveyard shift
in Boulder City as a patrol officer.

Kyle walked in at precisely 7:30 a.m., trying to look tough but only
appearing nervous and studious, thanks to the black leather planner he
carried under his arm. He greeted Ron and then went around the table
introducing himself again to the other team members. Mackenzie was
polite, but Lamar and Dozer looked at Kyle like he was an alien who'd just
beamed down from his UFO. Indeed, he had.

Jesse Lunden straggled in late and plopped down at the end of the
table, not bothering to make eye contact. Kyle half stood to offer his alien
handshake to Jesse when Ron called the meeting to order.

"All right, everyone. Welcome to Task Force Viper." Ron handed
Mackenzie a stack of stapled handouts to pass out. "As you know, this task
force was created to break up the auto-theft ring that's growing in the
metro area."

"This is why I tell homeowners that their garages aren't storage facili-
ties for all the things they buy and don't use," Mack said. "Once upon a
time they were for cars. I say donate all that stuff to Goodwill and park
the car in there."

"We'll try that campaign next year," Jesse said.

"You'll find the basic summary and stats on page two, as well as the demographic information," Ron continued. "You'll want to study these case files." Ron passed out folders with each of their names. "Lamar, Kyle, Mackenzie, here are your new identities. Jesse, Dozer, there's some stuff in there for you too. You've all been assigned new last names."

Kyle raised his hand. Jesse sighed and said, "This isn't grade school."

"Yes, Kyle?" Ron tried his best to stay serious. Kyle might put Jesse into an early grave.

"Why not change our first name too?"

"If you run into someone you know while working and they use your first name, you still have a chance to maintain your cover."

"I don't use my first name," Jesse said. "I go by Tony Ramone." Jesse folded his arms, expecting a challenge.

Ron ignored him. "There are two schools of thought on this. I happen to believe in using your real first name. I realize that there are those who think—"

"I was in a situation once," Jesse interrupted, "where, had my first name been used, I probably would've been shot. An old academy buddy saw me at a bar. He came up and said, 'Jesse, is that you?' I was going by the name of Tony, and I told the guy off, that I wasn't Jesse, and to stop drinking so much. If I'd have been using my real first name and he'd gone on about how we knew each other from the academy, I would've been toast, or at the very least, six months' worth of work would've been down the drain."

Ron didn't flinch. "Back in Chicago, we were all using different first and last names. We were inside a crack house, getting ready to cut a deal, when one of the new UC guys accidentally called me by my real name. Needless to say, the deal was called off, and we were lucky to get out of there alive." Ron intentionally glanced at the three newbies in the room. "This way nobody slips up."

Jesse sighed again and looked back down at his folder. "Yeah, well, we'll be lucky if names are all we have to worry about."

Kyle intently studied his folder. "This is no good."

"What isn't?" asked Ron.

Kyle gestured to his folder. "I mean…I'm kind of boring."

"This isn't *Mission: Impossible*. All they need to believe is that you're willing to do dirty deals," Jesse said.

"We don't want this to be too complex. The fewer details, the better," Ron said, hoping Kyle would quiet down. He'd just thrown something together to give him. It wasn't supposed to be real. "I've given you a basic rundown on your biography, but you'll have to fill in the blanks. Whatever you do, don't add anything that isn't real for you. If you end up hanging out with a bunch of guys who are in a garage band and you start talking about your guitar-playing days, chances are you'll be asked to play at some point. So make sure you really can play the guitar."

Kyle grinned, and his hand shot up again. "I can! I took lessons in high school. Acoustic only. Boy, what I would've given to be able to play the electric. I was also first-chair tuba." Kyle glanced around and cleared his throat. "But that probably won't be relevant."

"Oh, I don't know," Jesse said. "There's a huge black market for tubas."

Dozer laughed, and Ron waved at them to settle down. "Look, the point is, don't tell people you've been to places you haven't, or went to school where you didn't, or know someone you don't. Believable cover is critical. Getting caught in a lie could ruin it."

Jesse smiled. "Or in Kyle's case, *blow* it."

"It's called embouchure, and very few people can do it correctly," Kyle said.

Dozer shrugged. "He's right. I tried to play the thing and could never get my lips to vibrate like they were supposed to."

Jesse cut his eyes sideways but stayed silent.

"Your homework tonight," Ron continued, "is to write a twenty-page biography about yourself and know it front to back."

"How could we ever remember twenty pages about ourselves?" Kyle asked.

"Chances are you'll never use any of it, but you have to be prepared. You don't want to be caught off guard."

Jesse's smirk told the whole story—this was kindergarten work. Ron smiled to himself. Half of Jesse's battle was going to be getting through the training. Mackenzie and Lamar were studying the contents of their folders, and Kyle, in predictable fashion, was feverishly taking notes.

"In your packet you've got a driver's license, credit cards, and a social security card. When you put together your undercover wallet, make sure it looks real. Used. Worn." Ron looked at Jesse, who was sitting at the end of the table shaking his head. "Jesse?" Ron asked innocently. "Do you have something to add?"

Jesse threw up his arms. "I don't know, Sergeant Yeager. I mean, we still have to cover what to wear, how to act, how to talk, how to fit into Thug Universe." Jesse looked at Kyle. "Maybe Professor Khaki Pants isn't aware of this, but we're dealing with criminals here. According to Captain Gates, we've only got six months, and you're up here lecturing us on how to put a UC billfold together? What's next? Are you going to start handing out AC/DC T-shirts?" Jesse pointed to Mack. "Look at her. What is she, nineteen? From what I observed at that stupid cocktail party, she's not going to make it in undercover work."

Mack stood up. "I'm right here. If you've got something to say to me, then say it."

Jesse gave a nervous laugh. "Fine. What's your experience?"

"Egos make people blind and stupid."

"Ooh!" Dozer said, turning to Jesse. "Score one for the khaki team."

Mack glanced down at her pants and then back at Jesse. "You're judging me by what I wear to a meeting?"

Jesse tried to look unimpressed. "All I'm saying is that you don't have any experience and, from the looks of it, you aren't cut out for UC work."

Mack suddenly threw her folder. It slapped the table, slid to the other side and spilled into Kyle's lap. But nobody paid attention to the folder because they were all watching Mack's face turn red. She pointed her finger at Jesse. "I am so sick and tired of people like you. You think you're the best, that you can do anything. You have no idea who I am or what I'm capable of. Let me tell you something. You don't scare me. If I had to guess, I'd say you're terribly insecure, and if anybody knew the real you, they'd see someone a lot different, wouldn't they?" She glared at him, turned, and walked out the door, slamming it behind her.

A couple of tense seconds went by before people released a collective sigh. Jesse broke the silence. "Okay, maybe I was wrong," he said. "So she does have a little spunk. That's what we want to see."

The words had hardly left his mouth when the door swung back open again and there Mack stood, breathing heavily, her hands on her hips, her eyes focused on the carpet. "I'm sorry." She walked in and quietly shut the door. "I shouldn't have said those things. I have a temper passed down from my mother's side of the family, starting with my great-grandfather. As the story goes, he got so angry one day that he burned down his own house. That's neither here nor there. The point is…I shouldn't have shouted at you, Jesse, and I'm sorry."

Jesse paused, not sure what to say. But before he could open his mouth, Mack's remorseful look gave way to what looked to be another fit of—

"I said I'm sorry!" she yelled, then slapped her forehead. "See? There I go again!" She looked at Ron. "May I take a few minutes to compose myself?"

"Um…uh, yes. Sure."

Mack walked out, this time only firmly shutting the door. Everyone stared at Jesse.

"What?" he asked. "What did I do?"

"You should've accepted her apology," Dozer said.

The door opened again, and everyone tensed for another Mack attack, but Captain Gates entered.

"Good morning." She looked around the table. "So, this is my team?"

"Yes, ma'am," Ron said. "Minus one. Mackenzie. She'll be back in a bit. She's just…uh…"

"Ironing the wad out of her panties," Jesse said, grinning.

Dozer cracked a smile. "That's funny. Panties in a wad. That's"—he looked at Captain Gates and the smile dropped off his lips—"totally crude."

She looked them over, especially Kyle, who seemed to hold her interest.

"I came by to tell you we're going to have to move. I thought we could share floor space with the UC narcotics guys, but they've run out of room." Laura passed around folders. "Here's some info about the house where we'll be setting up operations. It's already been secured by the narcotics guys, but they don't use it. Stop by sometime today and check it out."

Ron said, "Move anything in there you think you'll need, but absolutely nothing that would identify you as a cop. We'll meet there tomorrow at noon."

Ron dismissed the group, then prayed Laura wouldn't mention Kyle until everyone had left. As soon as they'd gone, she shut the door. "Who's the guy in the khakis?"

"He's a decoy."

"A decoy?"

Ron smiled. "He's actually my pastor. I'm putting him into the group to see how they respond to something unexpected. Although," Ron said with caution, "Mackenzie is kind of doing a good job of that already."

"So who's your fifth officer?"

"Five's a crowd. Besides, Jesse's ego is big enough to count for two."

She smiled. "Don't worry. A few more years and that ego gets replaced by cynicism."

Chapter 13

J esse pulled his truck into the driveway of the house they would soon call headquarters. It looked like every other house in the neighborhood—old and rundown—except for the one across the street, with its fresh white paint, flower garden, and swept porch.

Jesse took the key from his folder and unlocked the front door. The house was furnished with two old couches, a television, and a few odd knickknacks to make it look lived in. By rule, you were never supposed to bring acquaintances to the house. You were friendly but not friends. However, on the off chance that it could happen, you had to be prepared.

He'd already changed out his issued weapon for one that didn't scream "cop." And he'd shaved his head, keeping only the goatee. It was time to get inside the mind of Tony Ramone.

Jesse set down his bag and pulled out a picture of Elvis. He chose one of the many nails pounded into the otherwise bare walls, hung the photo from it, then knocked knuckles with Elvis. "Don't let me down now."

Before Jesse could take a look around, he heard a knock at the door. He knew immediately it had to be the mild-mannered Kyle, who Jesse was sure didn't possess an alter ego. But instead of Clark Kent, a hunched-back woman in an aqua floral dress stood on the porch. Since the screen door was leaning against the wall next to the door, nothing stood between Jesse and the lady shoving a Saran-wrapped plate toward him.

"Cookies," she said in an unbefitting husky voice.

"Who are you?" he asked.

She pitched a thumb over her shoulder toward the house across the street.

"I've lived in that house for fifty-seven years. Had six children, three husbands, and killed a burglar over there. The day I die, this sorry neighborhood can go down the drain. But until then, I'm going to make sure that people like you don't drive it down. I'm bringing you a plate of cookies and telling you that I'm the president of the homeowners' association. The name's Ruth. Ruth Butler."

Neighborhood association? This neighborhood had associations, but not the neighborly kind. A car drove by, squealing its tires and blasting heavy bass that shook the windows. It had a shiny silver spoiler, fat tires, and four people hanging out the windows. Ruth gave them a nasty look, but then her attention was back on Jesse. "Keep your grass cut, furniture off the porch, cars off the lawn, and we'll have no problems. I like to listen to Buddy Holly, so if I hear so much as one lyric from a rap song, I'm going to come over here and beat some sense into you with a shovel. That's right, a shovel."

Clutching the cookies, Jesse spoke in a calm voice. "Listen, you have nothing to worry about. I'll stay out of your business."

"And I will stay in your business. Don't think I don't know what cars coming and going all hours of the night means. And just in case you didn't read the homeowners' association packet, this is a single-family dwelling, which means a man, a woman, and two kids. Oh, I know there are exceptions. A single mom with kids, or a man living alone. But a long list of people coming and going or coming and staying isn't acceptable, unless they're relatives or out-of-town guests. And if they are, I'd better see them carrying suitcases." She pointed to the plate of cookies. "Those are homemade triple-delight chocolate chip cookies. To remind you that what keeps a neighborhood safe is the fact that one neighbor can trust another."

Jesse smiled. "So I can trust you didn't put poison in them?"

They both turned to the sound of a car and watched a Subaru pull into the driveway.

"Who is this?" the old woman said, pointing to the car. But before Jesse could think up something to say, Mackenzie climbed out of the driver's seat wearing khaki shorts, a white polo, and a warm smile. Ruth Butler gasped and put her hand to her heart. "Is this your wife?"

Mackenzie sized up the situation as she walked toward them.

"Mackenzie," Jesse muttered.

"Isn't she precious!" the woman gushed, walking to the edge of the porch with her hand stuck out in front of her. "Welcome to the neighborhood!" she said.

Mackenzie looked at Jesse and then back at the woman. "Thank you," she smiled. "I'm Mack."

"Ruth Butler," the woman said. "Aren't you darling! You remind me of my granddaughter. She's studying to be a doctor."

"Thank you, ma'am."

"*Ma'am!* Oh! I could just squeeze you to death." She turned toward Jesse. "Apologies to you… What's your name?"

"Tony Ramone."

Ruth looked at them. "I was giving your husband a hard time. What with the earrings and tattoos, I just assumed he was a troublemaker. But you look as sweet as a peach." She glanced at Jesse. "Are you a musician?"

"No…ma'am." Maybe good southern manners went a long way.

"Well, I'm so glad to finally have a nice couple move in. You can't imagine the kinds of people I've had to deal with through the years. I've been praying for a nice young couple to move in. You are planning to pot some flowers, aren't you?"

Mack looked calm as she answered. "Maybe. We've got a lot of work to do inside first."

Ruth teared up. "I can't tell you how happy I am to have you here. Do you have any children?"

"No," they both answered.

"In due time, in due time. I miss having the babies around. All my family is scattered across the United States. Five boys and one girl. They hardly ever come to see me." She looked at Mackenzie. "Maybe we could have tea sometime?"

"Sure," Mackenzie said, patting her back. "Thank you for coming by to introduce yourself."

Ruth nodded, smiling, her dentures gleaming in the sunlight. "Good to meet you both. Enjoy the cookies." She walked back to her side of the street.

Jesse pulled Mack inside. "She's going to be a problem."

"Why?" Mack asked.

"Because she thinks we're a married couple, and the team is going to be coming and going all night. Without suitcases. And I don't think we're going to pass Lamar off as a relative."

Mack glanced out the front window. "She'll be okay. We're undercover officers. Surely we can make up a story to fool an old woman."

Jesse gestured toward her. "The tennis outfit is going a long way in helping with that."

"Too bad it didn't come with a racket so I could smack you in the head." Jesse didn't have time to retort before she sighed heavily. "I'm sorry. It's not fair of me to take advantage of the fact that I'm better at comebacks than you are."

Jesse's words froze on his tongue because she looked genuinely remorseful. "Uh…I'm good at comebacks."

"I know. I didn't mean anything by that. I really am sorry."

"Yeah, sure, whatever. Let's just drop it."

Mack was looking at the picture of Elvis on the wall. "What's that?"

"Nothing. Just leave it alone. Don't touch it. Nobody can touch it but me."

"But that Elvis is…you know, puffy. Why don't you have a younger picture of Elvis, when he was thinner and sang gospel songs?"

"Back away from Elvis, okay? He's off-limits."

"Whatever you say." Mack bit her lip. "Look, there's a Wal-Mart a few miles away. Why don't you come with me, help me pick out some clothes?"

"Go shopping with you?" Jesse dropped the cookies onto the table. "It's official. You're insane. I don't even do that with my girlfriend."

"You have a girlfriend?"

"Not anymore."

"Maybe you should've gone shopping with her."

"Surely you have a basic understanding of what people wear. I mean, it's not like you just got out of the academy."

"I know. But…well, there's a certain style. It may not be our style, or at least mine, but it's a style. I don't want to look like an imposter. I want to look real. I could probably pick out a few things, but I don't want to look like I'm just playing the part."

"Okay. You asked for it. First of all, you might want to think about getting your ears pierced."

"I'm not allowed to."

Jesse wanted to knock himself unconscious.

"I mean, when I was a kid."

"I guess a tattoo is out of the question."

"As is getting rid of that attitude."

"It's all about attitude. You have to look like you belong there, no matter what you're wearing. You have to stand in front of the bad guys and give the impression that you might be just a little crazier than they are."

"I have a lot of acting experience. I did children's…uh, theater."

"I've been doing this for three years. Before that, I trained at an elite undercover school in Louisiana. I served in special forces for four years. Don't you get it? You don't fit in. You won't ever fit in. And more than that, you're probably going to put our lives in danger."

The front door opened, and Lamar walked in. "Hey," he said.

"Hi, Lamar," Mack said.

"Call me Wiz."

"As in a high IQ?" Jesse asked.

"As in I need to pee a lot."

Jesse exchanged glances with Mack. Great. Not only did he have a partner with June Cleaver tendencies, now he had one with an overactive bladder.

Wiz glanced out the front window. "Who's the old lady out there waving?"

"Her name is Ruth. And you're a family friend with a lawn business, got it?"

Rhyne Grello was not a paranoid man, but he couldn't kick a nagging feeling about Mason. Something about the explanation of how he got out of jail seemed off. A guy named Craig bailed him out, so he said, but he wouldn't offer any more information. Mason often bragged about his connections. But other than the fact that he flew out of jail, there wasn't much to support his claims.

Josie's Bar, unusually crowded for late afternoon, kept Rhyne hidden in a corner booth. He watched Mason move from one table to another. Either he was being unusually social or he was looking to make a hundred and fifty bucks ratting one of these people out. Maybe even Rhyne himself. The word on the street was that informants could earn up to two hundred dollars and a get-out-of-jail-free card, just for an introduction.

Of course, Rhyne earned much more than that, and he hadn't even scored big. Yet. He had entrusted Mason with one of his biggest business secrets, but first he had wanted Mason to prove himself, that he had what it took. So far, Rhyne wasn't impressed. He left the booth and headed for Mason, who was hanging onto a woman like he might just tip over without her.

Rhyne pulled him toward the bathroom hallway. "What are you doing?"

"What does it look like I'm doing?"

"Having a good time."

"If it's that obvious, why are you asking?" Mason smiled.

Rhyne yanked him closer. "You are making me very nervous. I swear, Mason, if you are working as a snitch, I will find out."

Mason folded his arms. "What are you going to do?"

"Beating people up isn't terribly effective, Mason. Do you know why?"

"Because I could beat you up afterward?"

"It's the fear of being beat up that's effective. It's like saying you fear death. People don't fear death. When you die, you're dead. People fear dying. It's not what's down in the dark basement. It's what people think is down in the dark basement that causes them to run up the stairs."

Mason glanced around with a worried look. "Are you trying to tell me you're going to beat me up in a dark basement?"

Rhyne rolled his eyes. Mason wouldn't be waxing philosophical anytime soon.

"Never mind. Just focus, would you? We're here to do business."

Mason grinned. "I know. I just met Shannon, the brunette, and she drives a station wagon."

"Really?"

Mason nodded.

Rhyne saw her through the crowd and smiled, then looked back at Mason. "Well done."

Chapter 14

Jesse spent a restless night at the UC house. Back in Henderson, there had been a lot fewer rules, a lot less supervising, and lot more trust. Now he was working on a task force with lots of boundaries and even more inexperience. But Tony Ramone could handle it

The rest of the team planned to show up at noon, so Jesse got up in time to fix himself a breakfast of scrambled eggs and toast. Before he took his first bite, the front door opened, and Mack walked in. She looked surprised to see him.

"What are you doing here?" Jesse asked.

"I thought I should unload some stuff. I brought some groceries and a few outfits I bought yesterday." She looked down at herself.

Apparently she was wearing one. Or trying to. A cardigan partly covered a tucked-in tank top, and a denim skirt hit just above the knee.

"What?" she asked.

"It's just…it's not right. Too much prep school and not enough…uh, vamp." Jesse groaned, shoving his plate out of the way. "What sector did you patrol?"

"Northeast."

"I can't figure it out," Jesse said. "You don't fit the UC profile. How'd you get in? Get noticed? There are tons of guys itching to get into UC work."

She tried to look like she wasn't bothered. "The way everyone else makes it. By slacking off and wearing khaki."

"Funny. Maybe they're worried about demographics. Between you and Lamar, we've got every demographic covered."

"What demographic do you represent?"

"One of two cops who actually belong here." He gestured toward her. "Do you have any idea what a poor impression you make as a bad guy?"

"That's because I'm a girl."

"You look like you should be going to Mass."

Mack dug into a bag she was carrying and pulled out lipstick. "Maybe this will help."

"I think you're beyond help."

"I bought everything I need," she said, peering into her bag. "Eye shadow, eyeliner, blush, mascara, and red lipstick."

"Terrific."

"So, are you going to help me or not?"

"Help you what?"

"Use this stuff. If Cassie were here, she could help, but she's not, so…"

Jesse looked down at his untouched food, then up at her. "Help you with…your makeup?"

"Yeah."

"What do you mean? And who is Cassie?"

"She's my sister. And I mean show me how to put it on."

"You don't know how to put on makeup?"

"If I tried, I would look like a clown. Literally." She looked serious.

Fantastic. "Can you juggle, too? It might be a nice distraction when our cover is blown."

Mack turned noticeably red. "I can play the part."

"You can start by cutting four inches off that skirt and losing the cardigan."

"Fine. But I really do need help with the makeup. You'll just have to show me once. I'm a quick learner."

Jesse felt a headache coming on. "What makes you think *I* know how?"

"Surely you've seen a woman put makeup on."

"Fine. Let's get this over with." He walked into the bathroom and flipped on the light. Jesse grabbed the bag out of her hands and dumped the cosmetics on the counter. Mack watched him from the doorway.

Truthfully, he didn't really know what he was doing, either. But surely between the two of them, they could pull it off. He grabbed what he guessed was eye shadow and opened the case. It was blue.

"Put this on first."

"Okay." She barely swept the brush across her eyelid. "How's that?" she asked.

"I can't even see it." He pointed to her hand. "That wand thingy. Spackle it on real thick."

"Spackle? I'm not painting a wall."

"Just use short strokes."

She tried again.

"I still can't see any color."

She tried again. He stepped back to observe. "That's better. At least I can see something."

"It seems a little…blue."

"That's the point, isn't it?"

"I guess. Now what?"

Jesse stared at the cluster of cosmetics. "That black tube. Isn't that mascara?"

"Yeah."

They reached for it at the same time, knocking knuckles. He snatched it off the counter and pulled out the tiny brush. "You put it on your lashes." He handed it to her. She turned to the mirror, but every time the brush got close, her eyelid twitched erratically. She tried several times before Jesse grabbed it from her. "Just hold still." But every time he moved in with the brush, she blinked uncontrollably. "Can't you just hold your eye open for a few seconds?"

"Sorry, I can't help it," she said. "It feels like you're going to poke my eye out."

"With all that blinking, I might." He pointed to a pink container. "Maybe that will be easier."

Mack flipped it over. "It's blush."

"I know how to do this," said Jesse. "I watched my mother. You start at the corners of your mouth and go up to your temple in a straight line."

Mack stared at it.

"With that brush there."

Mack pulled out what looked like a miniature paintbrush. She swiped it across the blush and then with large strokes brushed the color onto her face in a straight line just like Jesse told her.

"Huh."

"What?" Mack asked.

"That doesn't look quite right."

"It doesn't?" She peered into the mirror.

"Maybe you need some lipstick."

Mack held up the tube. "This is not going to be easy."

"Did you buy a pencil?"

"Why would I need a pencil?"

"That's how they do it. They draw a line around their mouth so they won't color outside the line."

Mack began to look desperate. "Maybe if I'm careful?"

"I guess you could wipe it off if you messed up."

She removed the lid and after several nervous false starts, finally applied some on her top lip.

"Whoa," he said.

"What?"

"That's really...red."

"Well, that's what it says on the bottom. Glossy fire-engine red."

"I can hear the sirens already..."

Mack put her hand on her hip. "I don't need any of your lip right now."

"No, you're making quite a statement with your own."

Jesse heard a truck outside. He lifted the blinds to peer outside.

"Oh no."

The driveway was crowded, so Ron parked his truck on the street. His leg was giving him fits despite the four Aleve he'd taken with breakfast. He leaned on his cane and shut the door, trying to shake the kinks out, but it was no use. His leg wanted to stay home on the couch.

"Hello."

Ron turned to find an old woman peering up at him with a hyena-like smile.

"You must be that sweet girl's daddy."

"You have me confused with someone else."

She stood a little straighter. "Are you related to them? The young man that looks like trouble and his wife who looks as sweet as cream?"

"Who are you?"

"Ruth Butler. I live across the street. I've been the president of the neighborhood homeowners' association since 1976."

Ron glanced down the street. "*This* neighborhood?"

"That's right." She moved closer. "I know this is a rental house. All kinds of terrible people have come and gone, and I've said good riddance to 'em all." She gestured toward the cars in the driveway. "So are you his father or hers?"

The front door opened, and Mack hustled down the porch steps. Ron barely recognized her. She looked like she'd just escaped from Cirque du Soleil.

"What happened to you?" Ron asked as he gazed at her upper lip. Her very red upper lip. Which wasn't to be outdone by her very blue eyelids. Ruth looked curious as well.

"You've met Ruth?" Mack asked, trying to smile.

"Just now," Ron said.

"Is this your father?" Ruth asked.

Mack grabbed his arm. "Yes. Yes it is."

"Isn't that sweet," Ruth said, then gestured toward her face. "Dear heart, what in the world are you doing with all that makeup? You look like you belong at a street corner on the strip."

Mack couldn't hide her embarrassment. "Oh, it's nothing. Just having a little fun."

"I can see that. But honey, there's lip gloss and then there's Crisco. You're not getting ready to fry yourself in a pan, are you? Blot, honey. Always blot. And as much as I like blue, I'm surprised you can hold your eyelids up with that much on." She reached out and grabbed Mack's face. "You look like you've been slapped. What happened to you? Where's that lovely pink cardigan you were wearing?"

Ron saw the panic in Mack's eyes and said, "We're throwing a costume party in a few weeks. Mack was thinking about going as…as…"

"A hooker?" Ruth offered.

"See!" Ron slapped his hands together. "I told you it would work."

Ruth scooted closer to Ron. "Do you need a date?"

Ron's face flushed. "No thanks. My wife is going."

"Ah." She sighed. "The good ones are always taken. Or they don't live long enough. Been married three times and thanks to a love for donuts, french fries, or water-skiing, none of them made it past seventy." She looked at the cars in the driveway again. "Just don't get in a habit of parking on the street or in your front lawn. It's fine if you're throwing a party, but cars belong in a driveway." She turned toward her house. "Good to meet you. I best be going. It's almost time for tea. Care to join me?"

"No thanks," Ron and Mack said together. Ron followed Mack into the house and they both went directly to the kitchen for a drink of water.

"What was that?" Ron asked.

"That was Ruth Butler. She thinks we're a family moving in, and she wants to make sure we keep our lawn mowed and our—"

Dozer walked in the front door and nodded his head toward the window. "The last time I checked, it wasn't illegal to park on the curb, but you wouldn't know it in this neighborhood."

Ron and Jesse laughed.

"You've met Ruth," Mack said.

"Yeah. Lucky for me, Kyle pulled up, and I ran inside."

Everyone glanced out the window for a moment before Jesse groaned. "This lady is going to give me a—"

Suddenly the front door swung open, and Kyle rushed in looking panicked, overdressed, and surprisingly tan in his white *Miami Vice* blazer. His eyes held a wild shock. Ron was just about to tell him to breathe when Kyle said, "I might've blown it."

"Blown what?" Jesse asked.

Kyle shut the front door and closed the curtains to the street-facing window. "She just caught me off guard. I parked on the street because there was no room in the driveway, and the next thing I know, well…" He was gesturing as if his hands might do the talking. "I realize she's little and old and a lady, but…but…"

"But she threatened to mothball you to death?" Dozer asked with a smirk.

Kyle tried to hold a steady expression. "She asked me if I was related to the woman who couldn't put on makeup."

Jesse glanced at Mack. "I told you to use lip liner."

Kyle kept babbling. "I was confused because then she invited me over for Earl Grey—at first I thought she was talking about her husband, and it took me a second to realize she was talking about tea—and then she asked if I planned on getting my ears pierced too."

Jesse looked at Ron. "He can't even handle an old lady."

Ron held up his hands. "Settle down. Ruth is the least of my concerns right now. As long as you didn't tell her we're undercover officers, everything is fine."

Ron had seen a lot of people go pale—usually when he pulled out his badge or gun—but none had ever gone quite as pale as Kyle.

"You told her?" Wiz asked.

Kyle threw up his hands defensively. "She was berating me with questions! I think she already knew. She asked if anyone else was going dressed as a hooker, and I told her I would probably be disguised as a pimp."

Ron slapped his hands to his face. "Is that all you said?"

"No." Kyle looked mortified. "She was fretting that criminals were moving in next door so I was trying to reassure her."

"What did you say?" Jesse asked.

"That we…you…I mean, we are, you know, officers."

"Why did you do that?" Jesse roared. "The Las Vegas police department doesn't even know where we are located. Why would you tell a citizen?"

Ron's plan to use Kyle to help the officers cope with less-than-perfect circumstances was turning into a liability. And now he was going to have to deal with Ruth. Again.

Jesse's disapproving stare found Ron across the room. Ron kept an even expression. If Kyle were really a cop, it would indeed be a nightmare, but he still wanted to see how Jesse would handle the situation.

Uneasiness simmered in the air.

Ron gripped his cane. "Okay, I'm going to go over and talk to Ruth. I'm going to explain the situation, spout some legalese to make sure she understands she can't tell anybody about us. In the meantime, I want you all to review this folder. It details our plan of action. When I get back, we'll go over specifics and then talk about some of the training exercises we'll be doing for the next week."

Jesse looked genuinely exasperated with it all. Ron recognized his expression. It felt like watching a younger version of himself. This was agony for Jesse Lunden. And ultimately good for him too. Kyle's disruption would teach this team to work together under the worst circumstances. Ron just hoped it wouldn't get any worse than this.

Chapter 15

J esse felt like punching something. In all his years working undercover, this was the most ridiculous mess he'd ever seen. Old Man Ron had lost his mind. The guy was whacked out. Wiz looked like he might work out, but Mack and Kyle? These two were a danger to the team's safety.

"He made an honest mistake."

Mack moved toward Kyle.

"He didn't mean to," she added, turning to the other three.

"That's not the point, Mackenzie," Jesse said. "We don't have room to make mistakes. You make a mistake in the middle of an operation, and it could be the last mistake you'll make."

"First of all, it's Mack. I don't want to hear anyone call me Mackenzie again. Secondly, Kyle realizes what he did. There's no reason to make him feel worse." She looked at him. "You do feel bad, don't you?"

Kyle nodded.

"We're all going to make mistakes," she continued. "The question is, what are we going to do with those mistakes? Learn from them. That's what we're going to do."

It was hard enough to take Sergeant Yeager and his cane, but with Kyle and Mary Poppins along for the ride, he might as well have been sucked into a black hole.

"There's not much to learn once a bullet's in your head," Jesse said. He rolled his sleeve up, revealing a scar. "I made a mistake. It almost cost me my life. The second bullet hit an artery, and I nearly bled to death. The dealers thought I was already dead or they would've put a third one in me."

"Lucky for us, Ruth isn't a bad guy," Mack said.

"You haven't seen what old people can do with a gun." He sighed and plopped down at the table, shooting Dozer a look of frustration. Dozer nodded.

Mack said, "Let's just review these folders."

Jesse tossed one across the table toward Kyle. "Fine. Unless, of course, Kyle here would like to make copies first and hand them out in Tweekerville tonight."

Mack's face started to turn red. Again. "How would you like it if we treated you like this?" she said to Jesse.

"Treated me like what? A cop? In case you haven't noticed, we're all cops. We have a standard to live up to. Kyle here isn't exactly measuring up."

"You haven't given him much of a chance."

"I'm not trying to make friends. I don't want a liability."

"Look, I'm sorry, okay?" Kyle said. "I'm nervous. I didn't really… I didn't picture it like this. I'll do better."

Jesse opened his folder, hoping they'd both shut up. He read the first few paragraphs and looked up at everyone else around the table.

"A body shop," Wiz said. "Cool. We're opening up an undercover body shop."

A tingling excitement rushed through Jesse. Now *this* was what he signed up for.

"No ma'am. But thank you." Ron had already had two cups of tea, and Ruth was on her third as they talked in a sitting room filled with furniture that looked a hundred years old. And indeed it was, as Ruth explained forty-five minutes into the conversation when she told the story of how her father had settled on the very land on which this neighborhood was built.

She had also explained why neighborhood watch programs don't work and how she made certain everyone in the neighborhood paid their yearly dues. Ron couldn't imagine Ruth walking door to door collecting the money, but apparently she did, and nobody thought twice about not paying this one-woman association.

"What do you do with the money?" Ron asked.

"Pay teenagers to mow the lawns for these people who can't seem to do anything but sit on their porches. You might think parking your car on the lawn would kill the grass, but it doesn't."

Ron had come over to explain the situation across the street, but Ruth's entire life history had filled every second of his visit. Ron had faded about thirty minutes into it, his mind wandering to the task force. He'd been tuning in about every fiftieth word when he heard, "my tax dollars."

And then she stopped. Ron had no clue what she'd just said or what those three words meant, but Ruth was leaning toward him like she expected a reply. Ron nodded and smiled, but that didn't seem to do the trick.

"Well?" she asked, in the same impatient tone that introduced every sentence.

"I'm not sure I'm following," Ron said carefully, wishing he had some tea to sip.

"I'm a taxpayer. I demand to know what my taxes are being used for."

"Um…"

"You think that's unfair?"

"No…ma'am, I just don't understand what you're getting at."

She nodded toward her enormous front window. "So what are you all doing over there?"

Ron finally caught on, but he didn't want to give up too much information. "Ma'am, one of my officers let it slip that we're running an undercover operation out of that house."

"Let it slip? It came roaring out of his mouth like a lion."

Ron cleared his throat. "At any rate, we're undercover officers, and we need you to keep that information completely confidential. We can't have this location compromised. It could put our officers in a dangerous situation."

Ruth sipped her tea and eyeballed Ron. "Fair enough."

"I can't stress how important it is for you to not discuss this with any-one in the neighborhood or elsewhere. There could be legal implications."

"I understand."

Through the large window, Ron gazed across the street, wondering what his team was up to. Apparently Ruth thought he was looking at the shiny black Lincoln Town Car in the driveway. "I would park it in the garage," she said, "if I had room. I've got two Cadillacs already parked in there."

"Why so many?" Ron asked.

"They belong to my late husbands."

"What do you do with three cars? Drive a different one each week?"

"No. I don't drive. Never have. I take the bus to the grocery store. That's just about the only place I need to go. I have a daughter in Texas who comes to visit as often as the sun eclipses. But she does see to it that I have all I need."

"You don't drive any of your cars?"

"No. But I can't bear to sell them."

"They're meaningful to you, I'm sure."

"They remind me to eat my vegetables and that I'm not twenty-five anymore, a lesson all of my husbands could've learned." She sighed, ges-turing toward a small mantel that held three urns. "Ralph, Monroe, and Saul." She studied them for a moment. "The cars are under the corpora-tion. I don't want to have to pay the taxes if I sell them."

Ron stared at the car. Two others in the garage? Not being used? Back in his UC days, they used to borrow people's cars all the time—the cousin who owned the plumbing business, the uncle who drove the Corvette. But today it practically took a vote from Congress to borrow a car because of all the liability…unless they were held in a corporation's name, and then things got a lot easier.

"About those cars," Ron said. "What would you think of loaning them to my undercover agents?"

Ruth looked intrigued. "Why would I want to do that?"

"We need vehicles. If something happens to your vehicle while we're using it, your corporation will be reimbursed for it. It's called a citizen loan. It's done all the time." Okay, *all the time* was a bit of a stretch.

"So apparently my tax dollars aren't being used to supply officers with cars they need."

"They are, ma'am. But the narcotics division gets all the good ones."

Ruth raised a curious eyebrow but then said, "Why not? They're just taking up room." She stood and walked to the kitchen, where she pulled out a drawer, and then returned with three sets of keys. Before giving them to Ron, she turned toward the window. "So what *do* you do over there all day?"

"Comb the neighborhood for criminals."

Ruth dropped the keys into his hand and followed him out to her porch.

"Thank you, Mrs. Butler. We will return the cars as soon as we finish with them."

"All right."

Ron walked carefully; his leg wasn't fond of porch steps. As he crossed the street, she called to him. "Don't forget—keep your grass under three inches."

Ron's cell phone rang. It was Nan. "So, are you doing anything dangerous?" she asked.

Ron turned and gave Ruth a quick wave. "You have no idea."

Rhyne heard Mason rummaging in the refrigerator, but he had more important things on his mind than fretting about how Mason treated his house like a complimentary all-you-can-eat buffet. He adjusted his black silk shirt, combed his hair, patted cologne onto his neck, and walked out of the bedroom. Mason was sitting at the table eating a bowl of cereal.

"Why are you eating?"

"I'm hungry."

"I told you to be ready."

Mason glanced down at himself. "I'm ready."

"That's what you're wearing?"

"My tuxedo's at the dry cleaners," Mason said as he shoved more cereal into his mouth.

"Is this some sort of joke to you?"

Mason looked up at him. "I don't know, Rhyne. I don't know what's going on. You're not telling me anything, remember? You want me to go along with all this, but you're keeping a lot of information to yourself."

"That's because I don't know if I can trust you."

Mason's angry gaze turned back to his cereal. "Right. You never know, I could be a snitch." He grabbed his cereal bowl and put it in the sink. "Maybe you're the snitch, Rhyne. And maybe you're setting me up. Maybe that's why you're being so secretive."

"You don't know what kind of people we're dealing with. If you did, you would have more respect for the situation."

"What situation? All you told me was to get here at noon. And be ready. Be ready for what? A lecture on my dressing habits?"

With one shove, Rhyne knocked a chair over. It smacked the kitchen floor and got Mason up and scurrying toward the refrigerator.

"What are you doing?" he yelled.

"Getting your attention," Rhyne said. "I don't want you to blow it for us. For me."

"I don't know what I'm blowing. Why don't you bring me up to speed?"

Rhyne sighed. He still had his doubts about Mason, but on the other hand, Mason seemed too stupid to be any cop's informant. "You've heard of Vincent Ayala?"

"Yeah. Of course. He's rolling in money and has his hands in everything on the strip."

"This goes all the way up to Mr. Ayala."

"What does?"

"We're meeting with him this afternoon. For the past two months, I've been dealing with some of his guys. They put in a good word for me. They've noticed we're turning the vehicles we've acquired into major profit. That got his attention."

Mason looked genuinely impressed. "That's cool. But…it doesn't add up. I mean, Vincent Ayala has millions of dollars. Why would he be interested in stolen vehicles?"

"He's not." Rhyne smiled. "He's interested in what's inside."

Mason's eyes lit up. "The run we did in Arizona."

"There's more to come if we make a good impression." Rhyne saw a healthy fear in Mason's eyes. "Are you up for it or not?"

"We're actually going to meet him? I heard he punched a photographer once just for trying to take his picture. Very few people know what he looks like."

"We're about to be two of the few." Rhyne grabbed his wallet. "Let's go. And tuck in your shirt."

Mason stuffed his shirt into his jeans and followed Rhyne out the front door. But before he'd taken two steps, Rhyne gasped and quickly turned around, shoving Mason back inside. "Hurry! Hurry!"

Mason stumbled backward, hitting his shoulder against the door frame. Rhyne pulled the door shut and locked it while Mason tried to catch his breath.

"What's the matter?"

"We're just going to have to wait here for a while." Rhyne peeked out the curtain of his front window.

"Why?" Mason whispered.

"Her name is Ruth, and we're not leaving this house until she's back inside hers."

Chapter 16

"C aptain Gates, the files are ready, and they're on Sergeant Yeager's desk," Jackie said over the speakerphone.

"Thank you, Jackie." Laura rose but as she did, Mack knocked on her door. "Hey, Mack. Come on in."

The eagerness that usually shone in Mack's eyes had vanished.

"What's wrong?" she asked as they both sat down.

"You know," Mack began, "I was so excited to work on this task force. I couldn't imagine why I was selected, but I went into it with everything I've got." She looked up at Laura. "Captain Gates, I just don't know if that's going to be enough."

"You're a talented cop. You've got good instincts. I know you don't have any undercover experience, but the only way you get undercover experience is to do it."

"Detective Lunden said he went to some special school for it."

Laura smiled gently. "That's because Jesse works in Henderson and they have money flowing like a river over there. Most undercover cops just jump in feet first and go for it. Sergeant Yeager can tell you that."

"I like him," Mack said.

"You should. He knows what he's talking about." Laura leaned forward on her desk. "Mack, don't doubt yourself. You can do this."

"I'm just not fitting in."

Laura had never fit in well either. "It's not easy. The fact is that it's still a boys' game out there. If you're going to fit in with the boys, you've got to think like one."

"According to my mother, I should've been born one. So why don't I fit in?"

"I'm going to shoot straight with you," Laura said after a small pause. "Sometimes, well, it's just that you come across a little…"

"Yes?"

"Religious."

Mack nodded. "I know. And that confuses people when I lose my temper, doesn't it?"

"Um…I'm not sure the temper is the problem. Listen, there's nothing wrong with being religious," Laura said. "I admire that about you, Mack. I really do. You're a person with strong character and convictions. It's part of what makes you a good cop. But it doesn't really belong in the middle of what you're doing."

"If God wasn't in the middle of what I'm doing, I wouldn't be doing it. He made me who I am, gave me the desire to help people and bring criminals to justice."

"I understand," Laura lied. She didn't have the foggiest idea where Mack was coming from. "But you have to understand that it makes people uncomfortable."

"People are uncomfortable because they know they've messed up, and they don't have a way to make everything right. Believe me, I know. My sister Hayden has probably sinned a total of eight times in her entire life. Then there's me." Laura nodded and smiled like it all made sense. It didn't, but she wasn't going to let her apprentice slip away over sins, or whatever Mack was talking about.

"I can't be somebody I'm not," Mack finally said.

"That's the whole idea of undercover work."

"Yes. But you also can't lose who you are. Sergeant Yeager told us that yesterday. He said that we're playing a part, and we've got to make a distinction or the lines could blur, and then we would have a hard time distinguishing between right and wrong." She leaned back in her chair. "There would be a lot fewer problems to shoot down if people would step aside and let God control their lives."

Laura folded her hands together on top of her desk. "Mack, you can't save the whole world. There will always be car thieves and drug dealers."

"I'm not talking about criminals. I'm talking about cops. What I wouldn't give to see some fruits of the Spirit taught." Mack glanced at Captain Gates. "You look confused. Don't they teach that at your church?"

The white lie she told a couple of years ago when Mack invited her to church was coming back to haunt her now. Laura called up a pleasant smile. "Yes. We're very fond of fruit. Except for apples, of course." Laura tried to steer the conversation back on track. "Mack, we don't live in a perfect world, which is pretty much what guarantees our employment. Now," she said in a serious tone, "I know you can do this. You're just going to have to try harder. You and I both know church is important, but your job isn't to make everybody know that. Your job is to catch criminals. You're a good cop. Don't let the others make you feel inadequate. Don't make the same mistakes I did. Stand up for yourself and show them what you've got."

Laura smiled graciously, even though she felt like a complete failure. Her dreams had been swept away by people who knew how to get to her, and by one split-second decision she learned to regret…to loathe.

"Mack, promise me you won't quit. I picked you for the task force for a reason, and it wasn't because of your religious views. You've got instinct and determination. You know how to read people. It's a…God-given talent."

Mack lowered her eyes and smiled. "Sometimes it's a curse."

"How so?"

"Because I know when people are lying about going to church." She rose and thrust out her hand for Laura to shake. "If you ever want to come, I would be honored to have you as my guest."

Laura shook Mack's hand and worried about the dumbfounded look on her own face. Yet the warmth in Mack's eyes sent relief to her heart, which was a strange way to feel after being caught in a lie.

"Captain Gates, you're right. This is an opportunity of a lifetime. I'm not going to give up. I can do this. Thank you for the inspiration."

"Uh…yes, sure." Laura walked around her desk as Mack went to the door. "Mack," she said. Mack turned around. "You can't be seen here once the operation begins. You can't be seen anywhere near the police department."

"I know."

"I'll see you after it's over."

Mack nodded. When she'd gone, Laura took a moment to gain her composure. Nobody had ever called her a liar to her face before. But somehow, she felt…understood. She couldn't put her finger on what drew her to Mack, but it kept drawing her. If Laura were a praying person, she'd pray that Mack would rise to the top and do all the things Laura never could.

Laura walked down the hall to Ron's office. She checked the hallway to make sure nobody was around, then marched to the desk. She picked up the copies of the case files, slipped off the thick rubber band, and shuffled through until she found the five she needed. She took them back to her office, shut the door, and promptly buried the files under a tall pile of papers.

Jesse moved the curtains slightly and peeked out the window at Ruth's house. She'd been outside potting flowers when he arrived and he'd decided to pretend he didn't hear her call hello. But she was nowhere to be seen now.

Dozer and Wiz had already left, off to their lame training assignment. Jesse turned to Kyle and Mack. "Okay, look. I'm going to go along with all of this, if only to keep myself from getting killed when we start the real thing." He looked at the piece of paper in his hand. "All right, the coast is clear. Let's go."

Jesse settled into his seat and handed the piece of paper to Mack. They drove toward the freeway. "This address is in your patrol area, isn't it?"

"Yes. But I'm not sure which apartments these are."

"Shouldn't we find out first?" Kyle asked. "We need to be informed."

"Don't get too excited about this, okay? It's a training exercise. We go in there with our undercover identities and carry on a conversation about how we're interested in renting. We ask a few questions our alter egos might ask, and then we're done. It's to help you learn your identity. It's not a big deal." He glanced in the rearview mirror at Kyle, whose expression was filled with concentration. "Kyle, tell me about yourself."

Kyle's eyes darted to the rearview mirror. "Why?"

"If we're going to work together, we need to know each other." That line would never work on another cop, but Kyle wasn't any ordinary cop, and Jesse wanted to know why.

"Well, I grew up in the Southwest. My mom was a homemaker, my dad an accountant. I graduated from high school a year early and finished my undergraduate..." Kyle paused, then caught Jesse's eyes in the rearview mirror.

"You have a master's?" Jesse asked.

"Why would I have a master's?"

"Because people who don't have masters' degrees never refer to their degree as undergraduate."

Kyle didn't look like he knew what to say, so Jesse filled in the silence. "I don't care what kind of degree or degrees you have. None of it matters on the streets. Maybe you'd fit in better teaching courses at the academy. That's where most of the guys with masters' turn up. Or in the FBI."

"You're making some pretty broad statements. You don't know me."

Jesse shrugged and stared out the window. "A hundred bucks says you're the first one to make a blunder at the apartment." He looked at Mack to see if she was in.

"I don't gamble," Mack said.

"You're in the right city for that conviction." Jesse shook his head. "Let me guess… You don't drink, either. Let's hope that holds up at the billions of bars we'll be hanging out at." Jesse gripped the steering wheel with two hands. Agitation fired in him, and the only way he could release it was to do something constructive. "Mack, you and I will pose as boyfriend, girlfriend. I'm going to play the quiet guy who lets his girl-friend do all the yakking. Kyle, just hang back and observe, okay? Pose as Mack's brother. Ask questions a brother might ask. But not very many questions, okay?"

"I'm still not sure who I am. I mean, I've got a name and a driver's li-cense and all that, but I don't know what I'm supposed to act like," Kyle said.

"That's the whole idea. You've got to adapt. You become the person you need to be in the situation where you find yourself. You've got to think like bottom-feeders. You've got to try to understand their mentality, or at the very least, imitate it. You're in survival mode. You live for a fix day to day, or for the money that comes from selling what you steal. At the end of the day, you care about you and only you."

Kyle said, "Maybe they're not all so bad. Surely some of these people just made a lot of mistakes and find themselves with no hope."

Jesse could barely keep his eyes on the road. "Dude, you're making me nervous. I don't know where you came from and what you've done, but I'm willing to bet you've been behind a desk for a long time. If you want to help these people, go into social work. Otherwise, I want to know that you can shoot someone dead without running through a checklist first."

"So you're going by Tony," Mack said. "We call you Tony no matter what."

"Yeah," Jesse said. "Just keep your cool. You have to completely buy into the idea of who you are, or people will see right through you." Jesse turned onto Beckland Street. "Let me see that address again." Mack handed it to him. Jesse pulled his truck to the curb and looked out the window. The towering building across the street had four shiny gold letters above the grand archway that led inside: 7590.

"That's it?" Mack asked.

Jesse checked the address again. "This can't be it."

"What?" Kyle and Mack both asked at the same time.

"Clever. I'll give him that."

"Who?" Kyle was staring at the doorman dressed like he was part of a marching band.

"What's the contact name?" Jesse asked.

"Misty Delack."

Jesse laughed. Sergeant Yeager was definitely not going to make this easy. "Okay, look. Sergeant Yeager is trying to throw us…me, for a loop. He knew I'd expect we'd be going to a place where the scum I normally deal with might live. But here we are, at an apartment complex for rich people." He watched Mack's eyes look from the tattoo on his forearm to her own jean skirt. They both looked at Kyle.

"What?" Kyle asked.

"We need a new game plan. Mack and I don't fit the profile of the people inside that building." He looked at Kyle's khakis. "Do you see what I'm getting at?"

"But…but…I'm the brother. I don't ask a lot of questions, I just stand there." He looked at Mack. "Right? I just stand there?"

Mack said, "I think this is a good chance for you to show us what you're made of, Kyle."

Kyle was shaking his head. "I don't think this is a good idea."

"You're the only one of us who will be taken seriously. I can still be your sister, and Jesse can still be my boyfriend, but you'll have to take the lead because you're the one who looks most likely to blend in."

Kyle nodded. "Okay."

Somehow Jesse didn't feel relieved, but he wasn't about to go back to Sergeant Yeager with a failure report. "Kyle, the trick is to act like you belong there. Mack and I have to do the same thing. We have to carry ourselves with confidence. You're dressed fine, so the only thing you'll have to carry off is the fact that you're not lying through your teeth."

Kyle swallowed hard, then cried out, "I can't… I just can't do it!"

"I can't believe this!" Jesse shouted.

Kyle cracked a smile. "Like that? Was that a good lie?"

Jesse sighed. He opened his console, rubbed the bullet, knocked knuckles with the picture of Elvis he kept in his truck, then pushed open the door. "Come on. Let's go."

Chapter 17

Rhyne was an expert at reading people, but Vincent Ayala was a real challenge. Maybe Rhyne was distracted by the enormous amount of wealth that was just inches from his fingertips. He'd never been to the penthouse suite of a casino before. The view from the patio window gave him the impression that everything below was ripe for conquering and pillaging. Maybe he was worried he and Mason were playing the scene wrong.

More likely, Rhyne's confusion came from Vincent Ayala himself, who looked liked he'd just stepped out of a trailer in a remote Nevada town full of misplaced rednecks. Rhyne had a hard time taking the man seriously. Bright orange hair, frizzy by way of the gene pool, was pulled back into a ponytail. Large brown freckles dotted every inch of his skin. His outdated mustache sat crookedly across his top lip as he guffawed his way through some completely irrelevant and stupid story.

Rhyne stood silently, his hands clasped in front of him. Two men in suits flanked Ayala, their hands also clasped in front of them. Mason dug a finger into his ear while Vincent Ayala dug a finger into a can of Copenhagen. He pinched some between his fingers and stuck it inside his lip.

"Rhyne, you wanna drink? Something cold?"

"Sure. Thank you, sir."

"Whatcha want? Lone Star? I got Milwaukee's Best too."

Rhyne tried not to look as disturbed as he felt. Milwaukee's Best? Where was the caviar? The expensive scotch? The cigars?

"I guess I'm not so thirsty after all, sir. But I did want to talk about—"

Vincent waved his hand. "Business, business. Heck and high water,

Rhyne, it'll be around whenever we get to it. Let's go sit on the patio, have ourselves a nice chat."

Rhyne glanced at Mason, who, by Vincent's standards, actually looked classy. "Of course. Thank you, sir."

The size of the patio was impressive, but the furniture might as well have been stolen from Rhyne's brother-in-law's backyard. A patio set with an umbrella, a large ice cooler, and a grill that looked big enough to cook a whole cow rested on ornate Italian tiles. Vincent's hand plunged into the ice and emerged with a beer. He threw it across the patio to Rhyne, who barely caught it but not before it hit his chest with a thud.

Now he had a new problem: should he open the beer or wait for the fizz to settle? Mason had already made himself at home, his feet kicked up on the patio furniture and a Lone Star in his right hand. Rhyne joined them at the table.

"So," Vincent said, spitting into an empty can, "my men say you think you can get the job done for me."

"Yes sir."

"You know about big business, Rhyne?"

"My father worked the blackjack table all his life. He told me stories about the wealth to be had in this city." He had also told him there was no hope of elbowing his way in. The wealth was controlled by too many powerful people. But if Freckles had a chance, so did he. How could a guy who wears a tank top to a business meeting end up in a penthouse? "He died on the casino floor with only seventy-two dollars in the bank."

Vincent raised his beer to him. "So you swore you'd do better. And here you are, right, ol' boy?"

"I can do this for you. I've already done several runs."

"Small runs."

"Yes sir. That's true, but it's all about the method, and the method works. Sir."

Vincent picked his teeth with a thumbnail as he stared at Mason, who only seemed interested in the chips and salsa. "Let's do some more talkin' about this, Rhyne."

"Thank you, sir."

"Alone." Vincent looked at Mason.

"I'll meet you downstairs," Rhyne said to Mason, raising his brows to motion him along.

After grabbing a handful of chips, Mason was escorted away. Vincent picked up a chip, scooped a huge dollop of salsa onto it, and stuffed it into his mouth. "Let's get this thing rollin'," he said as chip shrapnel and a spray of salsa flew out of his mouth. "I don't want to be late for the buffet."

Misty's desk was adorned with red roses, plump and potent enough to make Jesse's nose itch. He stood a few feet behind Kyle, who clasped his hands behind his back. Jesse could see his fingers fiddling with his belt loop.

Misty's discernable and curious expression held a gaze that went all the way down to Kyle's shoes, then stopped at Mack and her miniskirt. As Kyle introduced himself, Misty's eyebrow lifted.

"I'm not what you expected?" Suddenly Kyle's hands popped into a questioning gesture. "And I suppose Bill Gates looks like a trillionaire?"

Jesse wanted to squeeze his eyes shut. This was painful.

"Right," Misty said, this time with a more pleasant smile.

Jesse had to give Kyle credit for trying. Though posing as a geek didn't seem like too much of a stretch for him, so far he was using it to the best of his ability.

"This is my wife," Kyle said, pulling Mack next to him.

His wife? That wasn't the plan. Mack and Kyle looked so mismatched they would surely raise suspicions.

"I see. Well, I'm sure you're anxious to see what we have to offer." She looked between Mack and Kyle, who were now holding hands like they were at a school dance. "And this is...?" Misty asked, looking at Jesse.

"My brother," Kyle and Mack announced in unison.

"Whose brother?" Misty asked.

Kyle and Mack turned to Jesse, both their faces red with embarrassment. Jesse looked at Misty and said, "The brother who couldn't afford a place like this if I sold my soul. Can we get on with it?"

"Uh...his name is Tony," Mack said.

Misty cleared her throat and tidied the papers in front of her. "Let's go take a look, shall we?"

"That would be fine," Kyle said, and turned, politely gesturing for Misty to go first. Jesse shot him a look as they followed her to the elevators. But Kyle was nervously stroking the front of his polo where a tie might be if he were wearing a suit.

Misty pushed a button for the twenty-fourth floor. Kyle cleared his throat and turned to Jesse. "When will you have my Ferrari fixed?"

Misty glanced sideways at them.

"Your Ferrari?" Jesse asked.

"It's been in the shop for over a week," Kyle said, his nose high in the air. He looked at Misty. "He's great at what he does. He can fix any car."

"I see." Misty's lips pursed with disapproval as she glanced at Jesse. "I drive a Ferrari."

Jesse's heart pounded. He knew nothing about Ferraris. Kyle's eyes grew wide as they passed the fourteenth floor in silence.

"Good for you," Jesse said in an unimpressed voice. He didn't want to start a conversation with this woman about cars.

She looked at Kyle. "Which model do you drive?"

Jesse decided to let Kyle handle this. They were in an apartment building, not a crack house. This was practice, and Kyle was doing a great job of completely screwing it up.

"The 612 Scaglietti."

She grinned. "Wonderful."

Thankfully the elevator doors opened. Jesse watched as Kyle took on a new air of confidence, gesturing like everyone was headed for the ball.

"Here we are," Misty said, and opened the door.

Jesse followed them in. Mack had hardly said a word. He was going to have to challenge her or she might just sit quietly and let Kyle do all the talking. They gathered at the large window.

"I could get used to this," Jesse said, elbowing Mack with loser-brother obnoxiousness.

Misty cleared her throat. "We have strict rules for our tenants. Guests are welcome, but they must be checked in and cannot stay for more than a week without prior approval."

Jesse was starting to enjoy himself. Three out of the four people in the room couldn't stop squirming and clearing their throats. He leaned against the spotless glass and crossed his arms. "Is that so?" Jesse asked. "I guess I'll just have to live in Kyle's Ferrari."

"Over here is the kitchen," Misty said as they rounded the corner. The kitchen, with cabinets all the way up to the twelve-foot ceiling, was clearly a focal point of the deluxe accommodations. Jesse eyed a small sink at the edge of the circular island. He jumped up and sat on the shiny marble.

Misty gasped. "Down! Please!"

Jesse smiled and looked at Mack, whose hand was over her mouth. Then he looked back at Misty. "You're not my mom." This was fun.

Mack dropped her hand, realizing Jesse was intentionally stirring the waters. She said, "You'll have to excuse him. He has the manners of a Pinto."

"Pintos don't have manners or etiquette," Jesse said. "Unless of course you're talking about pinto *beans,* and then you might be onto something, although it's still a mixed metaphor because technically, the pinto bean isn't going to be the one having to excuse itself."

Mack looked annoyed but asked Misty if she could see the master bedroom.

Jesse hopped down off the counter and trailed behind them. The master bedroom was furnished with a four-poster bed and included a bathtub that looked like a small pool. Kyle's hands remained clasped behind his back as he strolled around the room, feigning interest in mundane details. Jesse wondered for a moment what it would be like to live in a place like this. Never on a cop's pay, of course. Mack seemed taken by it all. Her wide-eyed wonder would've been enchanting, except that she was supposed to look like she was used to this sort of thing.

"Looks smaller than your last place," Jesse said.

Misty turned to him. "I think you should let these two decide for themselves."

Mack took a deep breath and regained her composure as a rich girl. She blinked slowly and fell back into the role.

They followed Misty to the dining room, where she pointed out the features of the wet bar.

"Do you have any questions?" Misty asked. She glanced at Jesse. "The two of you, I mean," she said, redirecting her attention to Kyle and Mack.

"I love the carpet," Kyle said, and suddenly he sounded more British. He pointed to a glass case on the wall. "Beautiful. Truly."

Mack stared at the carpet. "Is it...stain resistant?"

"Um...I think...I can check on that. I suppose that would be important if you planned on keeping company that might cause stains." Jesse smiled as her gaze moved to him. "Most of the flooring is wood, of course."

"Of course. Wood." Mack was starting to look uncomfortable again. Kyle, on the other hand, looked right at home. He studied everything from the light fixtures to the crown molding. "I like this," he said, pointing vaguely to his left. "And this," he said, pointing to the floor. Misty hovered next to him, pretending to understand what was so captivating. Mack tugged at her miniskirt and pushed the hair out of her eyes.

"Darling, what do you think?" Kyle asked Mack. Misty tried to remain expressionless, but Jesse could tell she'd had her fill of Mr. Money-Bags. Jesse just couldn't help himself. He made his way next to Misty.

"I may not drive a Ferrari," he said, "but I've got plenty of nice maneuvers."

Mack rushed over. "Excuse him," she said, tugging at his arm. "Mind your manners, will you?"

"Just being me," Jesse said with a wink toward Misty that he was sure made her skin crawl.

"You're not really made for off-roading," Mack said, "and she's too high up the mountain for you." This brought a self-satisfied smile from Misty, though Mack was still the one coming up with all the zingers.

"Love the bookcases," Kyle droned on. "And the walls. Exquisite. The paint. Divine."

Jesse rolled his eyes, a familiar activity for the character of Tony Ramone. He considered Kyle's performance thus far. So Kyle could pull off a guy infatuated with paint textures. That would in no way help their cause with auto thieves.

"Do we have any questions?" Misty asked.

"What's your phone number?" Jesse winked.

Kyle whirled and snapped, "Jesse, would you leave the poor woman alone!"

The room grew still. Jesse's heart rate rose as he looked at Misty's perplexed expression. "I thought his name was Tony?"

Kyle swallowed, cleared his throat, itched his nose, scratched his hairline, and tugged at his left ear like a novice at a high buy-in poker table, but he couldn't come up with anything clever to clear the sudden suspicion hanging in the air.

"That's…uh, yes. Of course. That's what I meant."

Misty didn't seem to be buying it.

"Jesse is his middle name. That's what we call him when he's misbe-having." Mack slapped Jesse on the arm. "Behave, will you?"

"Yeah. Sure." Jesse played along, but Kyle was squirming like a heat rash had overtaken his body.

"Yes, yes," Kyle started mumbling. "Jesse is his middle name. He hates it. I call him that when I want to make him mad. Mom called him that, too, when he got in trouble. She passed in 1994. Or was it '95? Anyway, as you can see, Tony is making nothing out of his life, and all he wants is a free ride. And you might think to yourself, who would name their child Tony Jesse? Obviously, those don't really go together because of the *e* sounds at the end. His real name is Antonio Jesse, which was what my father called him. My father was Spanish." Kyle paused. "I look more like my mother."

"Misty, I would really like to see that bathroom again," Mack said. "I'm curious about the closet space…"

Misty nodded but seemed distracted by Kyle. Everyone was distracted by Kyle.

"Is he okay?" Misty whispered to Mack.

"He's fine," Jesse said. "I may be the bad blood, but you broke Mother's heart when you started smoking. Don't kid yourself. Look how your hands are trembling. We all know you're trying to quit, but you just can't do it, can you?" Jesse pulled out the pack of cigarettes he always car-ried with him on undercover jobs. A cigarette and a lighter could get you a long way. He offered one to Kyle.

"I, uh…I…"

"Mackenzie can handle the questions from here," Jesse said, shoving the pack of cigarettes and the lighter into his hand. He wasn't about to let Kyle ruin the exercise for them, and he wasn't going back to Sergeant Yea-ger without a completed rental form. "Stop acting like you don't want this.

Go outside and get it out of your system. Can't you see you're making the women nervous?" Jesse smiled again at Misty, mostly for the effect and to get her attention away from the startled expression on Kyle's face. Misty's body language told Jesse that she was about ready to ask them all to leave.

"Misty, I want to thank you for the wonderful tour you've given us. I will be sure to tell my uncle." Mack said suddenly.

The word "uncle" snapped Misty back into focus. "You're quite welcome," she said, her eyes shiny with the prospect of who this uncle might be and what this uncle might do for her real estate career. "Let me show you how many shoes can fit in that closet."

Mackenzie followed Misty out of sight and Jesse grabbed Kyle by the shirt, shoving him into the hallway. He punched the Down button on the elevator. Kyle was about to open his mouth.

"Shut up," Jesse said. "Don't say anything. Just go downstairs and stand outside and wait for us. Do you hear me?"

"But—"

"But nothing. I don't want to hear it. You nearly blew it in there. What if, instead of a cute girl, you were facing a thug with a gun who is high on meth?"

"I'm so sorry. I really—"

"Go have a smoke." The elevators arrived.

"I don't smoke," Kyle said, looking down at the cigarette.

"Maybe you should."

"You really want me to smoke?"

Jesse sighed loudly, reached into the elevator, and punched the first-floor button. "Kyle, just go down and do whatever it is you do to calm yourself when you're on edge, okay?"

As the doors closed he heard Kyle say, "I eat ham sandwiches."

Chapter 18

B ologna. No mayo, extra mustard." Mason shelled out the money and waited for his name to be called. As he stared out the deli window, he thought about Brandi. He knew she wouldn't hesitate to sell every ounce of his blood for a ticket out of jail. He'd never trusted her. He didn't really trust anyone. But he missed her. He regretted planting the money and drugs on her. He didn't mean to get her in trouble. He merely meant to hide the money in her purse and make an excuse for why he didn't have all of it. He didn't like to give all the money up front. Sometimes the smaller dealers wouldn't even come back for the rest. He'd read that guy wrong. Really wrong.

His name rang out in the small shop. "Mason…" He picked up his sandwich and walked outside to an umbrella-covered table. He unwrapped his sandwich and scarfed it down, which killed about three minutes. Rhyne was still up in the high rise, undoubtedly thinking he was some kind of big shot, leaving Mason with nothing better to do than figure out how to get a bigger cut of the pot of gold Rhyne had been lucky enough to discover.

He leaned back and tried to relax. Next to him a man fiddled with a packet of mayo, trying to tear it open with his fingers for a good minute before giving up and using his teeth. He squirted the mayo on the sandwich, then stared at it for a moment. Mason watched with amusement as the man got up, went back inside for a plastic knife, then returned to his sandwich.

What an idiot, Mason thought. Who leaves a sandwich unattended? He could've snatched it in a heartbeat. He sure wouldn't have left his sandwich just to get a knife. He would've spread the mayo with the packet. Or his fingers. The man smiled and said hello as he sat down. Mason hated that. There was no reason to talk to somebody you didn't know. Unless you wanted something from them. And he did…a cigarette.

"Nice weather today," Mason said out loud, maybe to himself, maybe not. If the man responded, Mason would have his cigarette in no time. If he didn't, then he'd—

"Yes, it is. Sometimes it's a blessing, you know? Things can be going badly, but the warmth of the sunshine, a breeze in the air…it just settles things, puts things into perspective." He looked down at his sandwich. "But there's a lot to be said for a good ham sandwich too."

"Uh…right." Mason was regretting starting this mess, and he wondered what additional "happy feelings" nonsense he would have to endure just to get a cigarette. But he did need a cigarette. And badly. "Hey, could I bum a smoke off you?" Mason asked, nodding to the package on the table.

The man looked confused, then glanced down at the table. "Oh…a cigarette. Um…"

"I wouldn't ask if I didn't really need a fix. I'm having a bad day, and my bologna sandwich doesn't seem to be working wonders like the ham."

"Well, it is bad for your health." Suddenly the man smiled and tossed him the package and lighter. Mason was never one for dry humor, but he could fake it for a cigarette.

"Thanks." He shook one out of the pack.

"Take them all."

"Really?"

"Yeah. It's a pay-it-forward kind of deal."

"Right. Thanks." Mason lit a cigarette and leaned back in his chair. "You're trying to quit, huh? I wish the sunshine would do more for my mood. My business partner thinks he's smart, that he doesn't need me. So I'm supposed to wait down here while he calls all the shots." Mason shrugged. "What a jerk."

"I'm kind of in the same boat."

"Really?" Mason blew smoke. "What kind of business are you in?"

The man looked down. "I'm planning on opening an auto parts store. A body shop, I mean."

Mason studied him. He definitely didn't look like the kind of man who would be willing to pay for parts with no questions asked. But then again, if Mason could tap into a new body shop, maybe he could rake in more money. Sunshine might be on his side today after all.

"So…do you already have dealers? And do you have a source yet for…for things you couldn't ordinarily get under usual business circumstances…?"

The man leaned forward and engaged him with a grin. "Look, I don't want to mislead you. I'm not really opening up a body shop, at least not in the conventional sense."

"Uh huh."

"And I'm not really portraying myself as who I really am. I'm playing a part. I'm not really that good." He gestured to his slacks. "Take these, for instance. They don't exactly match my persona."

Mason finished his cigarette and stomped it out with his foot. "So you're trying to make people think you're someone you're not."

"I know, it sounds weird. I can't really divulge details. But let's just say it's much easier to be who you are than try to be someone else. That's why I'm down here eating a ham sandwich. I nearly blew it for my friends up there because I accidentally—" He looked at Mason. "Anyway, forget it. I'm not making any sense. It just amazes me what kind of paper trail you have to work around to do this stuff. "

"No, man, I'm tracking with you. My business partner is always thinking about himself. He's got a huge ego. He thinks he can do bigger and better. But there is money to be made right here and now, if you know where to look." He tried a smile. "Like with you, for instance. Maybe we can work out a deal."

"A deal?"

"Sure. You're in this for the money, right?"

"Uh…"

"Look, there's no pressure here, okay? But there's also nothing wrong with working things to our advantage. I bring the goods to you, you pay less than what you'd pay wholesale, you sell it at top price, we nix the paper trail, and we're both winners." Mason reached into his pocket for a pen and scratched down a phone number on a napkin. "Think it over. We can keep this between us. Nobody else has to know. Believe me, the fewer people involved, the better." He handed him the napkin. "What's your name?"

The man didn't answer. Mason smiled. This guy was for real.

"Call me when you're ready to do business. Keep this number to yourself. And keep up that clean-cut image too. It works for you. Maybe I'll give it a try." Mason laughed and held up the cigarettes. "Good luck turning over that new leaf."

"Can I come in?" Ron asked. Captain Gates looked up and waved him in.

"How's the training?"

"Good so far."

Laura set aside what she was working on. "You're keeping a good pace, I hope. I want well-trained officers, but we don't have much time."

"They'll be ready. We're still setting up the body shop."

She sighed. "I miss the streets. I miss that adrenaline rush. That's what kept me invigorated."

It's what kept him alive all those years. "Captain, I have to say, you don't really seem like the kind of person who would enjoy working in property crimes. Not that there's anything wrong with it—"

"Don't even get me started," Laura said, waving her hand. "Dad probably would have handpicked this job for me. But I wanted to work narcotics."

"Why aren't you?"

"Why aren't *you*?"

"I'm too old."

"Yeah, well, I guess I'm too female." She folded her hands together. "Sergeant, let me ask you a question."

"Sure."

"Let's say you get a domestic call. Neighbors heard screaming next door. On your way to the scene, you get word that the offender is an officer. When you arrive, police are there, an ambulance is loading a woman covered in blood. She looks about five or six months pregnant. Once inside, you find the husband, and he's the brother of your former partner." Ron watched the scene play out in her eyes. "He's sitting in a chair, crying. You call for the watch commander and a domestic violence detective. You're trying to find out what happened from this guy, and then over your radio, you get word that the baby has died and the mother is in critical condition."

"Okay."

"The guy asks you to call his brother. His brother turns out to be your former partner. You make the call and tell him what happened. Your former partner arrives at the scene about ten minutes later, and the two men ask you for permission to go to the hospital to see the woman." Captain Gates paused. "So, Sergeant Yeager, what would you do?"

Ron thought the scenario through, trying to understand what she was getting at.

Then she laughed like its importance had just diminished. "Forget it." She leaned forward. "What can I do for you?"

"Um…okay, just wanted to give you an update. The National Insurance Crime Bureau has agreed to loan us two people who have experience in collision repair. They'll work perfectly as court witnesses too, since they know what they're talking about with the cars. Also, Auto Insurance

Group of America has agreed to supply the heavy equipment we need. I just need your signature so we can move the paperwork through quickly." He handed the folder to Laura and watched her sign.

"What do you have your gang doing today?"

"Taking their UC identities out for a little walk."

Laura shook her head and handed the folder back to Ron. "You've got some wacky ideas, Sergeant Yeager."

"It's a wacky world out there."

"All right. Let's get this stuff pushed through. We can't lose an hour on it. The Title 3 paperwork is ready, right?"

"Yes. I'll keep you updated." Ron wondered if he should bring his concerns to the table. He hadn't been able to let them go. When his gut did the talking, it meant one of two things: either he was going to get himself into a lot of trouble, or he was about to find a big piece of the puzzle that could turn an investigation around. He called this gut feeling his Second Wife. She nagged twice as much and was worthless in the kitchen, but she had a gift for seeing through bull. "Listen, I wanted to talk to you about something else."

"Yes?"

"I was going over the reports you gave me. I was wondering why some of the files were pulled."

"What makes you think files were pulled?"

"A good detective doesn't rely on other people's research. I wanted to review all the stolen vehicle reports linked to this investigation, and I noticed there were several missing."

"I pulled the ones that seemed irrelevant. Remember, we're on a time restraint."

"Do you have them?"

She went to a file cabinet and took a stack off the top. "Here. I can't imagine what you'd want them for."

Ron sat down and opened them up.

"Just what are you looking for?"

"As you know, cars are stolen for four reasons." Ron said, holding up four fingers. "One, they're stolen and shipped internationally. Those are mostly exotic or high-end cars, sometimes muscle cars from the sixties. Two, they're stolen by desperate people who need transportation. The recovery rate for those is about 80 percent."

Laura interrupted him. "We've really lowered the crime rate for that. Since we started handing out bus tokens, we've seen a 45 percent drop. Uh, sorry. " She smiled. "I forget I don't have to keep selling the idea that those tokens work."

"Three, they're stolen by kids looking for a joyride. These usually end up trashed. Four, and probably most commonly, they're stolen for profit. They're stripped for parts."

"Exactly. Which is why we set up the body shop."

Ron pointed to the folders. "But these don't fit the norm. Minivans and a station wagon?"

"There are always exceptions."

"These aren't stripped. They're not vandalized. And they've all been recovered—completely intact—within a few days."

Gates folded her arms. "So this is what you're going to focus on? Recovered vehicles?" Then she held up her hands. "I trust you, Sergeant. If you think you need to look into these, then look into them. Now, I've got to get back to work."

Ron turned to leave the office, but his Second Wife nagged at him. "Captain, I have to ask…what did you do?"

"What are you talking about?"

"With your partner's brother. What did you do?"

A thin smile spread over her lips. "The same thing you did, Sergeant."

"I didn't really have a chance to think about it."

"Neither did I."

"You have to make split-second decisions sometimes. You do the best you can."

"Yeah? Tell that to the narcotics guys."

Misty held out a hand and said, "Thank you, Mackenzie. It was very nice to meet you. I'll be in touch in a few days. Here's your copy of the paperwork."

Jesse stood in the corner like a snotty teenager and watched as they shook hands. Outwardly, he looked like he couldn't care less, but inside he was breathing a deep sigh of relief.

Mack said, "All right, Tony. Let's go."

Jesse trailed behind her out of Misty's office. Then he heard, "Tony."

Both he and Mack turned. "Yeah?"

Misty held out her hand for him to shake. It threw him for a moment. But when he looked at her, she was smiling cordially. Maybe she was worried about impressing "the uncle." What would Tony do? He wasn't used to dealing with upper-class types.

He stretched a menacing grin across his face. "So I finally won you over. Maybe next time you can show me *your* apartment."

She kept an even expression. "Take care, Tony." She cupped his hand with both of hers, then turned back to her desk. Jesse walked into the lobby and opened up his right hand. Inside was a folded piece of paper.

"What's that?" Mack asked.

Jesse unfolded it.

"I scored her phone number."

"You've got to be kidding me."

"Too bad she had to meet Tony instead of me. Although Tony does have a way with women."

"Why would a woman be attracted to that?" She gestured toward him.

"What's not to like?"

"This is why I don't even try the dating scene anymore."

"You date?"

"No."

"You just don't seem the dating type."

"I'm not. Aren't you listening to me?"

Jesse held up his hands. "All right, settle down. If I didn't know any better, I'd think you were jealous."

"We need to find Kyle," she said through clenched teeth.

Jesse pointed across the street. "There are some shops over there. Maybe he's—"

Mack was five steps ahead of him. She walked—no, stomped—across the street. Jesse hustled to catch up with her. "You know, Mack, you did a really good job in there."

She stayed quiet but seemed interested in what he had to say.

"That was no easy task, but it was good practice. You've got to be able to think quickly on your feet. You did that. We really pulled it off. At least you and I did. Kyle, well, that's another story."

"He just had one bad moment."

"Why are you always defending him? I've never seen such a disaster."

"Sergeant Yeager must see something you and I don't."

"Right. Maybe Kyle has superpowers."

"You're a really cynical guy, you know that? Everyone has to live with evil in the world. We have to deal with bad people on a daily basis, but at least we're trying to do something about it."

"Criminals don't make me cynical."

"Then what does?"

"One time I arrived at a hostage situation. The man had his wife at gunpoint and was threatening to kill her in the next ten minutes. The

SWAT team and negotiators were on their way, but we only had about a minute left. Something told me this guy was for real. So while he was at the front window, peeking out at the police, I snuck in through the back door and shot him in the shoulder. The woman ran to the bedroom and the police stormed the place. You want to know what happened next?"

She stopped and turned to him, her arms crossed. "What?"

"The woman came tearing out of the bedroom, kicked me between the legs, and then hit me over the head with a vase." Jesse started walking again, taking the lead. "So excuse me if I don't see the world through rose-colored glasses."

"I live in reality too. I just choose to see the glass half-full."

"I suppose that's why you think Kyle's a good cop... He works because he fills up a glass?"

"Kyle works because he cares and he tries hard."

"It takes a lot more than that to make it in undercover work. Unless, of course, you plan to 'aw-shucks' the bad guys to death."

She stepped in front of his path. "Look, my dad always said there are two kinds of people in the world: the kind that let their problems beat them, and the kind that beat their problems. We can figure this out. Maybe Kyle has some strengths we just haven't uncovered. Give him time."

"We don't have time. And I don't want my name attached to a task force that crashes and burns before it ever gets off the ground." Jesse scanned the street. "What'd he do, go shopping?"

"You know what? I really don't like you. I'm trying...I really am. I usually give people the benefit of the doubt, but you seem to be beyond the benefit."

"Mack, I hate to break this to you but—"

"Shut up!" she shouted. "Just shut that stupid, egotistical, know-it-all mouth of yours. Every time you talk, my hair stands on end. I've been try-ing my best to get over this. I really have. I've prayed, I've confessed, I've read God's Word on the power of forgiveness. But dang it, Jesse, every time I'm around you, you make me sin!"

Jesse raised an eyebrow. "Lust?"

"Anger, you idiot!" She took a deep breath and threw up her hands. "See what I mean? I just blew it. Again. Last night I really thought I had a handle on this. I prayed and heard God telling me that you have no idea how obnoxious you are so I shouldn't hold you accountable to that." She looked toward the sky and then back at him, this time with less fire in her eyes. "I'm sorry."

Jesse held up a finger, about to retort, when Kyle stepped out from the deli shop.

"Hey," he said. He looked at the papers in Mack's hand. "You did it?"

"Yeah, no thanks to you," Jesse said. "Come on, let's get out of here."

"Um, guys. Wait."

Jesse turned. "What is it now, Kyle?"

"I might've messed up."

Chapter 19

Ron walked into the house where his team had assembled. He held up Ruth's car keys; he'd finally been given approval to use her cars. "Our friendly neighbor across the street has been kind enough to loan us her cars. You'll have to get all of yours back to your houses so you can start using these." He threw the keys on the table and sensed a nervousness in the room. "What's going on? How'd the training go?"

Jesse and Dozer stepped forward, and handed him their apartment paperwork. "Well done," he said, then looked at Jesse. "You pulled it off."

"You threw quite a wrench in," Jesse said.

"I didn't want this to be too easy for you. I wanted to see what you would do with it." He looked at Mack. "Good job, everyone."

"Thank you," said Mackenzie. "It was a team effort."

"Not exactly," Jesse said. He looked at Kyle. "Kyle messed up."

"What do you mean?" Ron asked.

"I don't really know what I mean. Something happened, but he wouldn't say anything else until he talked to you."

Kyle sat in a chair at the breakfast table, chewing his lip as his eyes darted around the room.

"Kyle?"

"Look, I'm in way over my head. It sounded like fun, but now I've gone and done something…I may have really screwed you all up. I think it's just time I quit."

"I agree," Jesse said.

Ron held up his hands. "Wait, hold on. First of all, Kyle, it's hard for me to imagine you could have screwed anything up too badly. This was a training exercise. Why don't you just explain what happened?"

"It all started when I called Jesse by his real name instead of his under-cover name. It nearly blew the operation—"

"Exercise," Ron inserted.

"I got flustered and Jesse sent me downstairs for a smoke."

"You smoke?" Ron asked.

"No…no, it was just an excuse to get me out of the room."

Ron looked at Jesse. "It seems that it all worked out. You and Mack were able to smooth things over, right?"

"There's more," Kyle said. "I decided to get a sandwich. I eat ham sandwiches when I'm nervous, and I saw this deli right across the street. I sat at one of the tables in front of the shop. The next thing I know, I'm having a conversation with this guy, who then asks if he can have a ciga-rette. Jesse had given me a pack, so I said sure, and then I told him he could keep the whole pack. And then I got the stupid idea that while I was sitting there, I should practice my undercover identity. I felt a little ridiculous doing it, so"—Kyle sighed heavily—"I don't really know how it happened, to tell you the truth."

"What happened, Kyle?" Jesse asked.

Kyle reached into his pocket, pulled out a folded napkin, and laid it flat on the table. Everyone leaned in to read it.

"A phone number?" Wiz asked.

Mack looked at Jesse. "Looks like you're not the only one who scored a phone number."

Jesse looked at Kyle. "I don't get it. Whose number is this?"

Kyle mumbled something nobody could hear.

"Speak up," Jesse said.

"It's the phone number for a guy who wants to sell stolen auto parts at a discounted price to a body shop I told him I wasn't *really* opening."

Ron grabbed a chair, pulled it next to Kyle, and sat down. "Kyle, what exactly are you saying?"

"That's the problem! I don't really know what I'm saying," Kyle said, his voice heavy with emotion. "I was sitting there telling this guy that I wasn't really who he thought I was, or who I thought I was, and that I wasn't opening a 'real' body shop, and the next thing I know, he's giving me his number and wanting to sell me illegal parts."

The room suddenly grew quiet, except for a strange noise that Jesse recognized immediately. "Dozer, wake up!" he shouted. Everyone turned to watch Dozer snap out of his catnap. Then everyone started asking Kyle questions at the same time. Ron settled them down.

He focused on Kyle. "Did you mention that this was an undercover operation?"

"I don't know. I mean, I was talking about how hard it is to be someone you're not—"

"Did you say the word 'undercover'?"

"I don't think so."

"What did you say about the body shop? Did you say where it was located?"

"No. I just said something about it not being a conventional body shop."

"But you didn't mention that it was an undercover job or that the body shop was a sting operation?"

"No. Not directly, anyway. I think he misunderstood me."

"What was this guy's name?" Jesse asked.

"He didn't say. Just wrote down his phone number."

"Did you say your name?"

"I wasn't exactly sure if I should say my real name or my undercover name or just make something up, so I didn't say anything. I'm sorry, okay? I'm sorry."

Jesse put both of his hands on the table and looked down. "Dude, you are some piece of work. Don't you understand what you've done here?"

"I said I was sorry!"

"Kyle," Jesse said, "you scored big. You got us the phone number of a guy who wants to sell us stolen parts. We're *in*."

Wiz said, "Except we're not ready. How long before we can open up the shop?"

"We're three weeks out, at least," Ron answered. "We still need the framing equipment."

"Why not open early? We could do oil changes and maintenance stuff, at least to get something up and running," Dozer said.

"If we don't have something to offer this guy, he may take his business elsewhere, and then we've got nothing," Jesse said.

"Okay, let's not get ahead of ourselves," said Ron. "The guys with the auto experience aren't available immediately. There is a mound of paperwork to do and at least four different agencies wrapped up in this. We need guys in there with experience or we're going to look like exactly what we are: undercover officers posing as a body shop crew."

"This guy's obviously desperate," Jesse said. "He approached Kyle, left him his phone number."

"Sarge is right. If we open up without looking authentic, we're going to raise suspicion," Wiz said.

"I say we make contact with him anyway. Tell him we're willing to deal under the table to get some parts in before we open up," Jesse said.

Ron said, "I'm not comfortable with that. None of you have enough experience with cars to make this work."

"There's no way to get one of these insurance guys in here quicker?" asked Mack.

Ron shook his head. "Believe me, four weeks is fast. This kind of thing can take upwards of three months. I'm already pulling all the strings I can to get them here in that amount of time."

"So we basically just need one guy who can be the front man, right?" Mack asked. "Someone who can speak the language."

"At least," Ron said.

"Okay," Mack said. "I have a brother. His name is Hank. He's really good with cars and used to work for a mechanic. And he's unemployed right now, so I don't think he'd mind coming out here."

Before Jesse could ask the obvious, indelicate question, Ron said, "Mack, what kind of disposition does your brother have? I mean, could he handle something like this?"

"He's quiet, but really reliable and knows what he's talking about with cars. I could call him, see if he could be here in a couple of days."

Jesse's gaze met Ron's, and Ron could tell the wheels were turning. Ron wasn't so sure. A certain amount of flexibility was necessary when working undercover, which was why the by-the-book personalities never made good undercover cops. But this could get out of control, and quickly. In fact, Ron thought as he looked at Kyle, it already had.

Dozer spoke up. "So we send Kyle in, make additional contact with this guy, and start the exchange."

Wiz said, "He's probably not the biggest fish, but I bet he can lead us to someone who is."

Ron stood, trying to figure out how he was going to break the news. He realized there was no way around this except to tell them. "Look, guys, here's the deal. Kyle is not an undercover officer."

"Finally," Jesse said. "I thought I was the only sane one here."

"He's not an officer at all." Bewilderment swirled across their faces. "Kyle's a friend. I asked him to participate in the training. The purpose was to put him into situations with you and watch how each of you handled...complications."

Now everyone was staring at Kyle, who looked relieved to have his secret out on the table.

"You've got to be kidding," Jesse said.

"Makes more sense now, doesn't it?" Ron said.

"So now what do we do?" Wiz asked. "Kyle's our 'in' with this guy."

"We get creative. We figure out how to bring in one of Kyle's associates—one of us—who would work the deal. I don't think it's going to be that hard," Jesse said. "Kyle can make initial contact, and then we take it from there."

"I'm not comfortable with that," Ron said. "The plan was never to send Kyle out to the field."

Jesse looked at Kyle. "It's just for one meeting. Kyle meets him, gets his name, then drops the name of the guy who handles the money, Tony Ramone. Then we've got him. From there, we work our way up and see where the trail leads."

Kyle said, "I can do this. I know I can. I know I've screwed up a lot of stuff, but I want to finish this. Jesse's right. This guy made contact with me. He's not going to deal with anyone else unless I vouch for them."

Ron leaned against the kitchen wall. It would be a gigantic risk. It was absurd. Ridiculous. Insane. Just like the six-month deadline for the task force. A huge shortcut was handed right to them. How could they pass this up?

Ron was reasonably certain that this guy was not at the top of the food chain. The real pros would never have handed out a phone number so easily. But it was a foot in the door, and that's what they needed.

Jesse stopped pacing. "What do you think?" he asked Ron.

"I'm not sure," he confessed. "There's a lot that could go wrong."

"No offense," Mack added, looking at Kyle.

Jesse approached Ron. "Come on, Sarge. This could work. We'll have teams standing by, we'll control the environment, the location. This could be huge. How can we pass this up?"

The room seemed to concur.

"Sarge, don't look so worried," said Jesse.

"I just don't know what I'm going to tell her."

"Captain Gates?"

"Nan."

Chapter 20

Across the smoke-filled living room, Rhyne watched Mason puff on a cigarette. Every time he took it out of his mouth, he would look at it like it was made of gold.

"I didn't know you enjoyed smoking that much," Rhyne said as he folded his newspaper.

"Sometimes I like it, sometimes I don't."

"Never heard of that. Most people are addicted or they're not."

"There's something to be said about smoking just for the pleasure of it. What about a nice cigar once in a while, huh?" *Yeah, what about it. Or caviar. Champagne at two hundred dollars a bottle.* Though Rhyne would never admit it, he was having a hard time getting over his meeting with Vincent. If ever there was a guy who needed to go by "Vinnie," this was that guy. Even "Bubba" would be more appropriate. What a letdown. Rhyne had finally made it to the top, or at least to the penthouse, and the boss was a redneck? A *redneck?* How did a guy like that make it?

Rhyne's grandmother used to tell him not to judge people by their looks, and Vincent certainly had credibility where money was concerned, but did he even *own* a suit?

"You okay?" Mason asked.

"Before long, we'll have more money than we know what to do with." Rhyne said, avoiding the question. He went to the window. "Then I can move out of this neighborhood. That lady over there drives me nuts."

"You're always standing at your window worrying about her. She's a little old lady. Smile and wave, and she'll be off your back."

Rhyne turned to him. "Don't smile. And don't wave. I don't want to give her any reason to come near this house."

"Fine. Whatever you say."

"We can't afford to screw this up. We're playing with the big dogs now." More of a mutt than a purebred, but a mutt with money.

"So you say."

"I'm practically carrying you to the pot of gold. If you want to settle for plain old pot, be my guest. But let me know now, because we're getting ready to sink deep into this thing and I have to know if you're with me or not."

Mason put out his cigarette. "They're using us."

"We're using them," Rhyne said with a smile. "We're using them to get out of a business that's saturated. Body shops don't need any more parts. You can strip a car down to its frame and you might get five hundred bucks off of it."

"Maybe you just don't know where to look."

"Trust me," Rhyne said. "I know where to look. There's nothing new under the sun." He turned to Mason. "So are you in or not? If you're in, you gotta stop hanging out with people who don't understand big business. We gotta cut old ties. Carefully. But we gotta cut them." Rhyne sighed. He wasn't sure if Mason understood the scope of his plan, but Rhyne could work that to his advantage. "Just promise me."

"Yeah, yeah. I promise."

Rhyne walked to his back door and stepped outside for some fresh air. It was time to adjust his thinking. He was a businessman.

A long, shiny cherrywood table stretched the length of the conference room, void of any personality except for a large vase of fake flowers in the corner and a tidy bookcase at the end. Ron looked at the six men and two women who sat around the table. He knew them all by name, had talked with them many times over the years, but now, in this room, each of their gazes felt as unfamiliar as the room. Ron stood at the end of the table with his hands clasped in front of him, trying to make the best impression he could without the help of a tie or a pocket Bible.

He glanced at Nan, who sat in the far corner by the flowers. He didn't bother smiling. He knew she wouldn't smile back. Or talk to him. The last words she'd spoken to him were, "This has to go through the ministry board." Lucky for him, they were meeting tonight, and Nan was the official note taker.

This was Kyle's baptism into the world of crime. And now, as Ron stood in front of the ministry board, he wondered how he could've made it sound more appealing. He did his best to link Kyle's proposed work in undercover to the Sermon on the Mount, which was difficult for many reasons, not the least of which was that undercover work wasn't meek, poor in spirit, merciful, peaceful, or pure.

He had to admit, the explanation did sound a little kooky. It seemed apparent by the bewildered expressions on their faces that nobody in the room suspected Ron's occupation was anything other than an eight-to-five desk job, which, of course, it had been until a few weeks ago.

Ron studied the room. One woman was looking over her notes like she was searching for something she might have missed. Three men were whispering back and forth. One guy looked to be praying, which was probably what Ron should be doing, though he wasn't sure he wanted to know which side of this issue God was on.

The man at the end of the table, Bert, who wore a flashy bow tie and a tired expression, finally broke the mumbling. "Ron, I don't know what to say. We've never had anything quite like this come to our attention."

Lilleth held a large plastic notebook open in front of her. "There are all kinds of statutes and clauses, dealing with everything from adultery to alcoholism, but I can't find anything in here that states what we should do in a case of…of… What is this a case of?"

"Exploiting a man of the cloth," Nan offered. Everyone looked at Ron.

"As you can see," Ron said, "my wife is completely supportive of the idea."

Nan's eyes narrowed. "Don't make me out to be the bad guy here. I warned you that this wasn't a good idea. But," she said, addressing the others in the room, "as you can see, he doesn't always listen to wise council. Or common sense. This is the same guy, mind you, who decided—after beating the odds and living through twenty years as an undercover officer—that it would be fun to race cars." Nan held up a stern finger as Ron started to respond. "He'll tell you it's because he needed an adrenaline rush. Why not join the over-forty softball team?"

"That was just a little too much adrenaline for me," Ron said from across the room.

Nan set down her pen and crossed her arms. "The point is that Kyle is completely inexperienced in this sort of activity. It's ridiculous to send him to the seediest part of town to interact with people who ought to be in prison."

"The way we get these people into prison is by catching them doing something illegal, which is what we're going to do if the ministry board will allow me to use Kyle. It will be a controlled situation. The chances of something going wrong are small. We'll have an experienced undercover officer with him, posing as the money man. The meeting will take fifteen, twenty minutes tops, and Kyle will be finished. We'll take over from there."

"I'm just not comfortable with our pastor having anything to do with drugs," said Lilleth. "That's giving the devil an unnecessary opportunity."

"This isn't a drug operation. It's stolen cars."

Otis, the eldest board member, said, "We could certainly justify his presence there; nothing breaks up crime like a purging of sins by the Holy Spirit."

"Indeed," Ron said with a reverent nod toward Otis while Nan rolled her eyes. "And if I'm not mistaken, Code LXVIII, which explains in detail the three-week sabbatical, orders the church to not interfere with any rituals the pastor chooses to undertake during that time."

"Rituals," Nan said with an exhaustive gesture. "You call this a ritual?"

"The truth is that I would've never involved Kyle had I known it would end up like this. Kyle was just looking for some…interesting perspectives on life, and I thought it would be a good fit. However, now that he has secured this potential lead, I don't want to pass up the opportunity. Kyle will be fine."

The head of the council, Les, threw down his pencil and blew out a sigh. "There's nothing to vote on here. We have no mandate for this kind of thing."

Nan stood. "I propose that we vote anyway. It would be helpful to see where everyone stands on this issue."

Les shrugged. "Fine. Who's for letting Kyle do this?"

All the board members raised their hands. Nan scowled and sat down.

Otis said, "Motion to proceed with the rest of the agenda."

"Second that motion."

"Motion approved." Lilleth looked at Ron. "Thank you for your time, Ron. We'll be praying for you. Let us know how it all turns out."

"I will. Thank you." Ron took his cue to leave. As he walked toward the exit, Les grabbed his arm and pulled him down to whisper in his ear. "Say, if you've got any more of these kinds of things going on, give me a ring. I fought in the Korean War."

Ron patted him on the shoulder. "Will do." He left the room and punched the down button for the elevator, but Nan got to him before the elevator did. The doors swished open.

"This is the most ridiculous thing I have ever heard of," Nan said. The elevator doors swished closed.

"I think you're making too big of a deal out of this."

"This is going to end exactly like the Bobby Fernando case."

Ron laughed. Bobby Fernando was a high-ranking mobster Ron had spent eight weeks with in deep cover before he was finally able to make an arrest. "That was fourteen years ago. And it ended with Fernando going to prison for life and the DA sending me a personal note of congratulations."

"Is that how you remember it? Because I remember you missing our anniversary, not calling, and sleeping on the couch the night before the trial began." She punched the down arrow. "There are extra pillows in the living room closet and a blanket in the cabinet."

Dimmer than dim lighting, dark wood, soft music playing in the background... Dennis Norton was definitely going to get the wrong idea. Laura began scanning the restaurant, pressing her lips together to even out the lip gloss she'd applied on the freeway. It had been dark for over an hour, and the hot desert air was starting to cool under a clear sky.

Though nearly everything on the menu was deep-fried in beer batter, the restaurant had nice decor. Laura saw Dennis waving her over to a booth. She smiled widely and approached him, sliding into the booth as a waiter brought her a menu.

"You look great," Dennis said. Of course she looked great. They were practically dining in the dark.

"Glad you were free."

"I wasn't," Dennis said, flashing that same annoying grin. "But I rearranged some things, and here I am."

Laura laced her fingers together and pretended to be flattered.

"It's been a while," he said, sipping his drink, which looked like something atrociously strong and alcoholic. Tonight she would stick with water.

"Yes, it has. I've been busy."

Dennis kept his eyes locked on hers, which absolutely drove her nuts.

He had an intense stare that followed every move she made and eyebrows that talked more than his mouth. They moved up and down independently, lay flat across his face, arched upward like they'd been professionally tweezed, and then crowded together like imminent danger lurked in every fourth word.

They'd dated for a month and a half. Nearly every member of his family was with the police department. He had connections from the crime lab to the coroner's office to the deli.

He'd been married three times, which was the least of his unappealing traits. He also came equipped with a conviction that women weren't treated fairly in the department and had taken this problem on as his personal crusade. Or more accurately, as his own personal dating service. Two of his ex-wives were now his superiors, but Dennis didn't seem to let that stop him.

He'd transferred with ease to narcotics four years ago after a two-year stint in homicide, where he happened to work the worst string of murders in thirty years. Luck was on Dennis Norton's side, at least career wise. Unlike most men she knew, he didn't take it for granted. He genuinely wanted to help. His personality, though, was disorderly. Not in a manic sort of way, but in a complete-lack-of-self-awareness sort of way, which became evident to Laura on their first date when he ordered the triple-garlic medallions.

He also seemed to have a Superman complex. "I can make it happen." She must've heard that catch phrase a hundred and ten times in the four-month period he'd dedicated his career to getting her into narcotics.

He didn't make it happen.

The waiter approached the table with a platter in hand and Dennis said, "I took the liberty of ordering an appetizer. Hope that's okay."

"Sure."

"The beer-battered onion rings, sir," the waiter said, setting the platter between them. Well, at least she could chow down. This wasn't a date, so she didn't have to worry about her breath or his.

"I'm curious," his eyebrows said before he did. "I don't suppose you're going to tell me why you called."

"It's been a long time since we've talked. We haven't really stopped to catch up."

He noticed her hand. "I see you're still single."

Laura glanced at his fingers, thankful not to see a ring. His second marriage ended because of adultery.

"And," he added as he slurped the tail end of an onion ring into his mouth, "we're not at Hippo's." She understood what Dennis's eyebrows were adding to this observation—this was more than a catch-up dinner.

She'd have to play along until she found what she was looking for. They chitchatted for a bit about the Property Crimes Bureau. Laura tried to make it sound as exciting as possible, bragging about the predictable hours and how nice it was to work with seasoned cops…so seasoned they couldn't taste their food anymore without adding a heap of salt. They were a nice bunch of folks, but she didn't envy them.

Laura ordered the baked chicken; Dennis, the evening-ends-after-dinner eight-bean chili. It was an easy transition into talk of narcotics. Dennis's eyes had started to glaze over with talk about the burglary rate.

"So," Laura said, "anything unusual coming through Vegas lately?"

"Naw. We got word four months ago there might be more mob activity, but nothing's surfaced. Bringing in black tar by the truckloads, but what's new?"

Laura chose her words, and her expression, carefully. "I read a few weeks ago about these minivans being used to transport cocaine."

"Minivans, huh?"

"Somewhere on the East Coast. Something about soccer-mom types lending their vehicles to crack dealers to transport the stuff in exchange for the drugs."

"Yeah. Hasn't made it our way yet, though." Dennis laughed.

Laura leaned back and laughed too. Dennis's eyebrows couldn't lie. This thing wasn't even on their radar.

Now she just had to figure out how to end the dinner as soon as possible.

Chapter 21

R on walked six blocks from the UC house to a pay phone to call the number scrawled on the deli napkin. He had no reason to walk except that he needed the exercise, which had suffered since he took charge of the task force. It felt good to stretch his back and legs, both of which were really sore from sleeping on the couch.

He'd tried to talk to Nan this morning, but she wouldn't listen. Like a three-year-old, she plugged both ears with her index fingers and made a humming sound on her way to the kitchen.

He hadn't seen her this angry in a long time. In her own way, Nan had been supportive of his undercover career. She never questioned his work, never judged him for it, never asked him to leave. But she did, on occasion, remind him how a stupid move on the street could make him suffer endlessly at home—if it didn't get him killed.

Nan was fully aware of what was involved in UC work. She didn't like it, but she accepted it. And she trusted Ron, which was the saving grace in their relationship. She never questioned why he came home at three in the morning instead of midnight, or why he smelled like he'd bathed in nicotine. When Nan had an idea in her head, though, there was no changing her mind—like the idea that the entire drug world needed to come to a screeching halt on their anniversary.

In Nan's mind, Ron had completely crossed the line by involving Kyle. Of course, in the original plan, Kyle was never supposed to get this involved, but Nan hadn't listened to any of the nine attempts he'd made to explain that. She hadn't spoken a word to him this morning.

It bothered him now more than it would've in the past. Maybe because in the past, when he left for work, he submerged himself in it and had no time to think about problems at home. Ron gave Nan plenty of credit, though. She had to play second fiddle to a demanding job that made no guarantees about delivering him home safely. She'd forgiven him for plenty. Ron understood why she was so angry. They'd made it through a lot together. Why would he want to go back to harder times?

Ron reached the pay phone. He needed to make a call to see if this number was real. Since the guy hadn't given out his name, Ron believed he was probably legit, and at least somewhat experienced in this sort of thing. Now the question was, was he stupid enough to give out his cell number?

The phone rang a couple of times before a male voice answered. "Yeah. Doodah's." Ron knew the bar. It was actually called Doodley's House, but over the years it had acquired the abbreviated nickname of Doodah's, not to mention a rough crowd. "Sorry, wrong number," he said and hung up. Ron understood immediately. The guy gave the number to a bar, a signal that business could be on the table, but Kyle would have to show up and recognize the man's face. It was a safe place for this guy, who probably had hordes of friends there. A crowded bar on his turf would send the signal that he was in control.

Ron started losing confidence in his plan. Sure, Kyle made a good first impression at the deli. But that was an accident. This was the real deal and things could turn sour quickly.

Of course, Kyle wouldn't be alone. Jesse would be there too. It wouldn't be long before Kyle would be safely out of the picture. The chances of something going wrong were small. Right?

His cane thumped rhythmically against the sidewalk as he walked back to the UC house. He hoped Ruth didn't mistake the sound for a mating call.

It took an entire night for Jesse to get over how Yeager had tricked the team with Kyle. It wasn't until 5:30 a.m., when his stomach rumbled with hunger and wouldn't allow him back to sleep, that he realized the brilliance of bringing Kyle into the training. It was a good training tool. He'd scarfed down three bowls of Cheerios until he finally felt relief that Kyle wasn't a real part of the team.

Somewhere during a sip of his orange juice he realized, with horror, that Kyle *was* a real part of the team. At least until they could make contact with the man desperately seeking a body shop.

By midmorning, Jesse, Wiz, Dozer, and Kyle sat around the breakfast table engaged in a ridiculous conversation, but then again, the whole thing was pretty ridiculous.

"So, any questions?" Jesse asked Kyle.

"Let me just see if I've got this straight. Order an import, not a domestic. It'll show I've got taste. But don't drink too much, because it's got a stronger alcohol content than domestic. Say something about how you can't get any good beers anymore and shove it to the side."

"You've got to sell the idea that you're not drinking because you like high-end beer, not because you've never tasted alcohol in your life." Jesse tried to say it nicely. He'd never met anyone who didn't drink. Even Chaplain Greer liked wine.

"I can do it," Kyle said. He looked at the list they'd made of German beers. "I'll memorize this."

"I think he should drink the penny beer," Dozer said. "I mean, you can't go wrong, it's in every bar in town. You have to drink eight to feel a buzz."

"Kyle doesn't really look like the penny beer kind, does he? We have to sell him as a business guy. I'm not comfortable letting him order hard liquor."

Kyle said, "This guy really liked cigarettes, and he thinks I'm trying to quit. Do I have to know how to smoke?"

"I don't think so," Jesse said.

"I don't know," Wiz said. "I mean, the guy may pressure him to have a smoke."

"It wouldn't hurt to have some on him," Dozer said. "It opened the door before. Might give him something to break the ice with."

"All we need is for the guy to see Kyle's hands shaking like crazy while he's trying to light it," Jesse said. He wanted to add that this was the very reason you don't say you know how to do something when you really don't, but they didn't have time for lectures.

Jesse sighed. "Okay, look. We'll give you the basics. If at all possible, I would avoid smoking. But just in case it is absolutely necessary, we'll teach you how to inhale without imploding."

Wiz threw a lighter on the table.

"Maybe I should use matches," Kyle said. "Lighters make me nervous."

"This is never going to work," Jesse groaned.

"It's perfect," Wiz said. "People's hands shake when they're craving nicotine. It will give him an excuse."

"Look, I can do this, all right? How hard is it?" Kyle took the cigarette that Wiz had laid on the table. "I light it." He lit it. "I put it in my mouth." He put it in his mouth. "You suck—"

What are you doing?" Ron stood at the front door with wide eyes and a fierce scowl. His cane hit the floor hard as he stomped toward the table.

"We're trying to teach your apprentice how to smoke a cigarette so he has a chance of not blowing his cover." Jesse spoke in a confident tone. He glanced at Kyle, who looked painfully guilty, then at Ron, who looked like he was trying to recover from seeing somebody naked. "Do you have a problem with that?"

Ron cleared his throat. "Sorry. Um…I overreacted."

Everyone sat down slowly, eyeing Ron.

Jesse looked over at Kyle. "Kyle, where's your cigarette?"

Kyle looked down at his hands. "I don't know."

"Smoke!" yelled Dozer.

Kyle jumped up and backward, swatting at his smoking pant leg. He then stopped, dropped, and actually rolled into the living room.

By the time Kyle had pinballed against the coffee table and back toward the kitchen, Dozer was bent over, grabbing his stomach, laughing. Wiz roared next to him.

"I'm fine," Kyle said, looking at the burn hole in his pant leg. He hopped up and tried to smile. "No biggie."

Jesse slapped his hands over his face. "I think we're going to have to sell the idea that you're trying to quit smoking."

"Good idea," Ron said, going over to examine Kyle. "Are you sure you're all right?"

Kyle nodded. "I'm great. These guys are really taking care of me. I've learned how to order German beer."

Dozer said, "I voted for Coors."

Ron held up a hand. "Okay, look, let's just move away from alcohol and cigarettes for a moment. I called the number. It's Doodah's."

"Doodah's! You're kidding," Jesse said.

"The guy's smart enough to give the number to a bar."

"Kyle will have to go in on Friday night and try to spot him," Dozer said.

Ron nodded. "We need to come up with a plan. Where's Mack?"

"She went to get her brother from the airport," Wiz said.

"That was quick," Ron said. "Good. We need somebody by this weekend."

Just then, the front door opened and Mack walked in. Trailing her was a man who almost looked like her identical twin, except he was slouching and his hands were buried deep into his pockets. Mack encouraged him toward the breakfast table. "Hey, everyone, this is my brother Hank."

Hank hardly managed to look up. He gave a quick wave and stared at the carpet.

"He's… He can be a little shy. Until he gets to know you," Mack said. "But he does know cars, and he's ready and willing to help."

Jesse sighed and leaned back into his chair. "He'll come in real handy as soon as we can teach him to speak."

By now, Jesse had figured out Ron's game. He was going to pair Jesse up with Mack as often as possible until Jesse finally accepted her as part of the team. While Wiz and Dozer went to file paperwork for the body shop, Jesse, Mack, and her brother, Dumbstruck, went to get lunch.

Mack's brother sat in the backseat of the Cadillac, staring out the window, while Mack pointed out the obvious: "There's a casino… There's a hotel…" Mack explained that Hank had never been to a big city. And that today was the first time he'd flown on an airplane.

Jesse looked in his rearview mirror. "How was your flight, Hank?"

"High," he replied.

Jesse looked over at Mack, who gave an apologetic smile. "So, Jesse," she began, "I'm curious. How do you separate yourself from your undercover identity?"

"When I'm with criminals, I'm Tony. It's not rocket science."

Mack glanced back at Hank. "His undercover name is Tony Romaine."

"Tony *Ramone*. I'm not a head of lettuce."

"I know," Mack smiled. "But I thought that was funny since we're driving by Caesars. Get it? Caesars salad?"

Jesse kept his eyes locked on the road. "Mack, I'm sure you're a great cop, okay? And there's no getting around it. You're on the team. But you see by now that you don't really belong in the undercover world, right?"

He glanced at her as she looked out her window. "I'm not trying to be harsh. I'm really not. There's a certain personality type made for under-cover work. I can see you working your way up to captain."

"Why do you think I don't fit?" Mack asked.

From the back, in a quiet voice, Hank said, "It's because you were homeschooled."

"You were homeschooled?"

"Yeah. So?"

Jesse whipped around the corner, narrowly missing the curb. "That's terrific."

"He doesn't know about the convenience store?" Hank asked.

"Was that your previous job?"

Hank leaned forward. "She saved a store clerk who was being held at gunpoint."

"Look, it doesn't matter what I did or where I went to school," Mack said. "This whole thing isn't going to work unless you trust me."

"This isn't personal, Mack. It's about the safety of the team. If you're not ready for this, you could put us in jeopardy."

"I'm ready for it. I've been ready for it my whole life. No, I don't have your experience, but I'm a fast learner, and if you could dial your ego back a notch, maybe you could teach me something."

Jesse tried to remain calm and not let his impatience get the best of him. "I have no problem with your inexperience. But is this the best time for you to jump into something like this?"

"Everybody has to jump in at some point."

Jesse pulled to the curb in front of Pizza House.

"It's going to take us all working together," Mack said. "As a team."

"There's no 'I' in team," Hank said from the backseat.

Jesse wanted to bang his head against the steering wheel. Mack and Hank might be good at undercover work…if they needed a duo to bust a pencil-theft ring in the fourth grade. "There's no 'we' in undercover," he snarled. "I'm going in to get the pizza." He slammed the door and found Mack waiting for him on the other side. He walked past her but she followed, stopping him at the entrance to the restaurant.

"I proved myself to you once. I won't be a liability. I promise."

Jesse folded his arms and glanced toward Hank, whose face was pressed up against the window. "Fine. What about your brother? You don't have a mute button; his seems to be stuck."

"He'll be fine. He's not a big talker, except when it's something he's interested in, like cars, and now, apparently airplanes. He couldn't stop talking about them on the way back from the airport."

Jesse couldn't put his finger on what made other people believe in her. Maybe because she was the kind of person many people wished would fill up the world. Of course, if that happened, he'd be unemployed.

"Okay, look. I'm stuck with you. I get that. Ron's calling the shots here and for some reason, he wants you on the team. There are some things you just can't control—"

"My dad taught me a prayer to help with those things: 'Lord, grant me the serenity to accept the things I cannot change, the courage to change the things I can, and the wisdom to know the difference.'" Mack smiled.

Jesse pushed open the restaurant door. "Is there something for keeping my sanity?"

Mack followed him in. "Try the New Testament."

Ron was trying to concentrate as he formulated the plan. His number one priority was to keep Kyle safe, so he arranged for a backup team to be ready outside Doodah's. He'd just confirmed that decision with Captain Gates. He could hear the eagerness in her voice. They were lucky to have this break, and everyone knew it. Now he waited for Jesse and Mack to return with pizzas, Wiz and Dozer to return with the Title 3 wiretap warrant, and Kyle to stop pacing the room.

Ron cleared his throat.

Kyle stopped pacing and sighed. "Sorry. I'm doing it again, aren't I?"

"You're supposed to be working on projecting a calm demeanor."

"I know. But every time I think about trying to be calm, I get nervous."

He couldn't fault the kid for being nervous. It was Ron's stupid idea to get him involved in the first place. "Kyle, tell me what is the most nerve-racking thing about your job."

Kyle gave it careful thought. "I suppose it would be the organist calling in sick on Sunday morning. That can take out the singing of hymns, the special music, and the altar time."

"Right. Okay, so…what do you do when that happens?"

"It's never happened. It nearly happened. Vera had the stomach flu once. But we just put a wastebasket next to the bench and prayed for reprieve."

"We don't have a backup organist?"

"We did. But she died on her eighty-seventh birthday. The only other musician I know of is Bulldog, and his instrument requires an amplifier. Apparently, 'Nearer My God to Thee' can't be played on an electric guitar."

Ron laughed. He knew Bulldog. Really liked the guy too. The church was warming up to his leather jacket, not to mention his ear, eyebrow, lip, and nose rings. He hadn't missed a Sunday since the day he crashed into the Jesus Saves sign on the front lawn with his motorcycle. A few feet to the left and he would have hit the church bus instead. Bulldog was Kyle's one postmodern claim to fame.

"Let's pretend then. What would happen if Vera couldn't make it? What would you do?"

"I guess I would…I would expand the prayer time, read the full

Scripture text instead of the abbreviated version, and"—Kyle smiled—
"do a little song and dance?"

"Undercover work is all about the song and dance, Kyle. You have
some idea about what's going to happen, but there are a thousand things
that could swing the pendulum. You have to adapt to the situation. The
plan is for you to be in that bar no more than fifteen minutes. Not a whole
lot can go wrong in fifteen minutes, but you'll need to be prepared. We'll
go through several scenarios tonight." Ron smiled. "It probably will be
pretty uneventful. In fact, you'll most likely be disappointed by the lack of
drama."

"Well, I can tell you that I'm excited. Nervous, but excited. How
many people can say that they set up a drug deal, right?"

"About eighty percent of the population in federal prison, but this
isn't a drug deal. Why don't you get out a piece of paper and start writing down some bio stuff, just so you're familiar with who you're supposed
to be."

"Sure." Kyle paused. "Listen, um, I wanted to ask you something."

"What?"

"I was thinking about asking Mack out."

"Excuse me?"

"I know, I know...we're really different. But opposites attract, right?"

"Look, Kyle, now's not really a good time to be thinking about this.
There's only one thing worse than two undercover officers dating, and
that is a personal relationship between a UC and a CI."

"What's a CI?"

"A confidential informant."

"A snitch?"

"Yeah...a snitch. Except we don't ever call them snitches, at least to
their faces. Criminals have egos too. That title, confidential informant,
gives them a sense of importance."

"Why would a UC and a CI ever date?"

"It happens more often than you think. A lot of emotions get stirred up during an undercover operation. Sometimes UC guys are alone for days on end; their only company might be a female informant. I can't tell you the number of operations that have been wrecked by officers getting involved with informants." Ron felt the walls around his emotions starting to crumble. It was years ago, but every time he thought of that day, he felt himself sinking to that low place he thought he'd never be able to climb out of.

"So...I can't ask her out?"

"What's the rush?"

"I start a fast on Wednesday. It's awkward when you're on a date and can't eat." He paused. "I just didn't know there were police officers like her."

"There aren't any police officers like her. Look, Kyle, just forget about it for now. We've got more important things to deal with. I'm sure you and Mack would get along just fine, but we can't go complicating this already very complicated situation." Ron glanced to the window. "Oh, great."

"What?"

"Here comes Ruth." Ron steered Kyle by the shoulders toward the front door. "Go out to the front porch. Handle Ruth."

"How?"

"Make up a story about your love for water-skiing. And your favorite food is french fries."

That should keep him busy for a few hours.

Chapter 22

M ason sat in front of the television clicking through the channels while Rhyne answered some important phone call that was going to secure his financial future and give him more voltage than all the casino signs in Vegas.

Mason's cell rang. He'd already missed one call. Glancing at the closed hallway door, Mason decided to take the call.

"Hello?"

A female voice said, "This is the county jail. Will you accept a call from Brandi Brown?"

"Yes."

"Please hold."

Mason held his breath.

"Hello? Mason?"

"Brandi, hey."

There was an awkward silence.

"Uh…how are you?" Mason asked.

"I'm in jail, Mason. How do you think I am?"

"I've been trying to come up with some money to post bail," he lied.

"It's not that much. Talk to Chris. Maybe he'll give you some extra hours."

"I got fired, Brandi. What did you think happened? I'm in Vegas now."

"Why? I thought we agreed you weren't going to hang out in Vegas anymore."

Even steel bars couldn't keep this woman from trying to control his life. "Look, Brandi, I've got a life to live, you know? I'm trying to make some money. Steady money, you know? I was out of options."

"No, Mason, *I'm* out of options."

"Things are complicated right now, okay, baby? You've got to understand that. It's nothing personal."

"What happened at the bar sure seemed personal to me. Why'd you do that?"

"It was stupid. I was just trying to hide the money, hoping he'd forget about the rest and let me off the hook. I panicked."

"You owe it to me to get me out of jail. You put me here."

"Like I said, I'm trying to work some things out."

Just then, Rhyne came strutting down the hallway. Mason snapped his phone shut as Rhyne rounded the couch and fell into the easy chair.

"What was that about? Was that your woman?"

"She's trying to hook back up with me."

"I told you to cut all ties."

"I'm working on it. You know how women are. Anyway, she's still in jail and won't be out anytime soon."

"Good. Be done with her."

Easier said than done, but Mason nodded anyway.

"What are you doing tonight?" asked Rhyne.

"I've got to go back to Henderson, take care of some loose ends."

Rhyne smiled. "That's what I like to hear." But his smile faded. "Just don't do anything stupid. Take care of your business and get out. And start looking for your own place too. I don't want a roommate forever."

"What are you doing?"

"Thought I'd hit the casinos. Might run into some people, you know?"

Mason stood. "I'll call you later." He walked out the front door, got in the car, and headed for Doodah's. He'd gambled too. If luck would have it, he'd be doing his own big deals tonight.

Ron parked one of Ruth's cars, husband number two's ride, in a tight alleyway. Jesse sat in the passenger's side, staring up at the four-story building that was peeking above the flat roof of the building next to them.

They got out and Jesse walked toward Seventh Street. Ron followed. As they emerged from the dark gloom of the alley, the bright morning sun accosted them. They slipped their sunglasses back on.

It was an empty street now, but come nighttime it was going to get crowded. Doodah's was stuffed in among a long row of old single-story buildings. Most were bars. The ones that weren't didn't have a good view of the front door. Ron pointed to the four-story building across the street. "We'd be a block away," he said, "and I don't like that. But we can have a team on the ground near the alleyway."

"I want Dozer as an eyeball," Jesse said.

"Fine."

"Let's see if we can set up in that window on the fourth floor. It should have a clear view."

"I hope so," said Ron. "Setting up there will give us a little elbow room. Moving around down here after sunset is going to be like trying to march an elephant through Mardi Gras."

"What is that building anyway?"

"A hospital."

"Perfect. Exactly where I'll end up after this is all over."

At undercover school, Jesse learned the fine art of reading body language. But it didn't require much training to read the language this morning. Everyone's body said the same thing: this was a bad idea.

Kyle's shirt was soaked with perspiration. He tried to look calm and collected, but "I'm about to pass out" trumped the "I'm cool" expression

Kyle attempted. They'd already proposed a number of possible scenarios. Most weren't likely to happen, but they wanted him to be prepared. The most important piece of the plan was getting Kyle out of there as quickly as possible.

That's where Jesse came in. He'd pose as the money guy, the one calling the shots. Kyle wouldn't introduce him until he felt he had gained the guy's trust. Then Jesse would take over and convince the man they'd be ready to deal next week at the body shop. Kyle's role was small, but it would take finesse—not a skill Kyle seemed to have much experience with.

"So," Kyle said to Wiz, "if you put your finger to your eyebrow and scratch, that means... What does that mean exactly?"

Wiz looked at Jesse.

"Kyle," Jesse said, "this isn't science. Think of it as art. It's all about interpretation. It might not mean anything. You have to look at the big picture and then bring into play the small things. There's no formula, but there are some telltale signs. If he's leaning forward, he's eager to do business. If his arms are crossed, he's not ready to let you in."

Kyle nodded. "Okay, got it. What about the eyebrow, though?"

"Forget the eyebrow. Eyebrows mean nothing. When he leans forward, when he looks engaged like he trusts you, then you call me over, and I'll take it from there. Don't flag me like I'm a race car. Do it subtly, like you're in control of the situation." Jesse glanced at the rings underneath Kyle's armpits. "But before you do anything, take a bath in antiperspirant and put a T-shirt on under your shirt."

Kyle swiped his forehead. "I get a little sweaty when I'm nervous. My robe usually hides it on Sundays."

Jesse glanced at Wiz, who shrugged. "What robe?"

He noticed Kyle's eyes grow wide. "My bathrobe, I mean."

"You sweat in your bathrobe?"

"Um...only on Sundays...when I run on my treadmill. I read somewhere it helps you lose weight if you wear heavy clothing because you sweat more."

"What do you weigh—a hundred and fifty pounds?"

"Then it must be working."

Jesse sighed and leaned back. Ron was back at headquarters, finalizing paperwork for Hank's involvement and getting things squared away for the body shop to open. Jesse thought about calling Ron to tell him to cancel the plan or come up with a new one—one without Kyle as the point man.

"I can do this," Kyle said suddenly. He looked at Mack. Mack high-fived him like he'd just conquered Mount Everest.

"That's the spirit," she smiled.

"That's the spirit?" Jesse threw up his hands. "This isn't the ropes course at summer camp. Even if he could master Body Language 101, his sweat glands will sell him out. Not even a bathrobe can hide that!"

"Look, Jesse, maybe you could be a little more encouraging here. Kyle is doing his best to help us out."

Jesse glanced to the couch for help from Dozer. Predictably, he'd fallen asleep.

Kyle spoke. "Maybe Mack can run through this with me a few more times. I think the more I practice, the better I'll do."

"The thing is that no amount of practice can prepare you for exactly what's going to happen. You've got to be able to think on your feet."

Kyle looked at Mack and smiled. "I am thinking on my feet."

Mack looked hopeful. Wiz excused himself to the bathroom. "All right," Jesse said. "Let's start from the beginning. I'll be waiting in the bar, you come in and find a table."

Kyle walked into the hallway, then turned around and pretended to enter the bar. He looked around with more confidence than any man who works out in a bathrobe should. He stopped to survey the room, then sat down at the table, drumming his fingers. At least he looked collected. Jesse nodded for Mack to approach. He watched as Kyle played the scenario out with a surprising coolness. Mack played the scenario by the book, but this time Kyle looked exactly like the kind of guy who could buy illegal body parts and pretend it was all legitimate business.

After a few minutes, Kyle waved Jesse over with two fingers.

"Okay, hold on," Jesse said. "Kyle, that's terrific. Exactly how you want to play the thing. But when it's time to call me over, you need to stand, get my attention and let your confidence wilt just a tad. This guy has to buy into the idea that you work for me, and that I'm the one who calls the shots. It's the only way we're going to get you out of the picture."

"All right. Let me try again." Jesse backed up and Kyle sat down. This time, instead of waving Jesse over, he stood and, offering a slight look of inferiority, got Jesse's attention.

"Perfect!" Jesse slapped his hands together. "That's what we want, Kyle. Just like that. Then I'll tell you I want to talk to this guy alone, and you'll be free to leave."

Jesse checked his watch. "I've got to go do something."

"We're meeting here at four," Wiz said.

"I'll be back in time. Keep working on this." He looked at Dozer. "And somebody wake him up before Ron gets back."

Captain Gates hung up the phone. "Okay, we're set with the backup team. I talked to the insurance company. They're trying to get their guys here ASAP, but there're a lot of hoops to jump through." She looked at Hank, who stood with his back against the far wall. "Hank, we appreciate your coming to do this for us."

Hank nodded.

"You've worked a lot with cars?"

Hank nodded again.

Gates looked to Ron for help. "He knows his stuff."

She signed off on a batch of papers. "Well, Hank, the world could use a few more quiet people, I can tell you that."

Ron said, "Jesse will be the front man on most everything."

"All right," Captain Gates said, handing Ron the papers. "This could be very big for us."

"I'm cautiously optimistic, but truthfully, it's still a long shot. The chances of this guy actually arriving at the bar tonight are slim, but if he does, we'll be ready. Jesse's good. We'll be able to feel out where he is in the food chain."

"He could lead us right into the middle of this ring."

"I know."

Captain Gates walked to the other side of her desk, where she sat down and pulled out a sheet of paper. She handed it to Ron.

"It came in this morning," Gates said.

Ron read over the report. "White minivan, found completely intact. No forced entry?"

"That's right. You'll have to excuse me," Gates said. "I'm running late for a meeting." She shook Hank's hand. "I appreciate your help, Hank. Ron, keep me updated. I want to know everything that happens."

"I will."

Hank trailed Ron back to his office.

"What's significant about the minivan?" Hank asked.

"So you do speak."

"When it suits me," Hank said with a half smile.

Ron checked his watch. He needed to get to the UC house by four. "It's just another stolen vehicle. Listen, I need to call my wife. I'll meet you down at my truck."

"Okay." Hank left, and Ron called Nan.

"Hi," Nan said.

"Well, this is a good sign. You answered my call even though you knew it was me."

"I'm in a calm mood. How is Kyle?"

"He's fine. We've been practicing with him all day. He's got a knack for this kind of thing." Lie. White. Survive.

"That's surprising," Nan said. "Behind the pulpit he looks like a mouse staring at a hundred pairs of cat eyes."

"I just wanted to call and check in with you. I'll be home late. I don't know exactly what time. I'll call you as soon as we're finished to let you know Kyle's okay."

"Have you taken your heart medicine?"

"Of course I have." He reached for his bottle of pills in the desk drawer. "Don't worry. This thing is going to run smoothly."

"They're lucky to have you. I'll talk to you later."

"I love you," Ron said, but she was already gone.

Jesse walked past the elevator and took the stairs, hoping the climb would invigorate him. Time crept by. Jesse felt ready for this. Almost ready. He still needed to see Chaplain Greer.

He needed to tell Greer that he'd be unreachable for a few months, until Task Force Viper was complete. It wasn't a deep-cover assignment, but Jesse still had to cut all communication. The chaplain knew the drill.

He paused at the fourth-floor landing for a moment to catch his breath. Plenty of time. The chaplain rarely left his office before five. Chaplain Greer's presence had a way of calming Jesse. He knew the chaplain would pray for him, and that's all he wanted. He always prayed the same prayer—something he said he prayed often for officers.

Jesse knocked quietly on the chaplain's door, even though he really felt like banging on it. For once, he didn't want to startle the man.

Jesse listened but heard nothing. He knocked again, a little louder. He grabbed the door handle, but it was locked.

"Chaplain?" Jesse banged on the door. "Chaplain, it's me, Jesse Lunden."

Nothing.

He inhaled, and looked down the hallway. Walking briskly toward an open office door, he found a secretary at her desk slurping ramen noodles.

She motioned Jesse in when she noticed him.

"I'm looking for Chaplain Greer."

She chewed quickly, waved a hand in front of her mouth, swallowed, then chased the noodles with a long sip of Diet Coke.

"Will he be back?" Jesse asked.

She shook her head.

"Do you know how I can reach him? I really need to talk to him."

"I'm sorry," she said. "He left a couple of days ago for a twenty-one-day cruise with his wife."

"Where?"

"Where?" she echoed.

"Where?"

"Um… I think the Caribbean, but—"

"Do you know what cruise line?"

The secretary stared back at him.

"The cruise line?" Jesse asked again.

"Who are you?"

"Detective Lunden."

"I'm sorry, Detective, but I don't have that information. Is something wrong? Is there a family emergency?"

Jesse trembled, his heart hovering between every beat. "No…it's just…it's…"

"Yes?"

"Nothing. Never mind." Jesse walked away. After he rounded the corner, he slammed his back against a wall, slapping his hand against the concrete. *What now?*

It was a sign.

He couldn't do this now. Not without his lucky chaplain.

Chapter 23

R on stood by the dresser in the back room and fiddled with a tiny microphone. "Back in my day, we didn't have all this fancy junk. When microrecorders came out, we thought we'd died and gone to heaven. You kids rely too much on this. Any criminal can be prosecuted without a single recording if you know how to do it. Which you will."

Ron glanced over his shoulder to see why it was suddenly so quiet. Dozer had fallen asleep on the bed where he'd been sitting.

"Hey!"

Dozer sat straight up. "Yeah?"

"You were asleep. Again."

"Oh."

"You okay?"

"Didn't sleep well last night... You know, thinking about this."

Ron turned to him. "I need you at the top of your game."

"I'll be fine."

"Wiz will run this," Ron said, pointing to the listening gear. "I hope he knows what he's doing."

"He seems to know his stuff," said Dozer. "And I think you're sending the right guy in with Kyle. Jesse is the best. He's got this...I don't know, sixth sense? And he's a brave son of a gun too. A couple years ago a drug dealer shot him. They thought he was dead. But even with a bullet in his shoulder, Jesse managed to tackle him, get the gun, and cuff him." Dozer paused. "I know he seems hard to manage, and I guess he can be difficult. But you can count on him. He'll give you his best in there and he won't let you dow—"

Mack suddenly rushed into the room, her expression causing Dozer to hop up from the bed.

"What's wrong?" Ron asked.

"It's Jesse. He's...he's..." She pointed toward the doorway. Dozer started out of the room, but Mack stopped him.

"He's what?" Dozer asked.

Mack hustled them back into the room and closed the door. "He's kind of...losing it."

"What do you mean?"

"I don't know. I'm not sure I'm following what the problem is, and he's claiming he doesn't have a problem."

"What did he say?" Dozer asked.

"He says we need to call off the operation. And he's sweating and pacing. He's making Kyle look like a yoga instructor."

Dozer started to leave the room again, but Mack held up her hands. "I'm just warning you, he seems to be in a...sensitive...state."

"Why?" Dozer asked.

"Something about a chaplain and a cruise ship. And he's going on and on about bad luck."

"Oh no..." Dozer exited the room. Ron followed and they found Jesse arguing with Wiz.

"What's going on?" Ron asked.

Wiz shrugged. "I have no idea."

Jesse pointed to a far wall. "That's *another* sign!"

Two pictures of Elvis hung side by side.

"What about it?" Ron asked.

Jesse stomped over to the pictures. "I hung *this* picture up." He pointed to the Elvis in a white jumpsuit. "And now...*this*!" Another Elvis, in his younger, thinner days, grinned back at them.

"Will someone please explain this to me?" Ron asked.

Dozer sighed, then walked over and removed the young Elvis photo.

"Hey!" Mack yelled. "What do you think you're doing?"

"*You* hung this picture up?" Jesse barked.

"Everyone—calm down!" Ron shouted, and the room grew quiet. "Sit down. All of you."

Everyone sat except Jesse, who stood defiantly next to jumpsuit Elvis.

"Now," Ron said, "Jesse, what is going on?"

"I know you all think I'm crazy. I'm not, okay? We need to abort the operation."

Ron struggled to speak in a gentle voice. "Did you get some intel?"

"When I was shot a couple years ago, the bullet hit a major artery. I almost bled to death. They were rushing me into surgery, and this man comes out of nowhere. Just his fourth day on the job. Chaplain Greer. He prayed for me. And I didn't die."

The room was quiet.

"Ever since then, me and the chaplain, we've been really close, you know? He prays for me, and every time I have to go on an undercover assignment, he prays this…this… It's the Bible, something from the Bible. It's about protection. Ever since then, nothing bad has happened to me." Jesse met everyone's curious stares with a serious expression. "And now he's gone."

"Who?" Ron asked.

"The chaplain! Chaplain Greer is gone!"

"Dead?" Kyle asked.

"No. On a cruise. I can't reach him for twenty-one days. And then… then I come back here and suddenly there are *two* pictures of Elvis. There should only be one. One!"

"I'm trying to understand here," said Ron, "but I don't."

"I can't go out there without…without *him,* you know…" Jesse's hands were making some weird motion they were apparently supposed to interpret. Then, barely above a whisper, he said, "Praying for me."

"Elvis?" Wiz blurted out.

"Why would I want Elvis to pray for me?" Jesse asked. "Elvis is just there for good luck!"

Wiz looked genuinely confused. "Sorry, man."

Jesse ran his palm over his bald head. "All of this…it's a sign. A bad omen. We need to call it off."

Ron's patience had hit bottom. "Jesse, I'm sorry your chaplain is on vacation and that skinny Elvis offends you, but we're not calling this off. Everything is set. We're going in."

Jesse shook his head. "It's a bad idea."

"Then I'll send Dozer."

Dozer looked at Jesse. "You're the one, Jesse. You're the best. We need you in there."

Jesse continued to breathe heavily. As every second ticked by, Ron's confidence in him drained like a bathtub.

"Jesse, what scripture was it?" Mack asked.

"Scripture?"

"The chaplain. He prayed something. You said it was from the Bible."

"Uh…" Jesse shook his head. "I don't know."

"He never told you?" Mack asked.

"Yeah, he did, I guess. I just never paid attention."

Mack, the only person in the room who looked enthusiastic, said, "Jesse, this is no problem. We can find that scripture."

"You can?" Dozer asked.

"Jesse surely knows some of the verses, right?" Mack asked.

"I don't know any verses." Jesse glanced around the group. "Look, I'm not religious, okay?"

"He's superstitious," Dozer explained. "He touches Elvis's picture, rubs the bullet that went into his shoulder, talks to Chaplain Greer, and then he doesn't change his lucky socks until we make an arrest, at which point he sets them on fire."

Everyone looked at Jesse's socks.

"Let's just start with the basics," said Mack. "What was the general idea of the passage?"

"Um…that I wouldn't die."

"Okay, good, nondying."

"It's pretty long," Jesse continued. "But it was all about keeping me safe."

"Was it in the Old or New Testament?"

Jesse shrugged.

"Was the Bible opened toward the front or toward the back?"

"More or less in the middle. I think."

"Hmm," Mack said. "Sounds like the Psalms."

Jesse nodded. "Yes, that sounds right."

"There are a lot of psalms. One hundred and fifty. Tell me some specific words or phrases."

Everyone waited in silence. "Okay, well, God…evil…angels…the plague…"

Ron looked at Mack, who scratched her forehead. "That narrows it down…a little. What else?" she asked.

Jesse looked frustrated. "It seems like maybe there was something about danger…terror…punishment…"

"Man," Wiz whispered to Dozer, "I think I would change my rituals if I were him."

"Anyway, it ends by saying I'll have a long life."

"Good, good," Mack said. "Anything else?"

Jesse shook his head.

"Come on," Mack walked over to him and put a hand on his shoulder. "Maybe something peculiar about it, something that stood out to you."

Jesse thought for a moment. "I know. Feathers."

"Feathers?" Wiz cackled.

"Shut up," Dozer said. "Let him concentrate."

"I know…thousands…that's my favorite part…a thousand will fall, ten thousand will die around you, something like that."

"Got it!" Mack announced. "It's Psalm 91."

Jesse nodded. "That's the one. I remember now."

Ron exhaled. "Terrific. So now Mack can pray that for you…"

"She can't. It's unacceptable. She likes 'Heartbreak Hotel' Elvis. It has to be International Hotel Elvis."

"What's that supposed to mean?" Mack asked.

"Elvis was at his best in Vegas. His month-long show at the International Hotel kick-started his career again. He was given a second chance—just like me."

"His best?" Mack retorted. "Do I have to remind you that he used his very first record deal check to buy his mother a pink Cadillac? What can be better than that?"

"His music got better once he came to Vegas."

"You're kidding, right? 'Blue Suede Shoes'? 'Love Me Tender'? 'Anyway You Wa—'"

Ron stepped between the two, waving his hands. "For crying out loud, people. This isn't *American Bandstand*. Just let Mack pray for you."

Jesse crossed his arms. "Sorry, won't work."

"It doesn't matter," Mack sighed. "I don't know it by heart anyway."

Ron asked, "I don't suppose anyone has a Bible here?"

"A chaplain has to say it," Jesse muttered, glancing around the room. "Or a pastor. Someone official like that. Or it won't work."

Kyle stepped forward. "I'm a pastor."

"You are?" several voices asked in unison.

Ron grimaced again. Kyle's cover was blown, but what was the point? Now Kyle could come in handy, so he asked, "Kyle, you know it?"

"I do."

"The whole thing?" Jesse asked.

"Yes."

"You're really a pastor?" Wiz asked. He turned to Jesse. "Surely *that's* got to be some sort of sign."

Jesse started pacing again. "I guess this could work. If you say the whole thing, you know, it would… He's got that special connection with God. He's like a priority caller."

"Jesse," Mack said, "You don't have to be a pastor to have God's ear."

"Trust me," Jesse said. "I don't have a direct connection." He looked at Kyle then at everyone else. "This is never going to work. Why would he do that? Leave town without telling me?"

Jesse eyed the jumpsuited Elvis picture and punched his fist into his hand while Dozer searched for someplace to hide the other Elvis. He attempted to hand it to Wiz, but Wiz refused it.

"Jesse, calm down," Dozer said. "I don't see the problem. They're both pastors."

"Okay, maybe. Yeah, technically, it should work." He glanced around the room. "If you guys could give us some privacy, there are a few things I need to confess first."

Kyle's pastoral expression faded. "Confess?"

"My sins," Jesse whispered.

"No, that's okay. I don't need to know."

"I have to confess everything I've done wrong before the prayer will work."

"No, you don't." For the first time, Kyle seemed adamant about something.

"Yes, I do."

"This is ridiculous," Ron snapped. "Jesse, Kyle said he's willing to pray this prayer, okay? Don't push it with details."

"These aren't details. If I don't confess my sins, the prayer won't work."

"Your sins are forgiven by God through Jesus Christ," Mack said. "Not because you're brave enough to tell them to a pastor."

"You wouldn't understand," Jesse said to her. "You don't have any sins, do you?"

"I'm sinning right now."

"You are?" Wiz asked, his expression growing curious.

"Yes," Jesse said, gesturing toward Mack. "Can't you tell? She's raised her voice a little. Stand back. Lightning might strike."

Mack's face turned red, and she snapped, "Is there any possibility of getting you to shut up?" Then she slumped. "I'm really sorry. I just have a lot of anger toward you. You don't deserve to be talked to that way."

Dozer smiled. "I don't know about that."

"Shut up, Dozer," Jesse said.

"You shut up. Can't you see you're making her sin?"

Mack held up her hands. "It's not his problem. It's mine. Jesus was surrounded by irritating people all the time, but he managed to keep his cool."

Jesse glared at her. "I'm irritating?"

"And unbelievably defensive, but again, I shouldn't take it out on you. I'm sorry." She looked at Kyle. "I apologize."

"It's okay, Mack," Kyle said gently.

"Why does *she* get to confess?" Jesse asked.

Ron stepped up. "Look, here's how it's going to go down. Jesse, you're going to sit on the couch. We're going to gather around and Kyle will pray for all of us so we can get on with this thing." No one moved. "Well, what are you waiting for? The Second Coming? Let's go."

Jesse knocked knuckles with jumpsuit Elvis, then took a bullet out of his pocket and rubbed it between his hands before joining Kyle on the couch.

"Let's just get this over with." Jesse sighed.

"Um, all right, let's all just…bow our heads and… Okay, Lord, we come to you today and ask that—"

"That's not how he does it," Jesse interrupted. "He just says the Bible part."

"Oh...sure. Um, go ahead and bow your heads again, and I'll just...okay...um..." Kyle took a deep breath. "'He who dwells in the shelter of the Most High will rest in the shadow of the—'"

A loud banging sound shattered the prayer. Ron reached for his gun. Everyone scrambled, trying to locate the source of the sound.

They found it. Ruth was peering through their front window.

"What's going on in there?" she shouted. "A séance?"

Chapter 24

Kyle walked toward Jesse and Dozer, balancing a cardboard tray of coffees. He set the tray down on the car.

"You got a triple shot in here, right?" Dozer asked.

"And decaf for me," Kyle nodded. "Didn't think I needed any help with the jitters."

"This is where the arrest team will be stationed—a couple blocks from the bar. They're really just here for backup. We have to catch this guy when he comes to the shop to sell his goods. But they're there if we need them. Ron, Mack, and Wiz are setting up surveillance on the fourth floor of that hospital right now."

"But you'll be in the bar with me, right?" Kyle asked Jesse for the fourteenth time.

"I'll go in before you. We can't be seen coming inside at the same time. We're new faces in there. It'll be up to you to watch the door to see if he comes in or is already there. I'll head in around eight. You'll go in around eight fifteen. We don't talk or look at each other until you call me over."

"What if he checks Kyle for a microphone?" Hank asked.

Jesse turned, surprised. Hank had a knack for listening without anyone noticing he was there. "It's a public place. He won't check him. Besides, I'll be wearing the wire."

"So now what do we do?" Hank asked.

"Wait."

Kyle sighed. "I'd love to, but I gotta deliver the rest of the coffees."

Ron could do nothing but watch through an office window as the two men argued. One of the men was a Mr. Collins, the assistant director of the hospital. He'd assured Ron that the fourth-floor room would be available. The second man, the one raising a stink, gestured with one hand as he pushed up his glasses with the other.

The office door finally opened, and the two men walked out. Neither looked pleased. "Sergeant Yeager, this is Dr. Gil Shapel. He's the director of our psychiatric unit."

"What's that got to do with us?" Ron asked.

"A pipeline burst—" Mr. Collins began, but Dr. Shapel cut him off.

"The fourth-floor room you need belongs to us. We use it occasionally for special events. Our recreational room is flooded, and there is no other space available. We need it tonight."

"But—"

"We have recreation from precisely 7:45 p.m. to 9:15 p.m.," Dr. Shapel continued. "Our patients look forward to it every day. It's a reward for them. It can't be missed."

"I don't see a problem. We'll be set up by the window and won't take up any space."

"I realize you're speaking out of ignorance, Sergeant Yeager, but the fact is, your presence could cause some real problems."

Ron turned to face Mr. Collins. "The operation is already in motion."

"I am sure we can work this out." He looked Dr. Shapel squarely in the face. "These officers are willing to comply with what you need in order to get what they need."

Dr. Shapel eyed Ron, then Mack and Wiz. "Fine. But you're going to have to abide by my rules so we don't create any problems for the patients."

"I don't think we'll be a bother," said Ron.

"Yes, well, you don't live in my world, where things can get 'bothered' rather quickly."

"Dr. Shapel," Mr. Collins said, "why don't you escort the officers up to the fourth floor? They can show you what they need and you can tell them all about those rules."

Ron, Mack, and Wiz stared silently at the dark walls of the elevator.

"Is this thing working?" Ron asked.

"Some of our patients have a fear of heights," answered Dr. Shapel. "This elevator is specifically designed to minimize all sense of movement. We don't want them to think they're leaving the ground level. That's also why we have heavy blinds on the third-floor windows and why we're putting them in now on the fourth floor. You'll have to work around that. Harold doesn't do so well when he gets a glimpse outside."

"What about the claustrophobics?" Ron asked.

Wiz and Mack smiled, but Dr. Shapel didn't look amused. He gestured toward the black elevator doors. "Some of our patients hate to see their reflections. We ban the use of mirrors or anything that could provide a reflection. Including windows."

Ron could feel Wiz breathing deeply beside him, like he might be instantaneously transforming into a claustrophobic. Thankfully, the elevator doors opened. Dr. Shapel guided them down the hall past orderlies who were moving tables and chairs into the previously empty room.

"Where do you want to set up?"

Ron opened the blinds to the middle window, then looked out the two left windows. "Here," Ron said. "This will give us the view we need." He turned to Dr. Shapel. "We'll just need a table and a couple of chairs."

"Fine. We can supply that. But you have to keep the blinds lowered. You can peek through them, but we can't have them opened."

"Okay. Is that it?"

Dr. Shapel looked amused. "Harold isn't the only patient with special needs. If you're going to be in my hospital, then you're going to have to comply with my rules."

Mack took out a pad and pen.

"All right. What do we need to do?"

"It's more about what you need to *not* do."

"Certainly, Dr. Shapel. We'll do our best," Mack said.

"You'll need to talk in a quiet, reserved voice. Many of our patients suffer from sensory overload. You need to be aware of Ned. Whatever you do, don't give Ned anything to drink. Not even a small cup of water."

"How will we know Ned?"

"You'll know."

Wiz sucked in a breath. "What happens if he drinks water?"

"He thinks he becomes intoxicated. It's not pleasant. Martha will also be here. Martha is one of our most unusual patients."

"Oh…" *So what is Ned? Normal?* Ron started to feel like Wiz looked.

"Martha has a phobia of certain words. It is imperative that you do not say the following." Dr. Shapel turned to Mack. "Nest. Cranberry. Telephone. Hair. Vacuum. Nostril. Humidifier. Canteen. Walrus." Dr. Shapel paused. "We work very, very hard to make recreational hours pleasant and rewarding for our patients, so whatever you do, avoid unnecessary commotion and do not, under any circumstance, make any sudden movements that might be distracting or induce anxiety."

Wiz whispered to Mack, "For us or for them?"

"In other words, don't do anything weird," the doctor continued.

"Of course," Ron said. "We'll set up the equipment before they get here, and we'll be respectful of your rules."

"I'll be in my office, but I don't like to be disturbed." He turned and walked off toward the elevators.

"He doesn't like to be disturbed? What's he doing in this business then?" Wiz said with a snort.

Mack closed her notebook. "I feel sorry for them," she said, gazing at the empty room as if it were filled with people. "I wonder if they get many visitors."

"You can worry about that on your day off, Hazard," Ron said. "Right now, we've got to focus."

The elevator doors swooshed open, and Kyle appeared, walking quickly toward them with a tray full of coffees.

"Thanks," Mack said, taking her green tea. Kyle handed Wiz his latte. Ron took his coffee black, no sugar, no cream. Ron still didn't understand the lure of lattes and green teas. In the old days, guys stayed up with thick, black coffee. Twenty years ago, a latte would've earned you a nickname you couldn't repeat in public.

"You okay, Kyle?" Ron asked.

"Yeah…fine. I accidentally got off on the third floor and ran into a lady carrying a bushel of…never mind. " He glanced around the room. "So, this is where you guys will be watching from?"

"Yep," Ron said.

"Man," he said with a half smile, "you guys don't know how lucky you are that this room is vacant."

Chapter 25

Wiz taped the microphone to Jesse's chest as a group of about twenty people walked into the room, all dressed in pajamas. They milled around tables that had been set up with games and activities.

"Keep an eye on your coffee," said Ron.

Jesse wondered if his nervousness was because of the UC operation or the warnings Mack had passed along about not giving patients drinks and avoiding certain words. It wasn't unusual to be nervous before going undercover. One of his instructors had said if you weren't nervous, you weren't engaged—the adrenaline kept you vigilant.

Ron approached him. "Jesse, I want you to—"

"I know. My number one priority is to keep Kyle safe. I'm not going to let anything happen to him."

"Too bad you can't just wear him around your neck," Ron said. "It would keep him safe and give you good luck all at the same time."

"What kind of gun are you carrying?" The team looked up to find a tall man in too-short pajamas, his eyes studying the gun in Jesse's holster. "That's a Glock 27, .40 caliber, isn't it?" he asked. "It's got eleven rounds, weighs less than two pounds. Six point two-nine inches long and a little over an inch thick." The man looked at Jesse. "Good choice." Then he walked away.

"Was that Harold? Or Ned?" asked Wiz. "How will we know?"

"Probably just an undercover cop who went insane," Dozer quipped.

"Why did he say 'good choice'?" asked Hank. Ron had nearly forgotten Hank was in the room.

"It has significant knock-down power with limited penetration," Ron said, as Jesse took off his holster and put the gun in his waistband.

"What does that mean?" Hank asked.

Jesse answered. "It means it'll kill the guy in front of you but probably not the guy standing on the other side of the wall."

"All right, everyone. It's just about time to get this thing rolling."

"Walk in the park."

"Yeah, Central Park—at night, with a bag of money and a sign that says, 'Rob Me,'" Hank said, then smiled a little at everyone's surprised faces. "I both talk and joke."

"What are you drinking?"

They turned to see a man hunched over like he was about to rub his hands together over a fire. He stared at their coffee cups.

Wiz whispered to Jesse, "What do we do?"

"What does he want?" Jesse asked.

"Is that coffee?" the man asked, his eyes widening with each word. "I love coffee. I love it so much."

"Sir, I'm sorry," Mack said. "You can't have any of our drinks."

Wiz peeked over Jesse's shoulder. "That's Ned!"

"Who is Ned?" Jesse asked. "Why is everyone acting all freaky?"

"Didn't you hear Mack talking about him?" Wiz whispered.

"Look, dude, I'm sorta busy here, okay?" Jesse said.

Ron pointed to Jesse. "Cool it, Jesse. Let's not stir up any trouble. We'll handle this."

But the only person backing off was Wiz, who'd backed up all the way to the window. Jesse joined him. Wiz whispered, "He gets drunk if he drinks any kind of beverage."

"Lucky him."

Mack gently guided Ned to a male nurse who sat behind a desk reading a newspaper.

Jesse checked his watch. "I can't wait to get down to the bar and join all the normal people."

"All right," began Ron, with an edge in his voice that Jesse hadn't heard before. "It's time. Kyle, you wait in the hospital lobby until it's your time to go, then use the alley to get to the bar." Ron looked at Kyle. "You okay?"

Kyle put on a brave smile. "Walk in the park."

Jesse and Kyle rode the elevator down in silence.

Jesse left Kyle in the hospital lobby and walked down the dark alley. With each stride, Jesse was replaced by Tony Ramone. Tony had a confidence in his walk that could command the attention of an entire room. It wasn't just his walk, but also the way he looked at people. His mother used to describe a look that he would give his kindergarten teacher every day when she dropped him off. He simply glared at Mrs. Henson and declared with his face, *"I hate you. And I hate school."* His mother said that look terrified Mrs. Henson for most of the first semester. "I've never seen a scowl like that," she'd told his mother. A pure Tony look.

Jesse reached the street, which stirred with people. Things wouldn't really get crowded until ten or so, but enough activity buzzed around him that nobody would have noticed him stepping from the alleyway. He looked back. It was only one block to the hospital, but it would probably seem like a few miles to Kyle. Jesse took a deep breath and stepped into the bar. Time to find a pool table.

The bar was more crowded than he'd expected, but a pool table opened up, and Jesse snagged it. A guy named Ed joined him. Luckily Ed wasn't much of a talker, so Jesse could concentrate on his surroundings. He watched the door without looking at it. One thing he knew about bars: people watched people, and before long, someone would spot him staring at the door. He played it cool and never looked at his watch.

At least twenty minutes had passed when Jesse saw Kyle in the doorway. Kyle's eyes weren't wide, and he didn't glance around wildly. A good start, anyway. Jesse had told him to think, "I own the place." He wasn't owning anything as he walked in, but at least he didn't look petrified. Ed said something about his cue stick and Jesse engaged. He didn't want Ed to think he was distracted. Jesse nodded and pointed out it was Ed's shot.

Jesse moved around the table, trying to find Kyle through the growing crowd. He spotted the top of his head moving toward a cluster of tables near the bar. Then he lost sight of him.

Jesse had to finish this game quickly. He concentrated, and within two minutes, the game was over. He let Ed win because he didn't want Ed to insist on another game. Jesse nodded toward the bar. "I want to beat the crowd."

"Know what you mean," Ed said, holding up a pint of beer.

Jesse walked to the bar. He climbed onto a stool and ordered a light beer. He turned and let his eyes scan the crowd as he looked between bodies for Kyle. Finally he spotted him, but didn't let his eyes rest there. Instead, he became a casual observer, but wearing an expression that told anyone who noticed that he wasn't in the mood for chitchat. Kyle sat at a table and nursed a beer, doing little more than trying not to gawk at the women who passed by. Jesse smiled to himself. These weren't the kind of girls you'd find at church.

Jesse began to think the man wasn't going to show when he saw someone making a beeline toward Kyle's table. Jesse sat up a little taller, and then it happened. Kyle's face registered recognition. His eyes widened. He stood up like he wasn't supposed to and offered a hand. Jesse could only see the back of the guy's head, but they shook hands awkwardly, and then both sat down.

Jesse gulped his drink. Rock and roll time.

"Good to see you again."

Mason tried to smile. He wasn't sure what was up with the manners. It reminded him of Rhyne's recent transformation. Better clothes, cleaner shave, and "good business manners." Whatever that meant.

"Uh…yeah. Good for both of us." Mason grinned. "So you're ready to do business?"

"Maybe."

Mason laughed. Great. This would take some finesse. Well, it wasn't the first time. And thankfully, this guy looked way more nervous than Mason felt.

"Maybe, huh. Okay, so what's it going to take? I've got a lot of…" Mason paused. Manners. That meant watching his language. "What do you want?"

"To make money."

He liked the way this guy thought. "I meant what kinds of parts are you looking for?"

"I know. I'm just messing with you."

"Money's good. If we work this right, we'll both be happy." Mason studied the man for a moment, then said, "What's your name?"

"Kyle."

"Mason."

"Good to meet you."

Mason sighed. He would never get used to this. "So what are you looking for? I got a little of everything, and the good stuff, too."

"First, I need to know who I'm doing business with."

"I already told you my name."

"Are… Well, are you the person I'm going to be doing business with?"

Mason felt a strange awkwardness. This guy was starting to suspect something.

"Look, I used to have a partner. He decided he wanted to go into the drug business. And not the small-time. I'm talking the kind that can get your head in a bowling bag, if you know what I mean."

"I don't bowl."

Mason grinned. "Exactly."

"So we'll deal with you?"

"We?" Mason asked, then watched as a flicker of panic crossed the guy's face.

Maybe it wasn't panic. Maybe this guy was just high-strung, or strung-out. Either way, his guard went up. "Kyle" didn't look like there should be a "we" with him.

And then, to Mason's surprise, the guy's hand went over his head and he waved.

Ron paced near the table where Wiz sat wearing earphones. Mack took notes. Dozer stood at the window with binoculars. Ron noticed Wiz looking around the room. He tapped him on the shoulder. "Pay attention to what you're doing."

"Sorry," Wiz said, pulling an earphone off one of his ears. "This place is freaking me out. This is like Tweekerville times ten."

"Nobody's bothering us," Ron said, glancing at Ned, who, after five attempts to score a drink, was now restricted to the corner where he concentrated on a game of checkers with an invisible opponent.

"Which one do you think is Martha?" Wiz asked, his eyes darting all over the room.

"I don't know. I don't care. Focus on your job."

"Nothing is happening. All I hear is Jesse breathing and Led Zeppelin blasting from a really bad sound system." Wiz continued to stare at the room full of patients.

"Maybe we need to order him a Xanax," said Mack.

"Don't get carried away there, Hazard, or you're going to have to start confessing things again," Wiz countered.

Mack smiled.

"I think it's the redhead," Wiz said, pointing to the plump woman nearby, who seemed to be sizing everyone up.

"What've you got down there?" Ron asked Dozer.

"Nothing, Sarge. They're still inside. It's getting crowded," Dozer said, his eyes still pressed to the binoculars. "So, Sarge, what's the weirdest place you've ever had to eyeball?"

"You're looking at it."

"Dang it!" Wiz said suddenly.

"What's wrong?" asked Ron.

Wiz sighed. "I've got to pee."

"What?"

"Sorry. I'm in horrible pain. I've got to go."

"He's living up to his nickname," Dozer said.

"Why didn't you go before we started?"

Wiz looked at the doorway. "I was afraid to walk through…them."

Mack gave him a serious look. "Bathrooms up here don't work. You have to go down to the third floor, through the doorway on your right, then take a left down a really dark hallway. The lights aren't working. Two rooms on your right have warnings about entering at your own risk. Don't go there. The bathroom—it'll be on your left."

Wiz looked terrified. "I think I'll use a cup."

Mack laughed. "I'm just kidding, Wiz. They're next to the elevators."

He looked at Ron. "Can I go? Nothing is going on here."

Ron nodded and ordered Mack to the chair. She put on the head-phones and listened with full concentration.

"Anything?" Ron asked.

She shook her head but then held up her hand. "Wait! I've got some-thing!"

Chapter 26

I got the signal. I'm going over," Jesse said quietly as he slid off the barstool. He moved through the crowd, past two women who wanted his attention. One look and they walked off. He was a few feet from the table, still maneuvering through people when Jesse got his first glimpse of this guy's face.

A shock of fear rippled down his body. *Mason Capps!* Jesse stopped midstride. If Capps saw him, their cover would be blown.

He had to think fast.

Capps had done nothing wrong, so he couldn't make an arrest, but if he walked off, it might kill the whole case. Not to mention leave Kyle hanging.

Jesse made eye contact with Kyle, who looked puzzled. Before Kyle waved again, Jesse walked briskly to the table, stumbled, bumped into the table, and knocked Kyle's drink with his hand. It spilled down onto Kyle's shirt and made him gasp.

"Sorry." Jesse mumbled and continued his fake drunken waddle down the short, dark hallway that housed a pay phone and the restrooms. He hoped Kyle would get the hint.

Within a few seconds, Kyle joined him. "What's going on?" he whispered.

Jesse didn't speak to Kyle first. "Wiz, you've got to get down here. Now. My cover is about to be blown. Kyle is on his own until you get here. Hurry. It can't be Dozer. Tell him it's Mason Capps." Jesse looked at Kyle. "Kyle, listen to me. I know this guy. He's going to know we're cops if he sees my face. You're going to have to take control of this situation. Is he looking at us?" Kyle glanced behind him and nodded.

"Hit me."

"What?" Kyle gasped.

"Don't look so scared. You have to convince Mason that you're in control here. I just spilled beer all over you. You're mad. Now pull back and punch me in the stomach as hard as you can."

"I can't do that!"

"You've got to, Kyle. Hurry up. Hit me!"

Kyle pulled back his arm like he was about to hit a tennis ball, then swung at Jesse, landing a weak punch in his stomach. Jesse bent over and clutched his stomach, pretending the punch knocked the wind out of him. "Harder!" Jesse said. "Hit me in the face!"

Kyle slapped his hand across Jesse's cheek. Jesse clenched his teeth in frustration. This wasn't a girl fight.

"Kyle," Jesse harshly whispered. "Don't slap me! Hit me in the nose!"

Jesse didn't have time to blink before he felt his face explode in pain. Within seconds blood dripped to the floor. Jesse kept his head down. "Grab my shirt. You're going to have to hang on a little bit longer. Wiz is on his way down. Do you hear me? Tell Mason you won't do business with him until you get a contact number. Tell him you'll call with the location of the body shop. You're going to have to go solo until Wiz can get down here. Now, take me by the arm and pull me toward that exit door at the end of the hallway." Jesse pretended to stumble along as they walked toward the door. Jesse pushed it open with both hands and met the darkness. "Go, Kyle. Get back in there. You can save this thing. Make him believe you. If you get into trouble, run out this back door. I'll be here." The door closed, and Jesse fell against the wall of the adjacent building, pulling his T-shirt to his nose to try to stop the bleeding.

"Wiz...can you hear me? They're at a table near the pay phone. Get in there!"

"What? Why?" Ron kneeled next to Mack.

"He said send Wiz down, that it's somebody named Mason—"

Dozer rushed to the table. "Mason Capps?"

"That's it," Mack said. "Then he told Kyle to hit him. It sounded like Kyle was hitting him hard."

Dozer's fingers tore through his hair. "He's making it seem like Kyle's in charge."

"But that puts Kyle down there alone," Ron said. His chest felt tight and he looked toward the elevators. The doors opened, and Wiz walked into the room.

Dozer swore under his breath. "I can't go down there either! I was part of the arrest team."

"Wiz, change in plans," Ron said, beckoning him over.

"What's going on?"

"Jesse's cover is blown. You have to go down there," Dozer said.

"Wait," Ron said, turning to the window for a moment. "Wait."

"What?" Wiz asked.

Ron paused for several seconds, then looked at Mack. "I want you to go."

"Me?" Mack asked.

"Listen carefully," Ron said, getting close to her. "You've got to go down there and distract Mason, make him forget what he's doing there. It's got to be sexy, Mack. That's our only hope for saving this deal. Another guy comes in and this guy will get suspicious. But women make men lose their minds. Do you get what I'm saying?"

"Yeah. I get it." Mack threw her badge on the table and put her gun in a holster around her ankle.

"Pose as a woman every guy wants," Ron continued. Mack turned and headed toward the door.

"I'm taking the stairs!"

"Where are they in the bar?" Ron shouted back.

Mack opened the door to the stairwell. "Somewhere near a telephone, I think!" Then she disappeared.

"Get on the headset," Ron ordered Dozer, who slid into the chair. Ron's cell rang as he grabbed the binoculars. "Yeah?"

"It's Jesse. I'm staying at the back of the building in case Kyle needs me. I told him to leave through this exit if he gets in trouble."

"Do you think Mason saw your face?"

"No. Is Wiz in yet?"

"It's not Wiz. It's Mack."

"What?"

"She can save this deal. She'll be there in two minutes. Hold on." Ron and Dozer turned at the sudden sound of loud commotion behind them. A small, mousy woman with dark hair wound into a disheveled bun was screaming at the top of her lungs. Two orderlies and a nurse rushed her, but she eluded them. She tipped over two chairs and knocked over an elderly man twice her size who was trying to get out of her way.

"Code nine! Code nine!" the nurse shouted.

"What's happening?" Dozer asked as they watched the once-quiet room shatter into disarray. A long beep sounded, and the doors to the room slammed shut. The commotion was so loud, Ron couldn't hear Jesse.

"I'm going to have to call you back!" Ron shouted.

"What's code nine?" Dozer yelled.

A doctor rushed through a side door carrying a large syringe and a small bag. The woman shrieked when she saw it coming, and began kicking and thrashing, knocking the nurse into a table.

"Secure her!" the doctor ordered. "What happened?"

The woman howled like a wild dog.

Dr. Shapel burst through the main doors.

"Martha!" Dr. Shapel shouted. "Calm down!"

A nervous chill worked its way down Ron's spine.

"No, Martha!" Dr. Shapel shouted. "The telephones are *not* coming to get you!"

Dozer looked at Ron. "Oops." Ron looked at Wiz, who was hiding under the table.

With his hands planted on the table and feet on the ground, Mason watched this unassuming man throttle the tattooed bald guy. He didn't look capable of killing a fly. Kyle emerged out of the darkness of the hallway. As he approached the table, Kyle looked at the blood on his knuckles. Then he looked at Mason. "Sorry about that."

"Uh…okay, yeah. No problem." Mason took his cue from Kyle, who seemed to relax as he sat down.

"Where were we?" Kyle asked, fussing with his beer-stained shirt.

Mason cleared his throat and pointed to Kyle's empty glass. "You wanna 'nother beer?"

"No. Thank you, though."

Mason gulped his drink and set it carefully back down on the table. He definitely didn't want to knock it over onto Kyle. He glanced toward the hallway, which was quiet and dark again. "Anyway, back to our bus—"

A pack of cigarettes landed on the table. "Care for one?" Kyle asked.

"Yeah, I guess." He pulled one from the pack. "You got a lot of willpower to carry them with you and not smoke."

"It'll trigger my asthma. I mean, at night. Night air triggers the asthma and then you add the smoke… I break out in hives everywhere, my hay fever kicks in. It's a meth. Mess, I mean."

Mason rolled the cigarette through his fingers. "You do drugs?"

"Only for the asthma," Kyle said, pointing to his lungs. "Geez, when are they gonna legalize that stuff, you know?"

Mason relaxed in his chair. "Let's get down to business."

"Hey, baby…" A woman with her thumbs hooked inside the back pockets of her jeans walked up. She swung her arm around Kyle's neck, which turned three shades of red, but she stared at Mason. He felt every ounce of this woman's flirt. "So, this is the guy?" she asked Kyle.

Kyle nodded. The girl plopped down on Kyle's lap and stuck out her hand. "I'm Mackenzie."

"Uh…Mason…"

"Mason. I like that name."

"Okay, yeah. Thanks."

"Did I already miss it?" Mackenzie asked Kyle.

"Miss what?"

"Oh, come on. Don't pretend like you don't know what I'm talking about." She smiled at Mason like Kyle wasn't even sitting there. "Baby, get me my drink, will you?" She stood up but Kyle looked perplexed. "My drink. You know the one."

Kyle clearly didn't. She sighed and rolled her eyes, glancing at Mason. "Men. Coke with a shot of vanilla."

"Oh…right…that…"

"You want a refill?" she asked Mason.

What weirdos. "No, thanks."

Kyle walked away and the chick slid into his seat, easing her elbows forward on the table toward him. "I hear you're the one I want to talk to."

"Where'd you hear that?"

"Word gets around." She paused and grinned at him. "My brother doesn't think the shop's ready yet, but I do."

"That's your brother?" This was getting even weirder.

"No," she said. "That's Kyle. We like to feel people out before we get down to serious business. Because we're only interested in serious business. And we're only in this for serious money."

"So, let's talk—"

Suddenly Kyle was back at the table. "Um…sorry to interrupt, but

the guy said that if you want Vanilla Coke, there's a hamburger joint down
the street."

Mackenzie giggled. "You're such a joker. You know that I meant Coke
with vanilla *vodka*."

"Oh. Right." Kyle left again.

"Let's be up front," she said. "Is there anything that could complicate
this?"

"Besides spilling a beer?"

"Like you being a cop."

Mason laughed. "You think I'm a cop?"

"Are you?"

"Lady, I just got out of jail. I'm trying to lay low, you know, until my
court date. Still, a guy's gotta make money, you know? I've got some parts
if you're interested. That's it. I'm not Vegas vice, and I'm not Steve Wynn."

Kyle returned with her drink.

"Go get me a napkin, will you, babe? And a pen?"

"Okay. Sure." Kyle was gone again. Mason didn't see a lot of women
in this kind of role. Her boyfriend just beat up a big tough guy, and this
lady was bossing him around like he was her cabana boy. What else was
she capable of? Brandi just did what she was told and shut up when she
needed to.

"Your brother runs the shop?" Mason asked.

"The part that doesn't require late-night meetings in bars."

Mason checked his watch. It wasn't even midnight yet. Maybe she was
being facetious.

He *did* need money.

Kyle returned with a stack of napkins and a pen. Mackenzie took one
and slid it to Mason, then set the pen on top of it. "I want a contact number. We'll call you and let you know when to come to the shop. If you give
us a fake number, that's the end of our business relationship. Don't ever
try to get in contact with us again. We're not here to mess around."

Mason hesitated. Mackenzie's smile faded. Kyle looked around nervously, then grabbed a napkin and blotted his beer-dampened shirt. Mason jotted down his number and slid it across the table. Mackenzie folded it and put it in her back pocket. "We'll be in touch."

"Yeah. Sure. Great." Mason grabbed the pack of cigarettes and looked at Kyle. "I guess you won't be needing these."

"Not at all. Go ahead and take them."

Mason laughed as he got up. These two were absolutely absurd. Somehow, though, that put him at ease. The last guy he dealt with may have looked the part, but he turned out to be a cop.

"Thanks."

As Mason walked away he overheard Kyle say to the girl, "So…do you want to sit on my lap again?"

Chapter 27

An hour later, the team was back at the house. Dozer had spotted Mason leaving the bar, but Kyle and Mack still took extra precautions to make sure they weren't followed.

Wiz was in a back room ordering pizza and mourning the fact that he missed an opportunity for action. Jesse didn't have much of an appetite. He was still reeling from how it all went down. What were the chances he would run into Mason Capps again? In Vegas, no less. Capps was known for doing deals in Henderson, but not much in Vegas.

Sergeant Yeager was on the phone, explaining to his wife that Kyle was all right. Kyle and Mack were discussing every detail of the event.

Jesse glanced out the window into the dark, quiet street. Framed perfectly in orange light from her living room, Ruth stood at a bay window with arms crossed. Jesse yanked the curtains closed.

"How long do we wait before we contact Mason?" Jesse asked.

"We'll move as quickly as possible, but we can't rush," Sergeant Yeager said, snapping his phone shut. "Hank's working around the clock to get the shop in decent working order."

"I just don't want to waste our big break or risk Mason losing interest. If this thing doesn't kick into high gear soon—"

"We don't want to look overly anxious," Sergeant Yeager said. "What happened at the bar is most likely going to make him extra cautious."

Jesse leaned back into the couch. He knew Mason was in it for the money. Everything he did was driven by his money problems. If this didn't turn out to be lucrative, Mason would move on.

"You were amazing," Mack said to Jesse.

"Amazing?" Jesse asked.

"How did you think that quickly?"

"It's all about thinking on your feet." He looked at Sergeant Yeager. "And taking a few risks."

"The biggest risk any of you will be taking for the rest of the night is with the double-sausage pizza Wiz ordered." Sergeant Yeager held up four blank pieces of paper.

"What's that?" Wiz asked.

"This will be your police report."

Jesse laughed. "You want us to draw what happened?"

"I'm going to introduce you to the four-corners doctrine," said Sergeant Yeager.

Jesse folded his arms. "Is this in honor of our resident pastor?"

"You young cops are going to learn how to write a police report. A real police report." He held up the papers again. "What do you see on this paper?"

"A cloud," Dozer said and laughed. "The absence of my childhood pet."

"I'll pass. I've had enough mental evaluation for one night." Wiz said.

Jesse stared at Sergeant Yeager. "Nothing. It's blank."

"No lines, no questions, no boxes to check." He passed out the paper. "Today, officers rely too much on forms. Back in my day, we didn't have fancy recording equipment. Didn't need it. Our testimony in a court of law was enough. The reason it was enough was because we wrote down everything that happened. If it isn't written down, then it didn't happen. My mentor taught me to use every inch of white space on the page. Now it's your turn. Fill your paper with every detail you remember from tonight. Don't stop writing until you're completely out of paper. Both sides."

Jesse shook his head. This was nonsense. If Sergeant Yeager had such a passion for this kind of basic training, why not teach at the academy?

He started writing anyway. There was no point in arguing about it. He didn't want to hear another lecture about the old days. His mind wandered as he wrote. He couldn't figure out why Mason was in Vegas. What was his connection? And why auto theft? Mason had no history of auto theft. He was a cocaine user who dabbled in dealing. Someone else must be driving him into this new venture.

With a long sigh, he tried to concentrate on his report. Maybe after they were finished, they could have milk and cookies.

Dozer smirked from across the room. "Wax on, wax off, baby."

A hole was about to burn through Laura's stomach.

Everything had started with a hunch. She overheard a conversation while on lunch break. Then another in the parking lot after work.

One thing led to another, and now she was tailing Detectives Byers and Bourquin under a dark sky into a neighborhood that was starting to confirm her suspicion. Streetlights highlighted neatly trimmed lawns and flowerpots filled with colorful flowers in front of all of the houses except the one where they parked. She watched the two detectives get out of their car, walk across a yellowing lawn, through a cluttered maze of children's toys, then up the sidewalk past a pot of dead flowers to the front door. Laura parked a half block away and waited in her car under the shadow of a tree.

After a few moments, someone answered the door. She couldn't quite see from her vantage point, but if her gut was right, it was a woman. The detectives stood outside and questioned her for about ten minutes, then left.

After they'd left, Laura drove up to the curb outside the home, got out, and walked up to the door. She knocked loudly, and the door opened quickly.

"What do you wa—" A young woman with heavy red eyelids and splotchy skin stared at her through glassy eyes. "Who are you?" When she spoke, Laura noticed the black rot to her teeth, probably from the acid in the meth.

"You drive a minivan, don't you? You reported it stolen yesterday."

"I just told the cops that. Are you a cop?"

"Yes."

"You guys need to get your act together." This coming from a woman who was wearing a blouse with pajama bottoms.

"How long after it was stolen did you wait to report it?"

"Look," she said, running a finger under her nose, "I was busy, okay? My boyfriend and I share the car sometimes. I thought he'd taken it. Couldn't get ahold of him. What good's a cell phone when they don't turn it on?" Laura nodded like she was buying her story.

"Thank you for your time," Laura said.

"That's it?" The woman's eyebrows came together.

"You're not the only one with cell phone problems. If my superiors would turn theirs on, we wouldn't have cops out here bothering you all night."

A small child emerged from behind the woman. He wore a Superman T-shirt and a diaper that had reached maximum capacity. The woman didn't seem to notice him.

Laura walked back to her car. She was right. She'd been right all along. These vehicles were being stolen or loaned to run drugs. There was no way she was going to let narcotics score this one. She was way ahead of them, and that was how it was going to stay.

No matter what.

Ron stood outside a small convenience store, cell phone to his ear, trying to explain the situation to Nan, though even he wasn't sure why Laura had wanted to meet him at this late hour. "I'm sorry. You know I can't control these things," he said to Nan.

"There are a lot of things that can't be controlled," she fumed, "which is why they have restrooms in five different locations at the mall." She paused. "Hold on, there's someone at the door."

Ron snapped his phone shut. He knew it was Kyle at her door. He'd sent him to deal with the fallout that would come with telling Nan he would be home later than he planned. Besides, Kyle kept lingering near Mack, who was trying to finish her police report. Ron made an overly dramatic plea to Kyle: "Nan is going to be upset about another late night. I would appreciate it if you would talk to her." He didn't warn Kyle that Nan would probably take out her anger on him, but the visit would still serve its purpose.

Ron had something more pressing to consider—like why Laura insisted on meeting him in a greasy diner at a remote convenience store.

Laura got right to the point. "Task Force Viper is going to take a big turn."

"Okay."

"I don't think this will surprise you. You seemed to be drawing your own conclusions."

"About what?"

"The minivans that are being stolen."

"The ones that you took out of the report."

"Yes."

"What about them?"

"I have good intel that says these vehicles are being used for drug running."

Ron nodded. "Makes a lot of sense. I suspected any damage they had was just to make it look like they were stolen for, at the very least, joyriding. But who steals minivans for joyriding, right?"

"There's another pattern—these vehicles aren't reported missing until at least twenty-four hours after they've disappeared."

"Crack rentals. They loan the car in exchange for dope."

"I've known this for a while," she said, each word carefully spoken. "Even before Viper."

"What do you mean?"

"I set Viper up for this."

"What are you talking about?"

"I want this, Ron. I deserve it."

Ron leaned back and stared at her. "You set up the entire task force for a drug bust?"

"It's going to be huge. This thing keeps growing. If we can get someone on the inside, I'm certain we can get all the way to the top."

Ron grew angry. "I didn't sign up for this."

"That's why I signed you up for this, Ron. I knew you could handle it. You have a lifetime's worth of experience in undercover drug work."

"That was yesterday, Laura. I came on board to bust up a car-theft ring. That's it."

"You *have* to do this. We have to do this. I can't let narcotics take this over."

"They don't know?"

"They're starting to suspect, but they're way behind the curve. They've been tied up with a huge heroin bust. If narcotics gets involved in this task force now, there will be so much red tape, we'll trip over it with every step. We're already in. We can move quickly. We keep going and we topple this thing."

"This sounds like a vendetta."

"You don't know what I've had to listen to for the past ten years. I deserved that position. It got ripped from me."

"Because of a cop's pregnant wife? Is that what you're talking about?"

"It could've happened to anybody. A lot of people would've made the same decision. They penalized me because I'm a woman."

"What decision?"

Laura sighed and drew back her intensity. "I let the cop see his wife."

"Your partner's brother, right?"

"Not my partner, really. Only my partner on paper. It was an accreditation test."

"This whole thing was over a promotional assessment? A policies and procedures test?"

"It wasn't just a test to me. It was my chance to get into narcotics. That scenario... I made my decision. It's all subjective, you know? And they failed me for that."

"Look, Laura, we've all gotten bad breaks here and there. So you didn't get narcotics because of one question on an exam. You're the head of a bureau. That counts for something."

"They don't respect me, Ron. And they won't until I can prove that I'm as good of a cop as they are."

"Are you talking about the narcotics guys or your father?"

"Leave my father out of this."

"I don't think you can."

"I read your file, Ron. I know what happened to your partner. He fell in love with an informant, turned on you, and you had to shoot him. Now *that's* a problem to worry about."

"That was a long time ago, and it doesn't have anything to do with the work we're doing here."

"I chose you because I knew this was going to be an extraordinary case. We have a chance to bring down some very powerful and dangerous people. Tell me, what's wrong with this scenario?"

"Motivation," Ron said.

"What's the difference if the job gets done?"

"Trust me. It makes all the difference in the world."

Laura squeezed her hands together to look calm, but her knuckles were turning white. "Are you with me on this or not? Of course, you're welcome to sleep on it." She glanced at his cell phone sitting on the table. "It's getting kind of late."

"That's a big chip you're carrying on your shoulder," Ron said. "My old partner carried one too. He got disgruntled, blamed the force, turned on us."

"We've all got motivations. You do. I do. Look at Mack. She cares that this world is going to hell in a handbasket. She thinks she can do something to help. Yes, I realize she's on the upswing of idealism, but I'm not sure she has a downswing. So what? It's all motivation."

"Narcotics changes the game. If the drug-running theory is true, we're dealing with a very dangerous group of people."

"That's why we need to get them. We have an open door. This Capps guy is known for dealing drugs, right?"

"Small-time. In Henderson."

"He could be connected to somebody bigger." Her eyes held a quiet desperation.

Ron rested his forearms on the table. "After we get Mason, if we want to push him for contacts, fine. If it leads us to drug dealers, though, I don't have the right people in place to do what needs to be done. We may need to pull in some guys from narcotics."

"Jesse is capable of handling it, and there's no reason we can't use Mason as an informant."

Ron slid out of the booth. "Right now, I've got to go home, see my wife, and get some sleep." Ron grabbed his cane and walked out into the still, dark night.

Laura Gates was in way over her head. But Ron knew, deep inside, he wasn't.

Chapter 28

J esse and Kyle scurried down the porch steps and sidewalk of Sergeant Yeager's home and jumped into Kyle's car.

"Well," Kyle said softly, staring forward and gripping the steering wheel. "That didn't go well."

That was the understatement of the century. Jesse wasn't exactly sure why Sergeant Yeager had sent Kyle to visit Nan, but whatever the reason, it had backfired.

Jesse hadn't really gotten to know Nan at the cocktail party since nobody was allowed to speak, but she seemed like a decent person. She had a bit of an edge to her, but that wasn't uncommon for cops' wives.

During the party, he'd even let his mind wander to thoughts of marriage. His had been a disaster. He wanted to believe there was a chance for something better down the road. But while he found that a lot of women liked the idea of dating a cop, when the reality of police life set in, off they went. On the rebound from his marriage, he'd started dating a beautiful woman named Lindsey. Then he got shot. She stood by his bed, carrying on about how brave he was…until they put in a catheter. She watched with her hand over her mouth, and he never saw her after that. Her parting thought was written all over her face: *He can't even use the restroom by himself?* Jesse shook off the thoughts and turned to Kyle. "What, exactly, did the sarge expect you to do in there?"

"I'm not sure. Usually I'm called in to people's homes to comfort them or offer counseling. But with the Yeagers, well…you never know."

"So what would you call that?"

"Possibly an exorcism," Kyle said with a wry smile as he started his car. "Nan can be pretty stubborn. She's the secretary for our ministry committee. She takes the job very seriously. But I've never really seen her like this. She's angry, and I think it's because she's really worried about Ron."

"Join the club," Jesse said with a sigh. "The guy is wearing me out."

Kyle pulled away from the curb. "Maybe he's just trying to pass on some traditions."

"We're not talking about Christmas, here."

"No, but wouldn't you agree that tradition is a big part of your occupation? It's certainly true in Christianity. Some of the traditions are good… some bad. But when the good is lost, it can be troubling. Tragic in some cases."

"Like what?"

"Well, for instance, studying the Scriptures. Decades ago, Christians knew and practiced the importance of reading God's Word daily. That's being lost more and more in the church and it shows. People aren't reading God's Word, and so they're not equipped when trouble comes knocking."

"Nan seemed perfectly equipped, if you define us as trouble."

"Well, with a mouth like that, who needs a weapon, right?"

Jesse laughed. "No kidding."

"You still haven't told me why you wanted to come along, unless it was to escape writing your report."

"I wrote it. I used big letters to fill up the page faster. It's a trick I learned in the fourth grade. I had to fight the urge to draw smiley faces and stick people." Jesse slouched into his seat. "I'm sure the sarge is a great guy. He's just not what I'm used to. If I were an old guy in his position, I'd make sure everyone knew I could keep up."

"Speaking of keeping up…"

"Yeah?"

"I need some advice."

"From me?"

"I need chick advice."

"*Chick* advice."

"I can name all the minor prophets in the Bible, I know the four gospels by heart and find Leviticus interesting, but when it comes to women, it's all Greek to me." Kyle laughed. "That's not really a good analogy, because I can actually read Greek, but you get the idea."

"Right…" Jesse fought to keep a straight face. "Well, it would be better if you knew French. It's more of a turn-on than Greek."

"Oh."

"It's really about confidence. When you ask a woman out, there can't even be a hint that you're afraid she's going to say no."

"But what if she says no?"

Jesse sighed. This wasn't going to be easy. "First, let me tell you why I asked to come along tonight. I wanted to talk to *you* about something." Jesse propped his elbow up against the window and leaned his head against his hand. "I know my thing with Chaplain Greer probably sounds weird. But it worked. I don't know what it was about him, but when he prayed, things happened. Good things. And now that he's gone and I'm working undercover with the Huxtables, everything is falling apart. That's what I wanted to talk to you about."

"What about it?"

"I need you to be Chaplain Greer. Just until he gets back from the cruise." Kyle started to speak, but Jesse interrupted him. "I realize you and I started off bumpy. It could've been worse. A lot worse. But now I think we could have something good here. Sort of like what I had with Chaplain Greer."

"Jesse, I don't have any special—"

"You're a pastor, right? And pastors are supposed to pray for their people. I'll come to church on Sundays if you'll do this for me."

"You'd better explain what 'this' is first."

"Whenever I go into the field, I need you to pray for me. And feel free to bless me too. Chaplain Greer used to do that, but he's been falling off a little in that area."

"You'll come to my church every Sunday?"

"Sure."

"*Every* Sunday?"

"Yes, yes. Every Sunday. I'll even wear a tie and carry a Bible if that makes you happy." Jesse folded his arms. "So is it a deal? You pray for and bless me, and I'll turn you into a chick magnet."

Kyle's face immediately flushed bright pink. "Well, I don't really need to be a magnet. Washable glue would be fine."

"I'm just saying, if you help me with my problem, I'll help you with yours."

"Okay...deal," Kyle said. "On one condition. You need to understand that I can't control what happens to you. I can pray for you and offer advice, but the rest is up to God."

"Okay. Same here—I can show you my moves, tell you to stop wearing fabric belts, and teach you some good lines, but at some point, you'll have to carry this thing yourself."

Kyle smiled and stuck out his hand to shake. "Now," he said. "Let's get started. Give me some good advice."

Jesse thought for a moment. "I'll never forget what my best friend in high school told me. We were eating lunch one day, and he just said out of the blue, 'Man, with girls it can be as simple as the difference between *a* or *the*.' So I ask him what he means, right? And he goes, 'It's the difference between telling a girl you're in *a* band or *the* band.'" Jesse laughed hard at the memory. "Isn't that hilarious?"

"I don't get it."

"What he meant was if you're in *a* band, you're in a rock-and-roll type thing, but if you're in *the* band, it means you're in the marching band."

"I was in the marching band!" Kyle said. "First-chair tuba!"

Jesse was suddenly certain he had the impossible end of this deal.

A perfect early-morning temperature greeted Jesse as he got out of his truck in front of the body shop. Three huge garages dwarfed the building on the right, which they would use as their office. Jesse bent down to peer inside one partially open garage door. It looked like a typical body shop, complete with grease stains on the floor that were evidence of a previous tenant—the shop had once been a tire store.

A bell chimed as he walked through the customer entrance. Colorful car brochures and paper-filled clipboards covered a small red counter. On the wall behind the counter, a collection of automotive repair licenses hung in crooked frames. Double doors on the left led to the garage, and a large glass window allowed customers to see the work being done on the cars.

Hank, wearing a blue mechanic's jumpsuit, came through the double doors holding a rag. "Hey, Detective Lunden."

"This place looks great."

Hank glanced around. "Yeah, I kind of wish it were my own shop."

"It will be for a while." He looked through the window into the work area. One of Ruth's cars was lifted up like it was being worked on, and one of the doors had been removed. "When do the insurance guys get here?"

"Maybe another week. Sergeant Yeager said that this kind of thing takes time, and you guys hadn't expected to move this fast."

"You here alone?"

"Mack's here," he said, just as she came through the door to the office behind the counter.

"Hey, Jesse." She smiled, but not as broadly as usual. Hank walked back through the doors.

"Where's everyone else?" Jesse asked.

"Sergeant Yeager had to go into the office to talk with the insurance guys. Wiz and Dozer went to get breakfast." She pointed to a pot of coffee in the small waiting room. "That's ready if you want some."

Jesse walked over, took a foam cup, lifted the coffeepot, and poured his way toward a brighter outlook. He took a sip. "You look tired," he said as Mack leaned down to put something away behind the counter.

She popped up. "Do I?"

"A little."

"I didn't get much sleep. I kept playing the scene over and over in my mind, you know? How could I have done it differently? What did I do wrong? What did I do right?" She yawned. "Sorry. Anyway, Kyle gave me a good perspective."

"Kyle?"

"Yeah, after you dropped him off last night, we talked for a while. I know, I know, we probably talked the thing to death, but that was my first real UC job." The megawatt grin was back. "It was exciting."

"It always is. It doesn't get any less exciting, but after a while, you get a little less idealistic." Why was he even trying? She didn't have a cynical bone in her body.

"You know, the whole time I was in that bar, I had this amazing calmness. It was weird. I figured my heart would be beating out of my chest, but it sort of felt like I was transformed into this other person. I *became* her, and talking to this Mason guy was just part of who I was."

"That's good," Jesse said, sipping his coffee. "You had to think fast, and you did. Not everyone can do that."

"I'm a little nervous about calling Mason. I need to really think about what I'm going to say and how I'm going to react to his questions."

"When are we making the call?"

"This afternoon. Sergeant Yeager wanted us to wait until he got back."

"Right." Wait. One of his favorite things to do. Jesse looked up to see if he could spot the hidden cameras. He knew there was recording equipment on the counter too. This was a state-of-the-art setup, thanks to money coming from the insurance companies. A small price to pay to save thousands of dollars in claims. He watched Mack for a moment. She shuffled papers and went about her tasks like they were the most important things anybody could do. Even tired, she was so dang plucky. "You know, Mack, I have a hard time picturing your life. Growing up, I mean. How did you go from that to this?"

"How do you envision my life?" she asked.

"I don't know. All I know is that you were homeschooled." Jesse leaned on the counter. "So maybe I'm stereotyping. It's not fair, I know. But it's life. We're all stereotyped in one way or the other. Take me. When people find out I work undercover narcotics, the first thing they wonder is if I have my own drug problem. It's a fair question. Some cops get pulled in. Even before they know that I'm a cop, they draw all kinds of conclusions about me based on my appearance." He pointed to the tattoo on his forearm, then crushed his foam cup and tossed it free-throw style into the wastebasket on the other side of the counter. "Undo your stereotype for me. I hear 'homeschooled,' and I think 'sheltered kid living in a commune with no idea what the real world is like.'"

"My life was nothing like that," she said, laughing. "I actually was raised as a clown."

Jesse smiled. At least she had a sense of humor about it. But she wasn't laughing anymore. "Please tell me there's a punch line coming."

"It was a family business," she continued. "My parents lost their jobs around the same time, and they were trying to support a large family, so they started this clown business. We were definitely not in a commune! We traveled all over, to county fairs and places like that."

"Are you being serious?"

Mack looked up. "Why?"

"You're not exactly helping dissolve the stereotype."

"What's stereotypical about that? How many clowns do you know?"

"Personally?" Jesse asked, unable to hide the taunt in his tone.

"Working as a clown has actually helped me in my career. Especially now in undercover work. I know how to act, and that's part of the job, right? Playing a role."

"It's definitely going to come in handy when we have to bring down those seedy circus trainers."

She put away some folders. "Well, it hasn't failed me yet. My parents were amazing people, and they taught me everything I needed to know about surviving in this world. Let me assure you, this job is a heck of a lot easier than entertaining forty five-year-olds."

Jesse laughed, and he wasn't sure if it was because of the absurd conversation or the mental picture he was forming of Mack in clown makeup.

Hank walked back through the doors wearing the first smile Jesse had seen on him. "You won't believe who is on the phone." He held his cell phone toward Mack. "Hayden. She wants to talk to you."

Mack snatched the phone away and quickly put it to her ear. "Hayden... I can't believe it... I'm so excited for you!" Mack rushed through the doors and down the hallway into a small office.

"Our sister. She just got engaged to her boyfriend, Ray," Hank explained.

"How many of you are there?"

"Seven."

"Ah." He studied Hank for a moment. "So...were you a clown too?"

"Mime."

Of course.

Wiz and Dozer came in carrying coffee trays and sacks. "Bagels, but no donuts," Dozer said with disappointment. "Wiz thinks diet is important."

Wiz walked over to the coffee pot and refilled his takeout cup.

"You've had two cups already. Sure that's a good idea?" Dozer asked Wiz.

"Stay out of my drinking habits," Wiz said. "And for the record, it doesn't matter what I drink. I just have a small bladder."

Jesse laughed.

"Shut up, Jesse, or I'll tell Ruth you've got a crush on her," Wiz said. Jesse's hands flew up in self-defense. "All right, all right. You have me."

"Good, because Ruth was about to have you at hello," Wiz said.

Dozer walked over to the waiting room and plopped down in a chair. "We need a TV in here."

The bell rang and Ron walked in, looking exhausted. "Everyone here?" he asked.

Dozer leaped to his feet.

"Yeah," Jesse said. "We're working like crazy."

Mack came through the doors beaming. Jesse felt a pang of envy. He couldn't recall beaming about anything when it came to his family.

Ron leaned his cane against the counter and placed a sack on the floor. "I've never seen so much bureaucracy in my life. These people can't even say 'maybe' without checking with four other people." He looked into the garage. "Well, at least we're starting to look like the real thing. We'll just have to play up the idea that we're adding on as we can afford it."

"What about body parts?" Wiz asked.

Hank laughed and leaned in to Mack. "I feel like I'm on *CSI.*"

"We've got some in the warehouse behind the shop. Enough for now, but Captain Gates requested more. Who knows how long that's going to take, though." Sergeant Yeager pulled out a two-way radio from the sack. "We need to put this in the shop."

"What's it for?" Mack asked.

"The likelihood that we'll need the radio is small, but we're putting it in the shop just in case someone we come in contact with is wearing a bug detector."

"A bug detector?" Hank asked.

"A counter-surveillance device," Jesse said. "They're small enough to carry in your pocket, and they vibrate if they detect a signal, like a recording device."

Sergeant Yeager patted the radio. "The signal put out by the two-way would confuse the detector and make our contact question whether it's picking up the two-way or something else. Besides, most body shops would use one of these to contact tow trucks and salvage yards." He handed it to Wiz. "Why don't you get it set up somewhere."

"No problem," Wiz said.

"When do we call Mason?" asked Jesse.

"In a little bit. We'll call him from the land line here so he can trace it if he wants to." He looked at Mack. "We'll rehearse it. You'll do fine."

"I feel ready," she said. "I've got a little bit of nerves going, but I'm confident I can handle it. I've been praying like crazy. I'm getting a sense that God is going to do some big things here, and we're going to get these guys. Aren't you guys feeling it?" She looked at Jesse, then at Sergeant Yeager.

"Yeah, sure," Sergeant Yeager said.

"Good," she said, slapping her hands together. "I'm going to go pray one more time." She hurried through the swinging doors.

Jesse gestured toward the doors. "What is that?"

"It's called childlike faith. It's just that most people don't take it literally."

Chapter 29

Rhyne slipped the tailored black jacket over his shoulders. He felt instantly powerful. Soon enough, he'd have the Rolex to match. He looked at himself in the door mirror, wondering how a man like Vincent Ayala could have so much money and not indulge a little. It was practically a crime not to. All Rhyne needed to complete the look was a cigar and a glass of cognac.

"You look smooth, man," Mason said as Rhyne walked into the kitchen.

Rhyne pulled a stack of money, neatly secured with a rubber band, out of a drawer. He handed it to Mason.

"What's this?" Mason asked. "You already paid me."

"Let's just call it a bonus."

Mason flipped through the crisp bills. "Really?"

"I told you we're going to be rolling in dough. Do you believe me now?"

Mason nodded, still staring at the stack of cash. Rhyne smiled at the expected response. "So, do you trust me now?"

Mason looked up. "What do you mean?"

"Do you trust me to run this thing?"

"Sure, Rhyne. You set this whole thing up. You got us the meeting with Ayala."

Rhyne slipped off the Armani and laid it carefully across the back of the couch. "Well, Mason, I don't trust you. That's why I had you followed Friday night."

"Why would you do that?"

"What were you doing at that bar?"

"Why would you follow me?"

"I have to know I can trust you, Mason. You're no good to me if I can't trust you."

Mason snorted. "Yeah, well, I don't know what it takes for you to trust me. All you do is worry that I'm a snitch."

"So what were you doing there?"

"Why don't you tell me, if you're so smart?"

Rhyne kept silent. He knew Mason would eventually keep talking.

"Look, man, I'm just trying to get out of your hair, okay? I just needed some extra cash." He sighed and glanced up at Rhyne. "Okay. You got me. I was working a deal to sell some parts. I've got a ton of stuff left over from last month, and there's a new place opening up. They're willing to deal under the table. They need everything." He looked at the cash in his hand. "I...I didn't know this was coming. I swear I wasn't trying to betray you, Rhyne. I swear it. I was just trying to get some cash so I could get my own place."

Rhyne blinked. He loved the power he had over Mason, who had been reduced to a blubbering idiot. "So, you had a meeting. How do you know these people?"

"I don't. I just ran into the guy when I was waiting for you the other day. We struck up a conversation, and he mentioned his shop."

"Interesting. Have you sold anything yet?"

"No, not yet. They're going to call me."

"They have your cell phone number?"

"It won't happen again. I promise. It won't."

"I want to believe you."

"It was stupid, man. I just thought it would be a quick way to get some cash. That's all." Mason's eyes pleaded for understanding.

"I hate being paranoid. It can destroy a person...or make a person destroy."

"I'm sorry."

"What else do they know about you, besides your cell phone number?"

"Just my…my name. My first name."

"You're sure about that?"

"Yes."

Rhyne exhaled a long, ferocious breath. "All right, Mason. I'll give you one more chance. But this is it. You mess up, and that money you're holding will turn into blood money." Rhyne studied Mason. He looked scared enough.

"Now, cancel your cell phone. We've got work to do."

"How do I know you're not a cop?"

Jesse leaned against a wall watching Dozer pepper Mack with question after question, each time piling more paranoia onto the character of Mason. Mack seemed to be handling herself okay, in a textbook sort of way. Her weirdness factor just might work to their advantage. One could hope.

Mack was offering an elaborate explanation about why she wasn't a cop when Sergeant Yeager interrupted her. "Mack, listen. Criminals never explain themselves to people they don't know. As far as you're concerned, *he* could be a cop. The way you handle this is to become just as paranoid. Turn all the questions back on him."

"But what if he won't back down?"

Jesse jumped in. "You've got to be able to make him think that you're about to walk away from the deal. Look, you know, in high school, the quickest way to get a date was to act like you didn't want one, right?"

Mack cleared her throat. "I'll have to take your word for it."

"You didn't date in high school?"

"I did. Once. A guy named Thomas."

"So did you play hard to get?"

"Um, kind of."

"Let me guess. He showed up at your doorstep only to be met by your dad and his shotgun."

"Well…not quite. He showed up at my door with his shotgun and totally freaked my mother out. We had a common interest in guns, and he was just bringing one to show me. Turned out I was a better shot than him, so the relationship didn't last."

Kyle appeared. "Hey, guys."

"What are you doing here?" Mack asked, standing to greet him with a hug.

"Just for support. For Jesse."

Everyone looked at Jesse, who shrugged. "It's complicated."

Sergeant Yeager walked back into the crowded office. His expression quieted the room as he focused on Mack. "You ready?" he asked.

"Um, yes." She tilted her head and looked closely at the sergeant. "Are you okay?"

"I'm fine. You have the number?"

"I've got it," Mack said.

"Wiz, recording equipment ready?"

"Yes. Tested twice."

"Just leave a brief message for him to call back if he doesn't answer. We're ready when you are."

"All right," Mack said in a calm voice. "Give me a moment." She bowed her head and prayed, mumbling to herself as if no one else were in the room. Wiz and Dozer shifted uncomfortably. Kyle just smiled. Jesse looked at Sergeant Yeager, who didn't seem to notice what was going on. He was staring at the wall, looking like he was a million miles away.

"We can't hear you," Dozer interrupted.

"That's okay. I'm not talking to you." She finished with a quiet, "Amen," and then took the phone in her shaking hand. Her eyes darted around the room. "Gentlemen," she said, "it's feeling a little crowded in here."

Sergeant Yeager gestured toward the door, and everyone filtered into the hallway. Jesse and the sergeant stood opposite each other, leaning against the walls with their arms crossed.

"You okay?" Jesse said quietly. The sarge looked up. "You seem a little out of it."

They heard the soft musical tones of a number being dialed. Several long seconds ticked by as they listened for Mack to say something, but instead she was suddenly in the doorway, looking disgruntled.

"What's wrong?" Jesse asked.

"The number is no longer in service."

Jesse tilted his head toward the ceiling. "So much for the power of prayer."

Mack seemed irritated. "Looks like there's more than one disconnection here."

Chapter 30

R on sent everyone to lunch. He needed time to think. So many things were going wrong. And Laura's admissions, among other things, complicated matters. He began to distrust his emotions. Pride tempted him with the idea that busting up a huge narcotics ring would prove every young jerk wrong who had told him he was long overdue to retire.

But bringing the narcotics factor into the equation made everything more dangerous. Knowing that this wasn't any ordinary auto-theft ring forced him to change his course of action. If the stolen vehicles were indeed crack rentals, it was almost certain they were dealing with the mob.

Back in Chicago, Ron had his fair share of run-ins with the mob, including a bust that went all the way to a suburban mayor and some of his cops. Sometimes the trials were scarier than the arrests. People all over the city started turning up dead whenever the mob was involved in a trial.

Busting an auto-theft ring meant arresting the guys who brought in the parts and then making deals with them to get to the bigger guys. That wasn't going to work if this was a mob operation. If his suspicions were right, the only way to make it to the top of this ring would be to get someone on the inside, most likely deep cover. That would take months. Ron had gone into deep cover once for two and half months. It had nearly gotten him killed…and divorced.

A white paper sack dropped onto the table in front of him. Ron twisted around to find Jesse, who handed him a coffee.

"Large, thick, and black," Jesse said.

"Thanks."

"Turkey, extra mayo."

"Don't tell Nan."

Jesse pulled up a chair and sat across the table from him. "I want to talk to you about something."

Ron unwrapped the sandwich. He suddenly realized how hungry he was. "Shoot."

"As you know, I've dealt with Mason Capps in Henderson. It was a small-time drug deal, nothing to do with auto theft. He doesn't have that long of a rap sheet."

"What about him?"

"Mason has always been well connected, not because he's smart, but because he has this ability to become everyone's loyal dog. People trust him just enough. And so he rides on the coattails of others' hard work."

"What does that have to do with our situation? Mason has cut ties with us. We have no way of contacting him."

"I know someone who can. His former girlfriend. We arrested her along with Mason in Henderson."

"And?"

"I'm positive she would agree to be a confidential informant."

Ron set down his sandwich. "Not a good idea."

"It would work. She's got it in for Mason, and I know I could get her to cooperate. He sold her out during the bust that we made."

"No. We're not using informants."

"Why?"

"They can become a real thorn in your side."

"I've used informants a dozen times. You just have to know how to control your snitch."

"You can't completely control informants, Jesse. They can create complicated situations. And in this instance, if you're talking about an informant who is out for revenge, you're doubling the likelihood that something could go wrong."

"Human intelligence, time and time again, has proven to be the most reliable asset we have in undercover work. The CIA started phasing out human intel in the early nineties and look what's happened to them."

"Look, Jesse, I'm working on this, okay? I realize a gigantic wrench has just been thrown into the situation. But Mason was a fluke to begin with. Our original idea was to send you guys into bars to start taking names and making contacts. That's still a feasible idea."

"Mason is a better line in. I can get him back. I'm certain I can get Brandi to work for us."

"Brandi, huh." Ron shoved the rest of the sandwich in his mouth and crinkled up the sack. He took his coffee, stood, and said, "No. We're going back to the original plan. Now let's get this body shop ready, okay? If we're up and running by next week, we'll still be ahead of schedule."

"Um…weren't we supposed to turn back there? I thought we were going to check out some bars."

"I'm supposed to be checking out bars. You're supposed to be going home and starting your real sabbatical." Jesse glanced at Kyle. "Don't look so innocent. You're not here just for me. There's something in this for you too."

"I've been praying all morning for you."

"For safety and protection? Did you pray that Psalm 91?"

"Yes. And about a dozen more. I also prayed that your heart would be open to hearing God's voice in your life."

"Why would you do that?"

"Don't you want to hear God's voice?"

"I don't have to," Jesse sighed. "I've got Mack. She's like his mouthpiece. I once worked with a partner—this guy named Fred who was infatuated with Celine Dion. Horrible. She's all he would talk about. I'm kind of missing Fred, if you get what I'm saying."

"You obviously believe in God and his power or you wouldn't want his protection."

"Yeah, but don't you think Mack takes it a little overboard? I mean, you're a priest—"

"Pastor."

"Whatever. The point is that if she wants to talk about it, maybe she should be a pastor, not an undercover cop. There are thousands of other occupations that would suit her just fine. Why a cop? Why an undercover cop?"

"It is rather exciting. I can see the appeal."

"Undercover work isn't for people who say things like 'rather exciting,' and it's definitely not for people who say, 'Blessed are those who are flexible, for they shall not be bent out of shape.'"

"That's clever."

"No, it sounds like the kind of thing you'd see on a church billboard. There's one by my house. And on hot days, they love putting this one up: 'Repent now or you'll be headed for a place hotter than this.'"

"Well, that's just tacky. From everything I've seen, Mack is going to be a great undercover cop. You should've seen her in that bar. She was amazing."

"That was one time."

"What does a cop need to do for other cops to give her a break?"

"I know this is hard for you to understand. There're just a lot of unspoken rules with cops. You've got it easy. You have the Ten Commandments, and if you follow those, you're in the club. We have a code of conduct and a badge that gives us authority, but we're bonded together by something more than those things. It's a sense of trust. I have to trust that the person I'm working with is going to make decisions that aren't going to get me killed. And if I'm in a dangerous situation, I have to believe they would die trying to save me."

"Mack seems like that kind of person to me. She scrambled to your rescue at the bar. When Ron asked her to go, she didn't think twice about it."

Jesse eyed him. "Why do you keep coming to her defense?"

"I suppose we Christians have our code of conduct too."

Jesse leaned back into his seat and kept his eyes on the road. "Don't get me wrong. She's nice. And a hard worker. Just because you can do all the right things doesn't necessarily mean you're the right person for the job. That's all I'm saying. But enough about that. I promised you some advice. So, is there a specific woman you're interested in or is the sky the limit here?"

"Uh, yeah, there's someone I'm…well, I'm interested in. I mean, I don't know her real well. I know she's… I don't know, I just like her. We seem to have a…connection, or maybe that's too strong of a word. Maybe it's more like a—"

"Kyle, we're off to a shaky start here. Women are looking for men who are confident. I'm not talking cockiness. Walk into any bar in America and you can see that approach crash and burn by the second. But confidence, that works."

"That's the problem. When I get around women, I lose my vocabulary and my voice. I start squeaking and then apologizing and then stuttering and next thing I know, she's saying, 'I'm sorry, you're going to have to excuse me.'"

"Just remember, they're as frightened of you as you are of them." Jesse decided to show one of his lessons-learned cards. "I've been married before."

"I didn't know that."

"I don't talk about it much. I told Chaplain Greer, though."

"How long were you married?"

"Eleven months." Jesse held up his hand to stop whatever comment Kyle might make. "I take full responsibility for it. I always have. I know lots of things can make a relationship fail."

"Why did yours fail?"

"Irreconcilable similarities."

"What does that mean?"

"I married a carbon copy of myself. Shanna. We came through the academy together, went to undercover school together, and worked on several of the same cases. I thought I had married the girl of my dreams, but basically I just ended up marrying myself, and two of me in one relationship was more than the 'I do' could handle." He glanced at Kyle. Chaplain Greer often had the same expression. It wasn't shock or disgust, or even pity, but something else Jesse couldn't quite put his finger on. "What I'm trying to say is that maybe the women you're trying to date are too much like you."

"Yeah…I see what you mean."

"What about this woman you like? Are you two similar?"

"I would've never dreamed of dating someone like her. It was a fluke that we met."

"There you go. Another rule of thumb, never date someone you work with."

Kyle's excitement diminished. "Oh."

"You work with her?"

"No. Not technically. I kind of worked with her on a… We did this thing together, but that's over. I guess, technically, we're not working together."

"It would be a bummer to lose it all over a technicality," Jesse said and smiled. Kyle didn't seem to find it funny. "I'm kidding. Lighten up."

"I can't. God is telling me some very strange things about you right now."

Jesse let off the accelerator. "What is he saying? Is it about my marriage?"

Kyle offered a small, wry smile. "I'm kidding. Lighten up."

Jesse blew out a breath and gripped the steering wheel. "Cute."

"So what do I do? The moment I think I'm going to ask her out, I clam up. Plus, there's a part of me that feels like she's going to think I'm a very unexciting person."

"Not anymore. When this job is over, tell her about your brief but galvanizing stint in undercover work."

Kyle slid down in his seat. "Uh, yeah. I don't think she'd be too impressed by that. What else?"

"Well, what do you do in your spare time? Something like bungee jumping or kayaking would be good," Jesse said.

Kyle thought for a moment. "I do like to pontoon. And I love motorcycle racing."

"Good! That's exciting. What kind of bike do you race?"

"Oh, I don't race them. I like watching it on TV."

Jesse pulled his truck to the curb and took out his wallet. He handed Kyle a twenty.

"Buy her dinner?" he asked.

Jesse laughed. "That's a start, but this is for a taxi."

"Why?"

"There's something I've got to go do, and you can't be with me when I do it."

"Why not?"

"Well, if you feel comfortable lying to a certain member of your church who helped you kill time during a sabbatical, then you're welcome to come."

Kyle opened the door. "Is it dangerous?"

"Not in a bodily harm sort of way."

Chapter 31

Captain Gates didn't look pleased to see him. "You're back," she said in a flat tone.

"Get used to it. I'm going to be here a lot until you can prove to me why this is a good idea."

Gates gestured for him to shut the door. "You are not backing out on me, are you? We've come too far."

"Our suspect broke contact."

"What happened?"

"I'm not sure. His phone was disconnected. Maybe he suspected something. Maybe he didn't pay his bill. Either way, we're back to square one."

Her jaw muscles quivered. "All right. So we're at square one. We can still make this thing work."

Ron sat down. "I don't feel good about it."

"You're just going to let everything they say about you be true. Is that it? You're too old for this job. You can't handle the pressure. Similar things that were said to me, but the difference is that I'm not buying in to it and you are." She leaned forward on her desk. "Ron, there's more talent in you than all of the UC guys in narcotics put together. You can do this."

"And I am going to do this. On one condition. That I do the UC work."

"What?"

"My team isn't experienced enough to handle a narcotics case. Since the body shop is now a cover for a drug investigation, I can't take my chances with a team that's not ready. They can cover me, but I have to make the contacts."

"That's ridiculous," Laura snapped. "You're going to stick out everywhere you go."

"I know how to work this thing, and I know how to get to whoever it is that's using these crack rentals."

Laura leaned back in her chair. "You're supposed to be on light duty, which means no suspect contact."

"True," Ron said with a small smile. "So if this doesn't work, you're going to be in a lot of trouble."

"You've got Jesse Lunden."

"Jesse has a lot of talent, but he doesn't have the finesse it's going to take to earn their trust. At least in the time frame we're talking about. Jesse is quick on his feet, and I'm obviously quite a bit slower, but slow and pathetic can work to your advantage sometimes." Ron could see the apprehension building on Laura's face. "This is nonnegotiable for me. Either I go in, or we don't go in at all."

"We're running out of time. How long will it take you to infiltrate?"

"Ordinarily, a few weeks of hanging out in bars and getting to know the players."

Laura groaned.

"But," Ron added, "I've already been doing that."

Laura looked up. "What?"

"In the evenings I've been hanging around a couple of bars, establishing myself."

"Why?"

"Because at the end of the day, the only person I trust to do the job right is me."

"Does your team know?"

"Not yet."

Laura ran her hand through her hair. "Just don't get yourself killed."

"I don't plan to."

"Keep me updated."

Ron stood and walked to the door. "There's a lot at stake here, Laura. I hope you know what you're doing, and that you're willing to reap the consequences."

"Or the benefits."

Jesse sat on one side of a stark white table that rested on a surprisingly shiny linoleum floor. A crisp, lemony scent filled the air. The room was empty except for one female prisoner talking with a boyfriend or husband.

The door opened, and a guard escorted Brandi by the elbow into the room. He let her go as Jesse stood. Brandi stared at him. "What are *you* doing here?"

"I wanted to talk with you."

Brandi looked suspicious.

"I want to help you."

"Yeah, right." Brandi slowly walked to the table and sat down, looking around the room, seeming to appreciate the openness of it. "What is it you really want? You need a prom date?"

Jesse sat across from her and tried to remain calm and professional. He had expected feistiness. In high school, her mouth got her into a lot of trouble. Her lips formed a stiff, embittered line across her face, causing her to look older than her thirty-four years. "Look, Brandi, I'm not sure what went down with Capps. All we know is what we found."

"So you don't believe that Mason set me up," Brandi said.

"Actually, I do. Which is why I'm here."

She leaned forward. "You're going to get me out?"

Jesse took in a deep breath, hoping he could explain all of this and make it sound appealing. "Right now your case is in the hands of the district attorney. Since you haven't posted bail, you have to stay in here until the trial. I will most likely be called as a witness."

"You'll tell them you think I was set up?"

"I'll be asked for the facts, and that's all I can give. If there's an opportunity, I can state my opinion. It'll be up to your lawyer."

"Al Hervett. The first time I met him, he had his tie tucked into his pants, and one side of his hair was sticking straight up. He smelled like he could use another drink." She looked at him. "So why are you here if you can't help me?"

"You know Mason has posted bail."

"Yeah, I know. I talked to him. He said he's working on getting me out, but I don't believe him. He doesn't care about me."

"We've been in contact with Mason. From what we can tell, he's up to no good. He's in Las Vegas, and we think he's involved in an auto-theft ring."

"That would've been handy before. It would've been pretty hard to stuff a car in my purse." She shook her head. "What a jerk. He gets out of jail and then decides to steal cars. I suppose it shouldn't surprise me. He was a loser, and I knew it. I don't know why I stayed with him." Her eyes filled with tears. "Look where it's landed me."

"I want to talk to you about helping us get Mason."

"Get Mason? What do you mean?"

"We had contact with him, but we lost it, and now we don't know where he is."

"What does that have to do with me?"

"We were hoping you might know where he is."

"If he's not at his apartment, I don't know. He got fired from the pub."

"Do you have any other way of contacting him?"

"His cell phone."

"It's disconnected."

Brandi shrugged her shoulders and avoided Jesse's eyes. "I dunno, then."

Jesse leaned in. "Brandi, if you're willing to cooperate on this, it could help your case. I can't promise you anything, okay? This isn't a ticket out of here. But it will certainly help your case at trial when I explain the lengths you went to so we could get the real bad guy."

"What lengths? What can I do?"

"Would you be willing to be a confidential informant?"

She thrust herself back in her chair and frowned like she'd just witnessed something horrifying. But she didn't say no.

"You locate Mason, help us figure out who he's connected to, and it could help your case."

Brandi's expression did all the talking. He read her train of thought like a large-print book.

"If Mason cared about you, Brandi, you'd already be out of here. This is your chance to set things right, to make him pay for setting you up."

"I don't think he realized it would be this bad."

"Who are you kidding? He wanted you to take the fall for the whole thing."

Tears dripped down Brandi's face, and she brushed them away. "I really thought he loved me. I know that it sounds stupid. I haven't had the best luck picking men." She glanced up at Jesse with an irritated scowl. "This problem dates all the way back to high school." She folded her arms. "Why should I trust you? You are, after all, a man. All men are self-ish. You used me at prom, and now you want to use me again. You're not so different from Mason, are you?"

"Brandi, I know what I did at prom, and it was horrible. But I was seventeen years old. I was an idiot back then."

"And you're not now?"

"I have a healthy respect for women. And I haven't been that lucky with love, either."

"Jesse Lunden with no love life? That is shocking."

"Look, as much as I would love to divulge all my secrets on how to stay single and lonely, I would rather get back to business. Here's the deal: you help us find Mason, and I will put in a good word about you to the DA."

She thought hard for a moment. Then suddenly she grinned.

"Okay, Jesse Lunden," she said, "I will help you. On one condition."

She wasn't exactly in the position to set conditions, but he played along. "Yes?"

"When I get out of this place, you take me on a prom date."

"What?"

"You heard me. I want a corsage, you in a tux, me in a gown, us at a fancy restaurant you can't afford. And a limo would be nice."

"Please tell me you're joking."

The grin faded. "Do I look like I'm joking? Do you have any idea how horrible it is to be dumped by your prom date the night of the prom? Can you imagine how humiliating that is?"

No imagination needed. She kept talking.

"I really had a crush on you, you know? I know I said differently. But I was so excited to be asked to the prom by Jesse Lunden, king of the jocks. I didn't feel worthy of going with you, but you asked. How could I turn you down? It was supposed to be the happiest night of my life. I drank because I was nervous. Then you dumped me five minutes into the prom."

Jesse wanted to explain that he had been scared off by all the hint dropping she did on the way to the prom about how much she wanted to find the perfect man to settle down with. That's terribly frightening to any man, but at seventeen, it's like telling a guy he's got three weeks to live.

"So that's it? That's how I can make this up to you?"

She nodded.

Jesse squeezed his eyes shut. Somehow this seemed like a really bad idea, yet if it would get him Mason, it might be worth it. But a tux? Maybe he could negotiate her down to a suit and tie. He'd have to buy one for church anyway.

"All right," he finally said.

"Good." She smiled. "It's going to feel good to get Mason back for what he did to me."

Mason wasn't the only one she was getting back.

Chapter 32

R on downed his third cup of coffee as he passively studied the meager bar crowd. The bartender, a guy named Tim, was beginning to recognize him after two weeks of regular visits.

"You want another?" he asked.

Ron turned on his barstool to face Tim. "Why not."

"Well, if you were drinking alcohol, I'd tell you it's because you have to drive home. But in your case, I'd say it's because all that caffeine is bad for your heart. At least that's what my doctor told me."

Ron laughed as Tim reached for the coffeepot. "I'll keep that in mind."

"I don't usually see many coffee drinkers in here. I keep it around for my wife. She likes to hang around here after she gets off work, but needs the caffeine to stay awake."

Tim poured Ron another cup. "You're new around here. Where are you from?"

"Chicago. My wife took off and left me with nothing. I'm starting over."

"Maybe you could use something stronger than coffee."

"Can't do liquor anymore. That's why she left me."

Tim smiled a little. "Well, you're a brave soul sitting in the middle of a bar."

"I'm not ready to start playing dominos with old people at McDonald's."

Tim laughed. "All right. I'll keep the coffee hot for you."

"Thanks."

Ron turned to watch the activity in the room. He was an expert at spotting dealers and users. He couldn't explain to Nan how he knew. He just *knew.* Big-time dealers were almost always clean-cut. They were in it only for the money. Users weren't hard to spot, for various reasons. He could also identify a con man in a crowd of twenty people. Something in his gut made the distinction. It was how he knew, all those years ago, that his partner had turned on him. Ron saw the change in his eyes. That's what Ron always studied: the eyes, the body language.

And right now, the body language of the guy sitting next to him was screaming, "Notice me!" He'd plopped down next to Ron with a mug of beer. Out of the corner of his eye, Ron saw the man staring at him. A clinger—a guy who didn't have any friends but came to bars hoping to make some. Sometimes clingers were useful. They often were familiar with other bar regulars. They liked to know other people's business. They also could be a detriment, because they couldn't read body language to save their lives, which meant they never got the hint to go away.

However, desperation could be useful in the hands of a cop. Ron took a sip of coffee and glanced at the man, who immediately offered a friendly smile. "How're you doing?" the man asked.

"Good. You hang out here a lot?"

"Yeah. Before I go to work. Night shift."

"Where do you work?"

"Caesars. In the kitchen."

Ron turned and put his arms on the bar, giving the man his full attention.

The man continued talking. "I heard you say you're not from around here."

"Chicago."

"What brought you to the desert?"

"My wife. She would have preferred I move to another continent, but she'll have to settle for a parched and dry land."

The man offered an understanding smile. "Divorced?"

"In the truest sense of the word. I always liked Las Vegas. So I took what little money I had, and I'm trying to start up a business."

"What kind of business are you in?"

"My dad owned a body shop, and I worked for him when I was younger. That's what I'm starting up. I'm still getting equipment, but I can do small repairs. And I'm always looking for parts."

The man stared into the crowd for a moment, then looked at Ron. Ron stuck out his hand. "I'm Ron, by the way."

"Doug."

"Well, Doug, it's time for an old fogy like me to get home." Ron chuckled. "Actually, I wouldn't call it home. Just a place to stay. I used to go nuts every time my wife would come home with some stupid new decoration for the house. Now I kind of miss those."

"Well, you're starting over," Doug said, raising his mug of beer. "Maybe you'll have better luck on this side of the world."

Ron nodded, then slipped his hand into his back pocket. "Here's my card. If you ever need any body work, give me a call."

"Thanks. See you around," Doug said.

Ron took his cane and headed toward the door, limping noticeably just for the effect. He could almost bet Doug would spread the news around. Soon enough, he'd be shaking hands with the real deal.

The house was unusually quiet. Nan was up later than usual, and her joints ached for her to get back to bed. But the pain was overshadowed by a quivering fear.

She hadn't cried about it yet, but with every passing day, her suspicions grew. It was nearly eleven thirty. Normally the sounds of Ron's harmonious snoring would drown out the hum of the air conditioner. Tonight, though, that's all she heard, until she opened the hall closet door, which let out its faithful squeak.

A musty odor floated out, reminding her she should clean it soon. She put boxes and sacks aside, mostly Christmas decorations and other rarely used items. She crouched, then against her better judgment, kneeled as if she were going to pray. She might have to petition for intervention in order to stand back up.

She'd seen the signs, but didn't want to believe them. Ron said he wasn't doing undercover work, and she wanted to trust him. But her gut told her something different. Ron often said undercover work was a young man's game. Even when he was in his late thirties, it seemed as if he'd outgrown it, but he stayed for a while longer.

There was no way to know if that had anything to do with Ron's partner losing his mind. But Nan couldn't help thinking that if Ron had gotten out sooner, Terry Bingham would've followed, and nothing would've happened to him.

Terry and Ron had been partners for many years, doing undercover work separately and together. Terry's wife, Melissa, was Nan's closest friend. Melissa was with Nan the night things fell apart.

The boys had been working a drug case for nearly eleven months. Terry had gone deep cover for weeks, and it looked as though they were going to bring down a huge operation that included corrupt politicians and government officials. They'd been using an informant, Jana, who had gone to jail on unrelated drug charges, but swore she could get them names and numbers of the big guns. It almost worked.

They didn't count on Terry falling for Jana. And they didn't know Jana was romantically involved with one of the bad guys. It became a complicated, emotional mess. Ron confronted Terry, and to Ron's shock, Terry pulled a gun on him. Ron shot first. The bullet hit Terry's spine, and in an instant, Ron's partner was a quadriplegic.

Nan broke the news to Melissa. Ron was never the same. He retired from undercover work and started racing cars. It took years for Nan to feel like a part of Ron was back. Although a different man than she married, he had found his way back to her side. Eventually, his sense of humor returned. Life would never be normal again, she knew, but at least it had quality and purpose. She could live with that.

Last week, while he sat on the back porch waiting for Nan to bring out their dinner, she saw certain expressions, glimpses of his game face. Hints of the man who would take Ron's place when he used to transition into a case. She passed it off as coincidence.

But she couldn't pass off the half-dozen additional times she had seen it since.

Then, two nights ago Ron said, "I can't sleep. I'm going to go watch some TV." Normally after Nan mumbled for him to keep the volume down, she would roll back over and fall asleep. Not that night. She lay in bed, her mind whispering with paranoia. She got up to go talk with him. As she shuffled down the hallway, she laughed to herself because she could tell by the sound he was watching a cooking show.

But then she heard a click. And another click. And another. She stopped and listened.

He was dry-firing his gun. Over and over and over. She turned and went back to bed, burrowing in the covers, refusing to admit that her fears had come true. He always had trouble sleeping when he was doing under-cover work. He always dry-fired his gun when he was having trouble sleeping.

Kneeling at the closet now, Nan knew how to confirm it. Back when their kids lived at home, Ron kept his personal guns in a safe. But now they were in a padded carrying case.

Nan tugged at the zipper and opened the case. She covered her mouth, fought the coming tears. Even in the shadowy closet, she could see three guns where four should be. The three remaining had been recently cleaned and oiled.

The sound of Ron's truck turning into the driveway broke the heavy silence. She quickly zipped the case and put it back in the corner of the closet. Then she shoved all the boxes and sacks back in, closing the door just as his keys rattled against the front door. She hurried down the hallway, her knees cracking, trying to keep her footsteps quiet. She crawled back into bed, rolled over to face the wall, and threw the covers over her shoulder.

His footsteps stopped in the hallway. She heard the creak of the closet door and some rummaging. After a moment, the door closed again, and he walked toward the bedroom.

Nan shut her eyes and slowed her breathing, as if she were asleep. Soon enough, Ron was in bed with her, carefully lifting up the covers, trying not to wake her. And within minutes, he was asleep.

"You did what?" Dozer suddenly didn't look the least bit sleepy. He sat up in the deck chair. "Please tell me you're kidding."

"Why would I be kidding?"

"Because that's something you would kid about." Dozer blinked. "You really did that?"

"You're being a little melodramatic about it, don't you think?"

"You just broke the golden rule."

"That I should love people as much as I love myself?" Jesse smiled. "That's going to be difficult."

Dozer scowled. "The golden rule of using informants."

"Which is?"

"Don't play stupid."

"That's a good rule."

"Stop joking around. You never, *ever* use an informant you have a personal relationship with. You know that."

Jesse leaned back and crossed his ankles. "You're overreacting. It's not like I'm using my ex-wife."

"Doesn't matter. You simply don't use informants where there's a personal history."

"I would hardly call five minutes at the prom a personal history."

"Maybe not for you, but what about for her?"

"She's already made it clear that I'm going to owe her."

Dozer threw up his hands. "That's the last thing you want."

"It's harmless," Jesse said. "She just wants me to buy her a corsage and take her to dinner when this is all over with, assuming I'll be able to get the DA to reduce the charges."

"And assuming she'll be able to help us out. What makes you think she can?"

"She's been in contact with Mason. Mason checks in with his grandfather every week. No exceptions. She said his grandfather would tell her how to contact him. I guess while she was dating Mason, she made the old guy coffeecake."

Dozer shook his head. "You're betting this whole deal on coffeecake?"

"Never underestimate the power of cinnamon and sugar. The point is, she can lead us back to Mason. Someone got to Mason first. And that someone probably has a lot of influence over Mason, which means we have a good reason to find out who it is. And yes, I realize this whole thing would've been easier had I shown Brandi the night of her life back in nineteen eighty-seven."

"I don't know, man. It's always risky using a female informant."

"They can be really good informants."

"Yeah. Unless their hormones are all out of whack. Remember that one chick who would cry every time we tried to send her in to make some contact? I've never seen anything like that in my life. She couldn't even tell us why she was crying. I swore after that I would never use another female informant."

"Please," Jesse said. "You have a short memory. It was all solved with chocolate." Jesse turned to him. "Dozer, this is our chance. If we make a big bust on this thing, we have a chance to work some really great narcotics cases in Las Vegas."

"We're not out in the cold yet. Yeager's got a plan. A good *by the book* plan." Dozer's eyes widened. "Oh no."

"What?"

"You've got that look."

"What look?"

"The one where you throw the book out the window."

"In case you or Yeager haven't noticed, we don't have much time to spare."

Dozer sighed and settled into his chair again. "I don't have narcotics ambitions like you do. That's why I joined this task force. Eventually, I want to leave undercover." He glanced toward the patio door. "Sarah worries about me all the time. I've had my days of excitement and adventure. It's time for a new chapter."

"I can't believe what I'm hearing," Jesse said. "You're gonna do some lame desk job?"

"That's not what I said. But my priorities have shifted. I want to come home at night to my children, be there for them. Who knows? Maybe I'll make lieutenant someday."

Jesse kept his mouth shut.

Dozer continued. "Look, man, why don't you put some of that energy into helping Mack? She's excited about undercover work. Maybe she could be good at this."

Jesse stared at the night sky. "Mack's an enigma."

"She's capable. She's shown us that already."

"She's capable of reciting the Bible like it's the Miranda rights. I'd like to remind her she has the right to remain silent."

"Dude, I don't get you. I mean, you're practically glued to Kyle, wanting these blessings and prayers and—"

"That's different. I'm not pushing my views on anybody. I don't sit there and order Kyle to go around the room and pray for everyone."

"Neither does Mack."

"Why are you so insistent on taking her side?"

He shrugged. "I'm not taking her side. I just think you're too hard on her, that's all."

"Well, that's the business. People were hard on me, and so it goes."

"All right, man. I can see there's no changing your mind. What did Sergeant Yeager say when you told him you talked to Brandi?"

"Uh…I haven't exactly told him."

"What?"

"I know what he'd say."

"You're going behind his back? That's career suicide!"

"I just want to get her out and see what kind of connection she can make. If she scores, then I'll let Sergeant Yeager know. If not, nothing's lost."

"That's going to send him through the roof."

"Maybe. But I'm willing to bet he's as eager to break through on this case as I am. He'll reprimand me on procedure, and then we'll do what we came here to do."

"Whatever, man. But we never talked about this."

"Yeah, I know."

Dozer stood. "I gotta get inside. I've been gone too much lately and Sarah's tired. We need to spend some time together."

"Right. Sure." Dozer followed Jesse into the house and then walked him to the front door. "I'll see you tomorrow."

Maybe he was a one-man show now. That was fine with him. He worked best by himself. Backed up by Elvis, Kyle, and the bullet.

Chapter 33

Ron watched Hank and Wiz remove the bumper from Ruth's Cadillac. Mack stood beside him with a clipboard. "The car's in good hands with Hank," Mack said with a smile. "He knows how to be careful."

"I'm glad he's here. He's moving things along quickly. When are we expecting the totaled cars from the insurance companies?"

"Should be in today, but they haven't exactly been on schedule," Mack said. "I talked to someone named Lisa who was certain they were on their way."

"Make sure everyone's wearing their shop uniforms. We should be expecting business anytime."

"Wiz and I spent the afternoon passing out the fliers where you told us to. And Hank's been giving Wiz, Dozer, and me a crash course in body shop."

"Is Hank comfortable dealing with the customers?" asked Ron.

"Yeah. He's enjoying this. He should be fine."

"Things could happen quickly. We need to be ready."

"We're ready," Mack said. "Hey, Sarge, I wanted to thank you."

"For what?"

"Giving me a chance. I know you took a gamble on me."

"Mack, you're a fine officer. With some additional training, you'll be ready for more undercover work."

Mack's smile faded. "Additional training? You said you didn't have any official training. You just got dropped into this and figured it out on your own."

"That was a long time ago. Things are different."

"What's different?"

Ron stopped watching Hank work and looked at Mack. "Jesse went to an undercover school. Training is a good thing. And by the way, where is Jesse?"

"Sergeant Yeager, I've always believed in gaining experience. My parents kind of sheltered me. Their intentions were good, but I had a lot to learn, and quickly, before becoming a police officer. I've gained a lot of experience on the streets. I think I'm ready for this. I proved it to you once. Do you think I can't do this?"

"Did I say that?"

"No, but I can read it on your face."

So she could read body language. Huh. That was a plus. She needed a lot more pluses.

"I'm not like Jesse. Believe me, I realize that. But I have my own strengths."

"What makes you think Jesse's got it all together?"

"He's confident. He can walk into any room and own it."

"And you think that's a good thing?"

"Well, you've got to make the bad guys think you're a bad guy, right? You've got to make them afraid."

Ron gave her a gentle smile. "Not all criminals have huge egos. Sometimes it's more effective to play the guy who doesn't seem like a threat. If you play it weak, they think they're running the show, and that's what you want. You want them to run their show right in front of you. In law enforcement, you have to find your niche. Not every cop is a great street officer. And not every cop is a great detective. You have to find your love. I knew a guy who hopped from one job to the next before landing in the K9 unit. He's been there a long time now."

She put her hands on her hips, and her eyes shimmered with disappointment. "Why don't you think I can do this? I want to know."

Ron bit his lip. How could he put it gently? A long stretch of silence passed, but Mack wasn't going to back down. Ron drew in a deep breath. "Mack, you've got more character in your little finger than most people have in their entire body."

"But?"

"You're dedicated to your faith. I completely respect that. However, you've got to be able to separate that from your work, and I don't think you can. Your faith encompasses you."

"Doesn't it encompass you? We share the same faith."

Ron looked at his feet. That was a difficult question. "I had to separate the two a long time ago, Mack. The people I became while doing undercover weren't real. My faith *is* real. I became a Christian when I was twenty-four years old, right before I started doing undercover work. But when I did undercover work, I had to become a completely different person to stay sane and to stay alive."

"Those two people never crossed paths? Not once?"

Ron paused. Who was he kidding? For every undercover deal he did, he lost a little piece of himself. It was a necessary sacrifice.

"I respect you," Ron evaded.

"But not as an undercover officer."

Ron felt horrible. He hated to shatter the dreams of a young officer, especially someone as nice as Mack. But he also couldn't live with himself if he got her hopes up on false pretenses. "I'm sorry."

Mack folded her arms. "I'm going to prove you wrong." Ron started to interrupt her, but she said, "There were plenty of people in the Bible nobody believed in. I know I'm different. Nobody has to tell me that. I figured it out a long time ago. Most of the time, it hasn't made my life easy, but—"

The sound of a phone ringing ended their conversation. The clank and whir of the body shop suddenly quieted. Hank and Wiz looked at Ron. He took a deep breath and motioned with his hands to keep the noise level going. He walked over to the phone and answered it. "Body shop."

"Ron Taylor?"

"Yeah. Who's this?"

"My name is Bobby. I got word you were looking for some body parts."

"What've you got?"

"What do you need?" Bobby asked.

That was a good sign. They'd ask for specifics to make sure the shop was for real.

"Parts without much trouble, if you know what I mean. I know I've got a Chrysler minivan coming in and a Toyota Sienna. What can you get me?"

"I'll have plenty for you to choose from if you don't feel the need to bury me in paperwork."

"I pay in cash and don't ask questions. And as long as you don't ask questions, we should be fine."

"We meet in person first. I'm in this for the long run. Let's just say I need a business partner. "

Ron took a deep breath. "Look, I don't know you. How do I know you're not setting me up?"

"That's why I want to meet you in person. Make sure we understand each other."

Ron let some silence go by.

Bobby spoke up. "I can take my parts elsewhere. But if we work together we could both make a lot of money."

"You working with anybody else?"

"Not at the moment."

"You know where Teddy's is?"

"Yeah."

"Meet me there at seven. You'll be able to spot me. I use a cane."

"Right."

Ron hung up the phone and turned to the eager crowd. "Looks like we got us a hot one."

Brandi rolled down the window, stretched her neck, and thrust her face into the wind. She closed her eyes and smiled, her hair rippling in the breeze.

"You want to eat bugs or something?" Jesse asked.

She pulled herself back into the truck. "Just enjoying my freedom."

"Don't get too excited. It's temporary."

"The DA will listen to you though, right?"

"You know I can't guarantee anything. Connect us with Mason, and we'll see. Tell me who he was running with."

"I don't know names. He didn't talk about that stuff. All I know was that he was going to Vegas a lot."

"You don't know what for?"

She sighed and rolled up the window. "Mason is a dreamer. He always thought he could do bigger and better, but he couldn't shake bad habits. Every time he'd get something good going, like the job at the pub, he'd blow it by doing something stupid." She glared at Jesse. "Don't give me that look."

"What look? I'm watching the road."

"You look down on me. You think I'm a loser for staying with this guy."

"I didn't say that."

"You don't have to say it. Look, Mason took care of me. Maybe he had a bit of a temper, but that was his only problem."

Jesse glanced sideways at her. "Mason's got more problems than a bad temper. But it's none of my business. I just need to find him." Jesse pointed to a street sign. "Is this where I turn?"

She nodded and Jesse headed down Miller Street.

"Eight-thirteen," she said. "There it is. The seventh one in this row." Some of the trailers were decorated with plants and flowers, but eight-thirteen was stark and white and as plain as they come, except for the metal bars across the windows.

"What's his name again?"

"Charles."

"All right. Remember, I'm a friend from high school; we were great buddies, etcetera, etcetera. I'm just trying to get back in touch with him."

Brandi started to squirm. "Um…there's something you should know about Charles."

"What?" Jesse asked.

"Well, you're probably going to have to repeat the questions a lot."

"Does he have Alzheimer's?"

"Not exactly."

"I thought you told me he would know where Mason is."

"He should know. I'm just saying, we're going to be here awhile."

"What's wrong with him?"

Brandi hedged and looked toward the trailer. "You're just going to have to see it for yourself."

Rhyne threw down his cards. "I'm out." He scooted back from the poker table and turned, hoping to find a lovely young lady carrying a tray of drinks. Of course, any lovely young lady, with or without drinks, would do. He wasn't one for premature celebrations, but this time, he was almost certain the deal was sealed. One day down to the Mexican border. One day back. And he was on his way to becoming a wealthy man.

"You look like you could use something to fill your time," a voice said from behind him.

Rhyne turned. "Bobby."

"I knew I'd find you here."

"You were looking for me?"

"Well, I have to come looking for you these days. You cut us off."

"Nothing personal," Rhyne said smoothly. "I'm just going a different direction, that's all."

"With your clothes, too, it seems." Bobby looked him over. "Luckily, I'm not one to hold grudges."

"Why would you have a grudge against me? You're doing fine without me."

"News gets around, doesn't it?" Bobby studied the large gold ring on his own finger, twisting it a few times. "Actually, I have a business proposal for you."

Rhyne smiled politely. Any business that Bobby was proposing couldn't possibly be better than what he had now. But he held out his hands expectantly anyway. "Are you going to keep me guessing?"

Bobby looked pleased. "I met with a guy tonight at Teddy's. He's opening up a body shop on the west side of town."

"I'm not in that business anymore."

"Hear me out. Kind of a desperate old guy, if you ask me. His wife divorced him after thirty-something years. Moved here to start over. He's willing to pay cash for parts."

"What kinds of parts?"

"He's got a Toyota Sienna with heavy front damage, including a busted up windshield, a Honda Civic with rear-end damage, and a Chrysler minivan that he says should probably be totaled, but he's going to give it a shot."

"What's the year on the Chrysler?"

"Two thousand and two."

Rhyne put his fingers to his chin, rubbing the stubble he forgot to shave.

"This guy's willing to pay top dollar."

"What do you get out of it?" Rhyne asked.

"A small finder's fee."

"How small is small?"

"Twenty percent. This guy will only deal with me. He doesn't even have to know you exist." Bobby's eager eyes glanced around the room. "We can make a lot of money off this guy."

Rhyne could always be tempted by cash. His arrangement with the minivan was working nicely, but what would the owners do if he just stole it? Call the police and tell them that the guy who was giving them drugs in exchange for borrowing their car to go get more drugs has buckled on their deal and stripped it for parts?

"I can hook him up with that Chrysler," Rhyne finally said.

"When?"

"Tell him we'll bring it by tomorrow morning for him to look at, but he can't have it for three more days."

"We?" Bobby asked.

"I want to come along, check this guy out. You'll do all the talking. I'll just hang back and observe. And yes, you'll still get your cut." He wasn't about to let the van out of his sight.

"Don't spread the word, okay, man? I mean, this guy's just starting out. He's gonna need a lot of parts, and if we get him what he needs, then we make a lot of money."

"This is a one-time deal for me. I've got a car he needs, and we can do business, but after that, he's all yours."

Bobby shrugged. "Whatever, man."

"Meet me at the corner tomorrow at nine."

Bobby looked at Rhyne's suit. "Whatever you're doing, it must be paying well. Never seen you dressed like that."

"You can't stay stuck in one thing forever."

Bobby grinned. "I know, which is why we gotta move on this thing."

"All right. I'll see you in the morning. Keep this between us."

Bobby nodded and disappeared behind the slot machines. Rhyne couldn't wipe the smile off his face. What a way to top it all off. He would consider it a little bonus.

Finally, a woman walked by with her tray of drinks. Rhyne snatched one, toasted the air, and headed for the blackjack table.

Chapter 34

C harles was barely five and a half feet tall and so skinny that his ribcage showed through his ratty undershirt. He had white and gray hair that stood up like he'd just been electrocuted. Every time he spoke, he pulled at his chin like there was a beard to tug on, but there wasn't. This was the first of many things that Charles seemed to think existed. He was explaining to Jesse why humans can't see the spaceships that are landing in the desert, and what that had to do with the four moons of Jupiter, when he suddenly stood, grunted, and walked to the closest of two small windows in his trailer. He turned the blinds and then yanked closed drapes that were thick enough "to block the rays of the bright star Sirius." He slowly opened his front door, looked outside, then quickly shut and locked it.

"Sorry 'bout that," Charles said, sitting back down in his recliner. "Sometimes in the evening right before sunset a few of them get restless, and they start wandering around." He noticed Jesse's baffled expression. "The aliens."

That clears things up. Jesse glanced at Brandi, who only shrugged and smiled.

"Charles," Jesse said quietly. The first time Jesse had used the man's name, Charles shushed them and explained how "they" have high-tech equipment that can listen through walls. Jesse resisted the urge to explain that nearly every law enforcement agency in the country had that same ability, but that would have done little to ease this man's paranoia. "I need you to listen to me very carefully. We're trying to find your grandson, Mason."

Charles's face lit up with delight. He pulled out a drawer in a nearby table. Then he held up a small picture frame. "Mason, he's special. I really enjoy that boy. His father wasn't much to write home about, but Mason turned out okay. He comes to see me every once in a while." Charles leaned forward with peering eyes. He spoke in a hushed voice. "I tried to explain it all to him, but I don't think he understands."

"Understands what, sir?" Jesse asked.

"That they're after me now, not him. He got abducted when he was eight. Doesn't remember it, of course. They gave him some memory-blocking serum. But when I described the inside of the spacecraft, he said it sounded familiar." Charles's eyebrows raised to indicate this was an important fact. Jesse nodded and tried to look fascinated instead of befuddled. "It was many years later before I even spoke 'bout it with Mason. His parents didn't want me to see him. I understood. We all knew I could be abducted at any moment."

"Um, yes... Well, again, about Mason. Do you know where to find him?"

"If I give you his coordinates, they'll hear us," he whispered.

Jesse tried to dial back the desperation in his voice. "Maybe you could write it down on a piece of paper," Jesse whispered back.

"Oh," Charles said, pulling at his imaginary beard. "That might be a good idea."

Charles reached into the drawer next to him and pulled out a small notepad and pencil. Jesse and Brandi watched him as he held the notepad close to his face and wrote slowly and carefully. Jesse gave Brandi a relieved smile, which she returned.

"Now," he said, ripping the piece of paper off the pad, "you can't, for any reason, let anybody know where he is. He's hiding. He has to, or they'll be back to get him."

"Is that what he tells you? That he's in hiding?" Jesse asked.

Charles nodded with a sad sigh. "I almost lost him once. I don't want to lose him again. I tell him that I understand. Every once in a while, he still comes by. Mostly I talk to him by telephone, which I rigged so it couldn't be tapped. Mason doesn't understand how dangerous his cell phone is, but I've talked until I'm blue in the face about it, so I guess he's never going to change." Charles stared at the piece of paper in his hand and, with a little reluctance, handed it over to Jesse.

Jesse read the note and folded it, stuffing it into his pocket. "You'll have to excuse me." Jesse stood. "I need to make a phone call." Jesse pulled out his cell phone. "I'm going to step outside for a moment."

"No, you're not!" Charles barked, startling Brandi. "What are you, crazy? Why not handcuff yourself to the roof with the television antennas and scream derogatory remarks about their technology? No. Go to the back bedroom. The phone there is safe to use. Never underestimate what they can do with a television antenna." He pointed to his television. "That's why I have cable. You got a satellite dish at home? You might as well pack your bags, because they're going to zap you up."

Without enthusiasm, Jesse said, "Oh. They don't *beam* people up anymore?"

"They've found it can cause second-degree burns on human feet."

"Right."

Jesse excused himself to the back bedroom, closed the door, turned the lock, and opened his cell phone. He dialed a number and held the phone close to his ear as he turned away from the door.

"Hello?"

"Kyle. It's Jesse."

"Oh, hi, Jesse."

"What are you doing at this moment?"

There was a long pause, and Jesse thought he could hear music in the background.

"Hello? You there?"

"I'm here."

"Then what are you doing?"

Kyle chuckled. "Well, my friend, I'm taking your advice."

"What advice?"

"About the band. I'm going to hire a band."

"You're going to do what?"

"Hire a band. Serenade her with a band. Well, more like a quartet. I'm thinking a couple of violins and a flute, but—"

"Would you like to know what I'm doing?"

"What?"

"I'm trying to track down Mason Capps. I've located his grandfather, who keeps in regular touch with him."

"That sounds promising."

"Doesn't it? In fact, his grandfather wrote down the exact address where I can find Mason."

"Great, then you can go get him?"

"There's one problem. Mason is in Callisto."

"Is that in Nevada?"

"No. It's four billion light years away. One of Jupiter's moons, and unfortunately my spacecraft is broken."

"Is this a cop joke? I love cop jokes. But I don't get it."

"We had a deal, Kyle. You were going to pray for me, and I was going to give you advice on how to handle the ladies. You're not holding up your end of the deal."

"I prayed for you this morning."

"When Chaplain Greer prayed for me, things went well. I never had to deal with aliens."

"Jesse, I'm not doing anything less than I do for my own congregation. I'm praying for you, praying God's Word over you, especially the psalm that you like so much. I mean, if you'd like to come in and talk about this—"

"I don't want to talk about it, Kyle. I want things to go smoothly. Are you praying that? That things would go smoothly?"

"Um…well, I can try. It's not like there's any guarantee, though."

Jesse's free hand balled into a fist. "Then you're not doing it right."

"Jesse, you sound very irritated. Why don't you meet me in the morning? We can talk through some of this and find out—"

"I don't want to talk! I want to find Mason Capps!"

"Um—"

"You know what? Forget it. Just forget it."

"What are you going to do about the grandfather?"

"I don't know, Kyle. What would Jesus do?"

Kyle paused. Leave it to him to give that serious thought. "He'd probably cast out a demon, but I can't be certain—"

"Right. Well, you'll have to excuse me. Radioactive particles could hit at any moment." Jesse switched off his phone and returned to the small living area where Charles was discussing Area 52.

"Isn't it Area 51?" Jesse interrupted, crumpling the map Charles had drawn him.

"The Area 51 people don't even know Area 52 exists."

"Let's go."

"Wait," Brandi said hastily. "Let's not give up yet." She looked at Charles with desperate eyes. "Charles, I need to find Mason. You know how close we were. Is there anything you can tell us that might help us find him? Like a phone number?"

"He calls me. The number's always blocked." Charles smiled. "I taught him that."

Brandi scooted to the edge of her seat and locked eyes with the old man. "Maybe he told you who he's been hanging around?"

Charles shook his head.

Brandi looked like she could cry at any moment. Jesse wasn't sure if it was a ploy for information or if it was because she thought Jesse would haul her back to jail if they couldn't find Mason. "Tell me the truth, Charles," she said. "Is there another woman in his life?"

Charles reached out and took her hand. "I know this is hard to understand, but the aliens are asexual. You have nothing to worry about."

Brandi looked at Jesse like she'd run out of ideas.

"Has he brought anyone when he's visited you?" Jesse asked.

Something registered with Charles. "Well, yes. He did. The last time he came by. There was a man with him."

Brandi and Jesse exchanged looks. "What was his name?" Jesse asked.

"Ryan." Charles looked certain.

"Did he have a last name?"

Charles started to speak, then paused, then started to speak again, only to be interrupted by another pause.

"Yes?" Jesse urged.

"It seemed like he liked Jell-O."

Jesse sighed. "Terrific. We've got it narrowed down to Ryan who likes Jell-O. What flavor?"

"Wait," Charles said, holding up a finger. "It rhymed with Jell-O. That's it. The best way to remember someone's name is to think of something it rhymes with. It's harder to do with alien names because they don't use vowels, but…" He looked up at Jesse. "I don't remember what his last name is. Just that it rhymed with Jell-O."

Brandi stood, glancing at Jesse. "That's good, right? You've got a database of some sort, don't you? You can type in that information and see what comes up?"

"Yes. It's called a Rhyming Computer. It comes in very handy when you've got this sort of information, or if you're trying to write a poem." He took Brandi by the arm. "Come on. We're leaving."

"Wait," she said as Jesse escorted her out the front door. "We can get more information out of him. It just takes time."

"Thanks for your help," Jesse said to the old man as he stared at them through the screen door. "Get in the truck, Brandi."

When he climbed into his seat, he was greeted with a tirade. "So that's it? That's the end? You're supposed to be good at interrogating people! What was that?"

"I'm sorry," Jesse said, glancing sideways at her. "They don't teach UFO interrogation until you get to the FBI."

"I'm not kidding."

Jesse pulled away from the curb. "Neither was he. That's the problem. He's a crazy old man."

"He didn't used to be that bad. I mean, he's always been into conspiracy theories, but I guess it's getting worse."

"What's getting worse is the fact that we have no credible information."

"What about Ryan?"

"Yes. Ryan who loves Jell-O. I'll see what I can do with that."

"His last name rhymes with Jell-O."

"I'd have more luck if his last name rhymed with pudding."

"You know, you were a lot better looking and a lot nicer back in high school, so that should tell you what I think of you now." She slumped in her seat and looked out the window with an icy stare. "Are you taking me back to jail?"

"I don't know. What else can you tell me about where Mason might be?"

"There's a bar."

"Yes?"

"Cracker Jack's."

"I know it. Tiny place. Does he go there a lot?"

"He goes there when he's depressed. He hasn't mentioned it in a while, though."

"When he's depressed? That's it?"

She shrugged. "I don't know why. I just know that's what he does."

He didn't know if Mason was depressed, but Jesse sure was well on his way.

Chapter 35

Ron checked his watch. It was nearly nine, late enough in the morning that even Jesse should be awake. "Where is he?" Nobody seemed to know, no matter how many times he asked. "Did you call him again?" Ron asked Dozer.

"I've called five times. You want me to run to the house, see if he's there?"

"No. Forget it. We've got to focus. Mack, you'll man the counter. Hank, Dozer, Wiz, you guys will be in the garage." Ron glanced into the garage. One of the vans arrived yesterday. It was already pulled apart, and the front end was smashed up. "When he comes in, it's fine to look up from what you're doing in the garage, but just act like you don't care who is coming and going. You've got a job to do." He looked at his watch again. "All right. We've got ten minutes. Wiz, make a final check on the cameras and recording equipment. The rest of you, position yourselves where you need to be."

Ron went into the small office to prepare and pray. This wasn't a particularly dangerous situation, but with one slip, they could blow their cover and scare the guy off. Ron wasn't too worried about that happening, though. Bobby seemed like the kind of guy who jumped first and looked later.

He closed his eyes, trying to calm his nerves. Why were his hands shaking? Guilt washed over him. He knew some of his nervousness was because he'd gone back undercover without his wife's blessing. Nan wouldn't have understood. How could he explain he was trying to keep them safe? Or that he was, in reality, doing something he shouldn't by agreeing to help Laura bust up a narcotics ring?

Nothing about this felt right. Everything was getting too complicated.

He closed his eyes and asked God for protection and wisdom, but that's all he had a chance to pray before his phone rang.

"Yeah?"

"Hey, Ron." It was Mack. There was a slight strain in her voice. "A guy named Bobby is here to see you."

"Be right out." Ron sucked in a breath, grabbed his cane, added the extra limp, and walked to the front desk. Bobby stood outside, next to the door. As he stepped into the morning air, he noticed a guy standing by a maroon Chrysler minivan. "Who's that?" Ron asked.

"He's okay. I can vouch for him."

"We had an understanding. Nobody else was supposed to be involved." Ron looked over Bobby's shoulder and gave the man a hard stare. The man pretended to be interested in what was going on in the garage, then walked that direction away from the van. Ron could hear the equipment noise and the chatter between the guys in the garage.

"Look, he's got a van. Just what you're looking for. The Chrysler."

"Really." Ron glanced over at the van.

Bobby smiled. "I've got good connections."

"What kind of condition is it in?" Ron said.

"Nearly perfect. But we can't deliver it to you for three days. After that, you get first pick of whatever you want off of it."

Ron stepped up to the van and looked it over. "Bring me in the hood, the stereo equipment, the engine. Bring it all. But no glass. No doors."

Ron looked at the stranger one more time, just to make everyone nervous. The man stomped out his cigarette, stuffed his hands in his pockets, and studied the activity in front of him.

"That'll work," Ron said.

"Great. You'll be dealing with me."

"Don't leave me hanging," Ron said. "I don't want to have to go scrambling for parts. If you don't deliver, we're done doing business."

"I'll see you in three days," Bobby said and turned to walk toward the van. Ron went back inside, catching Mack's eye as she looked up from the computer. He gave her a small smile and slipped into the office to wait for the men to leave.

Jesse slowed as he noticed the maroon minivan parked outside the garage. Sergeant Yeager was talking to a red-haired man, but he didn't seem to notice Jesse. Jesse parked as far away from the garage as he could. He had no idea what was going on, but didn't want to blow something that might be going down. He got out of his truck, grabbed some papers from his passenger seat, and pretended to look through them while secretly scanning the scene. A second stranger watched the activity in the garage. When they both started to head back to the van, Jesse carried his papers and walked slowly toward the shop. He listened intently as he neared the van, hoping to overhear a conversation.

"We got it," one said. "We just gotta show up with it on Friday."

"That seemed too easy," the other man said.

"It's easy because I made it easy. He trusts me. And you should, too, if you want this deal."

Jesse kept his head down and pretended to flip through the pages as he walked, when he heard it. The guy with the red hair seemed to call the other man Ryan. Or something that sounded like Ryan, anyway. His words were somewhat obscured by the sound of crunching gravel.

Neither of the men seemed interested in Jesse as they drove off. He went in the garage and found Hank under the car. Wiz and Dozer were messing with a door. "What just happened?" Jesse asked.

Dozer stood. "Where have you been? I've been calling you all morning."

Jesse checked his cell phone. He'd turned it off last night to save batteries and forgot to turn it back on. "What happened?"

"You would know if you were where you were supposed to be," a voice said.

Jesse turned to face Sergeant Yeager, who didn't look pleased. "All this 'busy work' you claim I'm making you do scored us a suspect, who is planning to deliver stolen parts on Friday."

"I'm sorry. I overslept."

"Out late last night?" The sarge didn't wait for an answer. He walked back into the office. Dozer shrugged. Inside, Mack was making coffee.

"You missed it!" Mack said as Jesse walked through the door. "It was great. Everything went down like it was supposed to."

Jesse looked back toward the office where Sergeant Yeager had disappeared. Should he tell him about his hunch that the two Ryans might be connected? Maybe it was a coincidence, maybe not. Suddenly he wasn't so sure a procedural reprimand was all Sergeant Yeager would give if he told him how he'd gotten his information.

"You okay?' Mack asked. "You look worried."

Jesse blinked away the dismay. "What's Sergeant Yeager been like today?"

Mack glanced to the doors then back at Jesse. "Fine. Seemed a little uptight, but he's been pretty focused on preparing for the meeting with our guy. The whole thing took ten minutes. Amazing." Mack looked curious. "You don't look okay."

Jesse leaned on the counter and gave Mack his full attention. "Not having Chaplain Greer around is throwing me. Kyle's an okay stand-in, but it's not the same. Things seem to be going really bad instead of really good. Maybe Kyle doesn't have the experience Chaplain Greer has."

"Jesse, it's not about experience. God is capable, and that's all that matters. The Bible tells us to give him our worries, so whatever you're worried about, you should talk to God."

Jesse gave her a short smile. "Yeah, well, I went behind Sergeant Yeager's back to get some information I thought we could use. How does God feel about liars?"

"The same way he feels about magic bullets."

"I wish I could see the world like you do. It must be some kind of trip to be inside your head." Jesse stared at the counter. "And I was pretty rude to Kyle yesterday too. I was mad and I took it out on him."

"I talked to Kyle today. He seemed fine, so don't worry about it."

"You did? When?"

"Maybe an hour or two ago. He called to ask me what kind of music I liked."

Jesse stared at her. "He… It's you?"

"What's me?" Mack asked, her eyes widening.

"Nothing. I, um, better go talk to Sergeant Yeager."

Mack touched his arm. "Jesse, everybody lies. It's human nature. If you go in there and tell Sergeant Yeager you're sorry, I think that will go a long way in patching things up. It probably wouldn't hurt to call Kyle, either. You'll feel better. Every time I apologize to you, I feel better."

If he didn't tell Sergeant Yeager about what he'd heard from Mason's grandfather, they might miss an important connection. Maybe Mack was onto something. If he went in and apologized first, maybe Sarge would be less likely to explode. Still, Jesse couldn't shake the disappointment in Sergeant Yeager's eyes just moments ago.

"Go ahead," Mack said warmly. "He's a reasonable man. He'll understand."

"You really think so?"

She nodded. "Once you sincerely apologize, there's nothing else you can do. And people grow as much by forgiving as they do by apologizing. Needless to say, I've been growing like a weed," she grinned.

Jesse felt a tiny surge of courage. Mack made it look so easy. He made a mistake. Everybody makes mistakes. Maybe, just maybe, this mistake would pay off. He walked around the counter and pushed open the door.

"You did *what?*"

Ron didn't need Jesse to repeat himself. He'd thoroughly explained it in three short, rapid-fire sentences. "I'm sorry," Jesse said, clasping his hands awkwardly in front of him.

"I can't believe you would do something like this."

"If you'll just let me explain—"

"There's nothing to explain. You disobeyed a direct order."

"Because you made an irrational decision!" Jesse's attempt at humility landed with a thud on the floor. "You had no reason not to use my informant. It was a solid lead. I know her, and I was sure she could at least—"

"You know her?"

Jesse paused. Ron stared at him, demanding an explanation.

"From high school," Jesse said hastily. "We barely knew each other."

"You went behind my back to get an informant, and then you broke the golden rule of using informants?"

"I've got good information on Mason Capps. That's why I came in here."

"I thought it was to apologize."

Jesse sighed. "Will you at least listen to what I have to say?"

Ron leaned back in his chair, folding his arms together and tapping his foot against the carpet.

"It's kind of a long story, but the gist of it is that Brandi Brown, Mason's former girlfriend, said that Mason keeps in regular contact with his grandfather. She knew where to find the grandfather, so I took Brandi with me to see what kind of information we could get out of him."

"And?"

"He came up with a name. Ryan. A guy Mason brought around once before."

"Does Ryan have a last name?"

Jesse hesitated.

"Well?"

"All he could remember was that it rhymed with...um...Jell-O."

"Terrific," Ron said. "So a fellow that rhymes with Jell-O. And the cow jumped over the moon." Jesse was getting upset, but Ron didn't really care. He knew Jesse was cocky, but he hadn't expected him to pull a stunt like this.

"The reason I'm telling you this," Jesse said, "is because I drove up when you were talking to the red-haired guy."

"I didn't see you."

"I saw the van and parked on the other side of the garage. I thought something might be going down. Did you see the other man?"

"Yes."

"I overheard the red-haired guy talking to him, and he called him Ryan. Or something like it."

"Something like it?"

Jesse seemed confused by his own words. "No, I think it was Ryan. I'm almost certain. Could be the same guy, right?"

"Where is the informant?"

"At a motel. She's willing to cooperate. Mason is not her favorite person, and she is hoping to get a deal."

"You left her there?"

"She's not going to run. She knows what's at stake."

"Which motel?"

"The Six. Off the interstate."

Ron stared at his desk, gently rocking back and forth in the squeaky chair, his hands folded in front of his lips. Jesse's eyes searched Ron for an answer, a clue. But Ron looked away.

"You're relieved of your duties," Ron finally said.

"What?" The color drained from Jesse's face.

"You crossed the line, Detective. I can tolerate a lot, but I can't tolerate this. You're reckless."

"I'm not reckless!" Jesse shouted. "I'm trying to solve this case! I'm trying to get Mason so we can get in."

"I told you *I* would get us back in." Ron gave him a cold stare. "How do you think they knew where to show up in the first place?"

Silence.

"I said we were going to work the bars, make the connections, and get names and numbers."

"Yeah, well, you're moving at a snail's pace."

"I worked the bars."

Jesse's jaw dropped. "You're saying you've been working undercover?"

"Go back to Henderson. You're off this task force."

Jesse cursed, flung open the door, and slammed it behind him. Ron heard the bell chime as Jesse blew out the front door. Within seconds, Mack stood in Ron's doorway. He held up a hand. "No questions. Just get back to work. Tell the guys we need to put those posters up in the garage. Make this place look used, okay? I need a half hour without interruption." Mack nodded and shut his door. A sharp blade of pain sliced through his head as he grabbed the desk phone. It was an old phone, big and black with a cord and a square full of push buttons. He used to love this kind of phone. Back in Chicago, he'd tuck his fingers underneath it and carry the whole thing around with the receiver cradled on his shoulder. Nan never understood why he didn't want a cordless phone at home.

Nan. He could see her face. In his mind, she looked happy. They were at Yosemite on vacation. She was smiling and really enjoying life. Why not? He'd put her through tough times in Chicago. It would break her heart if she knew he'd been back on the street again. That he was doing more than leading a task force from behind the relative safety of a desk. He closed his eyes. He knew what he was doing.

He put the phone to his ear, his fingers hovering over the number pad. And then he dialed.

"Captain Gates."

"Laura, it's Ron."

"What's wrong? You sound like something's wrong."

"I think we just got a huge break."

"What?"

"How many months has the LVPD been looking for Rhyne Grello?"

"The drug dealer? Six, at least."

"I think we've found him."

"You're sure?"

"Almost positive. We have an informant that put us back in touch with Mason. Apparently Mason's been hanging around Grello."

"He dropped out of sight for a while. You think he's behind the auto thefts?"

"Maybe. We don't have much information on Grello. But we have info on the guy he was apparently with today."

"Let's bring him in."

"He's delivering parts to us Friday. Maybe we should wait, see if Grello comes in with him, and make the arrest then."

"No. Narcotics has been close to Grello before, and he's always outsmarted them. It's our turn, Ron, and we need to move on this now. It might be our only chance."

Ron stared at the ceiling, thinking through the options. "All right. I'll bring in Bobby. We'll see what he knows."

He hung up the phone and went to see Mack. She was busy working on a laptop. "We got a trace on that number Bobby called from?"

"Yeah. It was a cell. But we've got his address."

Ron walked into the garage and called everyone over.

"What's going on?" Dozer asked. "I saw Jesse leave."

"Forget about Jesse. Right now I need you and Wiz to bring in Bobby.

Mack's got his information." He turned to Mack. "Please tell me he's got some parking tickets or *something* we can get him on."

Mack nodded. "Four unpaid speeding tickets."

"Good. Bring him to headquarters. Let me know when he's there." Mack handed Wiz and Dozer the information and they left.

He looked at Hank. "Hold down the fort. We may be getting calls today since we've been passing out fliers. Collect information from anyone who calls. I'll look into them later." Hank nodded and went back to the garage.

He turned to Mack. "I need you to go to the Motel 6 off the highway. There's a woman there named Brandi Brown. She's an informant. Get all the information you can from her. Then stay with her until I call. Don't mention this to anyone." Mack left without asking questions.

Ron walked outside and stood in the shadow of the garage. He wasn't superstitious, but he'd give anything if knocking knuckles with Elvis would make this thing work.

Chapter 36

Kyle sat on a couch that had been handed down from his grandmother. One lamp lit the small living room. As the television droned on, Kyle sat and stared. How had he come to this? He'd spent his entire youth serving God, spent every penny he had on seminary, and now here he was, wondering what it was all for. Wondering what got him up in the morning.

If he weren't on sabbatical, he would be in his office, reading a book by some megachurch pastor, wondering if his church would ever grow above a hundred and fifty people. It dawned on him that he'd never really been content or fulfilled. He got his bachelor's degree in three years, his master's at a prestigious school. He wanted a church. He got the church, but then wanted the people. He got the people, but then wanted more people. Why was he so desperate to fill his days with something else? Something more…exciting?

He clasped his hands and closed his eyes, trying to concentrate. He was restless, *and* he had a crush on a woman who could fire a gun. How could he match that excitement? He couldn't even fire his nearly deaf organist.

"I'm feeling useless." It was all he could pray. It was a statement, a call for help, a confession. He didn't have to say any more. God knew his heart, and Kyle felt ashamed of it. He'd lost his focus, his passion. Maybe he wasn't supposed to be doing this.

Then he heard a knock. Hopeful it was Mack, he opened the door to Jesse instead.

"Jesse…what are you doing here?"

"Are you certain there's not some sin you're dealing with that might be skewing this whole prayers and blessings thing?"

Kyle sighed. Just one? "Well...I guess I'm dealing with a little bit of...envy. Why?"

"About what?"

Kyle opened the door wider. "You want to come in?"

"I don't have any other place to be. I got fired from the task force today."

"What?"

Jesse looked around. "So this is a parsonage. Could use some work. It's a little small."

"Well," Kyle said, "I'm not Siegfried or Roy."

Jesse turned to face him. "So what's this envy all about?"

Kyle gestured for him to sit. "I've been doing a lot of thinking about ministry. Before I took this sabbatical, I was really bored. It seemed all I did was settle one argument after another and attempt to help people just get along with one another. I kept wondering if I was missing something. And then I got tied into this task force, and I suddenly felt alive."

"I'm glad you're figuring out your life, but how does this help me?"

"That's the thing. I don't have it figured out. I think I'd like to be the kind of guy who carries a badge and a gun, but that's just not me. I'm a pastor at heart. At least I think I am."

"I know you're hot for Mack."

Kyle froze. "How do you know that?"

"They don't call me a detective for nothing."

Kyle looked away. "Let's get back to you. Why did you get fired?"

"I lied. But for a good reason. If Ron would let me do what I do, I know we could break into this ring. But every time I make headway, Ron is nearby, waving his stick of distrust." Jesse kicked his feet up onto an ottoman. "Mack had a stellar idea. She said to come clean and ask Ron for forgiveness. You see where that landed me." Jesse glanced around. "In a parsonage."

"You want a Hot Pocket?"

Jesse groaned. "Hot wings sound better, but I guess I can't be choosy."

Kyle tossed a couple Hot Pockets in the microwave. "I usually eat at potlucks."

Jesse kept glancing around the room. "Sorry," Kyle called from the kitchen. "No Elvises around here, jumpsuited or otherwise." Kyle brought a Hot Pocket to Jesse and handed him a can of root beer.

"People like you, don't they?" Jesse said.

"Like me?"

"Yeah. You're well liked, aren't you?"

Kyle shrugged. "I guess."

"You're easy to like. Me… I just rub people the wrong way. Look what I do to Mack. By the time we're done, I might actually make her cuss." Jesse let out a sad laugh and guzzled the drink. "Who am I kidding? I'm already done."

Kyle leaned forward. "Jesse, you're a passionate guy. You're really good at what you do, and you love it. There's nothing wrong with that. It seems to me that this is your purpose. You were born to be a cop."

"I've never thought about it like that. But you're right. It's the only thing I'm good at, so I didn't want to blow it. Then I blew it."

"God made you who you are."

Jesse leaned back in his chair. "That's what I see in Mack. Everything's stacked against her, you know? She's awkward to be around, she's quick-tempered, she was homeschooled, she was a clown…but she's comfortable in her own skin. Who can be that comfortable?"

"She doesn't care what other people think of her. She trusts God. That's where her comfort comes from. It's really all about purpose. God has a purpose for Mack, and she embraces that."

"All that stuff I do," Jesse said. "The Elvis. The bullet. Chaplain Greer. You think that's nuts, don't you?"

Kyle smiled. "No…but Elvis is dead, and that bullet nearly killed you."

"I can't feel anything from God, but I can feel these socks on my feet."

"Here you are, on a Friday night, with a dorky pastor in his dumpy old parsonage, eating a Hot Pocket. God got you here somehow, didn't he?"

Jesse laughed. "Yeah, I guess." He gazed out the window. "I have a lot of questions, but I never had the courage to ask any of them. I was always afraid God wouldn't answer me."

Kyle watched as Jesse's confident eyes flickered with vulnerability. Sitting right in front of him was his answer. *His* purpose. Watching a broken man open up to the idea that God loves him—it couldn't get any more exciting than that.

Brandi sat on the end of the bed listening to this new detective explain that Jesse wasn't working the case anymore, but that they might still need her help.

Brandi felt sick. She hated this ratty motel, but it was better than jail. She'd thought about running, but then her life would pretty much be over. Besides, she didn't have any money.

Suddenly, they heard a knock at the door. The detective motioned for Brandi to stay still as she quietly went to the door, her hand on her gun. She peered through the peephole as a muffled voice came through the door. "Brandi Brown? You in there?"

"It's an old man," the detective whispered.

"It sounds like Mason's grandfather!" Brandi whispered back. The detective quickly moved to the bed. "Keep the chain hooked, but open the door. Find out what he wants. I'll be hiding in the bathroom. Do not, under any circumstance, let him in. And don't tell him I'm here."

"Brandi? You in there? It's Charles."

The detective slipped into the bathroom. Brandi took a deep breath and walked to the door, trying to calm her nerves. She hooked the chain, peeped through the hole, then opened the door.

"Charles? What are you doing here?"

"Sorry to scare you, darlin'. You look white as a ghost."

"I'm fine. You just startled me."

"You alone in there?"

"Yes. How did you find me?"

"I'm sorry, honey. I followed you last night. I had to. The guy you was with, I didn't trust him. I don't think you should, either. He's got that look in his eye. I seen it before. He ain't human. At least…not anymore." He paused and looked around the parking lot. "I saw him leave earlier. I thought he might come back. He didn't. So I thought you were safe. I headed home. But then I realized somethin'."

Brandi held her breath. "What?"

"I realized you're the right woman for Mason. He never had much luck with women. Here," he said, handing her a piece of paper through the crack in the door.

"What is it?"

"Mason's number. He told me not to give it out to nobody. I made up that bit about the number being blocked. But you're a good woman. You're good for Mason."

Brandi looked down at the piece of paper. "It's in code," Charles said, then his voice became a whisper. "Add five to each number. Start over after nine. That's his phone number."

"Oh, okay. Thanks."

"It's gettin' dark. I gotta get home."

"Okay."

"Keep this door locked. If that man you been with comes around again, you call…" He paused.

"The police?"

"No. They're aliens too. I don't like my phone ringin', but call me if you get in trouble."

"I will."

Brandi closed the door and turned. The detective walked out of the bathroom, and Brandi smiled while she tried to catch her breath. She held up the piece of paper. "We got it."

Laura had done her fair share of interrogations, one of the things she'd enjoyed most about being a detective. It was also something her father was best known for. He could suck a confession out of a brick wall. Some of his partners liked to yell and push papers off of tables. But her dad, he was always calm, subdued. He once told her that he liked to fool the criminal into thinking he could identify with him or his crime. Smile a little and nod, he told her. Let them see your eyes reflect understanding. Before long, a confession—or what the criminal thought was a justification— would come spilling out.

She wished her dad could see her now.

If the black-and-white monitor Laura watched was any indication, it wouldn't be hard to put fear in this young man. Bobby Jackson sat very still in the steel chair, his hands tucked underneath his legs and his eyes darting over every inch of the room.

Sergeant Yeager and Detective Stillman, "Dozer" they called him, stood beside her.

"I'm going to go in and question him." She looked at Ron. "He was alone when he was arrested, right?"

"Yeah. Nobody saw him get into the car." Ron turned to Dozer. "Go finish the paperwork, then get back to the shop. I don't care if we have to work all night. I want the shop ready. I've got Mack running an errand for me. I'll tell her to get there when she can."

"What about Jesse?"

"Worry about what's in front of us."

Laura went to the door and opened it. Bobby's head jerked up. He seemed surprised at first, probably at seeing a woman enter, but there wasn't any less terror on his face.

"What am I being charged with?"

"It's called a traffic ticket. Here's how it works. When you get one, you have to pay it. If you don't, we come and arrest you." Laura sat down casually and leaned forward. "Did the arresting officers read you your rights?"

"Yeah. Am I going to jail?"

"Most likely. Unless you can give me some information I want."

"What kind of information?"

"Were you with Rhyne Grello today?"

Bobby glanced at the wall, then at Laura. "No. I mean, I haven't seen him in a while."

"You're lying to me, Bobby. " Laura calmly crossed her arms. "If this is how you want to play it, I can take you straight to jail. Or you can tell me the truth and I can put in a good word for you. Lie to me again, all bets are off."

Bobby's gaze fell to the table. "I was with him. This afternoon."

"What were you doing?"

"We were…um…" He glanced up at Laura. "We were making a deal with a body shop. They needed some parts. We thought we might be able to help out."

"Help out, Bobby? You're into charity work, are you?"

Bobby paused, then met her eyes. "It was a business arrangement."

"Where'd you get the parts?"

"We just…"

"Remember, Bobby. No lies."

"Okay, okay. They are stolen parts. But they aren't mine. They're Rhyne's. I just linked him up with this body shop. I didn't steal nothin'."

"Did you sell the parts?"

"No. Rhyne needed the van for a couple of days. So we didn't do nothin' wrong."

"What kind of van?"

"A Chrysler."

"Why did he need the van?"

Bobby stared at the table again. "I don't know."

"Why don't you make an educated guess?"

"It's just rumors. That's all I know."

"Tell me."

Bobby leaned in a little. "The rumor is that Rhyne's doing drug runs to Mexico. Nobody's seen him do it. It's just what we been hearing."

"What about a guy named Mason Capps?"

"I know him a little, but we don't hang out much. He knows Rhyne."

"Do you know where Capps is?"

"No."

"But you do know how to get ahold of Grello."

"No. I don't have a phone number. I don't know where he lives. I found him at a casino. He likes to gamble sometimes."

"You're telling me you have no idea how to get in touch with him?"

"He said he'd call me. He didn't leave me a number or nothing."

Laura excused herself and found Ron waiting for her outside. "I'm getting somewhere with him."

Ron smiled. "We just got Mason Capps's phone number."

Chapter 37

Ron and Brandi sat in one of Ruth's cars, a block away from Cracker Jack's. She looped her hair around her index finger over and over again.

"All right, speak so I can make sure this thing is recording," Ron said.

"What should I say?" She looked nervously at Ron.

"Okay, we're good. There's a minor miracle. I can't even get my VCR to record." He glanced sideways at her. "I'm just beating you to the punch."

"What?" she laughed a little.

"You think I'm old."

"No," she said, smiling. "I was thinking how nice you are."

She smacked her gum. Ron held out his hand. "I don't want to hear that noise all night."

She spit her gum in his hand, and he wrapped it in a piece of scrap paper. "Are you sure you're clear about what to do?"

"I act like I want to get back together with Mason. I'm real nice to him."

"You want to know what he's been up to. Try to get him to tell you who he's been hanging out with, what he's doing. Why he was too busy to come get you out of jail."

"There's no good explanation for that," she growled.

"Remember, you're fishing for information. Don't make him mad and don't raise suspicions by asking too many pointed questions." Ron smiled at her. "You'll do fine."

"Yeah, if I can keep from throwing up when I see him."

"You get us the information we need, and I will personally talk to the DA."

"You will?"

"I promise."

Ron glanced at his watch. "I want you in there early. And I want you to get out first. Make sure he doesn't follow you, and then come back to the car. I'll be waiting."

"Okay."

"It's time to go."

Mason tried to convince himself he wasn't nervous, but his body kept trembling. He couldn't believe he'd said yes. He really wanted to see her again. He was tired of Rhyne making all the calls, especially about his personal life. Rhyne was busy living large with his new and more important friends anyway. As long as Mason showed up the next morning, everything would be fine. No harm done.

Besides, after their little trip to Mexico, Mason was going to take his money and get out of town. It would be enough to start over somewhere. He had learned to hate being Rhyne's whipping boy. The money might be good, but there was only so much a person could take.

He couldn't believe Brandi had gone to the trouble of talking with his grandfather to track him down. He figured it was over after their last conversation, but women like Brandi, they always come back for more.

He glanced at his reflection in the bar window, smoothing his hair down on the top and the sides. The room was crowded and loud. He grabbed a stool at the bar and ordered a beer. He wasn't going to wade through this crowd. She would find him. She always did.

Before his first sip of his beer, she appeared. She was wearing her hair down, just like he liked it. He hated the ponytail she wore sometimes.

"Hi," she said, smiling.

"You look good," he said.

"I could say the same about you." She glanced around. "Maybe we could find a table?"

"Nah. Just hop up here. I'll buy you a drink."

She climbed on the stool. "I don't want anything."

"Come on. The fun's just beginning."

"I wanted to see you," she said, staring at her fingers. "I want to know where we stand. You left me hanging out to dry."

"I was just in a really bad place, you know? Needed to sort things out. I'm glad you got out, though. Your ma help you?"

"You know she doesn't have any money. It was Alice. She sold her TV."

Mason got the bartender's attention. "She'll have a Coors."

"So, is there someone else?"

Mason turned on his stool to face her. "Baby, I swear it. There's nobody else."

"Then what have you been doing all this time?"

Mason wiped the sweat off his bottle. "You know me. I had to work some things out. I was broke. That's why I couldn't get you out."

"Are you still broke?"

"Not anymore," he said, grinning. "I've got this thing I'm doing. It's going to bring in a lot of money."

"What kind of thing?" Brandi frowned.

"Don't get all freaked out on me now."

"Tell me what you're doing."

That disapproving look on her face told him she wasn't going to be happy about it. But then she touched his arm. "Look, I don't care what you're doing just as long as you're doing it for us."

Mason looked at her. "What does that mean?"

"You know what that means."

"You always got mad before."

"Maybe it's because I didn't always understand. I understand now."

"Listen to me, baby. I'm going to do this thing, and I'm going to make a lot of money. Then we can get out of here. I hate this city. We can go somewhere and start over."

"You mean that?"

"Yeah. I mean it."

"How much money are we talking?"

"More than enough. But I gotta do it."

"What exactly is it?"

"It's a one-time thing, I swear. I do this, and I'm out. Then we leave."

"What are you doing, Mason?"

Mason glanced around the bar. Nobody was looking at them. "There's this guy, Rhyne Grello. I've known him since we were kids. We've done some business together here and there. He's hooked us up with a really big player. I mean, really big. We're going down to Mexico. Just for a couple of days."

"For drugs?"

"Keep your voice down."

"Well?"

"We're just delivering, baby. I'm not using. Rhyne doesn't use. We're big-time now. We gotta keep our heads straight."

Brandi looked genuinely interested. "You swear you're not using?"

"Yeah."

"How much money?" Her eyes lit up like they used to.

"A lot."

She smiled and wrapped her fingers around his. "I always knew you'd make it big."

Mason put his hand on the back of her head and pulled her closer. "Baby, this is nothing like you've ever seen. We're delivering for Vincent Ayala," he whispered.

Her eyes softened.

"Why are you looking at me like that?"

"I guess because I know how big this is for you."

"For us," he said, stroking her cheek. "This is big for us. Tomorrow our lives are going to change."

"Did you say Ayala? Vincent Ayala?" Laura asked.

Sweat poured down Ron's face. Fighting a shooting pain in his belly, he held his cell close to his ear. The city sounds were competing with the conversation. "Laura, listen to me. My team isn't ready for this. I can't send them in. Get the narcotics guys on this. They know Ayala. They've been trying to peg him for years. Call Williamson. He'll know what to do."

"I am not calling Williamson! Or anyone else in narcotics!" Laura yelled through the phone. "You find out where they're going. You trail them!"

"We're talking about the mob."

"Maybe the mob. Nobody has positively linked Ayala with the mob."

"Ayala is suspected of having two undercover officers killed in the last three years."

"Which is why we can't afford to lose this. You get a surveillance team together and—"

"A surveillance team? What? Who? We need at least ten officers to go to Mexico on surveillance. That will take at least forty-eight hours to put together."

"Then you're going to have to use your guys."

"I won't do it. It's too dangerous. Even if Ayala isn't with him, Grello could be a wild card."

"We've got Rhyne Grello and Vincent Ayala in our sights, and you don't think you can pull it off? Ron, I brought you on to this task force because I thought you *could* pull this off."

"You brought me on to a task force to break up an auto-theft ring. I never signed on for this." Ron took a deep breath. His heart suddenly started pounding. "I need to call you back." He listened to the headset for a moment. Brandi said her good-byes to Mason. Ron flipped open his phone and started to dial Dozer's number. But before he could finish, another horrific pain stabbed through his stomach and around his back. He clutched the steering wheel, his head fell backward in a dizzy fog, and then the noisy city went silent.

"Well," Jesse said, stretching his arms up to the lowest ceiling he'd ever seen in a house, "I guess I should let you get back to whatever it is you do."

"You're welcome to stay for a movie," Kyle said.

"No...uh, thanks. I've had enough drama for one night. Maybe another time." Jesse stood. "I've got to get up early and head back to Henderson, figure out what I'm supposed to be doing. I think you can officially stop praying for me now."

"I think I'll keep at it. But maybe you can start praying for yourself too."

Jesse smiled. "Well, I can't do worse than you."

Kyle laughed. "I guess not."

"Do me a favor, will you? Ask Mack out. You two are perfect for each other." Jesse was about to thank Kyle for his time when his cell phone rang. He looked at the number. "It's the sarge. Probably calling to chew me out some more."

"Or maybe he's calling to make things right."

"So far that formula hasn't worked out too well for me." But he punched the button and answered it anyway. "Yeah?"

"Jesse? Jesse?"

It was a woman's voice. She was crying and sounded hysterical.

"Hello? Who is this?"

"Jesse?"

"Who is this?"

"Brandi. Jesse, you've got to come quick," she said between sobs.

"What's wrong? Where are you?"

"Something has happened to your boss, Ron. I think he might be dead."

Chapter 38

J esse and Kyle arrived at the hospital just after the ambulance. Paramedics were rolling the gurney through the automatic doors and down a long hallway. Brandi leaned against a wall, looking shaken. When she spotted Jesse, she went to him. He guided her to a chair in a small waiting room that wasn't as crowded as the one in the ER.

"He didn't look good when I found him," she said, tears rolling down her face. "I was with Mason, and then…then…he…" She looked down at her blouse. "I still have the wire on me."

"Sergeant Yeager was using you as a snitch?"

Brandi pulled away and grabbed a tissue.

"An informant, I mean."

"Yeah, whatever." She blotted her eyes. "You were supposed to be there. Not him. But…he was nice. Reminded me of my dad."

"You met with Mason?"

She nodded. "I got his phone number. Charles brought it by. He didn't give it to you because he thought you were an alien." She blew her nose. "We set up a meeting with Mason. Mason told me he and this guy named Rhyne Grello were going to Mexico, something about drugs. When I came out, Ron was unconscious. I called 911. I didn't know what else to do."

"You did the right thing," Jesse said. *Rhyne Grello. Rhymes with Jell-O.* "Is he alive?"

She nodded. "I rode with him in the ambulance. They didn't know what was wrong with him, but he was breathing."

Jesse paced in the small waiting room. He was out of the loop, but how far out? And who was in the loop? He called Dozer.

"What happened?" Dozer said, before a hello. "Sarge said you were off the case."

"Dozer, listen to me. What do you know about tonight? Did Ron tell you what was going down?"

"Down? Nothing's going down. We're just getting the shop ready. He wants everything done by tomorrow. Everyone's here but you."

"I can't explain right now, but get everyone up to the hospital. To the ER. As soon as you can."

"What's going—"

"I'll call you back." Jesse hung up and called Captain Gates. Her phone went to voice mail. He left a message, then looked at Brandi. "You have a wire on. Sarge was recording this. There's got to be a tape somewhere."

Brandi nodded. "I think it was in the car."

Just then, like a storm blowing in, Nan Yeager whipped through the sliding doors. Her head snapped one way, then the other. "I need some help!" she yelled. "Where's my husband? Where's my husband?"

She recognized Jesse and made a beeline for him. "Where is my husband?" she demanded.

Just then a doctor stepped into the waiting area. "Are you Mrs. Yeager?" he asked.

"Yes," she said desperately. "Where's my husband? Is he okay? He's got a heart condition. Did he tell you that? He takes pills." She started naming them all. The doctor took her by the shoulders. "Ma'am, calm down."

Teary eyed, she looked up at him. "It's his heart, isn't it?"

"Your husband is in surgery right now. His appendix burst."

Mrs. Yeager's face went from desperation to confusion. "It's his appendix?"

"Yes. But we caught it early enough that the toxins didn't get far. He's going to feel pretty bad for a while. They're cleaning him out now."

"You're sure? Did you check his heart?"

"His heart is fine. He probably became lightheaded from the pain and that's what made him pass out. We're watching his blood pressure, but he should be better soon. He'll need a few weeks to fully recover. We'll keep you updated." The doctor walked away, and Jesse led Mrs. Yeager into the waiting room.

"Here," he said, guiding her to a chair on the wall opposite from Brandi. "You need to sit down."

She yanked her arm away. "I need to hit something."

Jesse prepared to duck.

The small square house with white siding sat on the corner of an unassuming street in an unassuming neighborhood. All the houses looked nearly identical, but she knew this particular house well. She'd stood on the corner many times, watching the man walk in front of the windows, doing whatever it was he did inside.

But she'd never crossed the street. More than anything, she wanted to cross the street, but she never had.

Wiping the tears off her face, Laura looked up, just in time to notice his silhouette walk through the living room.

He'd moved to Vegas eight years ago after retiring. She always kept track of him, even though they hadn't spoken in years. She thought he was coming to see her, to be with her. But he never called. He never tried to contact her. He just lived alone in this box of a house, twenty minutes away from his only child. Might as well have moved to another planet.

Laura wiped away more tears. She didn't understand this flood of emotion. Maybe she was having a nervous breakdown. Whatever it was, she couldn't stop crying. The task force was so close to success, so close to giving her the dream of a lifetime. But she knew it could just as easily end in disaster.

There she teetered, her future in the hands of people she hardly knew. And then it happened, an unexpected unraveling, a tightly wound string undone with one tug. She'd poured everything into her job. The pride that had gotten her this far was the same pride that kept her from calling her dad.

She realized tonight, after pacing her office and begging its empty walls to hand her this victory, that all she really wanted to do was sit at her father's feet, bury her head in his lap, cry for all the lost years, and try to reconnect with a man she didn't know. Why had this been so hard for her?

Laura thought of Mackenzie Hazard. The girl had a lot stacked against her. But there was a surprising peace in her eyes and a sense of joy in her words that didn't depend on a single circumstance in her life. She didn't have everything she wanted, but she had something more.

Laura stared at the warm orange light coming from the house, and without looking down, she stepped off the curb. And then she took another step. And another.

She reached his front door, and with all her strength, raised her hand and knocked.

Around three in the morning, Jesse, Mack, and Dozer stood outside the hospital room and watched Mrs. Yeager at her husband's bedside. Wiz walked up, balancing four cups of coffee. "Any change?" Wiz asked, passing out the cups.

"Nothing," Dozer whispered. "But that is one angry woman. I mean, the man's unconscious, and she's still yelling at him because it was his appendix and not his heart?"

"She's upset. She almost lost her husband," Mack said. "I don't think it's about his appendix or his heart. She didn't know he was doing actual undercover work."

"None of us did. What did this Brandi chick tell you?" Wiz asked.

"Just that she was supposed to get as much information as possible about Rhyne Grello," Jesse replied.

"I know who he is," said Mack. "LVPD has been trying to find him for months. He's a drug dealer. Not big-time, but big enough." Mack looked at their curious faces. "What? I read the department memos."

"Capps is in it with him," Jesse said.

"But what are they up to?" Wiz asked.

"We have to find out," Jesse said. "He told Brandi not to call him. He gave her his cell phone and said he would be back, that he would call her if there was trouble."

"We've got the number. Why don't we trace it? Maybe we'll get an address." Wiz said.

"I have a feeling it'll be a bogus address. Remember, he got rid of one phone already to cover his trail."

"And we have no idea where Rhyne Grello is."

"We can be sure that Mason knows," Jesse said, rubbing his temples. "They're leaving tomorrow morning. We've got to follow them, but how do we find them?"

Mrs. Yeager was standing in the doorway, mascara smudged a good half inch under each eye. Her cold stare stopped at each of them. "Why are you still here?" she asked. "Please leave. Just leave us be."

"Ma'am, is there anything we can do?" Mack asked, stepping toward her.

"This job sucked everything out of him. I told him not to do it, and he did. He lied to me, and now look what it has cost him. A useless organ. But an organ nevertheless." She glanced back at him, and more tears rolled down her face. "I spent most of my life keeping myself from worrying about what would happen to him, to us, if he didn't come home. These years, these are the years we're supposed to take road trips and enjoy our grandchildren." She wiped the tears off her cheeks.

"I'm sure he had a good reason for what he did," Mack said.

"Well, I hope it was worth that," she said, pointing to his bed. She was silent for a moment. Monitors beeped in the background. "Just go now. Go." She turned and went back to his bedside. Dozer and Wiz walked away. Jesse started to follow, but when he glanced back, Mack was still standing at the door, watching.

"Mack, come on. Let's go."

Mack shook her head. She looked at Jesse. "You guys go. Try to figure this thing out. I'm going to stay."

"She said to go."

"She needs someone. She's upset."

"Mack, we could use you. There's a lot to do. Don't you want to be in the middle of this?"

"Yeah. I do. I really do." She paused and stared back at the sergeant and his wife. "But you guys can handle it. I'm going to stay here. This is where I'm supposed to be right now."

"I'll never figure you out, Mack. But I'm not going to argue about it now."

Jesse thought about what kind of prayer he would pray if he were going to pray one.

Dozer had fallen asleep on the couch after taking Brandi back to the motel. Wiz was still working the computers, trying to find leads on Capps or Grello. They needed that recording, but he still hadn't found out which company towed Sergeant Yeager's car. Brandi had said Mason mentioned another man's name, but she couldn't remember it…or what it rhymed with. And Jesse still couldn't get in touch with Captain Gates.

They were stuck trying to pull a rabbit out of a hat. "I'm going to get some air," Jesse said to Wiz. Jesse stepped onto the small porch and sat down on the bottom step. The cool night air felt good, but pain pulsed through his temples, throbbing to the point he had to close his eyes. He rested his forehead against his knuckles and tried to wrestle a solution from his thoughts. There had to be a way to find Capps or Grello before they took off to Mexico.

In the darkness of early morning, with nothing to hang on to but prayer and a couple of Advil, Jesse hoped for the best. No…he prayed for it.

"You planning to throw a party?"

Jesse looked up. Standing above him in the darkness was the perfect cure for tranquility…Ruth Butler.

"Mrs. Butler, with all due respect, I'm not causing any trouble, I'm not making loud noises. I'm just sitting here. There isn't some sort of code against that in the neighbor association, is there?"

"Well, it's an ungodly hour, and by definition you are loitering, but I've been watching you and you look like you could use some cheering up." She pulled a sack of cookies from behind her back. "Maybe this will help."

Jesse tried a polite smile and took the bag. "Thanks."

"Where's that good-looking fellow?" she asked, peering past Jesse, trying to get a glimpse into the house.

"Dozer?"

"The one with the cane."

"Right. Well, he had to have his appendix removed."

"Oh no." She pulled her housecoat closed. "How terrible. Once they start removing organs from your body, it's all downhill from there. Is he going to be okay?"

"Yeah."

"No wonder you're upset."

Jesse offered his most tolerant smile. "There's just a lot going on right now. I need some time to think. That's why I came out here where it was quiet. So I could think."

Ruth chuckled. "Oh, honey, you're out of luck there. In about three and a half minutes, our neighbor Mr. Warren will start his truck and let it warm up for a good fifteen minutes. You've never heard a car make so much noise just sitting in a driveway. It's why I get up at four instead of four thirty now. I hated waking up to that racket. I asked him why he doesn't get another car. He says he can't afford it, and I believe him, to tell you the truth. The poor man can't afford clothes that fit. I offered him one of my husband's belts, but he never took me up on the offer. I think he used to play football. He's got a lot of football jerseys."

Jesse's eyelids became heavy as Ruth droned on.

"Anyhow," she continued, like the stars were an attentive audience hanging on her every word, "I told him that he should think about getting a mechanic to look at it. He told me he doesn't have time. So I suggested he talk to Mr. Grello, see if he could come over and—"

"What did you say?"

"He told me he didn't have time for a mechanic—"

"After that. You said Grello. Rhyne Grello?"

"Yes. That's him. He gave me some phony-baloney name when he first moved in. But I peeked at his mail one afternoon. He used to mess with cars in his driveway, sometimes at all hours of the night. I thought he might be able to take a look at Mr. Warren's truck to fix it, but I haven't seen him out much lately—"

"How do you know Rhyne Grello?"

"I make it my business to know everyone's business. That's why the association has stayed in existence—"

Jesse stood up. "Mrs. Butler, stop for a second. Just stop. How do you know Rhyne Grello?"

Ruth looked genuinely perplexed but pointed down the street. "Because he lives at eleven twenty-two. Three houses over on your side of the street."

Nan pulled a chair up to Ron's bedside and laid her head down next to him. She counted his breaths. Watched the monitors. Willed him to keep breathing. To breathe steady and strong.

She heard someone come into the room. It was one of Ron's officers, the girl. "Mrs. Yeager?"

Nan sat up, keeping her hand on Ron's. "Yes?"

"I wanted to see if you needed anything."

"What was your name?"

"Mack. Mack Hazard."

Nan ran her fingers through messy hair. "No, we're fine."

Mack came a little closer. "I've been in the chapel praying for you and for Ron. I know this is a difficult situation."

Difficult situation? Try a difficult three decades.

"I know what it's like to lose someone you love. My parents died in an accident." Mack looked at Ron, then back at Nan. "You still have him. He's a strong man. He'll be fine."

"I appreciate your prayers. But I need to be alone."

"Your pastor went to get you something from the cafeteria."

"I'm not hungry."

"I know," Mack said gently. "I didn't eat for days after my parents died. Everybody kept trying to shove food down me, like it would somehow fill up my heart instead of my stomach."

"I'm willing to bet Kyle brings ham."

Mack laughed. "That's a good possibility."

A groan escaped from Ron, and Nan pulled herself closer to his bed. "Ron?" Nan looked at Mack. "Go get a nurse."

Mack rushed out of the room. Ron looked like he was trying to open his eyes. "Ron? What's wrong?"

He turned his head, looking at Nan. She tried to calm herself as he squeezed her hand. She placed her other hand on his head. He felt warm. Mack returned with the nurse, who checked him over, while Nan stepped aside. "Mr. Yeager? Can you hear me? Are you in any pain?"

Ron didn't respond, but his eyes were open. Nan felt Mack's strong hand on her shoulder. The nurse checked the monitors, listened to his heart, and checked his IVs. She turned to them. "Everything looks good. I'll page the doctor, but he's doing fine. Keep him calm and still. I'll be right back."

Nan returned to his bedside, and a small smile crept onto Ron's face. "Hi," she said, squeezing his hand. "You're going to be fine. Everything's going to be okay."

He nodded a little, but then noticed Mack. He blinked like he was processing something, and then he mumbled, "Mack...come..."

Nan said, "You need to rest. Don't talk."

"Mack...," he said again and tried to lift his head a little.

"Please, Ron, don't move." Nan turned to Mack. "Come here. See? She's here. Everything's fine. Now stop talk—"

"Mack," he whispered. Mack looked at Nan, then leaned in. "Mack..."

"I'm here, Sarge."

"Listen to me." His voice was barely audible. "Mason is in with Grello. And Grello is..." He coughed.

"Sarge, we know. Capps and Grello are working together."

"With...Vincent...Ayala..."

Mack repeated him. "Vincent Ayala."

"Tell Jesse... Tell him..." Ron paused and looked at the ceiling. At first Nan thought he was in pain, but she realized he was searching for the words to speak. "I want him to do this. Tell him Grello's…making a run to…Mexico for Ayala. Tell him to be careful." Nan felt relief as Ron's gaze returned to hers. He gave her a wan smile, then closed his eyes and went to sleep.

Nan let out an anxious breath and looked at Mack. "I guess you better go find him."

Mack raced out of the room. Nan lowered her head back onto the bed, closed her eyes, and prayed his gall bladder would hold up.

Chapter 39

D ozer was chosen to watch Grello's house for any activity, which he could do by standing on the front porch of the safe house. Jesse ordered Wiz to make some coffee for Ruth, as that seemed to be the appropriate thing to do for an unpredictable old woman who was sitting in the living room in her housecoat. Her suspicious glare combed anything that moved. Wiz, trying to be helpful, came in with a platter of cookies. "Would you like a cookie?" he asked.

"I brought those over here, you idiot," she snapped.

Wiz offered Jesse an apologetic shrug as he retreated to the kitchen. "Sorry. I thought Mack made them." Ruth looked at Jesse again. "You're telling me that the fugitive you've been looking for all this time practically lives next door to you?"

"It's complicated, ma'am," Jesse said. "Rhyne Grello is very good at hiding."

"Hiding in plain sight, apparently," Ruth said. "Where's that coffee?"

Wiz hustled out carrying a plastic cup and a bent metal spoon, offering it to Ruth like it was fine china. Ruth took one sip and, with an exaggerated grimace, set it down. "Somebody needs to teach you how to make coffee."

"Mrs. Butler," Jesse said, pulling her attention away from the dirty socks on the floor, "how long has Grello lived there?"

"Maybe a year. Not a very nice fellow, but he knows who's in charge around here. And ever since July 22, he keeps his lawn tidy too."

"What happened on July 22?"

"He had a little visit from the head of the homeowners' association."

Jesse's cell phone rang. "It's Mack," he told Wiz. "I'll call her back in a minute." Jesse hit the silencer on his phone and turned back to Ruth. "You've talked to this guy? Often?"

"Not often. All I have to do is step out on my porch and look his direction. That takes care of things. I told him that if he didn't get his lawn under control, I was going to have the city come out, mow it, and send him the bill." She sipped the coffee. "And that was that."

Wiz came out of the kitchen, lingering in the back of the room, but Ruth spotted him anyway. "Young man," she said, "don't you know how to entertain a guest? Don't you have a platter of crackers and cheese you could put together? Or truffles? Anything?"

Wiz glanced at Jesse and sighed. He went back to the kitchen, and they could hear him digging through the pantry.

"I tell you," she said. "What are they teaching young people these days?"

"Ma'am," Jesse said, "this is an undercover house. We don't actually live here. We just use it for the purpose of meeting, and just in case someone follows us, we have a place to go other than our real residences."

"Well, don't you think that *someone* might grow suspicious if you don't have some decent food around?"

"What else can you tell me about Rhyne?"

"He smokes too much, he thinks couches make good porch furniture, and he has been dressing nicer lately. Oh, and he has a young man living with him named Mason who has overstayed his welcome."

"Mason Capps?"

Ruth's eyes narrowed. "Someone else you've been looking for?"

Wiz entered carrying a plate like a waiter. He lowered it to the table with a self-impressed smile. "We have a crispy, slightly sweet selection of whole-grain nuggets along with an entire array of rainbow marshmallows."

Jesse shot Wiz a look. "That's all you could find? Lucky Charms?"

Wiz shrugged. "The chip bag was empty."

Suddenly the front door slammed open, and Dozer frantically rushed in. "Jesse! Hurry! Come out—" He glanced at Ruth and immediately shifted his approach to lackadaisical. "Um, you might want to step out here for a moment. I think there's a, uh, rosebush that needs our attention."

"I'm glad you called. I didn't want to wait three days to hear from you again. Are you sure it's okay?" Brandi asked as Mason gathered a few of her things out of the car. "You said this guy didn't want me around."

"I talked to him. He's cool with it." Rhyne wasn't, but he had enough on his mind to keep him from getting too upset. "You'll stay here while we're gone, okay? Look after the house. I'll give you some money for food." He nodded toward the house. "Go on in. Fix me a sandwich, okay?"

"But he's in there."

"His name is Rhyne. Fix him a sandwich too, then." Mason paused and smiled. "A ham sandwich. Yeah, ham. Makes everything better." Brandi gave him a confused look. "Just play nice, and he'll be cool. All he's got on his mind is this Mexico trip."

She walked into the house, and Mason turned to finish gathering her things. He pulled out her duffel bag and was just about to close the trunk when a car traveling down the street came to a screeching halt, right in front of him. Even in the glare of the headlights, he recognized the driver. The blonde from Doodah's. Mackenzie.

Their eyes locked.

Throwing down the bag, he stepped in front of the vehicle, then went to the driver's side, yanked open the door, and pulled her out.

"What are you doing here?" he demanded.

"What are you…doing here?" Mackenzie stammered.

"I live here, but I suspect you already know that."

She trembled in his grasp. He grabbed the back of her shirt and forced her toward the house.

After flinging open the screen door, he pushed her inside. She stumbled forward, her shoulder hitting the wall. The commotion brought Rhyne around the corner.

"What's going on? Who is this?" Rhyne demanded.

"I found her outside."

"What was she doing?"

Mason grabbed her face. "What were you doing?" Brandi came around the corner and gasped. "Brandi, stay out of this." Mason grabbed Mackenzie's arm, pulled her into the living room, and pushed her onto the couch.

Rhyne glanced back and forth between at Mason and Mackenzie. His gaze locked on Mackenzie.

"How do you know her?" Rhyne asked Mason.

"Look, she was one of the people I'd talked to that night at the bar. But I cut all contact like you said. I haven't seen her or the other guy since."

"Why's she here now?"

Mackenzie glanced at Brandi, who was watching from the shadows of the hallway, and then said to Mason, "I followed you."

Rhyne cursed. "Mason! I told you to watch your back! To always make sure you weren't followed!"

"I did!" Mason yelled back. It was true. He's been cautious every time he returned to Rhyne's house.

"Why did you follow him?" Rhyne asked.

Mackenzie stood, causing both men to step forward. "One of you tipped off the police."

Rhyne looked at Mason, and a wave of nausea rolled through

Mason's stomach. He didn't know what this lady was talking about, but it couldn't be good.

"One of *us*?" Mason asked. He looked at Rhyne. "You know him too?"

"He came to our shop with a van."

Mason turned to Rhyne, and there was no hiding his guilt.

"So which one of you did it?" She glared at Rhyne. "Was it you?"

"We've got to get in there!" Jesse said. "They just pulled Mack inside!"

Dozer pushed Jesse back into the house. "Mack's met Mason before. At the bar. As far as we know, he has no idea that she's a cop."

"We've got to do something," Jesse said, walking in circles, his hands clasped on top of his head. He couldn't catch his breath. "If we call in backup, this could become a hostage situation."

From the couch Ruth said, "Are you talking about that delightful young lady I liked so much? The one who wears too much makeup?"

"Mrs. Butler, please be quiet. Wiz, try Gates again."

"We've been trying all night."

"Do it."

Jesse went outside and stood on the porch, facing Grello's house. The street was quiet. The black sky was warming to a soft orange hue at the horizon. Did Mack go in there by choice? Was she part of some grand scheme Sergeant Yeager cooked up? Or did she stumble upon Mason by accident?

He tried to play out all the scenarios. If he, Dozer, and Wiz kicked down the door with guns drawn, there was no telling what might happen. Someone could get shot. Or they might simply ruin a plan that was already in place. He suddenly remembered Mack had called.

"Jesse, it's Mack. Where are you?" She sounded anxious. "I just left the hospital. I don't know what this means, but Sergeant Yeager told me that Rhyne Grello is making a run to Mexico for Vincent Ayala. They're leaving this morning. He wanted you to do it, Jesse. That's all he said. I'm on my way to the house. Call me when you get this message."

Nothing seemed clear. Jesse's mind had never felt so cluttered, and he'd never felt so incapable of making a decision. He snapped his phone shut and ran inside. "Mrs. Butler, listen very carefully. I want you to stand at this door. If you hear gunfire, call 911 immediately."

"Finally, something I'm good at," Ruth said, moving to the door.

"Come on, boys. We're going to the backyard to jump some fences."

They started toward the back door, but Dozer stopped him. "What about Elvis?"

"I've got all I need. Let's go."

"Wait a minute!" Ruth shouted from the front door.

"What is it, Mrs. Butler?" Jesse asked impatiently.

"Another car is stopping in front of the house."

Kyle slowly pulled to the curb, shutting off his lights. His heart thumped heavily in his chest as he stared at Mack's car. The lights were still on, and the door was wide open.

Nan told him Mack had run off on Ron's instructions. Kyle tried to catch her, but she was already gone. While praying in the chapel for Ron, Kyle felt a strange sense that Mack's life was in danger. It didn't make any sense at the time. He looked anxiously at the house. The front door was shut, but the lights were on, and he could see shadowy figures through the curtains. "God help me," he whispered. He looked toward the UC house. All looked quiet. But then he heard shouting inside the other house.

He quickly got out of his car, moved up the neatly trimmed grass, and stepped onto the porch. He couldn't even think straight. What was he doing?

But then he heard Mack's voice, and before he could stop himself, he reached out to the door.

"Did someone knock?" said Rhyne.

Mason stared at Rhyne, who looked at the door. The room went completely silent. "I didn't hear any—"

There it was again. A knock. Mason and Rhyne pulled their guns at the same time. "You expecting anybody?" Rhyne asked.

Mason shook his head. They approached the door, and Rhyne peeked through the hole. "It's a guy."

"Let me see," Mason said.

Rhyne looked at Mackenzie. "Don't move."

"What?" Mason exclaimed.

"What is it?" Rhyne asked, looking back through the peephole.

"It's…it's…!"

"Who?" Rhyne asked.

Mason turned to Mackenzie. "It's your boyfriend!"

Rhyne lunged and opened the door, then yanked the guy in and slammed it shut. "Who are you?" Rhyne barked, pointing his gun from one person to the next. The guy Rhyne had pulled in was the only one with his hands up. *Kyle,* Mason remembered. The one with the manners—until you spilled a beer on him.

"His name's Kyle." Mason quickly explained how he knew both of them.

"I'm…I'm…" Kyle didn't look nearly as tough with a gun pointed at him.

Mackenzie suddenly gasped. Her eyes were wide as she stared at Kyle. "Please don't let him hurt me."

The three men standing there looked at each other. "Who are you talking about?" Mason finally asked.

Mackenzie nodded toward Kyle. "Him."

"Him? You were treating him like a trained dog the other night."

Tears dripped from her eyes. "You don't know what he can do."

Rhyne looked skeptical. Mason said, "I saw him beat up a guy over a spilled beer."

Kyle, with his hands still in the air, didn't look like he could beat an egg. Mason asked him, "What's the matter?" If *this* guy was spooked, there had to be a good reason.

"Um…I don't… I just… I wanted to…"

"Speak!" Rhyne shouted.

Kyle glanced at Brandi, who was holding two sandwich plates. "Is that ham?"

Rhyne watched Mackenzie sob as she looked at this Kyle guy. "Keep him away from me! You don't understand," she said, tears streaming down her face. "He was sent here to deal with me. Because I dealt with you two, and one of you tipped off the police!"

Rhyne glanced at Mason as he put both hands on his gun. "You've gotten us into a fine mess, haven't you?"

"I didn't tip off the police! I just talked to these two. You're the one that went to the shop with Bobby. Maybe Bobby did it! That loser would sell us out, and you know it."

"Well," Rhyne said, his voice calm, "I could shoot all three of you. That would make things easier, now, wouldn't it?"

Mason slowly raised his gun. "You may be a great businessman, but I'm a better shot."

The woman who had brought in the sandwiches suddenly started wailing. "Please don't kill him!"

Rhyne kept his eyes on Mason. "See what you've done? This is a train wreck. You've become a gigantic liability. Sometimes you just have to cut your losses…"

"Wait!" shrieked Mason's woman. "Don't kill him!" She pointed at Mackenzie and shouted, "She's the cop!"

Chapter 40

H urry up!" Jesse whispered. They leaped over the last fence and into Rhyne Grello's backyard. The grass was cluttered with auto parts. Jesse crouched, trying to figure how he could get a look inside. The two large windows most likely belonged to bedrooms. There was a small window in the back door. If this house was like the one that they were renting, it would lead straight into the kitchen. It might give them a view of the living room. Jesse signaled he was going to the porch. He pointed to the two windows for Wiz and Dozer. All three crept forward, weapons drawn, feet padding lightly through the tall grass.

Jesse listened, snuck onto the back patio, then peeked into the small rectangular window. At first he didn't see anything, but then there was movement. Mason. He was pointing a gun at another man. Must be Grello. Grello also held a gun, and was waving it back and forth. He couldn't see Mack. Suddenly Grello lurched forward and grabbed something. He heard screaming. Rhyne was dragging Mack by her hair to the center of the living room.

There was more screaming from someone else, another woman. Grello told someone to shut up. Jesse turned to Wiz and Dozer and held up five fingers. This situation was getting out of control quickly.

After explaining how she knew Mackenzie was a cop, Brandi said, "I swear, Mason, after we met that evening in the bar, I knew I wanted to get back together with you. And then you called me... I didn't mean for any of this to happen!"

Rhyne, clearly baffled as to whom he should be pointing the gun at, finally just gestured with it. "We have a cop *and* a snitch in our midst, Mason. A *cop*. A cop who followed *you*."

Mason held up his hands to try to get everyone to calm down, but he still had the gun in his hand, and everyone but Rhyne ducked. He quickly lowered his hand to his side and turned to Kyle. "Please," Mason began. "Just take it easy, Rhyne. Let's figure this out."

Mason wondered what Kyle was capable of, with the new discovery that his girlfriend wasn't who he thought she was. Kyle looked pretty shocked. Mason knew the feeling. "Listen, man," Mason said, "a chick turning on you—well, that can happen to the best of us. Seriously, you couldn't have known. But what are you going to do about it?" Mason said, gesturing toward her with his gun.

Rhyne sneered. "He's going to do nothing. Look at him. He's going to pass out."

"I know he gives that impression. But trust me, he's like Jekyll and Hyde. He's about to snap, I'm sure of it." Mason turned back to Kyle. "You're about to snap, right?"

"Uh, um. I just think…I…"

Behind them, Rhyne sighed.

"Give him some room. He's just processing all of this." Mason stepped a little closer. "You want me to spill a beer or something?"

"What does that have to do with anything?" Rhyne growled. Mason could tell his patience was growing very thin.

With two rapidly moving fingers, Mason beckoned Brandi over and then grabbed a sandwich off a plate. "Take this."

"No…no, I'm not, um, hungry…"

"It's ham. See? Ham!"

"Beer? Ham?" Rhyne raised his gun. "I'm getting annoyed."

"Just wait a second, okay?" Mason held the sandwich up to Kyle's mouth. "Go on, take a bite. Maybe it'll calm you down. Then you can take care of this situation for us. Get rid of the cop. It's ham, remember? A brighter outlook and all that?"

Rhyne shook his head and started pacing erratically.

"He can do this for us, Rhyne. No guns. No nosy neighbors calling the police."

Kyle chewed slowly and blinked with every bite.

"Well," Rhyne said impatiently. "Don't just stand there like an idiot. What do you have to say? Are you going to deal with this or not?"

The room grew silent. Kyle seemed to change right in front of them. He calmly set down the sandwich, looked around the room at each of them and then said, "'He who dwells in the shelter of the Most High will rest in the shadow of the Almighty. I will say of the LORD, "He is my refuge and my fortress, my God, in whom I trust."'"

"What the…?" Rhyne shouted.

"Shut up!" Mason said. "Let the man speak! He's coming around to a point here—"

"Surely he will save you from—"

A loud crashing noise suddenly shook the windows. Everyone looked up, but they realized too late that the noises came from behind them. Three men stormed into the room. Mason's gun was knocked away as he was forced to the floor. With his face pressed into the carpet, his arms were pulled behind him and a knee jammed between his shoulder blades. There was no question about it. He was under arrest.

So much for the ham.

Laura Gates sat on the back patio watching the sun rise. Her clothes were wrinkled and her hair was a mess, but she didn't care. The fresh morning air flowed into her lungs as she listened to chirping birds and barking dogs. The back door slid open. Laura rose to help her father carry two plates out to the table. He smiled. "Been a long time since I made breakfast for two."

"It looks wonderful, Dad."

He patted her on the cheek and sat down next to her. They'd talked long into the night, until her father had fallen asleep in his recliner. Laura had curled up on the couch.

When he'd opened the door to see her standing on his doorstep, she wasn't sure what to expect. Without hesitation, he pulled her into his arms and said, "My Laura! My Laura!"

They talked about everything. Her father listened intently as she told him about her career. How she got from there to here. He talked about his retirement, his loneliness, and how he'd truly hoped they could reconnect when he moved to Vegas. Tears filled his eyes as he told her he couldn't find the courage to call. He was afraid she didn't want anything to do with him.

Laura marveled at how twenty years of pain and disappointment were undone in a matter of minutes. As soon as he wrapped his arms around her, it all faded away. And here they were, eating breakfast together, enjoying each other's company like not a day was missed.

She'd talked to Sergeant Yeager that morning, learned about his appendix and the arrests of Rhyne Grello and Mason Capps. For everything that seemed to go so wrong, it ended up turning out perfectly right. What shocked Laura most was how little it meant to her now. She knew the accolades would come, but she already felt fulfilled.

She buttered her toast and said, "Hey, Dad, you want to hear about what went down last night? We got a big one."

He smiled, his eyes lighting with the excitement every cop felt when anticipating a great cop story. "You bet."

Chapter 41

Nan propped Ron up against some pillows. He felt drowsy, like he could sleep for another five days. Even blinking took a lot of effort. But nothing was going to stop him from smiling. Jesse, Dozer, Wiz, Kyle, and Mack were gathered around his hospital bed.

He'd made peace with Nan. She wasn't happy he'd lied, but she understood his reasons. And he couldn't be more thankful that his appendix had burst. That was one strange but welcome gift from God. Had it been his heart, he never would've heard the end of it.

He'd tried to promise her a trip to Hawaii. "If you want to make nice," she said, "rent me a convertible and come with me up the Pacific Coast Highway in September."

"Deal." He smiled. They'd done that on their honeymoon.

"We just finished filling out the reports," Jesse said.

"The DA said he couldn't believe we got Rhyne Grello," Wiz said.

"He thought they could get Grello to testify against Vincent Ayala too," Jesse added.

"I'm glad we didn't have to do surveillance all the way to Mexico," Dozer said. "I hate that."

Ron smiled at Mack. "I hear you took my advice."

"Yeah," Mack grinned.

"What advice?" Jesse asked.

"Sarge told me that sometimes it's better to play the weaker man. It bought me precious time in this little scenario."

Jesse looked down. "I never should've brought Brandi into the mix." Then he smiled. "At least I don't have to take her to the prom."

Ron waved his hand. "We got 'em, and that's all that matters. You all worked really hard. We broke into an auto-theft ring and busted up a drug-trafficking operation. Captain Gates told me to tell all of you thank you and that you did a good job." A nurse entered with what looked like Ron's dinner. She set the tray on the table next to him.

"We should let you eat," Mack said. "And rest."

"Wait a minute. Don't leave just yet. I have a little surprise for each of you. Nan, would you mind giving Dozer his?"

Nan handed a bag to Dozer. Dozer laughed as he peered into it. "A can of Red Bull and a bottle of Mountain Dew. Thank you. I'll put these to good use."

"Wiz, I didn't have to go far to find something for you." Ron reached next to his bed and lifted up a bedpan.

Wiz cracked up. "How…thoughtful."

"Beats a catheter, believe me," Ron smiled. "Mack, come over here."

Mack raised an eyebrow and looked at him suspiciously. He took a small sack from Nan and handed it to Mack. She pulled out a plastic bottle and held it up for everyone to see. "Makeup remover. Thank you." She laughed and shook her head. "I don't think I'll be using makeup for a very, very long time."

Ron pointed to his food tray. "And last, but certainly not least, Jesse and Kyle, why don't you come over here." He pointed to a large closed container on the food tray. "Go ahead, open it."

Jesse paused and glanced at Kyle before lifting the lid. "Are snakes going to come flying out?" he quipped, carefully pulling off the lid.

"What is it?" Dozer asked.

Jesse smiled. "A week's worth of Jell-O. Compliments of the hospital."

"And," Kyle said, "a ham sandwich."

The room echoed with laughter.

"All right, all right," Nan said. "You guys are going to have to leave. The pain medication he's on might make him start thinking he's Santa Claus, what with all the gifts he's handing out."

"You heard the woman," Ron said, taking her hand. "Ho, ho, ho."

"We'll check in with you later, Sarge," Mack said. "Get some rest."

They filtered out of the room, and the nurse quietly shut the door. Nan sat down in the chair she'd been glued to since the moment he'd become conscious after the surgery.

"Don't look at me that way," he said.

"What way?" she asked.

"The way that makes my heart skip a beat."

She gave him a wry smile. "It's going to take more than flattery and a missing appendix to get you off the hook." She leaned back and folded her arms. "What's next for you? Skydiving? Treasure hunting? What?"

He touched her hand. "I've already found my treasure."

"Oh, brother," she said, rolling her eyes. "I think they've got the oxygen turned up too high." She leaned forward. "It's time to let them go." She glanced to the doorway. "They'll be okay, you know. Every generation has to pass what they know to the next generation and trust they'll make it work." She stood. "You rest now. I've got to leave for a little bit."

"Where are you going?"

"To buy a chain."

"For what?"

She smiled. "To chain you to your desk for the next nineteen months."

Dozer, Wiz, and Jesse walked out of the hospital. Jesse said, "Hey, I'll catch up with you guys tonight at dinner, okay?" He walked briskly toward the parking lot where he could see Mack's head weaving through the cars. "Mack! Wait up!"

She turned and waited for him as he squeezed between two narrowly parked cars. "Hi," he said, a little out of breath.

"Hi."

"Listen, I just wanted to tell you...well...you did a good job. A really good job. I don't know how any of us would've reacted in that kind of situation. You handled yourself like a pro." He offered a gentle smile. "I'm sorry I gave you such a hard time. You proved me wrong. You're a great cop."

"You too, Jesse. Thanks for everything you taught me."

"I'm sorry I made fun of your...uh, religious side. I'm an idiot, you know? I shouldn't have made you feel small. And it turns out," he said with a laugh, "you were right."

"You didn't make me feel small. But I'm glad you're taking what I've said to heart."

"Between you and Kyle, I might just turn into a priest."

She laughed. "I think we'd settle for a regular ol' Christian."

"Right. I'll think about it. I'll be checking out Kyle's church. We kind of had a deal."

Mack looked at her watch. "Well, I gotta run."

"Hey, listen, the guys and I are meeting at a sports bar tonight. You should come. It'll be fun."

"Thanks, but I've got plans. A date, actually."

"Really? I've got to give it to that guy. He's got a lot of guts...and good taste."

"You know who it is?"

"Let's put it this way. If a quartet shows up at dinner, that wasn't my idea. But be sure to give him props for trying hard."

She stuck out her hand, and he shook it.

"I'm glad we worked together, Mack."

"Me too. Made me realize I have a lot to learn."

"You'll get it. This stuff is second nature to you."

She cracked a smile. "I meant about my temper. But nobody's perfect, right?"

"If that's the most you have to work on, I think you'll be just fine."

"I'll see you around, okay?"

She turned, but Jesse said, "Mack, wait." He dug into his pocket, found what he was looking for, and handed it to her.

She opened her hand. "Your lucky bullet?"

"Something to remember me by. I won't be needing it anymore."

She closed her hand and gave him a warm smile. "Thank you."

Jesse watched Mack walk to her car. And just for the heck of it, he said a little prayer for Kyle, that tonight would be the start of something wonderful. And that Mack would be a fan of ham.

Chapter 42

M ack sat next to a roaring, crackling fire and watched her family mingle and laugh. It was good to be home. She planned on making the most out of every minute she was here. Hayden and her fiancé, Ray, were hanging last-minute ornaments on the tree. She'd never seen Hayden so happy. Ray, who couldn't stop gushing about her, told everyone that Hayden was still a hit at the news station. And Hayden couldn't stop talking about her wedding plans. She asked Mack to be her maid of honor, which Mack agreed to, with the understanding that someone else would have to do her makeup, if she wore any at all. But Cassie had already rushed to the drugstore to gather samples for Mack to try, claiming it would be a Christmas miracle if they could see her in lip gloss. Little did they know. Later she would suggest that the bridesmaids wear pantsuits instead of gowns. But for now she just wanted to enjoy the moment.

The aroma of a Christmas turkey wafted through the house. Christmas music played softly in the background: Nat King Cole, her mother's favorite. Silver garland wrapped all the way up the staircase banister. A wreath with bright red berries hung over the fireplace.

It amazed Mack that she could be in this old house, full of memories of her mother and father, and still smile. There was a time when she thought she would never get over their deaths. But time healed and new life began, evident in the squeals and screams of her nieces and nephew.

"Hey," Hank said, sitting down next to her with a string of popcorn in his hand. "How's my favorite undercover officer?"

Mack smiled and leaned into him. "I haven't told the rest of the family yet, but I'm going back to patrol."

"Really?"

"I realized I miss helping people, talking to little kids about safety, helping elderly people get their cats out of trees, lecturing people about their speed, and turning on my sirens and chasing down the bad guys. It's where I belong."

"I've been doing some career thinking too."

"Oh yeah?"

"I've just hopped from one job to another, but nothing seemed to fit. I know a lot about cars, but I don't want to work with cars forever. I realized while working with you that I need more passion for what I'm doing." He glanced sideways at her. "I know, I know, I'm not the epitome of excitement, but I watched how much you love your job, and I want that."

"What kind of job do you think you want?"

"I'm not sure," he said, staring into the fire, "but I have to say, I really liked being sneaky."

"Like undercover work?"

"I don't know yet. I'm going to explore my options."

"As long as it's something that involves sneaking around?" Mack laughed.

Hank laughed too. "Yeah. And preferably something where I don't have to speak a lot. I really did like that airplane ride. Maybe I'll get into airplanes."

"You don't give yourself enough credit, you know," Mack said. "You're funny and fun to be around. Maybe it's time you came out of your shell."

Hank smiled and rested his chin on his hand. "That might help me with the ladies, huh?"

Mack leaned over and ruffled his hair. "You know your charm and good looks are enough."

"Yeah, right."

"Merry Christmas, Hank. I know you'll find the perfect job. The sky's the limit."

Acknowledgments

T his book was quite a labor of love. Right in the middle of writing it, I accidentally stabbed a knife into my hand while making, of all things, my favorite food in the world—guacamole. I severed the radial nerve. I'll spare you the rest of the details, but they weren't good. I'd like to thank my surgeon, Dr. Ghazi Rayan, who saved the use of my hand so that I could type again and finish this book! I'd also like to thank all my family, friends, and readers who prayed for me and helped me through what seemed like an eternal pause.

I'm certain it felt like an eternal pause for my publisher, who graciously waited for me to recover. I'm blessed to work with a talented team at WaterBrook. Special thanks to Shannon Hill, who helped me work this story out to what it needed to be, and to Laura Wright and the rest of the editorial team, who worked hard to help me get it just right. As always, many thanks to Dudley Delffs and Janet Kobobel Grant.

This kind of book can't be written without the help of professionals, which is part of the vision for this series. I was blessed to partner with my longtime technical advisor, Ron Wheatley, who went above and beyond the call of duty by letting me get a real glimpse into the life of an undercover officer. I wish I could've included in this book every fascinating detail of my research; what is here is only a fraction of what I learned. However, I gained an enormous amount of respect for the men and women in this profession. My deepest thanks goes to Ron's wife, Barb, who was kind enough to share her thoughts and stories about life married to an undercover officer. Their graciousness and hospitality were the very definition of Christian love. I'd also like to thank Jerry VanCook, fellow writer, former undercover officer, and author of *Going Undercover* for his help, as well as Lieutenant Jeff Treat and Sergeant Mike Knight and his wife, Sherri Knight, for their patience in helping me with the details.

Last, but definitely not least, I cannot write without the support of my loving family. Thank you, Sean, John Caleb, and Cate, for bringing such joy into my life. I love you. And thank you, Father, for the many gifts that you have given me, including this wonderful thing called writing.

About the Author

RENE GUTTERIDGE is the author of ten novels, including *Ghost Writer, Troubled Waters,* and the Boo series. She worked as a church playwright and drama director, writing over five hundred short sketches, before publishing her first novel and deciding to stay home with her first child.

Rene is married to Sean, a musician, and enjoys raising their two children while writing full time. She also enjoys helping new writers and teaching at writers' conferences. She and her family make their home in Oklahoma.

Please visit her Web site at www.renegutteridge.com.

Book One in
The Occupational Hazards series:
Old School meets New School
meets Homeschool.

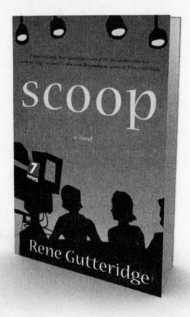

With unexpected twists and delightful humor, *Scoop* offers a hilarious
behind-the-scenes look at a local TV news team's desperate grab for
ratings—and the hazards of taking one's faith into the workplace.

Available in bookstores and from online retailers.

WATERBROOK PRESS
www.waterbrookpress.com